"The Vengeance of Ulios" by Edmond Hamilton—Would one woman's longing for immortality spell the doom of all Atlantis?

"The Double Shadow" by Clark Ashton Smith—When the wizard probed the secrets of Atlantis and other lost realms, would he win for himself powers beyond human ken, or reawaken horrors older than time?

"The Lamp" by L. Sprague de Camp—Was the lamp he'd brought a cleverly manufactured fake—or a key to vanished Atlantis?

"The New Atlantis" by Ursula K. Le Guin—Was the world on the brink of a new Atlantis, total destruction, or a warp that could exchange past and future?

From the glory and decadence of Atlantis to the final days of this great civilization to the traps it still holds for the greedy or unwary, here are masterful tales that make Atlantis live again in—

ISAAC ASIMOV'S MAGICAL WORLDS #9

D0890967

ATLANTIS

Isaac Asimov's Magical Worlds of Fantasy #9

Edited by

*Isaac Asimov,
Martin H. Greenberg,
and Charles G. Waugh*

*With an Introduction by
Isaac Asimov*

A SIGNET BOOK

NEW AMERICAN LIBRARY

Acknowledgments:

"Introduction: The Lost City," by Isaac Asimov. Copyright © 1987
by Isaac Asimov. Used with permission.

"Treaty in Tartessos" by Karen Anderson. Copyright © 1963 by
Mercury Press, Inc. First appeared in *The Magazine of Fantasy
and Science Fiction*, May 1963. Reprinted by permission of the
author.

"The Vengeance of Ulios" by Edmond Hamilton. Originally "The
Avenger from Atlantis" in *Weird Tales*, July 1935. Copyright
© 1935 by Popular Fiction Publishing Corporation. Reprinted
by the agents of the author's estate, Scott Meredith Literary
Agency, Inc., 845 Third Avenue, New York, New York
10022.

"Scar-Tissue" by Henry S. Whitehead. Copyright © 1946 by Ziff-
Davis Publishing Corporation from *Amazing*, July 1946.
Reprinted by permission of Scott Meredith Literary Agency, Inc.,
845 Third Avenue, New York, New York 10022.

"The Double Shadow" by Clark Ashton Smith. Copyright © 1939 by
Popular Fiction Publishing Corporation from *Weird Tales*, February
1939. Reprinted by permission of the agents for the author's estate,
Scott Meredith Literary Agency, Inc., 845 Third Avenue, New
York, New York 10022.

"The Dweller in the Temple" by Manly Wade Wellman. Copyright
© 1977 by Andrew J. Offutt for *Swords Against Darkness II*.
Reprinted by permission of Karl Edward Wagner, Literary Executor
for Manly Wade Wellman.

"Gone Fishing" by J. A. Pollard. Copyright © 1987 by J. A. Pollard,
by arrangement with the author.

"The Lamp" by L. Sprague de Camp. Copyright © 1975 by Mercury
Press, Inc. Reprinted by permission of the author.

"The Shadow Kingdom" by Robert E. Howard. Copyright 1929 by
Popular Fiction Publishing Corporation for *Weird Tales*, August
1929. Reprinted by permission of Kull Productions, Inc.

"The New Atlantis" by Ursula K. Le Guin. Copyright © 1975 by
Ursula K. Le Guin. Reprinted by permission of the author and
the author's agent, Virginia Kidd.

SIGNET TRADEMARK REG. U.S. PAT. OFF. AND FOREIGN COUNTRIES
REGISTERED TRADEMARK—MARCA REGISTRADA
HECHO EN CHICAGO. U.S.A.

SIGNET, SIGNET CLASSIC, MENTOR, ONYX, PLUME, MERIDIAN and NAL BOOKS are published by NAL PENGUIN INC., 1633 Broadway, New York, New York 10019

First Signet Printing, January, 1988

1 2 3 4 5 6 7 8 9

PRINTED IN THE UNITED STATES OF AMERICA

CONTENTS

INTRODUCTION:
THE LOST CITY

by Isaac Asimov

The time is 1500 B.C. The place is the island of Thera in the Aegean Sea, 65 miles north of the island of Crete. Few Americans have ever heard of it.

Of course, the city-state of Venice controlled the Aegean and parts of Greece during a portion of the Middle Ages, and there are alternate Italian names for some places. Thera is also known as Santorini, therefore. Few Americans have ever heard of that, either.

Thera is a round island with a peak in the center and in 1500 B.C. there was a city on it, very advanced for its time, rich, prosperous, and a great trading port. It had close connections with Crete, which was at the height of *its* civilization. Crete was the first maritime civilization, owned the first navy, and had cities without walls, for it relied on its fleet for defense. It had elaborate buildings, a cultured people, and (miracle of miracles) indoor plumbing.

Crete, with its Minoan civilization (for Minos, the ancient king of Crete in Greek legend) had existed for fifteen hundred years, traded with Egypt on an equal basis, controlled much of the Greek mainland. Thera shared in its power and prosperity.

There was a catch. That mountain on Thera was not

an ordinary mountain. It was an extinct volcano, which is a good thing. It doesn't erupt and its age-old lava is fertile. An extinct volcano is also a bad thing. Sometimes it isn't entirely extinct.

A volcano like Mauna Loa in Hawaii is only moderately dangerous. It has open vents inside which lava is always heaving and out of which it sometimes overflows—gently and slowly. It can sometimes destroy fields and habitations but people can get out of the way.

In an extinct volcano, magma slowly wells up from deep below and exerts a slow pressure against the long-solidified plug that blocks its vent. If it has its base on the sea, there may be a leak through which cold water can slowly penetrate. As it reaches the molten rock of the magma, it steams and the steam adds to the pressure until eventually, without warning, the rock plug gives way, half the mountain is blasted into the stratosphere and there is an explosion that puts even modern efforts with nuclear bombs (if you don't count radioactivity) to shame.

That is what happened in 1883 to Krakatou, a small island between Java and Sumatra. The explosion was called the loudest sound ever heard, for the atmospheric waves circled the world, the tsunami ('tidal wave') was felt half a world away, and three thousand people were killed by explosion, ash, and tsunami.

But Krakatou shrank into something minor compared to the explosion at Thera in 1500 B.C. and then again, even worse, some decades later. Thera was destroyed in a moment in that first explosion, its civilization was wiped out, its people killed. The island itself was torn apart and the sea rolled over where it had existed. What is left now are some arcs marking the rim of the island and a small peak in the center as the volcano grows again.

The first explosion virtually destroyed western Crete, and the second explosion got the whole island. The Cretan civilization was wiped out and it was not long afterward that the Greeks conquered and occupied it so that never again, *never* would it play an important part in world history.

In fact, the whole eastern Mediterranean world was thrown into turmoil, as settled societies collapsed, and invading rovers, fleeing their own lands, grabbed what they could. Egypt held its own, just barely, and was never again a great power until medieval times. The Hittite Empire was destroyed and successive waves of invaders took over Asia Minor. The Philistines and Israelites invaded Canaan (a small thing, but magnified by the Bible). It took centuries before the civilized world settled down again.

The world of 1500 B.C. was not yet very literate and there was no one in that troubled time who wrote up a careful description of what happened. At least there was nothing that survived very long.

However, it was too great a cataclysm not to remain in memory. The Egyptians, particularly, must have remembered. When matters are not written down in an authoritative and respected way, however, people have the privilege of distortion and embroidery and— people being people—full advantage is taken.

A thousand years later, the inquisitive and all-curious Greeks sopped up the tales fed them by the Egyptian priests, who had no objection to magnifying them for the benefit of people they no doubt considered pushy barbarians.

And eventually in the fourth century B.C., the tale reached Plato, one of the greatest minds and writers the world has seen. He told the event not as sober history, but as a cautionary tale intended to teach. The tale was never finished.

It is clear, nevertheless, that he magnified it, either because that was how he received it or because he wanted to make it more effective. He wrote of a civilized island that was destroyed in a day and sank beneath the sea, but it was not just a small island in the Aegean Sea. That was too mundane and the Greeks would not have believed it. It had to be a very large island, indeed a continent, and it had to be in the romantic distance where all myths and legends ought to be. To the ancient Greeks, one scene of wonders lay beyond the Pillars of Hercules (the Strait of Gibraltar) in the misty dimness of the Atlantic. And Plato called the sunken island "Atlantis."

Somehow Atlantis caught the imagination of the world. What Plato meant as a cautionary tale, as a fable, as a myth, became sober history to many people. Atlantis became a high-tech primeval civilization from which all the ancient civilizations, from Egypt to Mexico, derived their knowledge. Or it became a mystic land of powerful magicians and necromancy. Everyone snatched at it, and just a couple of decades ago the true tale of Thera was finally captured by archeologists who dug deeply into what is left of the island. But we can be sure that that won't stop the marvelous tales of Atlantis.

We have here a collection of those tales, from the sober realism of Sprague de Camp and the romantic semi-realism of Karen Anderson to the racing adventure of Edmond Hamilton and the morbid mysticism of Clark Ashton Smith. It is a broad sampling of the things that can be done with Atlantis and an example of how it stimulated the imagination in so many different ways.

But the cautionary tale remains. Atlantis (like Thera) was destroyed, unexpectedly, and suddenly, at the height of its power, and there is always the feeling that it was the punishment for arrogance and overweening pride.

Do we know another, nearer civilization marked by arrogance and overweening pride? And is there a well-known way in which, unexpectedly, and suddenly, at the height of its power, it, too, might be destroyed? And can we imagine some day in a galactic future, other species on other worlds speaking of a whole planet that suddenly, in a day, was destroyed? And might alien archeologists someday probe the slightly radioactive debris of the world in order to determine what really happened and whether the whole thing might not be a fable?

TREATY IN TARTESSOS

by Karen Anderson

Iratzabal's hoofs were shod with bronze, as befitted a high chief, and heavy gold pins held the coils of bright sorrel hair on top of his head. In this morning's battle, of course, he had used wooden pins which were less likely to slip out. As tonight was a ceremonial occasion, he wore a coat of aurochs hide dyed blue with woad, buttoned and cinched with hammered gold.

He waved his spear high to show the green branches bound to its head as he entered the human's camp. No one spoke, but a guard grunted around a mouthful of barleycake and jerked his thumb toward the commander's tent.

Standing in his tent door, Kynthides eyed the centaur with disfavor, from his unbarbered hair to the particularly clumsy bandage on his off fetlock. He straightened self-consciously in his sea-purple cloak and pipeclayed linen tunic.

"Greetings, most noble Iratzabal," he said, bowing. "Will you enter my tent?"

The centaur returned the bow awkwardly. "Glad to, most noble Kynthides," he said. As he went in the man realized with a little surprise that the centaur emissary was only a couple of fingers' breadth taller than himself.

It was darker inside the tent than out, despite the luxury of three lamps burning at once. "I hope you've dined well? May I offer you anything?" Kynthides asked politely, with considerable misgivings. The centaur probably wouldn't know what to do with a barley loaf, and as for wine—well, there wasn't a drop within five miles of camp. Or there had better not be.

"That's decent of you, but I'm full up," said Iratzabal. "The boys found a couple of dead . . . uh, buffalo, after the battle, and we had a fine barbecue."

Kynthides winced. Another yoke of draft oxen gone! Well, Corn Mother willing, the war would be settled soon. It might even be tonight. "Won't you, er . . . sit? Lie down? Er, make yourself comfortable."

Iratzabal lowered himself to the ground with his feet under him, and Kynthides sank gratefully into a leatherbacked chair. He had been afraid the discussion would be conducted standing up.

"I got to admit you gave us a good fight today, for all you're such lightweights," the centaur said. "You generally do. If we don't get things settled somehow, we could go on like this till we've wiped each other out."

"We realize that too," said the man. "I've been asked by the heads of every village in Tartessos, not to mention communities all the way back to Thrace, to make some reasonable settlement with you. Can you speak for centaurs in those areas?"

"More or less." He swished his tail across the bandaged fetlock, and flies scattered. "I run most of the territory from here up through Goikokoa Etchea—what men call Pyrene's Mountains—and across to the Inland Sea. Half a dozen tribes besides mine hunt through here, but they stand aside for *us*. We could lick any two of them with our eyes shut. Now, you take an outfit like the Acroceraunians—I don't run them, but they've heard of me, and I can tell them to knuckle under or face my boys *and* yours. But that shouldn't be necessary. I'm going to get them a good cut."

"Well, remember that if the communities don't like promises I make in their names, they won't honor them," said the man. He slid his fingers through the combed curls of his dark-brown beard and wished he could ignore the centaur's odor. The fellow smelled like a saddle-blanket. If he didn't want to wash, he could at least use perfume. "First, we ought to consider the reasons for this war, and after that ways to settle the dispute."

"The way I see it," the centaur began, "is, you folks want to pin down the corners of a piece of country and sit on it. We don't understand ground belonging to somebody."

"It *began*," Kynthides said stiffly, "with that riot at the wedding."

"That was just what set things off," said Iratzabal. "There'd been a lot of small trouble before then. I remember how I was running down a four-pointer through an oak wood one rainy day, with my nose full of the way things smell when they're wet and my mind on haunch of venison. The next thing I knew I was in a clearing planted with one of those eating grasses, twenty pounds of mud on each hoof and a pack of tame wolves worrying my hocks. I had to kill two or three of them before I got away, and by then there were men throwing spears and shouting 'Out! Out!' in what they thought was Eskuara."

"We have to keep watchdogs and arm the field hands, or we wouldn't have a stalk of grain standing at harvest time!"

"Take it easy. I was just telling you, the war isn't

over a little thing like some drunks breaking up a wedding. Nor they wouldn't have, if the wine hadn't been where they could get at it. There's blame on both sides."

The man half rose at this, but caught himself. The idea was to stop the war, not set it off afresh. "At any rate, it seems we can't get along with each other. Men and centaurs don't mix well."

"We look at things different ways, said Iratzabal. "You see a piece of open country, and all you can think of is planting a crop on it. We think of deer grazing it, or rabbit and pheasant nesting. Field-planting ruins the game in a district."

"Can't you hunt away from farm districts?" asked Kynthides. "We have our families to support, little babies and old people. There are too many of us to let the crops go and live by hunting, even if there were as much game as the land could support."

"Where can we hunt?" shrugged the centaur. "Whenever we come through one of our regular districts, we find more valleys under plow than last time, more trees cut and the fields higher up the slope. Even in Goikokoa Etchea, what's as much my tribe's home as a place can be, little fields are showing up." A swirl of lamp smoke veered toward him, and he sniffed it contemptuously. "Sheep fat! The herds I find aren't deer any more, they're sheep, with a boy pi-pipping away on a whistle—and dogs again."

"If you'd pick out your territory and stay on it, then no farmers would come in," said Kynthides. "It's contrary to our nature to leave land unused because somebody plans to hunt through it next autumn."

"But, big as Goikokoa Etchea is, it won't begin to feed us year round! We've got to have ten times as much, a hundred times if you're talking of Scythia and Illyria and all."

"I live in Thessaly myself," Kynthides pointed out. "I have to think of Illyria. What we men really want is to see all you centaurs completely out of Europe, resettled in Asia or the like. Couldn't you all move out of Sarmatia and the lands to the east? Nobody lives there. It's all empty steppes."

"Sarmatia! Maybe it looks empty to a farmer, but I've heard from the boys in Scythia. The place is filling up with Achaians, six feet tall, each with twenty horses big enough to eat either one of us for breakfast, and they can ride those horses all night and fight all day. By Jainco, I'm keeping away from them."

"Well, there's hardly anybody in Africa. Why don't you go there?" the man suggested.

"If there was any way of us all getting there—"

"Certainly there is! We have ships. It would take a couple of years to send you all, but—"

"*If* we could get there, we wouldn't like it at all. That's no kind of country for a centaur. Hot, dry, game few and far between—no thanks. But you're willing to ship us all to some other place?"

"Any place! That is, within reason. Name it."

"Just before war broke out in earnest, I got chummy with a lad who'd been on one of those exploring voyages you folks go in for. He said he'd been to a place that was full of game of all kinds, and even had the right kind of toadstools."

"Toadstools? To make poison with?" cried Kynthides, his hand twitching toward the neatly bandaged spear-jab on his side.

"*Poison!*" Iratzabal ducked his head and laughed into his heavy sorrel beard. "That's a good one, poison from toadstools! No, to eat. Get a glow on at the Moon Dances—same way you people do with wine. Though I can't see why you use stuff that leaves you so sick the next day."

"Once you've learned your capacity, you needn't have a hangover," Kynthides said with a feeling of superiority. "But this place you're talking of—"

"Well, my pal said it wasn't much use to men, but centaurs would like it. Lots of mountains, all full of little tilted meadows, but no flat country to speak of. Not good to plow up and sow with barley or what-not. Why not turn that over to us, since you can't send any big colonies there anyway?"

"Wait a minute. Are you talking about Kypros' last expedition?"

"That's the one my pal sailed under," nodded Iratzabal.

"No, by the Corn Mother! How can I turn that place over to you? We've barely had a look at it ourselves. There may be tin and amber to rival Thule, or pearls, or sea-purple. We have simply no idea of what we'd be giving you."

"And there may be no riches at all. Did this guy Kypros say he'd seen any tin or pearls? If he did, he didn't tell a soul of his crew. And I'm telling you, if we don't go there we don't go anyplace. I can start the war again with two words."

The man sprang to his feet, white-lipped. "Then start the war again! We may not have been winning, but by the Mother, we weren't losing!"

Iratzabal heaved himself upright. "You can hold out as long as we give you pitched battles. But wait till we turn to raiding! You'll have fields trampled every night, and snipers chipping at you every day. You won't dare go within bowshot of the woods. We'll chivy your herds through your crops till they've run all their fat off and there's not a blade still standing. And you'll get no harvest in, above what you grab off the stem and eat running. How are the granaries, Kynthides? Will there be any seed corn left by spring?"

The man dropped into his chair and took his head in trembling hands. "You've got us where we hurt. We can't survive that kind of warfare. But how can I promise land that isn't mine? It belongs to Kypros' backers, if anyone."

"Pay them off in the grain that won't be spoiled. Fix up the details any way it suits you. I'm not trying to make it hard on you—we can kick through with a reasonable number of pelts and such to even the bargain."

He looked up. "All right, Iratzabal," he said wearily. "You can *have* Atlantis."

THE VENGEANCE OF ULIOS

by Edmond Hamilton

The crowd of white-robed men and women in the Square of Science gave way respectfully before me as I and my servant approached. Bowing until their spotless robes swept the green marble paving, they hailed me and made an opening for me.

"Way for Ulios, for the Guardian of the Force!" they called.

And others cried, "Make room for the greatest scientist in Atlantis!"

"Friends, I thank you for your courtesy," I told them as I walked gravely through the respectful throng.

But in truth I was human enough to feel pride that they held me so highly. For in all Atlantis there was no one who did not know and honor the name of Ulios, the Guardian of the Force. And that was as it should be, since he who held the Force held Atlantis itself in the hollow of his hand.

The city seemed beautiful to me that spring morning. Under the blue sky, beside the blue sea, its snowy marble buildings towered in almost unreal splendor, a stainless beauty of white pillars and walls and porticoes. Over them hummed shimmering flyers, and through them ran the streets that were like rivers of green marble flowing into the lakes of the great squares.

All around me rose the great halls of science that bordered the Square of Science, towering alabaster structures that contained the laboratories in which our Atlantean scientists had wrested so many of nature's secrets from her. And at one side of the Square was a comparatively small building which outranked all the others in importance, the Hall of the Force, of which I, Ulios, was guardian and tenant.

Gathering my white robe around me, I walked up the steps of the Hall, followed by Sthan, my faithful servant. I entered and went through the corridors and courts inside to the white laboratories that were my own private workrooms. There Etain, my wife, was talking with my assistant guardian, Karnath. She ran toward me as I entered.

"Ulios, Karnath has been telling me of your experiments in transferring living brains!" she cried.

"Then Karnath has talked overmuch for my content," I told her, frowning at my underling and trying to frown also at her.

But I could not frown at Etain, nor ever be the least angry with her, and well she knew that it was so. She was not wholly of Atlantis. Her father had been one of our nobles but her mother had been of the savage tribes that dwelt in the great, wild continents to the east, and this savage woman's barbaric beauty had so entranced the noble's heart that he had captured her and then wedded her.

There was still something of the untamed in the beauty of Etain. Beautiful she was, with her night-black hair and soft black eyes that could flash yellow lights of passion, and with her white body that could be languorous and leopard-taut by turns.

And well she knew the power her beauty had over me, a power so great that even now her hand on my arm and the touch of her clinging white robe stirred my pulse.

Nevertheless I told her as severely as I could, "Etain, there are some experiments which it is well to conduct but not well to publish to others. This of the brain-transference is such a one."

Karnath stepped forward and said hastily, "I only thought that it would interest the lady Etain. I meant no harm."

"No harm has been done," I told him shortly. "But in future babble not of my work to anyone."

He bowed and left us, his dark, handsome face sullen and his black eyes narrowed in anger.

When he had gone, Etain asked me breathlessly, "But is it true, Ulios, that you could transfer a man's brain into another man's body? So that the first man would take up life in that other body anew?"

"I could, yes," I admitted. "I have done the thing many times with animals and corpses. But it would be an unholy thing to do it to living people and I never shall."

"Not even if I asked you to do it to *me*?" she cried.

I stared at her. "I do not understand you, Etain," I said finally. "Why in the name of all the gods should you wish your brain, your personality, transferred from your own lovely body into a different body?"

"I do not wish it now," she said. "But there will come a time when I shall wish it much, Ulios."

Her midnight eyes held my own anxiously. "Before many years my beauty will fade and I will become wrinkled and flabby and old. *Old!* A horrible fate that I dread above all others.

"But you could prevent that, Ulios! In a few years you could transfer my brain into some young and beautiful girl's body and so I would have youth and beauty again.

"And so could you regain youth yourself," she continued urgently. "You are already middle-aged, your dark hair graying and your keen eyes beginning to dull. You could take a young man's body in a few years, and we could live on so always, young and immortal."

"Etain," I told her sternly, "you know not what you say. Such immortality is not for men, and he who strove to live on in that way would be guilty of black unholiness. We are born to age and die, and not to steal the bodies of others so that we many live unendingly. Banish such thoughts as these from your mind."

Etain stared at me with an unchanging face; then she said, "I see you do not love me, Ulios," and went out of the room.

I turned to my work and told myself that she would soon forget her wild fancy and that I had told her nothing but the truth. Yet as I worked, her face came always before my eyes; so that at last I dashed down my instruments and went out to make amends for any hurt I had done her.

She was not in her own chambers, and I searched through the building until at last I found her down in the mighty vault underneath the building, the Chamber of the Force. This was a great domed cavern hollowed from the solid rock under the building.

At its center rose a mighty pillar of brassy metal, which was the top end of a great rod running far down into the bowels of the earth. Inside this pillar lay the keys to the Force, locked up by a door that only I, the Guardian, and Karnath, my assistant, could open.

Only two men in all Atlantis were ever allowed to know how to reach those keys, at one time. For this mighty rod tapped the colossal volcanic forces of the fires underneath our land, and while it was necessary occasionally to make use of those forces, we knew that a too careless handling of them would bring catastrophe upon us. So the Guardian of the Force and his underling watched and warded the keys.

Etain was standing beside the great brass pillar and Karnath was leaning eagerly toward her. He was talking to her and she was listening so intently that neither of them heard my approach.

"Were you my wife. I'd not refuse you what you asked as Ulios did," Karnath was telling her. "Why should you have to age and wither and die when immortal youth and beauty are his to give?

"*I* can give you such unending youth and beauty, Etain," he continued eagerly. "I have learned well the process of brain-transference from Ulios."

"Then it is the last thing that you will ever learn from Ulios," I said freezingly.

Karnath whirled, startled, and Etain looked up quickly, though her expression did not change.

I pointed to the door. "Karnath, go! You are not worthy to be the assistant of the Guardian of the Force, and tomorrow I will pray the Council of Atlantis to depose you from your post."

His face grew black with menace and he hissed, "You know that if I am deposed I will be slain also, since only two men may know the secret keys of the Force. You wish to kill me for your jealousy."

"Go, before I forget that I am the Guardian," I told him in a cold fury, and he went.

I turned to Etain. "Why were you listening to him?"

She smiled at me, unfrightened by my sternness. "He stopped me and poured out his wild talk to me before I could get away."

"Perhaps I should report him to the Council this very

hour," I said, frowning. "Karnath has revealed himself an evil man."

Etain told me, "He is a little angry, doubtless, but not dangerous. Let him go until tomorrow, Ulios."

Her soft white arms were slipping warmly around my neck and in her black eyes was that mysterious smile that always seemed to deaden my own will. I thought no more of Karnath that evening.

At midnight I was sleeping soundly in our chamber when an urgent tugging at my shoulder awakened me. I sat upright in the dark chamber to find that Etain was not beside me and that it was Sthan, my squat, faithful servant, who had awakened me.

"Master, she is gone!" he cried. "Gone with Karnath!"

A cold bell seemed to strike in my heart, and I grasped his neck and cried, "Whom do you mean?"

"The lady Etain!" exclaimed the servant. "I saw her but now run to the roof with Karnath and embark in a flyer! See, there they go now!" he added, pointing through the great open portico at the end of the chamber.

I rushed to the portico and peered out. Before me lay the sleeping white marble mass of Atlantis, crowded against the dark sea. Above it rose the sheer, blue-black heights of heaven, blazing with winking, twinkling stars. There across the star-specked skies drove a tiny light, heading eastward and rising on a long slant.

I cried in mad rage, "Karnath has offered her endless youth and life and she has fled with him!"

Then I whirled. "After them!" I shouted to Sthan. "I will overtake them and have vengeance!"

We raced up the marble stairs toward the roof of the building where the flyers were parked.

As we came out onto the starlit, gleaming roof, it and the whole building beneath us shuddered slightly. It shuddered again, a little more violently, as we ran toward one of the long, flat, stream-lined metal flyers.

"Master, the earth rocks!" cried Sthan fearfully.

"It is but a tremor—quick, start the flyer!" I shouted to him.

I swear by all the gods that I had no suspicion of anything else! Earth tremors were common enough in Atlantis, and had I dreamed that this was anything more, I would have forsaken my pursuit.

Or would I? Sometimes I believe that in my madness at that moment I would have held to my chase even had I known all. For mad I was with jealousy and rage against the fleeing pair as the flyer that bore Sathan and myself whirled up hummingly into the starlight.

"Head straight after them!" I yelled to Sthan as we lay flat on the little flyer's deck. "Follow their light."

"I follow, master," the faithful fellow cried.

With insane speed we plunged headlong across the sleeping city in pursuit of that receding speck of light. Suddenly terrific gusts of wind caught our flyer and began to bat it this way and that like a leaf in a gale. The air seemed to have abruptly gone mad, and only our safety-rings kept us from being dashed off the deck. Sthan yelled hoarsely and pointed back downward.

My blood froze as I looked back. The city of Atlantis and the dark countryside beyond it were rolling and heaving like waves in a heavy sea, the solid earth buckling and folding. A horrible grinding sound came up to us.

"Gods of Atlantis!" I screamed as I saw. "Karnath opened wide the keys of the Force before he and Etain fled! He has unchained the Force to destroy all our land so that there might be none left to pursue him and the traitress!"

My own black guilt crashed home to me. I, the Guardian of the Force, had deserted my post for personal vengeance when the Force I guarded was about to annihilate our land.

"Back—turn back toward the Hall of Force!" I yelled.

But Sthan, clinging to the deck, shouted, "The flyer will not obey her helm, master!"

Whirling and tossing high in the air, we saw the swift unfolding of the cataclysm back there. The whole city and land were heaving and rumpling wildly, rapidly shaking into fragments the countless splendid marble buildings. The little white block of the Hall of Force was suddenly blown into the air by a fiery, awful uprush of flaming lava.

The sky was lit with a lurid crimson glow from this spouting fire-fountain at the center of the city. We could glimpse tiny figures of men and women and children rushing into the streets to be killed by the downfall of molten lava or the crash of marble.

The volcano at the center exploded a mountain-mass of flaming rock skyward. There was a prolonged, world-shaking roar of direst diastrophism far below, and then we saw the whole land shaken violently for a last time. Then:

"Master, the land sinks!" screamed Sthan, his eyes dilated.

Frozenly, rigidly, I stared down at the land that was being destroyed because of my neglect of my duty. With terrible grinding and grating, a long and awful chord of solemn earth-agony, the land sank downward in the dark. The foam-maned stallions of the sea rushed in wild triumph across the foundering land, a charging host of new destruction. They met the flaming volcano, and sea and fire hissed in deadly battle, filling the air with steam.

Then as our wildly gyrating flyer was whirled downward by a freak of the mad air-currents, we glimpsed through a rift in the swirling stream the last of the land sinking under the waters. A single little point of land, and on it a small marble building that gleamed a last moment in the smothering darkness. Then it was engulfed, and under us the land was all gone, and where Atlantis had stood, the great deeps of the ocean now swirled and spun.

I lifted my arms toward the sky as our flyer began to cease its gyrations.

"Gods of Atlantis, the sin is mine!" I cried. "I am the Guardian who failed his land, and I will atone with my life for that sin. But first I will find those two who also sinned, and they also shall atone. Through all eternity I will pursue them, and the vengeance of Ulios shall strike them before Ulios takes vengeance on himself!"

Sthan, chattering with fear, clinging to the deck of the rocking flyer, caught my arm. "Master, where now? There is no more Atlantis—no more Atlantis for ever!"

I pointed a quivering hand toward the paling dawn. "Eastward, after the flyer of Karnath and Etain! From henceforth, the world holds only our quest for vengeance!"

So I, Ulios of Atlantis, began the quest of vengeance and atonement that was not to end for many a weary century.

First came Sthan and I to the wild, savage lands of North Africa. It was not long until we found the flyer of Karnath and Etain, discarded by them because of the depletion of its power.

We had shortly to discard our own flyer for the same reason. But Sthan and I went on on foot, following the trail through a thousand dangers. And the traitor and traitress were now aware of our pursuit, for they fled always before us.

Barbaric tribes, and monstrous beasts, and storm

and desert and mountain we conquered. A year passed, another and then another, and still we had not overtaken the two who fled before us.

Life to me had become but one thing—the quest. Somewhere, sometime, I would come up with the traitors, Karnath and Etain, who had destroyed my land for ever. I knew it. I would atone for my own sin, but first vengeance upon those two would be mine.

Sthan followed me like another shadow, stedfast and faithful, never faltering. We two, and the two we tracked, were the last four people of mighty Atlantis now left on the earth!

Year after year we hung to the trail, sometimes losing it for many months but always finding it again. I had lost all measurements of time, but knew that Sthan and I had become gray-haired.

Then one day we came upon a mound of earth near a small savage village. We dug into it and unearthed two bodies. They were the bodies of Karnath and Etain!

Karnath's hair had become gray and Etain's beauty had faded, but they were undoubtedly the two I sought. For a time I could only stare at them. How *could* I be deprived thus of my vengeance?

Then I turned their bodies over and saw that the brains were missing from their two skulls. I understood then, and wild joy filled me. I was not to be cheated of my vengeance after all.

"Sthan, look!" I told my servant. "The two we hunt are not dead after all!"

"But these are surely their bodies, master," he said, perplexed.

"Aye, but they no longer inhabit these bodies. Karnath has transferred the brain of Etain to some new, young body and has taught her how to transfer his brain likewise into a younger form. They think they will escape me by this means, live on past me. But I will find them! You and I, Sthan, will also take new, strong bodies for ourselves so that we may continue our search."

"But I could not do a thing of marvel like that, transfer your brain to another living body," the faithful fellow protested.

"I will teach you how, Sthan. And we will be able to take new bodies whenever we grow old, just as Karnath and Etain plan to do, and thus we will follow them down through time until we find them."

We settled near the village of savages and there for some time I busied myself in preparing instruments and in teaching Sthan the delicate, wonderful process for the transference of living brains. I was in no hurry. I knew that those I pursued could not go far enough to escape me, and that they would not die. My vengeance was sure.

When Sthan, after long practice, had become expert in the operation, we abducted two young warriors from among the savages and I transferred Sthan's brain into the skull of one of them.

Sthan's new skull healed and his new nerve-connections knit to his brain almost as I watched, due to the marvelous therapeutic powers of Atlantean science. He stood upright in his new body in an hour or so, and then Sthan moved my brain into the other young savage's body.

I awoke from that operation, no longer the gray, aging Ulios, but a new Ulios, one strong and young and filled with vigor.

"Now for the pursuit again!" I told Sthan.

The trail of Karnath and Etain led us farther east across the cruel wilderness of North Africa.

A generation passed, and another, and another,

while we slowly tracked the guilty pair through those
mighty wilds. Time had become meaningless to us, for
when we grew feeble we had but to stop and take new
bodies, and those we pursued were doing the same.

We lost the trail for half a generation in great
deserts and salt lakes far southward, but again we found
it. It led finally northeast toward a barbaric people
that had established a rudimentary civilization in the
lush, fertile valley of the Nile. These people, who
called their land Egypt, had but a few scraps of remembered knowledge left by Atlantean explorers long
ago for the basis of their civilization. The trail of
Karnath and Etain led us to a small town south of the
Egyptian capital of Memphis.

We entered this place of mud huts clustered beside
the tawny Nile, thronged with people in short white
kirtles, who looked with curiosity at our desert garb.

Suddenly there was a stir along the street and the
people bowed low as a palanquin borne by black slaves
swung past. In the palanquin lay a woman of dark
beauty clad in a fine, almost transparent robe, heavy
snake-bracelets of gold on her wrists. Her eyes met
mine a moment as she passed.

Concealing the sudden fierce joy in my breast, I
asked a villager, "Who was that lady?"

"She is the wife of the noble Kahotep. They came
here but recently, but have already won great favor
with Pharaoh."

I told my servant, "Sthan, our search ends here."

We went to the villa of Kahotep, a square brick
house surrounded by a high wall that enclosed green
gardens and arbors and a pool.

As we approached the door, a half-dozen armed
retainers suddenly spilled from it and overpowered us.
Two people came out of the square dwelling then, a

tall, powerful Egyptian with mocking eyes, and the woman I had seen.

"Greetings, Ulios!" said the tall noble mockingly. "I would never know you in that body, but Etain knew you, and so we were expecting you."

I looked at the dark, beautiful woman whom I too had instinctively recognized as Etain. Then I looked back at Karnath.

"Karnath, when your evil-doing loosed the fires that destroyed Atlantis, I and my servant alone were spared," I said. "The gods spared us because the sin of your evil deed was partly mine and to atone I must take vengeance."

Cruelly he laughed, and so too laughed Etain. "Great words for one who is in my power!" he said.

Then he continued mockingly, "Ulios, it is time that you and Sthan took new bodies. Your present ones are aging—as, alas! all bodies do—and I shall furnish you now with suitable new ones."

He uttered an order and the retainers brought two men into the courtyard. They were both very old. One of them was quite blind, without eyes, and the other was almost wholly paralyzed.

"These are the new bodies that I shall give you and Sthan," said Karnath. "Are they not strong, young, desirable bodies?"

He ordered us dragged into one of the rooms of the house, where were his instruments and preparations.

The thing was soon done. My brain he transferred into the body of the blind old man, Sthan's into the paralytic's.

"Now," said Karnath, "you shall be taken into the desert and there you many hatch new schemes of vengeance. And as you die, bethink you of Etain and me living on—forever."

The retainers took us far into the cruel, searing wastes of the desert and left us there. Blind and feeble, I felt the torturing blaze of the sun destroying my faint strength. But I did not despair.

"Sthan," I said to the living log that my servant now was, "we cannot die yet, for my vengeance is not achieved."

"Yes, master," whispered the faithful Sthan.

I took his paralyzed body in my arms and then, his eyes guiding my way, I started with tottering steps across the wastes.

I could not die yet—I knew it. The knowledge upheld my trembling, senile body through the terrible next two days.

How I endured in those days, without food or water, under the awful sun, dragging the paralyzed form of my servant with me, I know not. But at last we stumbled into an oasis of desert folk.

In superstitious awe of us, they treated us kindly. We soon recovered a little strength. In my blind mind still beat only one thought—Karnath and Etain! We must procure new bodies. Paralyzed, Sthan could not effect the transference of brains, so I must do it first to him. But could I, blind as I was?

I did it, the gods alone know how. Blindly, gropingly, I moved his brain into the body of the young desert dweller I had managed to ensnare and capture. When Sthan recovered, he easily secured another young man and transferred my brain into his body.

"My vengeance still waits!" I cried, young and strong once more. "Sthan, we return now to that village."

But when we re-entered it, Karnath and Etain were not there. Egypt was rent by war, dark invaders from Ethiopia advancing on the land, and like the other terrified Egyptians, the traitor and traitress had fled down the Nile for safety.

I followed with Sthan, but nowhere in lower Egypt could I find them. The Ethiopian invasion had swept away their trail, and for four full generations Sthan and I searched before we found it again.

It led eastward and northward across the great deserts into nearer Asia. Inexorably, relentlessly, we followed it, using body after body, even as those we followed passed from body to body. Generations became centuries as we searched up through nearer Asia for those two.

Years had become like hours to us; a generation seemed but a short time. It seemed that no sooner did we assume new, young bodies than they were old and worn out and it was necessary to take still other ones.

One thing Sthan and I were ever wary of, and that was that neither of us should be killed by accident. For if but one of us were left, there would be nobody to transfer that one's brain to a fresh body and so he must die in that body.

Through peoples, wars, cities without number, we followed the trail. The rude civilizations rising in the world meant nothing to us who had seen Atlantis in her glory. Never, except perhaps in thousands of centuries, would wrecked Atlantis be equaled.

The trail led finally to a great new city in the northeast, called Babylon. On a spring evening Sthan and I, in the guise of two Hittite chiefs, passed across a bridge over the Euphrates, dotted with round boats of skins and reeds, and approached the thick walls of Babylon.

"Sthan, our quest draws to an end. I feel that Karnath and Etain are in this city," I said.

"Then we shall find them, master."

We passed through Babylon's brass gates into streets of big mud-brick buildings thronged by the dark

Chaldeans. They were dressed in long white tunics of linen and wool and wore turbans over their long hair. To our left rose the brutal bulk of the Temple of Marduk, squat and square and mighty. Farther beyond it lay the flat, extensive palaces of the king.

I stopped a passer-by and asked him, "Friend, can you tell a stranger one thing? Who is reputed the most beautiful woman in Babylon?"

He stared disdainfully at my Hittite garb and said, "Only a stranger indeed could be ignorant that Tocris, the queen of our king Nabonidus, is the most beautiful woman in Babylon and the world."

"Sthan," I said, "the two we seek have become a king and queen. For well I know that this Nabonidus and Tocris must be Karnath and Etain, since Etain would ever choose for herself the most beautiful body she could find."

That day I asked for an audience with the great king, saying that I brought homage to him from my Hittite tribe.

It was many days before my audience was granted. And when I was finally ushered into the presence of Nabonidus, they permitted only me to enter, and searched me for weapons. I chuckled grimly at their precautions, for I had a copper knife so cunningly hidden in my hair they could not find it.

Nabonidus sat on a carven stool in the cool green hanging gardens of the palace roof, overlooking the Ishtar Gate.

He had a long, dark face and suspicious eyes, and beside him sat Tocris, his queen, a tall, beautiful woman with slumbrous eyes. "Etain!" my brain shouted.

I crawled slavishly forward, bumping my head upon the cold tile flags as the chamberlains had instructed. My heart was bursting as the moment of my age-old vengeance approached.

I raised myself, apparently overcome by awe. Nabonidus leaned forward impatiently. Instantly the knife flashed into my hand and stabbed forward at his heart.

Tocris was too quick for me. Her brooding eyes had read my intention and with tigress swiftness she knocked my arm aside.

There was a wild shouting of officers and running of guards. Held helpless by soldiers, I faced the king and queen.

Nabonidus looked more closely at me, and then his dark face smiled. And so too smiled Tocris.

"Welcome, Ulios," he said. "It was our thought that sooner or later you would come."

"Aye, and it is your thought too that sooner or later the gods will permit me to wreak their vengeance on you both," I said.

I saw haunting fear ripple swiftly over their faces a moment, the ever-present dread that had followed them down the centuries.

"You were ever a learned fool, Ulios," mocked Tocris-Etain. "Your gods will have to find a new instrument of vengeance, for here your quest ends."

"Aye, and this time there will be no escape for you as in Egypt," Nabonidus said. "All Babylon watches you die in torment tomorrow morning."

They locked me in the deepest of the palace's dungeons and set guards at my door five deep.

I slept calmly on the brick floor. I knew that I would not die.

Two hours before dawn I was awakened by a chipping and scratching. A hole appeared in the mud-brick wall and widened, and there came through it the dusty, anxious face of my servant Sthan.

"Master, I feared I could not dig to you in time!"

"You have done well, Sthan. Now we leave this hole."

"To seek out Karnath and Etain, master?"

"They are too well guarded now. We go first from this city to get new bodies, and then we will come back."

We stole out of Babylon by devious ways and made our way to the bleak plains to the north. There amid the fierce, nomadic peoples of the Medes and the Persians we acquired new bodies. I saw that these people were war-like and numerous, and I got the ear of their ruler, a powerful barbarian named Cyrus.

By dint of repeated narrations of the richness and weakness of Babylon, I so inspired him that in a short time he and all his horsemen and bowmen were pushing south toward Babylon. Sthan and I rode in the van of the Persian horse, and oh, it was sweet to be sweeping south with them toward my long-delayed vengeance on Karnath and Etain. It was sweet for us to crash through the smoking streets of terrified Babylon with the conquerors, amid whizz of arrows and death-cries of men and shrieks of fear-mad maidens, right up into the mighty, dusky throne-room of Nabonidus himself.

There Sthan and I burst in, red swords in our hands, and there we found Nabonidus and Tocris lying dead on biers.

I ran forward. My worst fears were realized. Their bodies lacked brains—they had escaped me again!

A terrified eunuch gasped, "When your forces came near Babylon, the great king and his queen shut themselves up and called for a young warrior and a young maiden. Later the warrior and the maiden came out and went, we know not where. But we found the king and queen thus, dead."

I shook my fist amid the thunderous uproar of falling Babylon. "I will find you, Karnath and Etain! Ulios and the vengeance of Ulios still will search you out!"

* * *

Sthan and I walked the streets of another city.

"Sthan, this is Rome, Mistress of the World and Light of the Universe. What think you of it?"

"It seems a poor huddle of a place beside Atlantis, master."

"Aye, but unless I am wrong we shall find Karnath and Etain somewhere in this place."

We two, now wearing the bodies of Greek sailors, were pushing through the motley, noisy throngs in the Suburra. Hard, brutal-looking legionaries, ill-fed, scrawny paupers, oily Syrian merchants and snaky Egyptian dancing-women crowded us in the narrow way. From the squalid booths along the street came the smells of sour wine and onions and fish frying in oil. Cobblers bawled the excellence of their wares, and two soldiers staged a drunken fight a little ahead, while from the windows over our head, women brown and black and white leaned down and entreated us to enter.

"Let us get out of this madhouse, Sthan. We shall not find Karnath and Etain in this part of the city."

Six centuries had passed since Sthan and I had crashed into Babylon with Cyrus, and found our prey escaped. A dozen or more bodies had we occupied since then, as we pushed over nearer Asia and Europe in pursuit of Karnath and Etain. Through the city-states of Greece and the isles of the Aegean we had sought them, with remorseless thoroughness, but always they seemed warned of our coming in time to escape. The growing greatness of this city Rome had brought us here, since it seemed to me the traitor and traitress would have come here.

Sthan and I were struggling out of the squalid Suburra when a hand tapped my shoulder. I turned and looked into the hard brown face of a helmeted captain who led a squad of legionaries.

"You are arrested by order of Tiberius Caesar," he said, and the clanking soldiers seized us.

"We have done no wrong—we landed only this morning," I said.

"You can explain your innocence to Caesar," he said shortly. "I am to take you before him."

An hour later we were marched under heavy guard into the presence of the lord of Rome in his great house on the Palatine. Tiberius stared at us with bulging, glassy eyes. He had a bony, gray, twitching face and a vein in his forehead throbbed continually. He was an old man made older by debauchery. Beside him stood a sleek, smooth, dandified Roman with deep subtle eyes, and a woman of superb, indolent beauty.

Her beauty gave me the clue, and I said quietly to her: "So you and Karnath were waiting for me this time, Etain?"

"Aye, Ulios, we grow weary of your stupid chase," she said, with merciless mirth that veiled in it a hint of her dread.

Karnath was telling Tiberius Caesar, "This is the man, Caesar. A sorcerer who has come here to Rome to poison you."

Tiberius stared at me with his glassy eyes and said menacingly, "What have you to answer to the accusation of Maximus?"

"Caesar, I came to Rome to kill, but not you," I told him. "It is Maximus himself whom I came here to take vengeance on. If you are wise, you will deliver him to me. For otherwise you will find that he is a snake who will soon sting you."

"It is a lie!"

Tiberius told me, "Maximus has taught me modes of pleasure I did not know before. He stands next to me in Rome, and the word of no prowling poisoner like yourself can harm him."

I understood the situation now. Karnath had secured his hold upon this old debauchee of an emperor by imparting to him some of the lore of evil pleasures he had picked up during the ages.

I smiled. "Caesar, it is true that I am a sorcerer, but I came not to Rome to kill you," I said. "I came to give you new life."

He frowned. "What do you mean?"

I told him, "I can transfer you from that old, worn-out body of yours into another body, a young, strong one."

Tiberius' glassy eyes widened with vicious eagerness. "By my ancestors, if you could do that—" he whispered.

"But he cannot!" cried Maximus hurriedly. "Listen not to his blandishments, Caesar!"

"I swear that I can do it," I told the emperor. "And for my pay I ask only—this man and woman to be given me!"

I saw Karnath and Etain pale at that, but Tiberius waved impatiently aside their outburst of denial and remonstrance.

His bulging eyes fixed on mine, Tiberuis told me, "There is a virtuous young relative of mine who is to succeed me as emperor. All Rome is waiting for me to die so they can have him for an upright sovereign. Could you transfer me into *his* body?"

I bowed. "As easily as into any other body, Caesar."

Tiberius burst into wild laughter. "What a joke on the people of Rome it would be, that!"

He rose. "Sorcerer, you will come to Capri with me

and effect this transference. If you succeed, this man and woman are yours."

"But they will escape—I want them now! I said.

"You will get your reward only when your work is done," he snapped. "They will be well guarded while we are gone."

I went to Capri with the old debauchee, though I misdoubted much leaving Karnath and Etain, even under guard.

The body into which I transferred Tiberius' brain was that of a young kinsman named Caligula. All Rome loved him for his modesty and virtue, and was waiting for him to succeed the evil Tiberius.

Once I had transferred the old emperor's brain into Caligula's skull, we allowed the dead body of Tiberius to be found. It was reviled by all, and Caligula was joyfully acclaimed emperor.

The new Caligula laughed and laughed. "They will soon find out what kind of emperor their virtuous pet will make."

In fact, Caligula's infamies and nameless vices began almost at once to astound the people who had hailed his accession.

"Caesar, remember now your promise," I reminded him impatiently. "Maximus and the woman are to be mine."

But when I returned to Rome with him, I found my worst forebodings realized. Karnath and Etain had escaped. It had not been hard for them, with their craft of many ages, to outwit their guards, and none knew whither they had fled.

"Forget them," Caligula told me. "You shall stay here and give me new bodies when I need them. You shall be second to myself."

I pretended to accede, but Sthan and I left Rome

that very night. Again we sought vainly for the trail of Karnath and Etain.

"Sthan, do you grow weary of this long search?"

"No, master. Wherever you lead, I shall follow."

We marched through a thick beech wood growing dark in the sad northern twilight. Snow was sifting from the dusky sky. Sthan and I, two blond Germans wearing helmets and hauberks of chain-armor on our tall bodies, led a hard-bitten crew of a hundred of the worst desperadoes that existed in Tenth Century Saxony.

Sthan pointed up through a break in the trees to a square gray castle with turrets at its four corners and a high surrounding wall, standing out boldly on a projecting cliff against the darkening sky.

"That must be the castle of Count Otto, master! They told us he and his lady ruled all this region."

"Aye, and this Count Otto and his lady are the two we have sought so long," I said, feasting my eyes on the castle.

I turned then to our hard-bitten followers.

"We halt here," I ordered. "Sthan, bring the minstrel garbs."

Before many minutes I and my servant had shed our armor and were attired like wandering minstrels, in brown cloaks and leggings, and carrying small lutes.

Then I asked the leader of our scoundrelly crew, a battered murderer named Eckhard, "Is it clear to you what you must do?"

He nodded his surly head. "I and my men are to creep up to the castle after dark and wait for your servant to open the postern gate inside. But all the loot of the castle is to be ours!"

"The loot shall be yours," I promised. "Sthan and I want none of it."

We two left them in the snowy beechen forest and

pushed up a rude track through the gathering darkness toward the castle. Once more my heart beat high with expectation. For once more I had come within reach of the vengeance that must me mine. Thirty generations had passed since Karnath and Etain had escaped me in imperial Rome. Rome had crashed beneath barbarian assaults as for century after century Sthan and I followed these two.

Twice had I almost had them in my power: once in Byzantium when Jovian ruled, and once in Cordoba where I found Karnath in the body of a Moorish emir. Both times they had given me the slip. But Sthan and I had always taken their trail again, assuming and discarding bodies every twenty or thirty years, and now we were close again to the two false ones. I swore they would not escape this time, as we climbed through the dusk and falling snow to the castle.

Count Otto's men-at-arms permitted us two wandering minstrels to enter before they closed the great gates for the night. We sat that night amid the servants in the great, gloomy stone dining-hall and devoured big shins of half-cooked beef, flinging the bones down into the rushes for the dogs to fight over.

Up at a raised table at the hall's end sat Count Otto and the lady Garda. Flushed with insolence of power was his handsome face and very fair and beautiful was the lady Garda—always Etain had chosen the fairest bodies. But I sensed dim undertones of dread in their pride, the haunting fear of the pursuer that had accompanied them these thousands of years. And I hugged to myself the thought of the dagger in my breast which I, Ulios, would soon bury in Karnath's brain.

As the meal drew to an end I made a slight signal to Sthan and he stole out of the hall. Then, as I had expected, Count Otto called for music from the minstrels who had come to the castle that night. I stepped forward until I stood just below their dais, my lute in my arms. Looking squarely up into their faces, I plucked the lute's strings and sang.

"Far away and long ago was a land in the western sea," I sang, and saw them look up, startled.

Count Otto's face became strange, and doubt gathered and gathered in the lady Garda's eyes as I sang on.

"Sin destroyed that land, and they that sinned had fled," I sang, and then Count Otto leaped to his feet.

"Ulios!" he cried, and his men-at-arms ran to him.

"Yes, Ulios at last!" I exclaimed, flinging down my lute and snatching out my dagger.

"Seize him!" he yelled to his men, but there smote across his order a gurgling death-cry from elsewhere in the castle, and with rush of clanking feet my hundred scoundrels poured into the hall.

Sthan was at their head, and he and that loot-lusting wolfish crew swept down the men-at-arms like chaff.

With my dagger gleaming, I sprang up onto the dais at Count Otto. One moment more and my five thousand years' search for vengeance would have ended, but I forgot his lady—I forgot Etain. She darted behind me as I sprang at Karnath, and then the shouting hall rocked in light as her own jeweled little knife drove into the back of my neck.

I sank, choking blood. With failing sight I saw Karnath and Etain leap through a hidden door at the back of the dais. My wolfish followers were too intent on looting to notice.

Sthan's frenzied face bent over me. "Master!"

I pointed a quaking finger at the hidden door and choked, "Follow them—follow—"

"No, master," he cried. "you are dying—I must get your brain into another body instantly or you perish."

I pointed again at the door, then all darkened.

When I awoke, Sthan was still bending anxiously over me, but I was lying now on a couch in the castle.

I looked down at myself. A big-boned body, in chain-armor. In the mirror Sthan handed me I saw the battered face of Eckhard.

"Master, I was not one moment too soon," Sthan told me. "I stunned Eckhard and put your brain in his skull just before you died."

"And Karnath and Etain?" I asked, sitting up.

"They got away by a secret passage that no doubt they had ready for such an emergency. But we will find them again, master!"

We will find them, Sthan."

The Duc d'Harcourt politely offered me a silver box that contained but a few last grains of snuff. Then he sat down beside us on one of the few benches that were permitted us in this big general room of the prison.

"It is one of the worst features of this Reign of Terror that we are not even permitted to die decently. Madame la Duchesse and I are not even given any snuff for these last days remaining to us."

Then his handsome, high-bred face smiled at me. "But I suppose we must not complain. We have long lorded this rabble that now rules France, and it is no doubt only fair that they should have a turn."

I told him, "I can understand their sending you aristocrats to the guillotine. But why should they condemn myself and my valet, two wholly innocent foreigners just arrived in France?"

The Duc looked at me and Sthan with interest. I was in the dress of a Swedish physician.

"Paris is a dangerous place for foreigners these days," he said. "More than yourselves have been condemned without reason. No doubt some enemy of yours in

Paris had accused you to the Revolutionary Committee of being a reactionary."

"It may be so," I said slowly. "I have an enemy who is in Paris, I know, though I do not know just where he is."

It was true, that, for Karnath and Etain, I was sure, were somewhere in the city. I did not know what identities were theirs now, what names they had, but their trail had led Sthan and me here. It might be that Karnath was the one who had had us condemned to the guillotine, though I had been sure he could not know us in our latest guise. Or maybe only idle rumor had been the cause. In any case, I cursed the fate that had brought us to die here with my vengeance unsatisfied. Would it ever be satisfied? Would those two ever elude me, mocking phantoms I could not grasp?

Since the night eight hundred years before, when they had fled from Count Otto's castle, we had followed them through generation after generation, body after body. In Italy, Spain, across Europe and nearer Asia we had pursued but had never again been so close to them. Now in this year 1793, this red summer when France was blazing with the Terror, it seemed our search was to end forever.

The Duc d'Harcourt rose to his feet, interrupting my dark revery.

"I must return to Madame la Duchesse. I trust that your wait for the tumbrils will not be too torturingly long, *monsieur*."

"While we wait, we live," I reminded him.

He bowed smilingly. "And while we live, we hope, even though we know hope is quite useless. *Adieu, monsieur*."

When he had gone I turned to my servant: "Do you too think that hope is useless, Sthan?"

"You will get us out of here, master," Sthan replied

with the calm confidence of the past six thousand years.

On the very next morning a stir ran through the prison and there was a shouting and running of guards. An excited fellow prisoner told me, "The Duc and Duchesse d'Harcourt were murdered horribly during the night. A turnkey and his wife are missing and it is believed that they did it."

The bodies were brought through the general prison room at that moment. My eyes fixed on them, dilating. The skulls of the Duc and Duchesse were opened, their brains missing!

I cried in crazy rage to Sthan, "The Duc and Duchesse d'Harcourt were Karnath and Etain! They did not know us, nor we them! And they have transferred their brains into the bodies of the turnkey and his woman and have escaped us!"

"If I had only known!" said Sthan. "He sat here beside me!"

When my first wild rage cooled, I said, "They must have instruments and materials they needed smuggled in to them by some of the guards. If they did it, we can do it, Sthan."

We did it, and one night we walked out in the bodies of two of the guards. Feverishly we searched Paris, but Karnath and Etain were gone.

The crash of exploding bombs rocked London in the darkness, drowning out ever and again the warning, wailing sirens and frantic bells that urged the hurrying people about us into underground shelters. In the distance great fingers of light searched the sky, sweeping back and forward. Then they held steady on a long, fish-like gray shape high in the sky above, a steadily moving Zeppelin from which high explosives continued to rain downward on the great city.

"Sthan, they are learning how to fight more efficiently as time goes by. What think you of these warriors?"

"We have seen many wars, master, but this one is the most terrible of all."

"Aye, but let them fight to their heart's content," I said. "Our business is not with their childish wars. Only I hope that none of these bombs kill Karnath and Etain. They must not die that way."

"Are you sure they are here in London, master?"

"Almost sure. We shall know in another half-hour whether this trail is false or true."

Sthan and I, two inoffensive Spaniards in appearance, walked steadily along that darkened street of London's West End, paying no attention to the crash of bombs still moving south across the city.

The sirens continued to wail, and airplanes droned by overhead in hot haste to attack the monster above. No lights showed in the whole metropolis, and one seemed abroad on the street but us.

For a century and a quarter Sthan and I had hung grimly to our search for the two whose track we had last lost in revolutionary Paris. In all that time we had not come up to them. The far-spread tumults of the Napoleonic wars had confused our hunt for years, and then all through the Nineteenth Century the guilty two had continued to elude us. Once in the Russia of the Czars we had almost had them, but adroitly they had escaped. For a dozen years we had lost their trail utterly; then it seemed to lead us toward a British politician, whose fashionable home I and my servant were pressing now.

"Sthan, somehow I feel that our long pursuit is approaching its end," I said.

"I too feel something of that, master—a feeling I have not had before."

We rounded a corner of the dark street. The noise of bombs was now receding but no one had yet ventured abroad. Then suddenly, as we passed the mouth of a black alley, I glimpsed in it the glint of two pistols pointing straight at my head.

I could not save myself by any movement of my own, I knew. I had a lightning-instant of agonized knowledge that here my pursuit ended indeed, with lost Atlantis unavenged, my sin unatoned.

The pistols spat fire and lead. But Sthan had glimpsed them in the moment I did, and had sprung in front of me.

"Master, beware!" he yelled as he sprang, and then the roar of the pistols came and he sank to the ground.

"Sthan!" I cried, and tore the pistol from my own pocket and poured a stream of shots across my servant's prone form.

The two in the black alley who had fired at us fell as my shots struck them. I bent over Sthan's limp form.

One look was enough. Both bullets had torn through his skull and into his brain. I had lost my companion for ever.

Dazedly, I looked at the two dead men in the alley. They were of a familiar type, burly, brutal London criminals.

I knew then that Karnath and Etain had become aware of our approach and had set these men to kill me. There was no use hunting now for Karnath and Etain in London. They would have fled, I knew.

So it proved, for when I came to look for them I found that the British politician and his mistress had disappeared.

Before I started on their track, I had my loyal, stedfast companion of sixty centuries buried in an English churchyard. Over his grave I placed a stone in

which was cut the legend, "STHAN OF ATLANTIS—A FAITH-
FUL SERVANT."

I started once more on the trail, and now with the
terrible knowledge that I must find those I sought
soon, or not at all. For I had now no Sthan to transfer
my brain into a new body when my present one grew
old. Nor could I teach anyone else how to do that,
since only an Atlantean had the mind and skill to
comprehend and execute that operation. None of these
people could ever do it.

My present body was over forty years old. unless I
found Karnath and Etain in the next twenty or thirty
years, I would die without finding them.

Alone—alone, now, for ever—I started on the last
of my age-old quest for vengeance.

"John Hardwick is the most powerful man on earth!"

I turned a little toward the speaker, one of two
young men sitting at the little table next to mine on
that Paris boulevard.

It was spring dusk and the chestnut trees above us
were white with blossoms.

"Kings and princes are puppets to John Hardwick!
And twenty years ago he was nobody."

I walked over to the table of my two neighbors, and
said, "Your pardon for intruding, gentlemen. But I
would like to learn something of this man Hardwick."

They looked up, two doubtful young men who saw
in me an elderly Spaniard with graying hair and a
lined, yellow face.

One of them said, "I thought everyone in the world
knew of John Hardwick."

"I have been traveling a great deal during the last
few years," I explained. "I have not read the daily
journals."

"Well, Hardwick is an American who is the world's

richest man," he said. "His fortune runs into billions, they say, and he lives in New York as though it was the capital of an invisible empire. Twenty years ago, at the time of the World War, he was just an obscure young clerk in an American city. Suddenly he began to show amazing far-sightedness and wizardry in finance, and rapidly vaulted up in power until today he is real ruler of half the world."

"And furthermore," the other added, "the husband of just about the most beautiful woman in the world."

I caught my breath. "The wife of John Hardwick is beautiful?"

"Stunningly so," he told me. "He married her shortly after he began his rise to power."

When they had gone I sat at my cafe table, thinking rapidly. Could this John Hardwick and his wife be Karnath and Etain?

It seemed more than possible. For the last twenty years, since I had lost my faithful Sthan in war-time London, I had found no trace of either of the treacherous twain. I had searched fiercely through Europe for them, while my body grew older and older, my strength slipping from me. Agony of soul was mine as I saw the inexorable approach of death, whom I had cheated for so long, robbing me of my rightful revenge.

It could well be that Karnath and Etain had fled to America and there, with their millennium-gathered wisdom, had risen to power and wealth while I searched vainly for them in the Old World. Yet if I went and found them not there, the time lost might be fatal.

I stood up suddenly. I had decided to go, to gamble my vengeance on the chance that John Hardwick was Karnath.

Two days later I was aboard a huge liner bound from Marseilles to New York, heading for my last hope of finding revenge and atonement before I died.

On the broad forward decks were twinkling lanterns and an orchestra's throbbing music, and happy young men and women dancing. Back in the darkness of the stern I stood at the rail, looking down with aching heart into the black, rushing waters. Far down there in the dimness and ooze and slime lay the wrecked marbles of the land of which I, Ulios, had been Guardian. In all the slow-revolving years they had rested there in silence and darkness, their only tenant the crawling squid.

A young man and a girl, flushed with dancing, came and leaned over the rail in the darkness near me.

"Do you know, the legended Atlantis is said to lie under these very seas we're sailing," I heard him tell her.

"A city down there—how wonderful!" she exclaimed. "Is there any truth to the legend?"

"Of course not, it's just a pretty fairystory," he said indulgently. "People used to believe it, but they know now such a city could never have existed."

Atlantis, Atlantis, shall the world ever see your like again, city of stainless white beauty beside the dark blue sea? Shall proud men and beautiful women ever again walk earth such as walked your green streets in the days of your glory?

The man and girl turned away to dance again, but I remained looking down at the rushing black waters.

The faithless twain who had cast my loved land down to doom beneath those waters still lived, still gloried in their evil. I prayed that I might be granted this last chance of vengeance and atonement.

When I reached New York, my hopes withered. For this John Hardwick and his wife who I hoped were Karnath and Etain were well-nigh utterly inaccessible. Their home was a great castle-like penthouse set on the top of a colossal skyscraper. When they were in it, armed guards watched every possible entrance. Even airplanes were forbidden over it. When John Hardwick or his wife went out of it, their car was guarded by other cars and by a dozen disguised bodyguards. The offices of the billionaire in lower New York were as heavily guarded.

For weeks I found it impossible even to see their faces. Yet I did not despair, for all this convinced me that they were so guarded because they feared something or someone greatly. And if they were Karnath and Etain, it was I, Ulios, whom they feared!

At last I had a momentary glimpse of them as they emerged one day from their great limousine. I knew at the first sight of John Hardwick's square, hard face and brilliant eyes, at the first glimpse of the woman's faultless features and secret gaze, they were Karnath and Etain.

My heart shouted thanksgiving within me. But still I was as far as ever from vengeance. How could I, a single, weak, aging man, hope even to gain access to this all-powerful pair?

Plan after plan I made, and had to discard. There seemed no way past the guards that always protected them. Then a plan came finally to me, one that was a slender reed indeed, but I decided to risk all upon it.

It was impossible to penetrate John Hardwick's penthouse castle when he or his wife were there. But I found it possible to enter the place during their absence. In the billionaire's study, I swiftly and secretly did that which I had planned. Then I left without anyone seeing me.

That night I went up to the door of that high stronghold again. John Hardwick and his wife were there now, and the place was ringed with guards who stopped me at once. In answer to their questions, I wrote the single word "Ulios" on a card and sent it in to the billionaire.

In a few minutes he who had taken the card in came quickly back. John Hardwick had ordered me brought in. They searched me first for weapons, so thoroughly that no tiniest one could have been concealed on me. Then they took me in.

John Hardwick sat with the woman in the study whose windows looked out across the blinking lights of New York. He took a heavy pistol from his desk and, pointing it calmly at my head, ordered the guards all to leave.

When they had gone I stood, a gray, thin old man, looking at this man and woman I had pursued across the ages.

"Well, Ulios," said Karnath to me, "what have you to say to me before I slay you?"

"Slay him now, at once!" cried Etain, her eyes wide with hate and fear as they watched me. "I trust him not!"

"Fear not, Etain—he cannot harm us now," Karnath reassured her, and said again to me, "Why do you come openly like this, Ulios?"

My voice was cracked and quavering as I answered desperately, "I came because I wish to call truce to this world-old feud of ours. Why should we hate each other for ever, Karnath? It is long ago since Atlantis sank and died, and was forgotten. Why should not we forget our hate and live in amity through time to come?"

He laughed, and the silver, scornful laughter of Etain chimed with his. And their eyes were glad with triumph now.

"Ulios, you do not deceive me," he said. "Twenty years ago we had your servant Sthan killed, and now you have no one to help you to a new body, nor can you teach any of these barbarians how to transfer your brain to another body, and you know that soon you must die forever in that body unless one of us takes pity on you. Well, I will take pity on you, Ulios! I will end your life here and now without further waiting, and we shall be rid of your pursuit for ever, and Etain and I shall live on and on while the world lasts. Think of that, Ulios, and die!"

His finger pressed the trigger as he spat the words. But there was only an empty click from the pistol. His face suddenly fearful, Karnath pressed the trigger again and again, but no shots came forth.

It was my turn then to laugh, and laugh I did as sickly fear spread across the faces of the two.

"The bullets in that pistol will never fire, Karnath," I said. "I saw to that when I entered this room secretly today."

"Guards! Guards!" yelled Karnath, but again I only laughed.

"You sent them away yourself, so that they might not hear you kill me. Now they will not hear me kill you."

Etain darted to the door but I was ahead of her and flung her back and locked the door swiftly. Then I turned.

Karnath came out from behind his desk, raising a heavy lamp wildly to dash down upon my head.

I caught his wrist and forced him to drop it. We struggled there, and though he was the younger by many years, he was a child in my grasp. I was no longer a trembling old man. The strength of every arm in doomed Atlantis seemed in my arm.

My thin hands held his throat with a steely grip he could not break. The woman watched in frozen, paralyzed horror as I stalked steadily, remorselessly, with struggling Karnath to the windows. I forced his head back down over the ledge of the open window, his protruding eyes staring wildly up at me.

"Gods of Atlantis, look down on a sacrifice and an atonement!" I thundered, and flung Karnath clear of the window.

I saw his body go whirling downward through the darkness, and then I turned.

Etain was flattened against the wall, her eyes dilated with awful fear, her beauty all lost in horror. But she came forward, glided fearfully closer to me, her eyes pleading.

"Do not slay me, Ulios!" she begged in frantic fear. "You loved me once!"

She came closer, breathlessly wheedling and insinuating.

"Only you and I are left now, Ulios—but we two can still live on immortally. We can still transfer each other's brains to new bodies at need. I will love you, as no woman has loved before. You will do it, Ulios? You will spare me and live on with me?"

I looked at her, and smiled. I took from my pocket a tiny black tablet which I put into my mouth and swallowed.

"What are you doing?" cried Etain.

I told her, "I have just swallowed a subtle poison. In an hour I will be dead, for my vengeance and atonement are finished. You are part of that atonement, Etain. You are not going to die, you are going to live on by yourself in that body, and grow old in it. Yes, you shall experience that thing you feared most of all in the world, that to prevent which you betrayed Atlantis. *You shall grow old!*"

I walked to the door and unlocked it. "I go now to complete the record of my sin and my atonement which I have written, and then to die. Farewell, Etain."

"Ulios!" she cried, and as I went out of the door and closed it behind me I heard her hoarse scream again.

"Ulios!"

SCAR-TISSUE

by Henry S. Whitehead

"What is your opinion on the Atlantis question?" I asked my friend Dr. Pelletier of the U.S. Navy, as he relaxed during the afternoon swizzle hour on my West gallery. He waved a depreciating hand.

"All the real evidence points to it, doesn't it, Canevin? The harbor here in St. Thomas, for instance. Crater of a volcano. What could bring a crater down to sea-level like that, unless the submergence of quadrillions of tons of earth and rock, or the submergence of a continent?" Then: "What made you ask me that, Canevin?"

"A case," I replied. "Picked him up yesterday morning just after he had jumped-ship from that Spanish tram, the *Bilbao*, that was coaling at the West India Docks yesterday morning. She pulled out this afternoon without him. Says his name is Joe Smith. A rough and tough bird, if I ever saw one. Up against it. They were crowding him pretty heavily, according to his story. Extra watches. Hazing. Down with the damned gringo! Looks as if he could handle himself, too—hard as nails. I've got him right here in the house."

"What are you keeping him shut up for?" inquired

Pelletier lazily. "There isn't anybody on his trail now, is there?"

"No," I said. "But he was all shot to pieces from lack of sleep. Red rims around his eyes. He's upstairs, asleep, probably dead to the world. I looked in on him an hour ago."

"What bearing has the alleged Joe Smith on Atlantis?" Pelletier's tone was still lazily curious.

"Well," I said, "Smith looks to me as though he had one of those dashes of 'ancestral memory,' like the fellow Kipling tells about, the one who 'remembered' being a slave at the oars, and how a Roman galley was put together. Only, this isn't any measly two thousand years ago. This is—"

Pelletier straightened in his lounge-chair.

"Good God, Canevin! And he's here—in this house?"

Twenty minutes later Smith stepped out on the gallery. He looked vastly different from the beachcomber I had picked up near the St. Thomas market-place the morning before. He was tall and spare, and my white drill clothes might have been made for him. He was cleanly shaven and his step was alert.

Pelletier did most of the talking. He established a quick footing with Smith with an obvious view to getting his story of the "buried memory" which the fellow had mentioned to me, and which pointed, he had hinted, at Atlantis.

At the end of ten minutes or so, Pelletier surprised me.

"What was your college, Smith?" he inquired.

"Harvard and Oxford," he answered. "Rhodes Scholar. Took my M.A. at Balliol. Yes, of course, Dr. Pelletier. Ask me anything you like. This 'buried memory' affair has come on me three different times, as a matter of fact. Always when I'm below par physically, a bit run down, vitality lower than normal. I mentioned it to Mr. Canevin yesterday—sensed that he would be interested. I've read his stuff, you see, for the past dozen years or so!"

I was getting interested myself now.

"Tell us about it," invited Pelletier, and Joe Smith proceeded to do so:

"It began when I was a small boy, after scarlet fever. I got up too soon and went swimming, had a relapse, and the next three or four days, lying in bed, I 'realized' that I was *memoriter familiar* with a previous life in which I wore clothing of animal skins and used stone-headed clubs. I had the ability to run long distances and go up and down trees without much effort, and could easily club a bear to death. The thing passes off, dims out, although the recollection remained quite clear, as soon as I was well again.

"The second time was after the Spring track-meet with Yale when I was twenty-one. I had run in the 220, and then, half an hour later, I put everything I had into a quarter-mile, and won it. I lay around and rested according to my trainer's orders for a week— not even reading a book. Then I 'remembered'—not the cave-life this time—but Africa. Portuguese and Negroes; enormous buildings, some of them with walls sixteen feet thick. Granite quarries and the Portuguese sweating the Blacks in some ancient gold mines. There were two rivers. I fished in them a great deal, with a big iron hook. They were called, the rivers, I mean, the Lindi and the Sobi.

"Curious kind of place. There was one enormous ruin, a circular tower on top of a round hill which was formed by an outcropping in the granite. There was a procession of bulls carved around the pediment. Yes, and the signs of the Zodiac."

"Southern Rhodesia!" I cried out. "The Portuguese controlled it in the Fifteenth Century, before Columbus' time. Why, man, that place is the traditional site of Solomon's gold mines!"

"Right!" Smith remarked, turning an intelligent eye in my direction. "It was pronounced, in those days— 'Zim-baub-weh'— accent on the first syllable. I've often wondered if it wasn't the Romans who carved those bulls, they had the place first, called it *Anaeropolis*. Plenty of legionaries were Mithraists, and the bull was Mithras' symbol, you know."

"And the last one, Smith," Pelletier cut in. "You mentioned Atlantis, Canevin tells me."

"Well," began Smith once more, "the fact that it was Atlantis is, really secondary. There is one item in *that* 'memory' which is of very much greater interest, I should imagine.

"I don't want to be theatrical, gentlemen! But—well, I think the best way to begin telling you about it is to show you this!"

He rose and loosening his belt, pulled up his shirt and singlet, exposing a bronzed torso. Beginning a half-inch above his right hip-bone and extending straight across as though laid out with a ruler across the abdomen, ran a livid, inch-wide scar.

Joe Smith tucked in his shirt, tightened his belt, and sat down again. "That's where it begins," he said, and, as my house-man. Stephen Penn, appeared at this moment with the dinner-cocktails, he added: "I'll tell you about it after dinner."

It was Pelletier who started things off as soon as we were settled on the gallery again, with coffee and Chartreuse before us.

"I want to know, please, how you happen to be alive."

Smith smiled wryly.

"I never told this before," he said, "and if I was

somewhat preoccupied during dinner it was because I've been figuring out how to put it all together for you.

"It's hard to put into words but it seemed as if I were walking through a short enclosed passageway, rather wide, stone-flagged, and low-ceilinged. In front of me, beside me, and behind me, walked eighteen or twenty others, all of us armed. Up in front of us, in bronze armor, and closing our rear, marched eight legionaries of the Ludektan army assigned to us as guards.

"We came out into the drenching sunlight of a great sanded arena. We followed our advance guard in a sharp turn to the right and wheeled to the right-face before a great awninged box full of the Ludektan nobles and dignitaries, where we saluted sharply.

"Do you get that picture? Here we were, prisoners of war—after a couple of months of the hardest training I have ever known, in the Ludektan gladitorial school, about to shed our blood to make an Atlantean holiday!

"The really tough part of it was the uncertainty. I mean a fellow might be paired to fight one of his friends. But I was fortunate that day. I was paired with a Gamfron—a nearly black Atlantean mountain lion, an animal about the size and heft of an Indian black panther—Bagheera, in Kipling's Mowgli yarn! I had been armed with a short, sharp, double-edged sword and a small bronze buckle. Otherwise I had been given choice of my own accoutrement and I had selected greaves, a light breastplate and a close-fitting helmet with a face-guard attachment with eye holes, covering practically my whole face and the back and sides of my neck.

"When it came my turn to step out on the sand and wait for the lion to be released, I asked the official in charge for permission to discard the buckler and use an additional weapon, a long dagger, in my left hand. I received the permission, and at the signal-blast which was made with a ram's horn, walked slowly towards the cage-entrance. I had noted that the sun was shining directly, full against that particular iron door.

"My strategy worked precisely as I had hoped.

The great beast came out blinking. Before its cat eyes became adjusted to the sun's glare I launched myself upon it, and when I sprang away, the hilt of that dagger was sticking in the Gamfron's back. The beast rolled over in the sand, hoping, I suppose, to dislodge the dagger. The hilt was twisted, I noticed, when the Gamfron again crouched for its leap at me.

"In the split seconds before it launched itself at me I could hear the wild tumult from the stands. The crowd swayed hysterically—screaming for blood. Mine.

"I side-stepped as the beast charged, but instead of trying another slash, I whirled, and as the beast plowed up the sand beside me, I threw myself upon it and, thrust my sword into the soft flesh of its throat, severing the jugular. Then, my feet and legs wedged hard under the animal's flanks. I reached under its jaws, swinging backward from the fulcrum of my knees and hauled the Gamfron's head backwards towards me.

"The snap could be heard throughout the arena. The great beast relaxed under me. I recovered my sword, stood up, placed my right foot upon the carcass and held up my sword toward the notables in the rigid salute signifying victory.

"The next thing I was directly conscious of was a hand falling on my left shoulder. I relaxed, let down my sword, and heard the voice of the official in charge of the gladiators telling me that I was reprieved. I stumbled along beside him around the edge of the arena under a continuous shower of felt hats and gold and silver coin until I felt the grateful shade of a stone passage-way on my almost melting back, and a minute later, with my armor off, I was being doused from head to foot with buckets of cold water.

"It was perhaps twenty minutes later when the official in charge of the gladiators came into the small stone-flagged room where I was tying the thongs of my sandals.

" 'The people demand your presence in the arena,' he announced from just inside the doorway. I rose and bowed in his direction. A public gladiator in Ludekta had the status of a slave. Then the official announced: 'You have been chosen to fight Godbor as the day's concluding event—come!' "

"Half way along the passageway the official stopped and turned to me, whispering with earnestness and vehemency directly into my ear. And when he had finished I was a new man! Gone now were all the feelings of rebellious hatred which his announcement at the rubbing-room door had raised up in me. He turned and led the way out into the arena. And I followed him now gladly, eagerly, my head up and my heart beating high.

"A thunderous roar greeted us, and the massed thousands rose in their seats like one man. A black slave stepping towards us from the barrier handed a bulging leather sack to the official. He took it and spoke to me over his shoulder. 'These are your coins that were thrown into the ring. I will keep them safely for you!

"Then we proceeded to a point directly before the great canopied enclosure of the nobles. Here, after saluting with my arms and hands straight up above my head and not giving their spokesman an opportunity to address me, I put into immediate effect what my un-suspecting friend, had whispered in my ear.

" 'I will fight Godbor to the death,' I shouted.

"A deafening howl went up from the multitude. I waited quietly until the tumult died, and then as soon as I could be heard once more I addressed the nobles.

" 'My Lords, I have proclaimed my willingness to please you despite the Ludektan Law which requires no man to fight twice in the arena on the same day. I beseech your nobility therefore, in return for this my good will to meet your desire, that you accord me my liberty, if I survive.'

"There was a deathly silence about the arena, while the nobles consulted together.

I stood there, rigid, waiting for this decision which meant far more than life or death to me. I could see the right arms of the members of that vast concourse being raised in the Ludektan voting gesture of approval.

"Then, as Bothon, who had been generalissimo of all the Ludektan armies, rose in his place to give me my answer, that sharp humming sound stilled and died and twenty thousand men and women leaned forward on their benches to hear the decision. Bothon was both terse and explicit.

" 'The petition is granted,' he announced.

"Remembering clearly all that the arena official had told me, I waited once more until I could be heard, and when that instant arrived I saluted the nobles and said:

" 'I would gladly slay the traitorous dog Godbor without reward, o illustrious, for not even yourselves, who deprived him his Ludekatan citizenship and condemned him to the arena, are better aware of his infamy than we of Lemuria who refused to profit by his treachery. I petition you that the rules which are to govern our combat be stated here, in his presence and mine, that there be no treachery but a fair fight.'

"At this, which had been listened to in a dead

silence that was almost painful, the mob on the benches broke out again.

Watching the nobles' enclosure I saw Bothon turning his eyes to those about him. When he had gathered their decisions he turned to me and made the sign of approval.

"Back in the preparation rooms with the chief official himself over-looking every detail, I got myself ready for my last fight in the arena. I was very well aware that I was now confronted with the most serious ordeal of my life. Not only had I spent most of my strength in that conflict with the wild beast, but also I was about to encounter in the traitor Godbor, one of the most skillful and tricky hand-to-hand fighters that the Ludektan army had ever produced. He would be fresh, too.

"At high noon, Godbor who had been similarly prepared in another room, walked beside me in the usual form of procession, proceeding through the passageway and into the blinding glare, shortly to stand side by side listening to Bothon repeat the rules of the combat.

"And then on a great square of freshly pressed and dampened sand we two stood facing each other tensed for a conflict from which one or the other would never leave.

"At the single blast from the herald's horn I leaped at my enemy. He had started forward at the same instant himself. I caught his descending blade squarely on the knob of my bronze buckler, relaxing my left arm to lessen the shock of the blow, at the same time delivering a thrust above Godbor's buckler. The fresh-ground razor-like point of my sword struck his upper shoulder, severing the tendon and rendering his left arm useless. I made a rapid recovery, but the equally swift forward leap of Godbor brought him breast to breast with me. He managed to shift his sword into a dagger-like position, and I was barely able to divert the stabbing stroke which he aimed for my left side.

"We backed away from each other then for, according to the stated rules of the combat, our initial attack-and-defense was completed. Then I lowered my sword as I saw Godbor drooping forward, his knees sagging under him, his eyes closing. As I stood there, waiting for him to recover himself, he suddenly dropped off the buckler from his left arm, and, launching himself forward, drove the bronze helmet he wore against my chest.

"I went crashing down under the terrific blow and I could hear very clearly, rising above everything, the howl of rage which rose from the spectators on every side.

"Then, Godbor was upon me, his face a distorted mask of hatred. His sword slashed into my right hip bone and across the lower and unprotected edge of my ribs.

"A dull-red cloud descended upon me, and a vicious stab of pain that swelled with each second. My fast-dimming eyes caught the edge of the strange spectacle of the people of the benches leaping down on the sand in their dozens and scores and hundreds, pouring over the barriers into the arena like cascades.

"And, with the dimming chorus of their massed roars of hate in my ears, I let go of life."

Joe Smith ceased speaking, rose, and walked over to the center table. I noticed that his hands trembled as he poured himself out the second drink he had taken since he had been in my house. Deep lines, too, that had not shown before dinner, were in his clean-shaven face. It was evident that the telling of his strange tale had done something to him. He settled in his chair again before either Pelletier or I offered any comment.

"I imagine Godbor didn't survive you very long," I said. "That mob probably took him apart."

Smith nodded. "He was very unpopular-execrated, in fact."

Pelletier's comments were in an entirely different vein.

"I beg of you, don't misunderstand me, Smith, but most people would say it's a wonderful yarn, as a yarn, but that's all. Atlantis, Zimbabwe, that caveboy stuff! That scar of yours for a point of departure; well-known facts, open to any reader, abut the ancestral memory theory; and all of 'em worked up into a yarn that is, I grant you, a corncraker! Exactly right, you see, for a couple of fellows like Canevin and me, known to be interested in out-of-the-ordinary matters. That, I say, is what the majority of people would say. I'm not insulting you by putting it that way myself. I merely call attention to the fact that there isn't a thing in it that couldn't have been put together by a clever story-teller."

Smith merely nodded. "Precisely as you put it," he said. "Precisely, except for this."

And he rose from his chair, once again loosened his belt, and exposed that frightful scar.

Pelletier, the surgeon uppermost at once, got up, came over to Smith, and peered closely at it.

"Hm," he remarked, "the real mystery isn't in that yarn, Smith. It's in how you ever survived this! The breadth of this scar shows that the wound must have been several inches deep. It cut straight through the intestines and just about bisected the spleen. Such a cut would kill a man in a few minutes."

"It did, as I told you," said Smith, a little crisply.

"My dear man!" protestingly, from Pelletier.

But Joe Smith remained entirely unruffled.

"You know, of course, what scar-tissue feels like to the touch," he said. "Run your hand over this, Doctor. Then tell us if you ever felt any other scar-tissue like it. It *looks* like any other scar, of course."

Pelletier did as requested, his attitude plainly skeptical. But he straightened up from this examination with a very different look on his face.

"Good God!" he breathed. "There's nothing to feel! This thing only *looks* like scar-tissue! What—?"

Smith carefully tucked in his shirt.

"It's precisely the way I told it to you. I was born without any appearance of a scar, although it falls within the classification of so-called 'birthmarks.' It did not begin to appear until I was twenty-seven. That was my age when I died there in the arena, from that wound in the same place, just as I told you."

Pelletier looked at Joe Smith in blank silence. Then he asked, "Did you have it on you during those two other 'memory-experiences' you spoke of, as a caveboy, or there in Africa in the Fifteenth Century?"

"No," Smith replied. "I suppose the reason is that I was not yet twenty-seven years of age in either of those two experiences."

"Well, I'll take your word for it all, Smith," said Pelletier. "It's been mighty interesting."

The two of them bowed to each other, Pelletier smiling whimsically, Joe Smith's tired, lined face inscrutable.

Just after this Pelletier took his departure.

Half an hour later—it must have been about eleven—Smith rapped on the door of my bedroom. He was in pajamas and bathrobe, and wearing a pair of my spare slippers.

"Would you like to hear the rest of it?" he asked, coming in and taking a chair. He placed something he had been carrying beside him on the wide chair's cushion.

"There isn't much more of it," he remarked, "but I'd rather like you to hear it all together."

"Fire away," I invited, settling myself.

"That 'birth-mark' of mine," he began, "isn't the only thing I could have shown you this evening. I had *this* around my waist, too!"

He reached down beside him and unrolled the thing he had brought into my room. It was a pigskin money-belt.

"There's between seven and eight hundred pounds in this," he remarked, laying it on the table beside him, "in Bank of England notes. I though you might put it in your safe until tomorrow, and then I'll put it in the bank. And now, here's the rest of my story.

"I'd been on board the *Bilbao* nearly two months when we struck this port of St. Thomas to coal. It was, to be precise, the fourteenth of August when I went on board her, in Santander. Three days before that, while I was sitting eating my dinner, a big fellow came in and took a table across the room from me. I didn't particularly take note of him except that he was big. He had an ugly face that seemed vaguely familiar.

"Then quite suddenly, it broke upon me. I knew who he was! It was 'Godbor,' Canevin—Godbor to the life! The man who had killed me in the arena!

"I sat there, and just sweated. I remembered putting my face between my hands, my elbows on the table, and feeling just plain sick.

"And then he moved over to my table and sat down.

"He was civil enough. His name was Fernando Lopez. He was the first mate of the *Bilbao*, just arrived in Santander harbor, expecting to clear for Buenos Aires three or four days from then.

"Lopez proposed that we eat together. Somehow I couldn't refuse. There was almost a weird fascination about the man. While we ate I told him I was a painter and required as much time to myself, including meal-time, as I could get. I spoke, of course, without trying to insult him, but nevertheless giving the impression I wanted to be alone. But it was no use.

"We drank together, and within a few hours I had passed out. When I awoke it was morning—the morning of the day the *Bilbao* was to clear from Santander, about seven o'clock. And then I found my money-belt gone! Fernando Lopez, too, was gone! He had probably gone on board, I figured, ready for the ship's departure, confident that he had made a clean getaway.

He saw me, as soon as I came on board. I charged him flatly with the theft. He made no bones about it, admitted he had taken the money-belt from me after I passed out, and had it down in his cabin. I demanded its return and he shrugged, walking toward his cabin.

"As I walked in after him, something struck me over the head. I came to in a berth, with my hands ironed, and a head that seemed too big for my body.

"For three days I sweated through a period that was like a nightmare.

"The captain, an old man named Chico Perez, who was Lopez' uncle, forced me to sign on. I was watched every minute and given the work of two men to do.

"They ironed me again the day we put into Buenos Aires. Lopez was taking no chances on my jumping ship and reporting him. Then, two days after we cleared from there, the old captain disappeared. I have no doubts in my own mind about what happened to him. Lopez probably threw him overboard.

"That fact, I imagine, saved me. You see, the entire crew had sailed with the old man, who was a part owner of the ship. Lopez, while he now commanded the *Bilbao*, did not dare to risk a mutiny if another member of the ship's company 'disappeared' in the same manner.

"We made four or five other South American ports, Cartagena last of all, and then we were to put in to St. Thomas for coal. This was the first American port of the voyage. I picked up a little hope.

"We were actually in sight of St. Thomas when I got my chance. It was about five o'clock in the evening, four days ago. I was on deck, and we had just made our landfall. Lopez was coming towards me across the deck. I waited until he was within a few feet of me, and then I lunged forward. My fist hit Lopez' jaw, knocking him flat on the deck.

"He was up almost instantly, snarling, and a knife appeared in his hand. I ducked his first rush and tripped him as he swept by me. His knife clattered on the deck as he hit it.

"I lunged forward and my fingers closed over the blade. I don't know what happened next, but suddenly the knife was imbedded in Lopez' back and I was on my feet, trembling with a cold sweat.

"One by one the crew members walked up. They all seemed to be smiling at me.

"I watched the knife being withdrawn from Lopez' body by one of them, and then, five men quietly heaved the body overboard.

"Nothing was said to me. There was no report, no investigation after we anchored in St. Thomas Harbor.

"I had gone straight down to Lopez' cabin after the money-belt, put it on, and came back on deck.

"No one stopped me when I went ashore. I imagine that that ship's family was only too glad to get rid of the fellow who had relieved them of Fernando Lopez. The rest of it you know, Canevin. I might add that I haven't the smallest possible regret over killing Lopez.

If those 'ancestral memories' of mine are authentic, I have killed before, but never in *this life*, certainly."

Joe Smith sat silent, and I sat across from him and looked at him. The only thing I could think of to ask, seemed an incongruity after what I had listened to that day! However I had to ask it.

"What is your real name, Smith?" I inquired.

He stared at me.

"Joe Smith," he said.

I nodded then. "I'll put your money in the safe and we'll go to the bank with it in the morning."

I saw him out, and picked up the money-belt from the table and carried it over to my house-safe standing in the corner of my bedroom.

I opened the safe and was about to lay the belt inside when I felt something rough against my hand. I turned it about and looked. A name was embossed upon the fine pigskin leather of the other side. I held it up to the light to read it. I read:

JOSEPHUS TROY SMITH

I put the belt inside and closed and locked the safe.

Then I came back and sat down in the chair where I had listened to my guest's recital of his recent adventures aboard the Spanish tramp steamer *Bilbao*.

Josephus Troy Smith. It wasn't so vastly different from "Joe Smith," and yet what a different viewpoint that full name had given me! Josephus Troy Smith, America's foremost landscapist! Josephus Troy Smith! I realized now whom I was having the honor of entertaining in my house on Denmark Hill, St. Thomas, Virgin Islands of the U.S.A. He was the eccentric artist, Josephus Troy Smith—or was he . . .

THE DOUBLE SHADOW

by Clark Ashton Smith

My name is Pharpetron, among those who have known me in Poseidonis; but even I, the last and most forward pupil of the wise Avyctes, know not the name of that which I am fated to become ere to-morrow. Therefore, by the ebbing silver lamps, in my master's marble house above the loud, ever-ravening sea, I write this tale with a hasty hand, scrawling an ink of wizard virtue on the grey, priceless, antique parchment of dragons. And having written, I shall enclose the pages in a sealed cylinder of orichalchum, and shall cast the cylinder from a high window into the sea, lest that which I am doomed to become should haply destroy the writing. And it may be that mariners from Lephara, passing to Umb and Pneor in their tall triremes, will find the cylinder; or fishers will draw it from the wave in their seines of byssus; and having read my story, men will learn the truth and take warning; and no man's feet, henceforward, will approach the pale and demon-haunted house of Avyctes.

For six years, I have dwelt apart with the aged master, forgetting youth and its wonted desires in the study of arcanic things. Together, we have delved more deeply than all others before us in an interdicted lore; we have solved the keyless hieroglyphs that guard ante-human formulae; we have talked with the prehistoric dead; we have called up the dwellers in sealed crypts, in fearful abysses beyond space. Few are the sons of mankind who have cared to seek us out among the desolate, wind-worn crags; and many, but nameless, are the visitants who have come to us from further bourns of place and time.

Stern and white as a tomb, older than the memory of the dead, and built by men or devils beyond the recording of myth, is the mansion wherein we dwell. Far below, on black, naked reefs, the northern sea climbs and roars indomitably, or ebbs with a ceaseless murmur as of armies of baffled demons; and the house is filled evermore, like a hollow-sounding sepulcher, with the drear echo of its tumultuous voices; and the winds wail in dismal wrath around the high towers, but shake them not. On the seaward side, the mansion rises sheerly from the straight-falling cliff; but on the other sides there are narrow terraces, grown with dwarfish, crooked cedars that bow always beneath the gale. Giant marble monsters guard the landward portals; and huge marble women ward the strait porticoes above the sea; and mighty statues and mummies stand everywhere in the chambers and along the halls. But, saving these, and the spirits we have summoned, there is none to companion us; and liches and shadows have been the servitors of our daily needs.

All men have heard the fame of Avyctes, the sole surviving pupil of that Malygris who tyrannized in his necromancy over Susran from a tower of sable stone; Malygris, who lay dead for years while men believed him living; who, lying thus, still uttered potent spells and dire oracles with decaying lips. But Avyctes lusted not for temporal power in the manner of Malygris; and having learned all that the elder sorcerer could teach him, withdrew from the cities of Poseidonis to seek another and vaster dominion; and I, the youth Pharpetron, in the latter years of Avyctes, was permitted to join him in this solitude; and since then, I have shared his austerities and vigils and evocations . . . and now, likewise, I must share the weird doom that has come in answer to his summoning.

Not without terror (since man is but mortal) did I, the neophyte, behold at first the abhorrent and tremendous faces of them that obeyed Avyctes: the genii of the sea and earth, of the stars and the heavens, who passed to and fro in his marmorean halls. I shuddered at the black writhing of submundane things from the many-volumed smoke of the braziers; I cried in horror at the grey foulnesses, colossal, without form, that crowded malignly about the drawn circle of seven colors, threatening unspeakable trespass on us that stood at the center. Not without revulsion did I drink wine that was poured by cadavers, and eat bread that was purveyed by phantoms. But use and custom dulled the strangeness, destroyed the fear; and in time I believed implicitly that Avyctes was the lord of all incantations and exorcisms, with infallible power to dismiss the beings he evoked.

Well had it had been for Avyctes—and for me—if the master had contented himself with the lore preserved from Atlantis and Thule, or brought over from Mu and Mayapan. Surely this should have been enough: for in the ivory-sheeted books of Thule there were blood-writ runes that would call the demons of the fifth and seventh planets, if spoken aloud at the hour of their ascent; and the sorcerers of Mu had left record of a process whereby the doors of far-future time could be unlocked; and our fathers, the Atlanteans, had known the road between the atoms and the path into far stars, and had held speech with the spirits of the sun. But Avyctes thirsted for a darker knowledge, a deeper empery; and into his hands, in the third year of my novitiate, there came the mirror-bright tablet of the lost serpent-people.

Strange, and apparently fortuitous, was our finding of the tablet. At certain hours, when the tide had fallen from the steep rocks, we were wont to descend by cavern-hidden stairs to a cliff-walled crescent beach behind the promontory on which stood the house of Avyctes. There, on the dun, wet sands, beyond the foamy tongues of the surf, would lie the worn and curious driftage of alien shores, and trove that hurricanes had cast up from unsounded deeps. And there we had found the purple and sanguine volutes of great shells, and rude lumps of ambergris, and white flowers of perpetually blooming coral; and once, the barbaric idol of green brass that had been the figurehead of a galley from far hyperborean isles.

There had been a great storm, such as must have riven the sea to its nethermost profound; but the tempest had gone by with morning, and the heavens were cloudless on that fatal day when we found the tablet, and the demon winds were hushed among the black crags and chasms; and the sea lisped with a low whisper, like the rustle of gowns of samite trailed by fleeing maidens on the sand. And just beyond the ebbing wave, in a tangle of russet sea-weed, we beheld a thing that glittered with blinding sun-like brilliance. And running forward, I plucked it from the wrack before the wave's return, and bore it to Avyctes.

The tablet was wrought of some nameless metal, like never-rusting iron, but heavier. It had the form of a triangle and was broader at the widest than a man's heart. On one side it was wholly blank; and Avyctes and I, in turn, beheld our features mirrored strangely, like the drawn, pallid features of the dead, in its burnished surface. On the other side many rows of small crooked ciphers were incised deeply in the metal, as if by the action of some mordant acid; and these ciphers were not the pictorial symbols or alphabetic characters of any language known to the master or to me.

Of the tablet's age and origin, likewise, we could form no conjecture; and our erudition was altogether baffled. For many days thereafter we studied the writing and held argument that came to no issue. And night by night, in a high chamber closed against the perennial winds, we pondered over the dazzling triangle by the tall straight flames of silver lamps. For Avyctes deemed that knowledge of rare value (or haply some secret of an alien or elder magic) was holden by the clueless crooked ciphers. Then, since all our scholarship was in vain, the master sought another divination, and had recourse to wizardy and necromancy. But at first, among the devils and phantoms that answered our interrogation, none could tell us aught concerning the tablet. And any other than Avyctes would have despaired in the end . . . and well would it have been if he had despaired, and had sought no longer to decipher the writing. . . .

The months and years went by with a slow thundering of seas on the dark rocks, and a headlong clamor of winds around the white towers. Still we continued our delvings and evocations; and further, always further we went into lampless realms of space and spirit; learning, perchance, to unlock the hithermost of the manifold infinities. And at whiles, Avyctes would resume his pondering of the sea-found tablet; or would question some visitant from other spheres of time and place regarding its interpretation.

At last, by the use of a chance formula, in idle experiment, he summoned up the dim, tenuous ghost of a sorcerer from prehistoric years; and the ghost, in a thin whisper of uncouth, forgotten speech, informed us that the letters on the tablet were those of a language of the serpent-men, whose primordial continent had sunk aeons before the lifting of Hyperborea from the ooze. But the ghost could tell us naught of their significance; for, even in his time, the serpent-people had become a dubious legend; and their deep, ante-human lore and sorcery were things irretrievable by man.

Now, in all the books of conjuration owned by Avyctes, there was no spell whereby we could call the lost serpent-men from their fabulous epoch. But there was an old Lemurian formula, recondite and uncertain, by which the shadow of a dead man could be sent into years posterior to those of his own life-time, and could be recalled after an interim by the wizard. And the shade, being wholly insubstantial, would suffer no harm from the temporal transition, and would remember, for the information of the wizard, that which he had been instructed to learn during the journey.

So, having called again the ghost of the prehistoric sorcerer, whose name was Ybith, Avyctes made a singular use of several very ancient gums and combustible fragments of fossil wood; and he and I, reciting the responses to the formula, sent the thin spirit of Ybith into the far ages of the serpent-men. And after a time which the master deemed sufficient, we performed the curious rites of incantation that would recall Ybith from his alienage. And the rites were successful; and Ybith stood before us again, like a blown vapor that is nigh to vanishing. And in words that were faint as the last echo of perishing memories, the specter told us the key to the meaning of the letters, which he had learned in the primeval past; and after this, we questioned Ybith no more, but suffered him to return unto slumber and oblivion.

Then, knowing the import of the tiny, twisted ciphers, we read the writing on the tablet and made thereof a transliteration, though not without labor and difficulty, since the very phonetics of the serpent tongue, and the symbols and ideas expressed in the writing, were somewhat alien to those of mankind. And when we had mastered the inscription, we found that it contained the formula for a certain evocation which, no doubt, had been used by the serpent sorcerers. But the object of the evocation was not named; nor was there any clue to the nature or identity of that which would come in answer to the rites. And moreover there was no corresponding rite of exorcism nor spell of dismissal.

Great was the jubilation of Avyctes, deeming that we had learned a lore beyond the memory or prevision of man. And though I sought to dissuade him, he resolved to employ the evocation, arguing that our discovery was no chance thing but was fatefully predestined from the beginning. And he seemed to think lightly of the menace that might be brought upon us by the conjuration of things whose nativity and attributes were wholly obscure. "For," said Avyctes, "I have called up, in all the years of my sorcery, no god or devil, no demon or lich or shadow, which I could not control and dismiss at will. And I am loath to believe that any power or spirit beyond the subversion of my spells could have been summoned by a race of serpents, whatever their skill in demonism and necromancy."

So, seeing that he was obstinate, and acknowledging him for my master in all ways, I consented to aid Avyctes in the experiment, though not without dire misgivings. And then we gathered together, in the chamber of conjuration, at the specified hour and configuration of the stars, the equivalents of sundry rare materials that the tablet had instructed us to use in the ritual.

Of much that we did, and of certain agents that we employed, it were better not to tell; nor shall I record the shrill, sibilant words, difficult for beings not born of serpents to articulate, whose intonation formed a signal part of the ceremony. Toward the last, we drew a triangle on the marble floor with the fresh blood of birds; and Avyctes stood at one angle, and I at another; and the gaunt umber mummy of an Atlantean warrior, whose name had been Oigos, was stationed at the third angle. And standing thus, Avyctes and I held tapers of corpse-tallow in our hands, till the tapers had burned down between our fingers as into a socket. And in the outstretched palms of the mummy of Oigos, as if in shallow thuribles, talc and asbestos burned, ignited by a strange fire whereof we knew the secret. At one side we had traced on the floor an infrangible ellipse, made by an endless linked repetition of the twelve unspeakable Signs of Oumor, to which we could retire if the visitant should prove inimical or rebellious. We waited while the pole-circling stars went over, as had been prescribed. Then, when the tapers had gone out between our seared fingers, and the talc and asbestos were wholly consumed in the mummy's eaten palms, Avyctes uttered a single word whose sense was obscure to us; and Oigos, being animated by sorcery and subject to our will, repeated the word after a given interval, in tones that were hollow as a tomb-born echo; and I, in my turn, also repeated it.

Now, in the chamber of evocation, before beginning the ritual, we had opened a small window giving upon the sea, and had likewise left open a high door on the hall to landward, lest that which came in answer to us should require a spatial mode of entrance. And during the ceremony, the sea became still and there was no wind, and it seemed that all things were hushed in awful expectation of the nameless visitor. But after all was done, and the last word had been repeated by Oigos and me, we stood and waited vainly for a visible sign or other manifestation. The lamps burned stilly in the midnight room; and no shadows fell, other than were cast by ourselves and Oigos and by the great marble women along the walls. And in the magic mirrors we had placed cunningly, to reflect those that were otherwise unseen, we beheld no breath or trace of any image.

At this, after a reasonable interim, Avyctes was sorely disappointed, deeming that the evocation had failed of its purpose; and I, having the same thought, was secretly relieved. And we questioned the mummy of Oigos, to learn if he had perceived in the room, with such senses as are peculiar to the dead, the sure token or doubtful proof of a presence undescried by us the living. And the mummy gave a necromantic answer, saying that there was nothing.

"Verily," said Avyctes, "it were useless to wait longer. For surely in some way we have misunderstood the purport of the writing, or have failed to duplicate the matters used in the evocation, or the correct intonement of the words. Or it may be that in the lapse of so many aeons, the thing that was formerly wont to respond has long ceased to exist, or has altered in its attributes so that the spell is now void and valueless."

To this I assented readily, hoping that the matter was at an end. So, after erasing the blood-marked triangle and the sacred ellipse of the linked Signs of Oumor, and after dismissing Oigos to his wonted place among other mummies, we retired to sleep. And in the days that followed, we resumed our habitual studies, but made no mention to each other of the strange triangular tablet or the vain formula.

Even as before, our days went on; and the sea climbed and roared in white fury on the cliffs, and the winds wailed by in their unseen, sullen wrath, bowing the dark cedars as witches are bowed by the breath of Taaran, god of evil. Almost, in the marvel of new tests and cantraips, I forgot the ineffectual conjuration, and I deemed that Avyctes had also forgotten it.

All things were as of yore, to our sorcerous perception; and there was naught to trouble us in our wisdom and power and serenity, which we deemed secure above the sovereignty of kings. Reading the horoscopic stars, we found no future ill in their aspect; nor was any shadow of bale foreshown to us through geomancy, or other modes of divination such as we employed. And our familiars, though grisly and dreadful to mortal gaze, were wholly obedient to us the masters.

Then, on a clear summer afternoon, we walked, as was often our custom, on the marble terrace behind the house. In robes of ocean-purple, we paced among the windy trees with their blown, crooked shadows; and there, following us as we went to and fro, I saw the blue shadow of Avyctes and my own shadow on the marble; and between them, an adumbration that was not wrought by any of the cedars. And I was greatly startled, but spoke not of the matter to Avyctes, and observed the unknown shadow with covert care.

I saw that it followed closely the shadow of Avyctes, keeping ever the same distance. And it fluttered not in the wind, but moved with a flowing as of some heavy, thick, putrescent liquid; and its color was not blue nor purple nor black, nor any other hue to which man's eyes are habituated, but a hue as of some unearthly purulence; and its form was altogether monstrous, having a squat head and a long, undulant body, without similitude to beast or devil.

Avyctes heeded not the shadow; and still I feared to speak, though I thought it an ill thing for the master to be companioned thus. And I moved closer to him, in order to detect by touch or other perception the invisible presence that had cast the adumbration. But the air was void to sunward of the shadow; and I found nothing opposite the sun nor in any oblique direction, though I searched closely, knowing that certain beings cast their shadows thus.

After a while, at the customary hour, we returned by the coiling stairs and monster-flanked portals into the high house. And I saw that the strange adumbration moved ever behind the shadow of Avyctes, falling horrible and unbroken on the steps and passing clearly separate and distinct amid the long umbrages of the towering monsters. And in the dim halls beyond the sun, where shadows should not have been, I beheld with terror the distorted loathly blot, having a pestilent, unnamable hue, that followed Avyctes as if in lieu of his own extinguished shadow. And all that day, everywhere that we went, at the table served by specters, or in the mummy-warded room of volumes and books, the thing pursued Avyctes, clinging to him even as leprosy to the leper. And still the master had perceived it not; and still I forbore to warn him, hoping that the visitant would withdraw in its own time, going obscurely as it had come.

But at midnight, when we sat together by the silver lamps, pondering the blood-writ runes of Hyperborea, I saw that the shadow had drawn closer to the shadow of Avyctes, towering behind his chair on the wall between the huge sculptured women and the mummies. And the thing was a streaming ooze of charnel pollution, a foulness beyond the black leprosies of hell; and I could bear it no more; and I cried out in my fear and loathing, and informed the master of its presence.

Beholding now the shadow, Avyctes considered it closely and in silence; and there was neither fear nor awe nor abhorrence in the deep, graven wrinkles of his visage. And he said to me at last:

"This thing is a mystery beyond my lore; but never, in all the practice of my art, has any shadow come to me unbidden. And since all others of our evocations have found answer ere this, I must deem that the shadow is a veritable entity, or the sign of an entity, that has come in belated response to the formula of the serpent-sorcerers, which we thought powerless and void. And I think it well that we should now repair to the chamber of conjuration, and interrogate the shadow in such manner as we may, to inquire its nativity and purpose."

We went forthwith into the chamber of conjuration, and made such preparations as were both necessary and possible. And when we prepared to question it, the unknown shadow had drawn closer still to the shadow of Avyctes, so that the clear space between the two was no wider than the thickness of a necromancer's rod.

Now, in all ways that were feasible, we interrogated the shadow, speaking through our own lips and the lips of mummies and statues. But there was no determinable answer; and calling certain of the devils and phantoms that were our familiars, we made question through the mouths of these, but without result. And all the while, our magic mirrors were void of any reflection of a presence that might have cast the shadow; and they that had been our spokesmen could detect nothing in the room. And there was no spell, it seemed, that had power upon the visitant. So Avyctes became troubled; and drawing on the floor with blood and ashes the ellipse of Oumor, wherein no demon nor spirit may intrude, he retired to its center. But still within the ellipse, like a flowing taint of liquid corruption, the shadow followed his shadow; and the space between the two was no wider than the thickness of a wizard's pen.

Now, on the face of Avyctes, horror had graven new wrinkles; and his brow was beaded with a deathly sweat. For he knew, even as I, that this was a thing beyond all laws, and foreboding naught but disaster and evil. And he cried to me in a shaken voice, and said:

"I have no knowledge of this thing nor its intention toward me, and no power to stay its progress. Go forth and leave me now; for I would not that any man should witness the defeat of my sorcery and the doom that may follow thereupon. Also, it were well to depart while there is time, lest you too should become the quarry of the shadow and be compelled to share its menace."

Though terror had fastened upon my inmost soul, I was loath to leave Avyctes. But I had sworn to obey his will at all times and in every respect; and moreover I knew myself doubly powerless against the adumbration, since Avyctes himself was impotent.

So, bidding him farewell, I went forth with trembling limbs from the haunted chamber; and peering back from the threshold, I saw that the alien umbrage, creeping like a noisome blotch on the floor, had touched the shadow of Avyctes. And at that moment the master shrieked aloud like one in nightmare; and his face was no longer the face of Avyctes but was contorted and convulsed like that of some helpless madman who wrestles with an unseen incubus. And I looked no more, but fled along the dim outer hall and through the high portals giving upon the terrace.

A red moon, ominous and gibbous, had declined above the terrace and the crags; and the shadows of the cedars were elongated in the moon; and they wavered in the gale like the blown cloaks of enchanters. And stooping against the gale, I fled across the terrace toward the outer stairs that led to a steep path in the riven waste of rocks and chasms behind Avyctes' house. I neared the terrace edge, running with the speed of fear; but I could not reach the topmost outer stair; for at every step the marble flowed beneath me, fleeing like a pale horizon before the seeker. And though I raced and panted without pause, I could draw no nearer to the terrace edge.

At length I desisted, seeing that an unknown spell had altered the very space about the house of Avyctes, so that none could escape therefrom to landward. So, resigning myself in despair to whatever might befall, I returned toward the house. And climbing the white stairs in the low, level beams of the crag-caught moon, I saw a figure that awaited me in the portals. And I knew by the trailing robe of sea-purple, but by no other token, that the figure was Avyctes. For the face was no longer in its entirety the face of man, but was become a loathly fluid amalgam of human features with a thing not to be identified on earth. The transfiguration was ghastlier than death or the changes of decay; and the face was already hued with the nameless, corrupt and purulent color of the strange shadow, and had taken on, in respect to its outlines, a partial likeness to the squat profile of the shadow. The hands of the figure were not those of any terrene being; and the shape beneath the robe had lengthened with a nauseous undulant pliancy; and the face and fingers seemed to drip in the moonlight with a deliquescent corruption. And the pursuing umbrage, like a thickly flowing blight, had corroded and distorted the very shadow of Avyctes, which was now double in a manner not to be narrated here.

Fain would I have cried or spoken aloud; but horror had dried up the front of speech. And the thing that had been Avyctes beckoned me in silence, uttering no word from its living and putrescent lips. And with eyes that were no longer eyes, but had become an oozing abomination, it peered steadily upon me. And it clutched my shoulder closely with the soft leprosy of its fingers, and led me half-swooning with revulsion along the hall, and into that room where the mummy of Oigos, who had assisted us in the threefold incantation of the serpent-men, was stationed with several of his fellows.

By the lamps which illumed the chamber, burning with pale, still, perpetual flames, I saw that the mummies stood erect along the wall in their exanimate repose, each in his wonted place with his tall shadow beside him. But the great, gaunt shadow of Oigos on the marble wall was companioned by an adumbration similar in all respects to the evil thing that had followed the master and was now incorporate with him. I remembered that Oigos had performed his share of the ritual, and had repeated an unknown stated word in turn after Avyctes; and so I knew that the horror had come to Oigos in turn, and would wreak itself upon the dead even as upon the living. For the foul, anonymous thing that we had called in our presumption could manifest itself to mortal ken in no other way than this. We had drawn it from unfathomable depths of time and space, using ignorantly a dire formula; and the thing had come at its own chosen hour, to stamp itself in abomination uttermost on the evocators.

Since then, the night has ebbed away, and a second day has gone by like a sluggish ooze of horror. . . . I have seen the complete identification of the shadow with the flesh and the shadow of Avyctes . . . and also I have seen the slow encroachment of that other umbrage, mingling itself with the lank shadow and the sere, bituminous body of Oigos, and turning them to a similitude of the thing which Avyctes has become. And I have heard the mummy cry out like a living man in great pain and fear, as with the throes of a second dissolution, at the impingement of the shadow. And long since it has grown silent, like the other horror, and I know not its thoughts or its intent. . . . And verily I know not if the thing that has come to us be one or several; nor if its avatar will rest complete with the three that summoned it forth into time, or be extended to others.

But these things, and much else, I shall soon know; for now, in turn, there is a shadow that follows mine, drawing ever closer. The air congeals and curdles with an unseen fear; and they that were our familiars have fled from the mansion; and the great marble women seem to tremble where they stand along the walls. But the horror that was Avyctes, and the second horror that was Oigos, have left me not, and neither do they tremble. And with eyes that are not eyes, they seem to brood and watch, waiting till I too shall become as they. And their stillness is more terrible than if they had rended me limb from limb. And there are strange voices in the wind, and alien roarings upon the sea; and the walls quiver like a thin veil in the black breath of remote abysses.

So, knowing that the time is brief, I have shut myself in the room of volumes and books and have written this account. And I have taken the bright triangular tablet, whose solution was our undoing, and have cast it from the window into the sea, hoping that none will find it after us. And now I must make an end, and enclose this writing in the sealed cylinder of orichalchum, and fling it forth to drift upon the wave. For the space between my shadow and the shadow of the horror is straitened momently . . . and the space is no wider than the thickness of a wizard's pen.

THE DWELLER IN THE TEMPLE

by Manly Wade Wellman

This country would have been beautiful to Kardios even if it hadn't been totally strange to him. It looked and felt and sounded the more beautiful in contrast to that long, cleftlike pass through the mountains where heavy twilight hung, where gaunt trees had moaned *Careful* to him, and toadstool clumps had seemed to echo *Careful*, and the advice was good. Now he tramped a moss-carpeted road between green thickets with flowers as big as his big hand. A bird twittered, prompting Kardios to sing himself. Tall, tanned, black-maned, he unslung the harp from behind his broad shoulder and smote the strings. He improvised his own words and melody, while his long sword thumped his leg as though joining in:

> "Who, whether he is small or grand,
> Brings happiness along
> And offers me a friendly hand,
> For him I have a song.

> "Who comes in enmity and wrath
> To make all men afraid,
> Who threatens me and bars my path,
> For him I have a blade."

The trees on both sides seemed to burst into cheers.

"Beautiful!" cried a voice.

"What brilliant music!" shouted another.

"More, sing more!"

They came out upon the road, a dozen of them, clapping their hands.

Kardios felt embarrassed that he had not known of people so near. They were all young men, slender and tall, though none was as tall as Kardios. They wore such rich fabrics, so gracefully cut, as he had not thought existed since he had barely escaped from drowning Atlantis. Like Kardios, they were smooth-shaven. Their heads wore plumes. They thronged around him, smiling and slapping the hafts of their javelins.

"Three times welcome, my lord," said a spokesman. "We'll escort you to your city."

"City?" echoed Kardios, keeping a hand near his sword hilt. "What city? I didn't even know there was one."

"Just over the hill yonder," said the spokesman, pointing. "Your city of Nyanyanya."

"It must be a fine one for you to name it two or three times," said Kardios. "But I never heard of it until this moment."

"Come and reign there, as was foretold."

They closed around him like a guard of honor, or perhaps just a guard. Those sharp-pointed javelins rode at the ready. "Come," the spokesman said, and they escorted him between flowering trees to the top of the ridge. There, a city presented itself to view in the cuplike valley beyond.

Walled, turreted, set with spires, that city gave a sense of soft, rich color. It was built of gray stone with a touch of rose to it. Here and there above the walls sprouted roof gardens. It was not a large city, but it was beautiful, a grateful refuge for a tired traveler. Kardios smiled.

"If it's my city, I invite you to enter," he said to his companions.

They were on a pavement of smooth blocks now, heading toward a pillared gateway with great open gates of nut-brown timber. The man who had first spoken to Kardios ran ahead.

"He comes!" he cried. "Our great king!"

Guards stood at the sides of the gate, their scaled armor worked with silver, ornamented spears in their hands. They came to attention as the party drew near. From the gate emerged someone in a plum-blue robe. He carried a staff with a device at the top, and held his other hand above his head.

"That's Athemar, our high priest, coming to greet you," a helpful voice spoke at Kardio's elbow. "Pardon, my lord, but I don't know your noble name."

"I'm Kardios. How should you know it? I tell you, this is strange to me, and I should be strange to it."

The party halted as the priest came close. Kardios saw a smile wreathed in a white beard, a lofty bald brow, twinkling eyes.

"This is Kardios, Lord Athemar, come to rule us," said the one who had asked for the name. "See, reverend father, how kingly he stands."

"Kardios," repeated Athemar resonantly. Kardios saw that the device on the staff was a grotesque frog or monkey shape, twined on a crosspiece. Athemar drew from under his robe a golden circlet studded with bright jewels of at least four colors. He bowed.

"Royal Kardios," he said, "it's my happy duty to crown you."

Kardios bowed in turn. Athemar set the glowing circlet upon his black hair. It seemed to fit perfectly.

"Sir," Kardios said, "I begin to think that these hospitable fellows aren't joking with me, after all."

"We wouldn't dare joke, great Kardios," murmured one of them.

"Never," Athemar assured him. "You see, we have an interesting way of choosing our kings. When one departs, another is mystically brought to us, by decree of the Dweller in the Temple. A committee meets him and brings him to us. It's been like that since Nyanyanya became a city." He stroked his beard. "That was lifetimes ago. But your palace waits for you."

Again Kardios was aware of the javelins. He thought of breaking and running, but smiled the notion away. He would never be happy without knowing the end of this quaint adventure.

"As you wish," he told Athemar grandly.

They entered at the gate. The guards saluted with their tall spears. Inside, throngs of people shouted from either curb of the street. Handsome people they were; Kardios noticed several attractive women. Flowers floated out to sprinkle the pavement on which he walked.

"He is King Kardios!" cried Athemar in a bell-like baritone.

"King Kardios!" came back a multiple echo.

"How royal, how handsome!"

The onlookers yelled so many compliments that Kardios could not sort them out. He smiled to this side, then that. The shouts grew louder.

"They love their king," said Athemar, his staff tapping. Again Kardios wondered at the strange, warped image upon it.

They came to a graceful building of the rose-gray stone. Its door was plated with copper, aged softly green. Athemar stepped ahead to swing the heavy gold knocker. The door opened inward and an armored guardsman saluted as Kardios and Athemar walked in together.

The entry was hung with interesting pictures of flying men and women. Athemar conducted Kardios into a spacious room with a central fountain, chairs and tables and divans, and a red-cushioned throne that seemed made chiefly of emeralds. At Athemar's courtly gesture, Kardios sat down.

At once, girls entered, spectacularly beautiful girls, gold-haired, jet-haired, jasper-haired, smiling. Their rich, clinging costumes were as brief as the very soul of wit.

"Here are some of your subjects, awaiting your orders," Athemar said to Kardios. "Whatever you may command of them."

"May I suggest food and drink?" asked Kardios. "It was a long walk today, after many days of walking, ever since I left the seacoast."

Athemar smote his shapely hands together, with a sound like a cracking whip. Yet another girl hurried in. She was smaller than any of the winsome first comers, did not seem dazzled by herself as they all did. Her hair fell in brown curls at either side of her shy, round face.

"Food and wine for the king," commanded Athemar. "The best."

"Bring enough for all of us," put in Kardios.

The small girl genuflected, whirled and hurried out again. "Be seated, Athemar," bade Kardios. "You too, ladies."

"You honor us," said Athemar, and took a low seat beside the throne. "Thank you, thank you," breathed the beauties musically, seeking places on a great divan and nearby couches, where they sat in the most studiedly becoming of attitudes.

"King Kardios, you come from a far country," ventured Athemar.

"From Atlantis," said Kardios.

"I thought that Atlantis was lost in the sea, that no Atlantean survived."

"I did, somehow," Kardios told him. "I was in audience with Theona, the queen. An old legend was mentioned—how, if anyone dared kiss her, Atlantis would die. She said it was a fanciful myth, and told me to kiss her."

"Kiss the queen of Atlantis, Lord Kardios?" squealed a lovely blonde.

"A queen's word is law," Kardios reminded her. "I kissed her, and down went Atlantis like a bucket in a well. How long I was washed and swept over the sea I can't tell you, but I came ashore somewhere else, and here I am."

"What a fine sword you have," observed Athemar.

Kardios drew it from its sheath and handed it to him. Athemar studied it expertly. "What metal is it?" he asked.

"I can't exactly say," admitted Kardios. "It came from the stars, so I was told by the Nephol, a tribe of giants. It was too small for a giant, so they lent it to me to kill something called Fith, and then they gave it to me for pay."

"And your harp, great king," said a gorgeous brunette. "Did the giants give you that, too?"

"No, it's from a little town called Swarr. A big wild boar named Malyhl was wasting their gardens and orchards and killing anyone who came out to make it stop. So I killed it—enough ham and bacon and ribs for all Swarr. I liked the harp and they let me have it."

He flung off his mantle of gold-worked black and touched the harp's strings.

"Play!" besought his audience of charmers. "Sing us a song, King Kardios."

"Well," he said, "I was working on this yesterday." He smote a chord and sang:

"Where is the ghastly Fifth of the star-born race?
The giant boar Malyhl, and the ape-bat, where?
What has become of Kru with his black-tusked
*   face*
And Ryohlar, the thing with claws like a bear?

"I looked in their evil eyes and they crouched
*   like cravens,*
I showed them my sword, and they trembled
*   and louted low.*
I gave their bones for food to the rats and
*   ravens,*
And I pray the gods for another and fiercer foe."

Storms of applause, more than Kardios thought the song and singer really deserved.

The little serving girl was back with great trays of dishes. She set them on a carven table before the throne, then dashed away to return with two tall flagons and an armful of green cups. She drew back as though to await further orders, while Kardios and Athemar and the worshipful bevy of beauties gathered around the table. There were legs and wings of birds, delicately roasted, buns of white and brown bread, a bowl of various fruits. Kardios ate hungrily, while his lovely companions watched him with eyes like jewels. When he had done, the serving girl brought him a silver basin to wash his hands and gave him a fleecy towel.

"Now, may I ask," said Kardios, "what are my duties here?"

"Only to be your royal self," replied Athemar. "We have a simple but efficient government. You can trust your councillors to administer it for you. Otherwise, graciously permit your subjects to love and honor you, and to afford you whatever pleasure is in their power to help you to enjoy."

"Pleasure?" repeated Kardios.

"If, for instance, any of these young ladies might divert you—"

"Choose me!" cried a statuesque girl with stormy black hair and eyes like forest pools.

"Don't look at her, mighty Kardios, until you've considered me," pleaded her neighbor, a superbly proportioned creature whose hair was as pale as frosted gold.

"Me, royal master!"

"Me! Me!"

Kardios smiled from one to another to another.

"Choose two, " invited Athemar. "Choose more than two."

"Me! Me!" besought all the girls at once.

Kardios leaned back, cuddling his harp. The serving girl came to gather up the dishes.

"Ladies," said Kardios, "I won't offend any of you by choosing another. Suppose I say instead, let me make choice of this good little one who has so well served a hungry man and his companions."

The serving girl straightened her slim body and stared. A cup fell from her hand to bounce on the floor. Kardios saw her closely for the first time. She wore a simple frock the color of dead leaves. Its wide collar slipped down from one bare shoulder which, Kardios decided, might well be the third or fourth most beautifully turned shoulder he had ever seen. Her wide eyes shone like blue stars.

"But she's only a kitchen servant, gracious majesty," protested Athemar. "She's good at that, but in the matter we're discussing she's not to be compared to these others. Every one of them is pastmistress of the arts of love, trained by the most able and experienced teachers."

"I'd feel inadequate with any companion so brilliantly schooled," said Kardios. He spoke to the serving girl. "What's your name, child?"

"Yola." He could barely hear her say it.

"That's a pretty name. But I should have asked how you might feel about my suggestion."

"The king's wish is my command." That was only a trifle louder.

Kardios laughed, hoping that he sounded kindly. "Very well, then."

"I am honored, dear majesty," Yola managed to say.

Athemar rose, his beard stirring on his chest. "Tomorrow morning, I ask you to give audience to your council," he said. "Now we'll be so tactful as to leave you. Come, you others."

They departed with Athemar, all those blooming girls, with coy pouts of what really might have been disappointment. Alone with Yola, Kardios wondered what to say next. Yola stood before him, her hands held out submissively, palms up.

"By heaven," said Kardios suddenly, "Athemar took my sword with him."

He reached for Yola's hands, but they lifted and her slim, round arms went around his neck.

At dawn, Kardios wakened on the cushioned divan where most of the lovely girls had perched, and wondered why Yola was not beside him. Then he saw her, prettily disshevelled, standing with a tray.

"Breakfast," said her soft voice.

He sat up eagerly. She gave him a goblet with what he judged was a mingling of tangy fruit juices. A platter held slices of toasted bread. Upon these she broke lightly boiled eggs and set aside the freckled shells. Kardios ate appreciatively, and she ate with him.

"I hope you weren't displeased with me," she ventured. "I'm not one of those girls carefully trained to love and be loved."

"You have a splendid natural talent that profits by experience," Kardios said honestly. "I gloried in you last night. These are good eggs, Yola."

"I cooked them for us."

"You'll cook no more if I'm king and you're my consort," he declared. "Wait, though, cooking's another gift and grace of yours. The kitchen staff can prepare big court dinners, but sometimes when you and I eat together in private, only we two——"

"Oh," she cried, "I thank you, I thank you."

"Don't thank me, I was thinking of my own comfort." He drank fruit juice and so did she, and they kissed, a strong, swimming kiss. "Athemar didn't say much about religion yesterday, and I haven't had time to ask you. What's this Dweller in the Temple you worship here in Nyanyanya?"

"Tongbi," she whispered fearfully.

"Tongbi," he repeated the name. "What sort of god is he?"

"A great god. Great and dreadful."

"Why dreadful? Does he kill your people?"

"No." Her hair tossed as she shook her head. "I don't think he ever killed a single citizen of Nyanyanya."

"Where is he worshipped?" Kardios asked her.

"His temple is just behind the palace here. A corridor leads to it. Athemar performs all that is needed."

"I'll have to ask Athemar," decided Kardios.

"He and the council members will be here for their audience in two hours."

"That leaves us time enough, Yola."

He took her in his arms, and she was glad to be taken.

Presently, Kardios bathed in the fountain and put on his loincloth and sandals and tunic. Yola trotted out of sight somewhere, and he sat on the emerald throne when Athemar came into the throne room, bowing low, followed by three councillors. They were all grave old men, dignified in robes and sashes. At Kardios's gesture, they sat before him. Athemar took the seat beside the throne.

"What is your royal will?" Athemar asked him.

"I'd like my sword back," returned Kardios shortly. "You carried it off yesterday."

"Only to have a proper sheath made for so fine a weapon," said Athemar. "Skillful smiths and jewellers are at work on it."

"Another question," pursued Kardios. "About the worship of Tongbi."

Athemar frowned. "That girl told you his name."

"And said that he was powerful, and has never yet killed a citizen of the town. That's to his credit. How ancient a god is this Tongbi, and how is he served?"

A councillor cleared his throat and tweaked his spearpoint beard. "You're our king, mighty Kardios," he said. "The king isn't called on to vex himself with religious matters. Athemar and his junior priests do the worshipping and serving of Tongbi."

"How ancient is Tongbi?" asked Kardios again. "As old as Nyanyanya?"

"Older," said Athemar. "Our ancestors came wandering here and saw the place would be good for a city. But a tribe of strangers—savages, history says, not desirable for friends and neighbors—was camped here. Our fathers were better armed and drove those savages out. But Tongbi, their god, stayed in the shade of a sacred tree. You might say that Tongbi persuaded our people that he would stay there. So the first building in Nyanyanya was a temple, around his tree and him. That's why he is called the Dweller in the Temple."

"What does Tongbi look like?" was Kardios's next question. "That is, if he can be seen, if he isn't one of those disappointing invisible spirits."

"I've never truly seen him," replied Athemar. "I bow low in his presence."

"What else do you do in his presence?"

"I ask him to accept the offerings of our people, and to continue to grant us peace and prosperity."

"That sounds like a good, intelligent sort of worship," Kardios approved. "Then, as king, I'm not expected to go near Tongbi."

"Oh, but the king must," said the spear-bearded councillor. "Once, at least, it's proper for each king to meet Tongbi face to face."

"State and religious matters have a certain relationship," added another. "When shall our beloved ruler visit the temple, Athemar?"

"Tonight, after the state banquet where you will meet your courtiers," Athemar informed Kardios. "That will be held in the great hall next to this throne room. Music, dancing by our most gifted performers, and high honor to your presence. When it's over, I'll conduct you to the temple."

"Very well," granted Kardios. "What other duties must I perform?"

"Only to show yourself at the window yonder," said Athemar. "Your subjects wait for a look at you. Put on your crown."

Kardios set it on his black thatch and strode to the window. Two councillors opened it right and left. Outside waited a throng. At sight of Kardios, they howled in admiration. Women threw flowers in at the window. Men waved banners. Kardios bowed and stepped away. After that, Athemar and the councillors respectfully shuffled backward and out at the door.

Alone again, Kardios sat down and tried the tuning of his harp. He played and sang the song of fighting adventures with which he had entertained the flock of girls the day before. As he finished, he was aware that Yola stood beside him, listening.

"What brave deeds you have done," she said.

Kardios laughed. "To be honest, my dear, I put in a couple of things for the sake of rhyme, but I did kill most of those creatures. I'd say the most profitable were killing Fith, who truly plagued the poor Nephol, and butchering Malyhl, whose flesh must still be feeding the town of Swarr."

Her eyes widened. "A giant boar, you said."

"He'd have been as big as an elephant if his legs hadn't been so short," said Kardios. "There was a horn on his nose and his eyes were wicked enough for ten thousand devils. His hide hung in folds on him. In Swarr they said it protected like armor."

"How did you manage to conquer him?"

"I stood and he charged me. Heavy and clumsy as he was he ran like a race horse. I let his horn almost touch me, than I dodged aside and made one downward cut with my sword. His neck was stretched out and the sword went straight through it. Then I called the people of Swarr out to help themselves."

"I'd have been afraid to eat that meat."

"It was very good. I had some before I came away and finally reached here." He rose from the throne. "Those councillors said I wouldn't be disturbed for a while, Yola."

She smiled up at him. "You want me again?"

"I've wanted you ever since you came into the room."
He led her to the divan.

Yola's shyness had departed. Her conduct was such
that Kardios felt that he must praise it.

"I remember women from time to time in the past,
Yola, but— "

"Please," she begged, "don't remember other women
to me."

"Only to their disadvantage, my dear."

Afterward they swam together in the fountain. Little coppery fish flicked around them. Getting out, they
dried on big towels. Kardios took up his harp again:

> *"They offered me gifts, and I did not refuse*
> *A city, a people, a crown, and a throne:*
> *They offered me beauties, and which did I*
> *   choose?*
> *Yola, no other, just Yola alone.*

> *"Yola is gentle and Yola is fair,*
> *Her voice is as soft as the voice of a dove,*
> *And Yola has torrents of spice-colored hair,*
> *Yola is filled with the sweetness of love.*

> *"And if they should bring from the east or*
> *   the west,*
> *Every fair woman from every land known,*
> *Which would I choose, and forsake all the rest?*
> *Yola, no other, just Yola alone."*

She burst into tears.

"Oh, you blind, dumb fool!" she quavered.

He dropped the harp and jumped to his feet. "Did
you say dumb fool or damned fool?"

"You can't know, you can't see," she cried at him.
"You'll be taken to Tongbi and that's the end of

you—devoured by Tongbi—that's why you were brought here to be king."

"I don't understand," he protested.

"Of course not, how could you? You weren't told that the king of Nyanyanya is always called from outside, and always he's given to the Dweller in the Temple to save us here in town—"

He had to hold her close to quiet the storm of agonized weeping.

"You must go," she said when she could talk. "Slip away as soon as it gets dark. I'll give the guard at the door a drink of wine with something to send him to sleep."

"Oh, think of the poor fellow," he argued. "Asleep at his post while I escape, what would happen to him? But my mind's working slowly. Why is the king sacrificed to Tongbi?"

"It was done by the people who worshipped him before our fathers drove them out and built Nyanyanya. They sacrificed their kings to Tongbi under his sacred tree, or he'd come into the open and do terrible things."

"He has to eat a king to keep him quiet," said Kardios, with the utmost interest. "You're a sensible people, making strangers into kings for Tongbi."

"Yes, dearest Kardios. That's why Athemar carried your sword away, so that you'd be unarmed before Tongbi."

"And that," said Kardios suddenly, "may be the answer."

Yola stared miserably. "Answer?"

"If they took my sword, they're afraid it might make a difference with Tongbi," he pointed out. "That means that Tongbi isn't utterly invincible. I wish I had my sword back—but you can't know where it is."

"But I do. Servants know so many things. It's in Athemar's chamber, where the corridor runs from the palace to the temple, under some folded robes on a shelf. I saw it when I was cleaning there today."

Kardios creased his face in thought. Then he took up his cloak and gave it to her.

"Carry that, as if you were going to wash it or mend it," he said. "If Athemar isn't in his quarters, bring the sword back with the cloak wrapped around it. What drug will you give the sentry?"

"I brought it with me." She fumbled in her belt pouch and brought out a leaf folded around some dull red dust.

Kardios filled the handsomest cup on the table with wine. Into this he put the dust and stirred it with his forefinger.

"Go ahead and leave the sentry to me," he said.

She departed with the cloak. Kardios stepped out behind her, the cup in his hand. The sentry, splendid in silvered mail, brought his spear to respectful salute.

"My lord the king," he said deeply.

"I thought I'd ask you to drink with me, friend," said Kardios.

The sentry gazed at the cup with relish. He was a sturdy fellow, snub-nosed and dark-browned. "Against the captain's orders to drink on duty," he protested, not very strongly.

"He's the captain, I'm the king," smiled Kardios. "I countermand his orders."

"Will my lord Kardios drink first?"

Kardios gazed at him, at the cup, then lifted it and took a mouthful and handed it over. The sentry turned it up and gratefully drained it. Kardios caught the cup back and eased the sentry down in a musical clatter of mail and weaponry. Then Kardios spat out the wine he had kept in his mouth. His ears sang a trifle, but that went away as he straightened the fellow's limp legs and crossed his hands on his armored chest. Then

Kardios went back inside and filled another cup of wine for himself.

Yola pattered in. From the folds of the cloak she produced his sword. Happily Kardios bent the springy blade so that the point almost touched the hilt. He plucked a brown hair from Yola's head, dangled it and sliced it through with a flick of the blade. He grunted in satisfaction and returned the sword to his scabbard.

"Now," he said, "show me the way to the temple."

Out they went again, past the profoundly sleeping sentry. Yola led the way past an archway, beyond which servants set ranks of tables in a great chamber. She brought him to a hallway strung with handsomely carved doors and put her finger to her lips for silence as they tiptoed past what must be Athemar's quarters. A broad, bronze-clamped door was at the end of the hall. At Yola's gesture, Kardios tried the big latch. They entered a narrow, gloomy passageway.

"This leads to Tongbi?" asked Kardios.

"They say it does. I've never been here before."

"Go back," he urged her, but she shook her head furiously.

Their footsteps echoed together on stone flagging. The walls to either side were adorned with carvings of creatures overabundantly supplied with wings, claws and fangs.

They may have walked a hundred paces before they came to another door, seemingly hammered of dull metal and flanked with stout wooden facings. It had a latch knob and a huge keyhole. Kardios tried it but it would not open.

"We can't get in where Tongbi is," said Yola's daunted voice.

"Oh, the lock looks primitive."

Kardios inspected the wood of the facings. Drawing his sword he hewed away two long, thick splinters and sharpened each to a flat point. Again he gave his attention to the door, pressing upon it and testing the solidity of its hinges. Finally he forced the point of his sword between door and jamb, pried carefully, and inserted one of his makeshift wedges at a point above the lock. Forcing it well in, he used his sword again below the lock to shove the second wedge there.

Again he sheathed his sword, took hold of the wedges and surged against them with all his strength. The metal of the door gave way a little, the wood of the jamb rather more. Again he forced the wedges in. Finally he voiced a short, harsh chuckle of triumph.

"The catch is far enough out for me to open it," he said. "Yola dear, go back at once to the palace, before anyone knows you're here."

"No," she wailed. "I'm going in with you."

"Not you," he said sternly. "I'm the king, and I order you not to go in. You can stay out here until I come back."

"What—if you don't come back?"

"Don't worry about me. I won't be in there any longer than I'm needed."

He dragged the door open. The wedges fell free. He stepped across a threshold faced with beautifully polished onyx, and drew the door shut behind him as far as it would go.

Light was in there, enough to see by, fight by. The temple's ceiling was lofty, probably was vaulted high up there. Closer to the floor were set three windows, barred with heavy metal slats that let a sort of twilight through.

"All right, Tongbi," called Kardios politely. "I'm the latest one tricked into being king of Nyanyanya on your account. Here I am."

He was able to see that the floor was of hard black earth, with strange footprints in it. At its center sprouted a tree, its smooth bark black, with drooping branches all around. The leaves had a soggy, purplish look. Kardios hefted his sword in his practiced hand.

"I didn't wait until I was brought, Tongbi," he said. "You can't be much of a god if you don't recognize my presence."

A creak of the low-hanging branches, a stir of the leaves. Something moved among them, something dragged its considerable bulk toward the light, toward Kardios. Peering, he saw what must be Tongbi.

Tongbi was black and shiny like the tree, stood up taller and broader than Kardios on what seemed to be three many-jointed legs. His thick body poised erect. His head was spiked with four, maybe five horns. Tongbi had arms too, and extended them with spread fingers. Those fingers had points as sharp as daggers.

"I see why they wanted to bring me after dark," Kardios addressed him. "You're so classically ugly. Maybe I look that ugly to you, if you have eyes."

Tongbi had glittering patches of eyes, on either side of a ridge that suggested a nose. Tongbi came forward, the dagger-fingers fiddling and questing.

Kardios slid forward his right foot and slashed at Tongbi's nearer arm. The edge struck and glided off, like a foot slipping on ice. Kardios danced back out of reach.

"You're wearing lubricated armor," he said. "Unfair advantage, Tongbi. I deplore it."

Tongbi lumbered forward again. His dagger-fingered hands groped, his head sank as though he would charge with the horns. Kardios remembered Malyhl, the swift giant of a boar with one horn. Maybe the same tactics would work. He stood almost against the wall and spread his arms with his sword well out of line.

"Come get me, Tongbi," he invited.

Tongbi made a scrambling rush, head down and

taloned hands forward. At the last instant, Kardios broke to the right and clear. Tongbi struck resoundingly against the wall. Kardios sped a lightning slash at what seemed to be the neck.

Again his sword slid away, unable to bite in. Kardios had a moment to see Tongbi's ungainly body, on which a dark integument lay snug except for seams at the joints. Kardios reflected that armor of such a design might be made for use in battle. Tongbi whirled upon him. His unspeakably strange face shoved close, patchy eyes glowing. Kardios saw the mouth, round and set with champing plates, like the mouth of a cannibal insect.

"You'll eat nothing better than king's meat, eh?" he mocked. "I'll feed you my sword."

His edge scraped away across the plated jowl of Tongbi and Kardios leaped backward again, among the low boughs of the tree. Dark leaves brushed him. Tongbi pursued.

Dodging, Kardios slashed. He missed his mark and the keen edge of the sword drove into the trunk of the black tree, so deeply that he had to tug mightily to free it.

As he did so, Tongbi cried out, half a squeal, half a stammering bray. He stopped and staggered. Kardios moved into the open.

"Hurt you, did I? But I struck the tree."

Tongbi straightened up and faced him.

"Struck the tree," Kardios said again. "And it hurt you."

He drew away from the drooping branches, Tongbi pursued, but Kardios dodged away and darted in toward the trunk. He chopped at it powerfully, chopped again. A great jagged slice of the trunk fell away, and the naked wood gleamed as white as a piece of nicely boiled fish.

Tongbi's tortured voice rose so shrilly that Kardios felt his nerves tingle. He put all his strength into another slash at the tree, biting deeply into it. Tongbi wailed behind him, or bubbled. Kardios spared a look. Tongbi was coming desperately in. Kardios circled the tree, chopping, chopping.

Those dagger talons clutched at him and ripped his tunic as he drove in a final blow. The tree splintered at the place where he had hewn it almost through. Swiftly Kardios danced off toward the rear of the enclosure. Behind him, the tree went down with a squashy noise of branches and leaves.

He turned. The tree was down. Tongbi stood. But Tongbi barely stirred. At last he brought himself painfully around. Kardios approached, right foot advanced, ready for conflict.

Tongbi did not move to meet him. Inside that shell of slippery armor the grotesque, unhappy being seemed to hunch, to crumple. The three legs wavered in all their joints. Kardios came near.

"Too bad I had to cut down your tree," he said to Tongbi. "Somehow your life is the tree's life. But it was a case of you or me, and you know which I had to choose."

Still there was movement in Tongbi, an effort to be dangerous. The arms pawed painfully. Tongbi tried to make a step forward, and fell uncouthly among the outlying twigs of the prone tree. He rolled over on his back, and Kardios stepped to his side.

The arrangement of plates in the mouth worked feebly together. Carefully, very carefully, Kardios slid his point right into that mouth and drove down hard. The plates clinked against it. Kardios felt the point piercing toughness. Tongbi quivered all over, and arms and legs went slack.

Kardios studied him carefully. Tongbi suggested

something of a giant insect, something of a water monster. Whoever may have tried to sculpt him on Athemar's staff had fallen short of his baleful duty. And Tongbi was dead. Like the tree, he was fallen and dead.

"That's all they'd have had to do to you, long ago," Kardios said, quite gently, to the silent form. "Those founders of Nyanyanya—all they'd have had to do was cut down your tree. It was your life, whatever your life is, wasn't it, Tongbi? That's why you went down with it."

His swordpoint was smeared with gluey green. He thrust it into the hard earth to cleanse it, and slid it back into its sheath. At last he went to the door and opened it.

"You're hurt," said Yola outside. "You're pale."

"I'm not hurt, just thinking," said Kardios. "I disposed of Tongbi. Come on, let's get out of here."

They went back along the corridor. Again they walked softly past Athemar's door and came to the place where the sentry slumbered peacefully. Kardios knelt and studied him and finally slapped his cheeks smartly, one cheek and then the other.

"Mp," grunted the sentry, stirring. He looked up at Kardios, abashed. "Did I sleep on my post?" he asked.

"Only a little while," Kardios reassured him. "Come on, get to your feet." He held out a hand to help. "Forget about it and so will I. No need for your captain ever to hear about it."

He and Yola went into the throne room. "Now," said Kardios, "let's get ready for that banquet tonight."

"Aren't you going to slip away?"

"I don't want to disappoint all those good people," he said. "It was sweaty work in there with Tongbi; I think I'll have another bath in the fountain. Why don't you swim with me?"

"Gladly," she said, and gladly she did.

The sun set outside the great window when Athemar knocked discreetly at the throne room and entered, followed by the three grave councillors. Kardios and Yola lounged on the divan, talking about inconsequential things. Athemar bowed so low that he could have touched the floor with the palms of his hands.

"Beloved and all-powerful King Kardios, we are here to escort you to the state banquet," he announced.

"I heard dishes clattering in yonder," said Kardios, rising. "By the way, gentlemen, Yola here will sit beside me as my consort."

A councillor looked at Yola so fixedly that she blushed. "She's only a kitchen maid, Magnificence," he said.

"You're behind the times," rejoined Kardios. "She stopped being a kitchen maid a little while after I arrived yesterday." He looked levelly from one face to another. "So long as I rule in Nyanyanya, she is my close and honored companion at all public gatherings."

"Of course," said Athemar drily, stroking his long beard. "As long as you are king—that is agreed."

"Agreed, agreed," echoed the others.

Kardios did not smile. He wanted them to think the hidden meaning was lost on him. "Understood, is it? Then let's go."

He set the crown on his head, draped his cloak, and took Yola by the arm. They paced to the door and through it. Kardios winked at the sentry, who braced more stiffly to attention.

Guests stood in groups in the banquet hall. They bowed respectfully as Kardios and Yola proceeded to the table of honor and took two chairs at its center. Athemar pronounced an eloquent benediction, after which all sat down. Men and women servants, apparently chosen for looks and deftness, served the dinner from great dishes made from agate, lapis lazuli and rose quartz, such dishes as would have done credit to the table of Queen Theona who was drowned with all Atlantis except Kardios. Wine gushed into goblets of silver-banded gold or gold-banded silver. The food was excellent. Kardios ate with the appetite of one who has spent the day in various active employments.

When fruits and nuts and puddings were brought for dessert, Athemar rose to speak of how happy and lucky Nyanyanya must feel to have a ruler like Kardios. In response, Kardios praised the manners and generosity of all he had met in the town, predicted glory and tranquility, and said that he had already striven to do his subjects a certain service to be discussed later. That brought admiring applause. In came a band of musicians, skilled with the lute and flagolet and various sorts of drums. A group of dancers performed. Kardios thought he recognized several of the bewitching girls offered for his refreshment when first he arrived. So enticingly graceful were their steps that the councillor with the spiked beard got up and danced with them.

Afterward came a call for Kardios to sing. He borrowed a harp from a musician, tuned it to his own method, and sang the three songs he had most recently composed, finishing with the one about Yola. She buried her face in her hands, utterly embarrassed, while cheers rang out.

The occasion drew to its end, with last lord bowing before Kardios and the last lady pleading to kiss his hand. Kardios returned to the throne room with Yola. Athemar and the councillors followed them.

"You've reflected shining credit upon Nyanyanya, royal lord," said Athemar. "Now, I remind you, there remains a significant event for tonight. You are to go from here to the temple and meet its all-powerful Dweller."

"Our great god Tongbi," amplified one of the council.

Kardios tilted his head. "Your great god Tongbi? Oh, gentlemen, that's been attended to. I met him earlier."

"Met Tongbi?" they cried in a breath, as though they had rehearsed it.

"That's what I said."

Athemar looked puzzled, for the first time since Kardios had met him.

"But King Kardios—I mean—" he swallowed, and his beard trembled. "But here you are, alive, not even—"

"Not even scratched, you were going to say?" laughed Kardios. "You're right, Athemar, as a priest should strive to be. He didn't even nick me with those sharp claws. I'm happy to report that the same can't be claimed for him. I killed him."

He twitched his sword hilt forward from under his cloak. "I took this little friend along," he said. "It wasn't Tongbi so much I needed it for, it was that tree of his to which his life was bound. The tree's dead, too. You know, it would have been so simple for you to cut that tree down long ago."

All they could do was goggle.

At last Athemar cried out something that might have been a prayer or an oath, or a mixture of the two. Without apology he scampered out of the throne room. Kardios poured out a finger's breadth of wine and courteously invited the councillors to do the same. When they only kept staring, he pledged Yola in the cup, held it for her lips to touch, and drank.

Athemar came hurrying back, robe and beard flowing.

"It's true," he gulped. "Tongbi is dead. What hero could have overcome him?"

"I did," said Kardios. "Permit me to develop what I hinted earlier about a service I did Nyanyanya. Your ancestors built here and took Tongbi to worship. He was a peril unless you sacrificed your rulers to him, and you were driven to that clever expedient of crowning one stranger after another as sacrifice time came around." He spread his broad hands as though to emphasize his words. "That's over now. You're free of Tongbi."

"Frec," muttered a councillor, as though not sure of the word. "What can we worship, great king?"

"Athemar's an accomplished student of religion. He can find you another god, not so bloody or so difficult."

"You may have brought Tongbi's curse upon us," whined another councillor.

"Not on you," amended Kardios, "for none of you had anything to do with it. I went to him without consulting you. Any curse would have to fall on me. Why don't I just leave Nyanyanya tomorrow morning, and take whatever curse there is along with me?"

"What royal generosity," babbled Athemar. "Would you do that for Nyanyanya, mighty Kardios? Abdicate?"

"Not exactly abdicate," said Kardios. "I thought rather of establishing a regency here in my absence."

He put his arm around Yola. He felt her tremble against him.

"After so many kings have been unlucky here, a queen might do better," he said. "Yola has had a chance to convince me of her considerable talents, in ways I won't explain. I leave her in my place here, gentlemen. She'll rule you. Give her the benefit of your support and advice."

"We will," promised Athemar, and, "We will," agreed the councillors.

"Thank you for that promise, and let me make you a promise of my own," said Kardios. "There's a lot of this world, and I hope to see some of it. But I might come back to Nyanyanya at any moment. When I do, if I gather any sense that Yola hasn't been properly treated and honored, you'll find yourself in worse trouble than Tongbi could ever have accomplished for you."

"Agreed," they said submissively. "Agreed."

"So then, will you excuse us?" Kardios said. "Go and confer somewhere about how you'll help Yola. Maybe you can even decide on what god to worship here; there are so many gods. But Yola and I have important matters to discuss in private."

As the sun rose, Kardios strode away with his sword and his harp. Athemar, the members of the council, the court, the people, gathered to raise a chorus of affectionate farewells.

Only Yola was not there. Sitting on the emerald throne that now was hers, she grieved.

GONE FISHING

by J. A. Pollard

All day long the Atlanteans slalomed through the water netting, casting up their baskets through the waves—into the world-beyond-worlds the Old Ones said—waiting for the prey to learn its capture. And then, at night, down through the darkening layers they would haul the silver threads, haul the floats, haul them down and down into the purpled recesses where the phosphorescent fish came out; and in the net would be the body of some lifeless creature which they would turn over and over and cut apart and share together.

It had been another slow day. "The populations grow thinner," the Old Ones said. "The populations depart. Hunger will stalk the deeps."

And the nets increased as the people increased and the fishing grew even poorer and the voices muttered, "It can't be possible."

"So we have overnetted," some said. "And now we must dwindle."

"The answer is more nets," the puerile complained.

And so it was that Hilyar and Frago drew the silver strands through the current, letting out the line and watching the silver floats rushing upward into the world above: up into the unknown where the world was faded, where all color lost its savor and dark was tattered.

"What is it like?" she whispered.

"There is nothingness," Frago declared. The scree of bubbles followed his words following the lines. Deftly he twisted the netting together, carefully he applied his craft. Very swiftly then the net with its floating bells struck upward; and they sat in the coracle on the bottom waiting, fanning the outer edges of their gills, hoping.

There was a tugging finally, a thrashing down the silver lines like shouting. Synchronized, they drew together, hauling the net toward them like a little elevator. Yet the thing caught would not give up but slowed their progress until at length all they could do was glance at one another and move their gills until they were red and hurting, and haul, and glance again.

Until finally the net billowed down before them and within they saw the black body of a creature darting now here, now there, its rage immense, its sleekness covering all angles and vision. And from the sight they stumbled backward over the edge of the coracle until they felt themselves sliding ever deeper; and then their curiosity took them and they returned, slipping over the edge to peer again within the net.

The creature sat on the bottom of the coracle with its strange limbs holding off the net. It had crossed its lower extremities and now the black flippers stuck out at either side. A single eye shining faintly in the dimming light looked out. And its upper limbs—its incredible upper limbs—it used its upper limbs to investigate everything. It thought through its upper limbs. She could see that immediately. She called to Frago, "It thinks with its hands!" and the idea was as frightening, intimidating, as if she did not know her brain controlled all action.

"Yet it thinks with its hands," she insisted.

For even now as it glimpsed them, it ceased struggling, the hands stopping with all the ten strange appendages at the ends curling and uncurling, gesturing, pointing, asking . . . then silently waiting. And in the waiting, she imagined, there was more danger than in all the rest. For it was dangerous, she perceived. It was sleek and black, and it was dangerous.

It had come down from the faded world above all in darkness, with its single shining eye focused and unblinking. It was not a skin-being but a creature of eyesight. What would it be like to live with visual perception paramount?

Warily she turned around. Warily she felt along her sides. Tenderly she moved herself, reading all the messages her skin would bring. She arched her neck, she moved her back, she curled and circled, watching Frago where he hovered, thinking.

He had taken out his sacred emblem. The object lay within his keeping, shining in the coming dark.

And now the black thing in the net perceived it, watched. She felt the black thing watching, felt the tension all along her sides until the nerve lines purpled on her silver flesh. She gasped . . . and sent a scree of bubbles floating past it, till the creature turned.

She knew their eyes were looking at each other. There it was; here, she. And yet their eyes sank into one another till she knew it knew; it knew she knew; until the emblem trembling there in Frago's hand was a barrier between them. Then she said to Frago, "Put the thing away. It understands, I tell you."

"Nonsense!"

"I say it understands."

"It can't!"

But even Frago hesitated.

"No, I say it can't", he said as if to reassure himself.

"But are they usually black?"

The words came out of her before she had looked into them. The words lay there in the shallows, on the floor of the coracle, turning orange and silver.

And the creature stirred, its limbs touching the netting now here, now there, stirring, uncrossing its lower extremities, moving its fins and pressing its single eye into the netting.

Frago moved.

"No! Don't!"

"But it's alive," he told her.

"But they are usually dead!" she warned him. "When they come down they are in various shades of brown from light to dark, and their limbs are shrunken with descent and their bodies crushed and they are dead and . . ."

Here she felt the nervelines on her sides like molten jade.

"They never live!" she said.

"Then I must kill it!"

There was a swirl. There was the netting parting. There was Frago moving in, the emblem with its sharp, smooth mouth agape; and there was in the net a rush of limbs, of fins, of single eyelid never blinking, and of bubbles rising, screaming, rising . . .

Frago swirled. The black thing dove away. He spun. Again it moved. The net was trailing from its fins, the single eye turned on her, back to Frago.

"Stop!" she cried.

And Frago halted, lolling on his side, for anything so strange had made him weak.

And then they saw the emblem in the black thing's hands; they saw the glint of light on ebbing light. The creature moved before them, pulling off the silver netting with its ten strange digits, holding in the digits something long and smooth and slick. They hovered, looking. Frago swirled to come at it again. But Hilyar moved her silver belly in between the two, and wavered there, the jade-green sidelines thumming in a wild insistent squeal.

The thing had paused. Its angles floated still before her. Eye met eye. Each eye saw pain and wonderment and fear . . . and more than that . . .

And more than that, she thought. And more than that. The thing had swum away, had bolted upward as her people bolted downward from the light and from the shark; held in its hand an emblem sleek and smooth, and waved it as it made the plunge beyond them, up and up into the fading world where life must end. Where life would end, the Old Ones said. Where light fades flesh and fin and scale, where waves pound on the endless reaches of the outer fringers of the universe.

"There is no life out there," they told her. "None. We catch the low life on the rim within our nets. That's all. Beyond the crashing and the golden glaze which few of us have seen there is a fire. Heat dissolves the soul. The fire eats the flesh. Up there is where the world comes to its limit. Only death remains."

"What of the mountains rising up beyond the waves?" she asked.

They smiled.

"They dry up, shrivel, die. The pounding of the world around their tips destroys them."

Then The Thing would be destroyed, she thought. And yet . . . she saw it bolting upward, looking back, the single eye unblinking, looking at her eyes. It knew, she thought. It knew. I know. She turned to Frago in the coracle.

"It understood," she said.

THE LAMP

by L. Sprague De Camp

I stopped at Bill Bugby's Garage in Gahato and got young Bugby to drive me to the landing above the dam. There I found Mike Devlin waiting for me, in an aluminum row-canoe with an outboard motor. I said:

"Hello, Mike! I'm Wilson Newbury. Remember me?"

I dropped my gear into the boat, lowering the suitcase carefully lest I damage the box I was carrying in it.

"Hello, Mr. Newbury!" said Mike. "To be sure, I remember you." He looked much the same as before, save that the wrinkles on his brown face were a little deeper and his curly hair a little grayer. In old-fashioned lumberjack style, he wore a heavy flannel shirt, a sweater, an old jacket, and a hat, although the day was warm. "Have you got that thing with you?"

I sent the car back to Bugby's to keep until I needed it again and got into the boat. "The thing Mr. Ten Eyck wanted me to bring?" I said.

"I do mean that, sir." Mike started the motor, so that we had to shout:

"It's in the big bag," I said, "so don't run us on a stump. After fetching that thing all the way from Europe, and having nightmares the whole time, I don't want it to end up at the bottom of Lower Lake."

"I'll be careful, Mr. Newbury," said Mike, steering the boat up the winding course of the channel. "What is that thing, anyhow?"

"It's an antique lamp. He got me to pick it up in Paris from some character he'd been writing to."

"Ah, well, Mr. Ten Eyck is always buying funny things. After his troubles, that's about all he's interested in."

"What's this about Al's having been married?" I asked.

"Sure, and didn't you know? Although born and reared in Canada, Mike still sounded more Irish than most native-born Irishmen. I suppose his little home town in Nova Scotia had been solidly Irish-Canadian. "He married the Camaret girl—the daughter of that big lumberjack." Mike chuckled, his faded blue eyes searching the channel ahead for snags. "You remember, when she was a little girl and the teacher in Gahato asked all the childer what they wanted to be when they grew up, she said: 'I want to be a whore!' It broke up the class for fair, it did."

"Well, what happened? Whatever possessed Al—"

"I guess he wanted a husky, hard-working cook and housekeeper, and he figured she'd be so pleased to marry a gentleman that she'd do what he wanted. Trouble was Melusine Camaret is a pretty hot piece—always has been. When she found Mr. Ten Eyck couldn't put it to her night and morning regular, she up and ran off with young Larochelle. You know, Pringle's foreman's son."

A big blue heron, disturbed by the racket of the outboard, flapped away up the channel. Mike asked, "How was the Army, Mr. Newbury?"

I shrugged. "Just manning a desk. Nobody both-

ered to shoot at me. I sometimes feel I was lucky the
war ended when it did, before they found what a
nincompoop they'd put into an officer's uniform."

"Ah, sure, you was always the modest one."

The channel opened out into Lower Lake. The lake
was surrounded by the granite ridges of the Adirondacks, thickly clad in hardwoods and evergreens—mostly
maple and pine. Here and there, a gray hogback or
scar showed through the forest. Most of the market-
able timber had been cut out early in the century and
its place taken by second growth. The postwar short-
ages, however, had made it profitable to cut stands
that theretofore had stood too far back from transpor-
tation to be profitable. While much of the land there-
abouts had gone into the Adirondack State Park and
so was no longer cuttable, enough remained in private
hands to keep the lumber trucks rolling and the saws
of Dan Pringle's mill in Gahato screaming.

We cut across Lower Lake to Ten Eyck Island,
which separated Lower Lake from Upper Lake. On
the map, the two lakes made an hourglass shape, with
the island partly plugging the neck between them.

Alfred Ten Eyck, in khaki shirt and pants, came to
the dock with a yell of "Willy!" He had a quick,
nervous handshake, with a stronger grip than I expected.

We swapped the usual remarks about our not having changed a bit, although I could not say it sincerely
of Alfred. While he had kept his slim, straight shape,
he had pouches under his eyes. His sandy hair was
graying; although, like me, he was still in his thirties.

"Have you got it?" he asked.

"Yes, yes. It's in that—"

He had already grabbed my big suitcase and started
for the old camp. He went up the slope at a pace that I
almost had to run to keep up with. When he saw me

lagging, he stopped to wait. Being out of condition, I came up panting.

"Same old place," I said.

"It's run down a bit," he said, "since the days when my folks entertained relays of friends and relatives all summer. In those days, you could hire help to keep it up—not that Mike doesn't do two men's work."

The trail was somewhat overgrown, and I stumbled on a clump of weeds. Alfred gave me a wry grin.

"I have an understanding with Nature," he said. "I leave her alone, and she leaves me alone. Seriously, anytime you want to help us clear out the trails, I'll give you a corn hook and tell you to go to it. It's all you can do here to keep ahead of the natural forces of growth and decay."

Camp Ten Eyck was a big two-story house, made of huge handhewn logs, with fifteen or sixteen rooms. There was a tool kit beside the front door, with tools lying about. Mike and Alfred had evidently been re-placing a couple of porch boards that had begun to rot.

Most Adirondack camps are of wood, because lum-ber is relatively cheap there. The Adirondack climate, however, sees to it that a wooden house starts to fall apart almost as soon as it is completed. Some of the big logs that made up the sides of Camp Ten Eyck had spots so soft that you could stick your thumb into them.

While I caught my breath, Alfred said, "Look, I'll show you your room, but first would you please get *it* out? I want to see it."

"Oh, all right," I said. I set the suitcase on one of those old-fashioned window seats, which filled the cor-ners of the living room, and opened it. I handed Alfred the box.

"You'll notice it's properly packed," I said. "My

sister once sent us a handsome antique luster vase from England, in just a flimsy carton, and it got smashed to pieces."

Alfred cut the cords with shaking hands. He had to go out to get a chisel from his tool chest to pry up the wooden lid. Then he burrowed into the excelsior.

While he worked, I looked around. There were the same old deerskins on the couches and window seats, the same deer heads staring glassily from the walls, the same stuffed fox and owl, the same silver-birch banisters with the bark on, and the same lichens on whose white nether surfaces amateur artists had scratched sylvan scenes.

I surprised to see that the big, glass-fronted gun case was empty. As I remembered it from the thirties, the case had held an impressive array of rifles, shotguns, and pistols, mostly inherited by Alfred from his father and grandfather.

"What happened to all your guns?" I said. "Did you sell them?"

"The hell I did!" he said, working away. "You know that no-good cousin of mine, George Vreeland? I rented the place to him one year, and when I got back I found that he had simply sold most of the guns to the *natives*." (Alfred always snarled a little when he said "natives," meaning the year-round residents of the country.)

"What did you do about it?"

"Nothing I could do. George was gone before I got back, and the last I heard he was in California. Then, when I was away last winter, one of our local night workers made off with the rest, including my sailing trophy. I know who did it, too."

"Well?"

"Well, what? No matter how good my proof was, do you suppose I could get the goddamn *natives* to convict him? After what happened to me with Camaret?"

"What about Camaret? I don't know this story."

"Well, you knew I'd been married?"

"Yes. Mike mentioned it."

Alfred Ten Eyck gave me a brief account of his short-lived union with Melusine Camaret. He said nothing about his own sexual inadequacy, for which I cannot blame him.

"The day after she flew the coop," he said, "I was walking along the street in Gahato, bothering absolutely nobody, when Big Jean comes up and says: 'Hey! What you do wit my leetla girl, *hein?*' And the first thing I know, he knocks me cold, right there in the street."

(That was not how the folk in Gahato remembered the event. They say that Alfred answered: "Now look, you dumb Canuck, I don't know what that floozie has been telling you, but—" and then Camaret hit him.)

"Well," Alfred went on, "when I came to, I swore out a warrant and had the trooper run Jean in. But the jury acquitted him, although half the village had seen him slug me. I heard they figured that if Big Jean wanted to belt his son-in-law, that was a family fight and none of their business."

(The villagers' version was that, since Jean Camaret was built like a truck and had a notoriously violent temper, anyone fool enough to pick a fight with him deserved what he got.)

Waving an arm to indicate the surrounding mountains, Alfred glowered at me. "They can't forget that, fifty years ago, everything you could see from here was Ten Eyck property, and they had to get a Ten Eyck's permission to so much as spit on it. Now the great Ten Eyck holdings are down to this one lousy little island, plus a few lots in Gahato; but they still hate my guts."

In fact, several members of the Ten Eyck family still held parcels of land in Herkimer County, but that is a minor point. Alfred did not get on well with most of his kin.)

"I think you exaggerate," I said. "Anyway, why stay here if you don't feel comfortable?"

"Where should I go, and how should I earn a living? Jeepers! Here I at least have a roof over my head. By collecting a few rents on those shacks on Hemlock Street in Gahato—when the tenants don't talk me out of them with hard-luck stories—and now and then selling one of the remaining lots, I get by. Since I can't sell them fast enough to get ahead of my expenses and build up some investments, I'm whittling away at my capital; but I don't seem to have any choice. Ah, here we are!"

Alfred had unwrapped the page from *Le Figaro*, which enfolded the lamp. He held up his treasure.

It was one of those hollow, heart-shaped things, about the size of the palm of your hand, which they used for lamps in Greek and Roman times. It had a knob-shaped handle at the round end, a big hole in the center top for refilling, and a little hole for the wick at the pointed or spout end. You can buy any number of them in Europe and the Near East, since they are always digging up more.

Most such lamps are made of cheap pottery. This one looked at first like pottery, too. Actually, it was composed of some sort of metal but had a layer of dried mud all over it. This stuff had flaked off in places, allowing a dull gleam of metal to show through.

"What's it made of?" I asked. "Ionides didn't seem to know, when he gave me the thing in Paris."

"I don't know. Some sort of silver bronze or bell

metal, I guess. We'll have to clean it to find out. But we've got to be careful with it. You can't just scrub an antique like this with steel wool, you know."

"I know. If it has a coating of oxide, you leave it in place. Then they can put it in an electrolytic tank and turn the oxide back into the original metal, I understand."

"Something like that," said Alfred.

"But what's so remarkable about this little widget? You're not an archaeologist—"

"No, no, that's not it. I got it for a reason. Did you have any funny dreams while you were bringing this over?"

"You bet I did! But how in hell would you know?"

"Ionides told me that might happen."

"Well, then, what's the gag? What's this all about?"

Alfred gave me another glare from his pale-gray eyes. "Just say I'm fed up with being a loser, that's all."

I know what he meant. If the word "loser" applied to anybody, it was Alfred Ten Eyck. You know the term "Midas touch"? Alfred had the opposite, whatever that is. He could turn gold into dross by touching it.

Alfred's father died while Alfred was at Princeton, leaving him several thousand acres of Adirondack land but hardly any real money to live on. So Alfred had dropped out of college and come to Herkimer County to try to make a go of the country-squire business. Either he lacked the right touch, however, or he had the most extraordinary run of bad luck. He sold most of the land, but usually on unfavorable terms to some smarter speculator, who thereupon doubled or tripled his money.

Alfred also dabbed in business of various kinds in Gahato. For example, he went partners with a fellow who brought in a stable of riding horses for the summer-visitor trade. It turned out that the fellow really knew very little about horses and imported a troop of untrained crowbaits. One of his first customers got bucked off and broke her leg.

Then Alfred put up a bowling alley, the Iroquois Lanes, with all that machinery for setting up the pins after each strike. He did all right and sold out at a handsome profit to Morrie Kaplan. But Morrie was to pay in installments. He had not had it a mouth when it burned up; and Morrie, who was no better a businessman than Alfred, had let the insurance lapse. So Morrie was bankrupt, and Alfred was left holding the bag.

Then came the war. Full of patriotic fire, Alfred enlisted as a private. He promptly came down with tuberculosis in training camp. Since antibiotics had come in, they cured him; but that ended his military career. Maybe it was just as well, because Alfred was the kind of fellow who would shoot his own foot off at practice.

"Okay," said Alfred, "let me show you to your room. Mike and I just rattle around in this big old place."

When he had settled me in, he said, "Now what would you really like to do, Willy? Drink? Swim? Hike? Fish? Or just sit in the sun and talk?"

"What I'd really like would be to go for a row in one of those wonderful old guide boats. Remember when we used to frog around the swamps in them, scooping up muck so we could look at the little wigglers under the microscope?"

Alfred heaved a sigh. "I don't have any more of those boats."

"What happened to them? Sell them?"

"No. Remember when I was in the Army? I rented

the island to a family named Strong, and they succeeded in smashing every last boat. Either the women got into them in high heels and punched through the hulls, or their kids ran them on rocks."

"You can't get boats like that any more, can you?" I said.

"Oh, there are still one or two old geezers who make them through the winter months. But each boat costs more than I could afford. Besides the outboard, I have only an old flatbottom. We can go out in that."

We spent a couple of very nice hours that afternoon, out in the flatbottom. It was one of those rare days, with the sky crystal-clear except for a few puffy little white cumulus clouds. The old rowboat tended to spin in circles instead of going where you wanted it to. When, not having rowed for years, I began to get blisters, I gave my place to Alfred, whose hands were horny from hard work.

We caught up on each other's history. I said, "Say, remember the time I pushed you off the dock?" and he said, "Whatever happened to your uncle—the one who had a camp on Raquette lake?" and I said, "How come you never married my cousin Agnes? You and she were pretty thick. . . ."

I told Alfred about my inglorious military career, my French fiancee, and my new job with the trust company. He looked sharply at me, saying:

"Willy, explain something to me."

"What?"

"When we took those tests in school, my IQ was every bit as high as yours."

"Yes, you always had more original ideas than I ever did. What about it?"

"Yet here you are, landing on your feet as usual.

Me, I can't seem to do anything right. I just don't get the hang of it."

"Hang of what?"

"Of life."

"Maybe you should have gone into some line that didn't demand such practicality—so much realism and adaptability. Something more intellectual, like teaching or writing.",

He shook his graying head. "I couldn't join the professorate, on account of I never finished college. I've tried writing stories, but nobody wants them. I've even written poems, but they tell me they're just bad imitations of Tennyson and Kipling, and nobody cares for that sort of thing nowadays."

"Have you tried a headshrinker?" (The term had not yet been whittled down to "shrink.")

He shook his head. "I saw one in Utica, but I didn't like the guy. Besides, chasing down the line to Utica once or twice a week would have meant more time and expense than I could afford."

A little breeze sprang up, ruffling the glassy lake. "Oh, well," he said, "time we were getting back."

The island was quiet except for the chugging, from the boathouse, of the little Diesel that pumped our water and charged the batteries that gave us light and power. Over drinks before dinner, I asked:

"Now look, Al, you've kept me dangling long enough about that damned lamp. What *is* it? Why should I have nightmares while bringing the thing back from Europe?"

Alfred stared at his Scotch. He mostly drank a cheap rye, I learned, but had laid in Scotch for his old friend. At last he said:

"Can you remember those nightmares?"

"You bet I can! They scared the living Jesus out of

me. Each time, I was standing in front of a kind of
chair, or maybe a throne. Something was sitting on the
throne, only I couldn't make out details. But when
it reached out toward me, its arms were—well, kind of
boneless, like tentacles. And I couldn't yell or run or
anything. Each time, I woke up just as the thing got its
snaky fingers on me. Over and over."

"Ayup, it figures," he said. "That would be old
Yuskejek."

"That would be *what*?"

"Yuskejek. Willy, are you up on the mythology of
the lost continent of Atlantis?"

"Good lord, no! I've been too busy. As I remember,
the occultists try to make out that there really was a
sunken continent out in the Atlantic, while the scientists
say that's tosh, that Plato really got his ideas from Crete
or Egypt or some such place."

"Some favor Tartessos, near modern Cadiz," said
Alfred. (This happened before those Greek professors
came up with their theory about the eruption of the
volcanic island of Thera, north of Crete.) "I don't
suppose a hard-headed guy like you believes in anything supernatural, do you?"

"Me? Well, that depends. I believe what I see—at
least most of the time, unless I have reason to suspect
sleight-of-hand. I know that, just when you think you
know it all and can see through any trick, that's when
they'll bamboozle you. After all, I was in Gahato when
that part-time medium, Miss—what was her name?—
Scott—Barbara Scott—had that trouble with a band of
little bitty Indian spooks, who threw stones at people."

Alfred laughed. "Jeepers Cripus, I'd forgotten that!
They never did explain it."

"So what about your goofy lamp?"

"Well, Ionides has good connections in esoteric circles, and he assures me that the lamp is a genuine relic of Atlantis."

"Excuse me if I reserve my opinion. So what's this Yuskejek? The demon-god of Atlantis?"

"Sort of."

"What kind of name is 'Yuskejek,' anyway? Eskimo?"

"Basque, I believe."

"Oh, well, I once read that the Devil had studied Basque for seven years and only learned two words. I can see it all—the sinister Atlantean high priest preparing to sacrifice the beautiful virgin princess of Ongabonga, so the devil-god can feast on her soul-substance—"

"Maybe so, maybe not. You've been reading too many pulps. Anyway, let's go eat before I get too drunk to cook."

"Doesn't Mike cook for you?"

"He's glad to, when I ask him; but then I have to eat the result. So most of the time I'd rather do it myself. Come along. *Mike!*" He roared. "Dinner in twenty minutes!"

By mutual unspoken consent, we stayed off Atlantis and its lamp during dinner. Instead, we incited Mike to tell us of the old lumbering days and of some of the odder lumberjacks he had known. There was one who swore he was being trailed, day and night, by a ghostly cougar, or puma, although there hadn't been one of those animals in the Adirondacks since the last century. . . .

We let Mike wash the dishes while Alfred and I settled down in the living room with the lamp. Alfred said:

"I think our first step is to get this crud off. For that, suppose we try an ordinary washcloth and a little water?"

"It's your gimmick," I said, "but that sounds reasonable."

"We have to be oh-so-careful," he said, wetting his cloth and rubbing gently. "I wish we had a real archaeologist here."

"He'd probably denounce you for buying looted antiquities. Someday, they tell me, governments will clamp down on that sort of thing."

"Maybe so, but that time hasn't come yet. I hear our brave boys looted half the museums in Germany during the occupation. Ah, look here!"

Much of the mud had come off, exposing a white, toothlike projection. Alfred handed me the lamp. "What do you make of it?"

"I need a stronger light. Thanks. You know, Al, what this looks like? A barnacle."

"Let me see! Jeepers Cripus, you're right! That means the lamp must have been under water—"

"That doesn't prove anything about its—its provenience, I think they call it. It could have been a lamp of Greek or Roman times, dropped overboard anywhere in the Mediterranean."

"Oh," said Alfred, dampened. "Well, I wouldn't dare work on it longer this evening. We need full daylight." He put the thing away.

That night I had the same nightmare again. There was this throne, and this dim character—Yuskejek or whatever his name was—sitting on it. And then he stretched out those rubbery arms. . . .

A knocking awoke me. It was Alfred. "Say, Willy, did you hear something?"

"No," I said. "I've been asleep. What is it?"

"I don't know. Sound like someone—or something—tramping around on the porch."

"Mike?"

"He's been asleep, too. Better put on your bath-robe; it's cold out."

'I knew how cold Adirondack nights could get, even in July. Muffled up, I followed Alfred downstairs. There we found Mike, in a long nightshirt of Victorian style, with a lantern, a flashlight the size of a small baseball bat, and an ax. Alfred disappeared and, after fumbling in one of the chests beneath the window seats, reappeared with a .22 rifle.

"Only gun on the place," he said. "I keep it hidden in case the goddamn *natives* burgle me again."

We waited, breathing lightly and listening. Then came the sound: a bump—bump—bump—pause, and then bump—bump—bump—bump. It sounded as if someone were tramping on the old porch in heavy boots, the kind everyone used to wear in the woods before the summer people started running round in shorts and sneakers. (I still like such boots; at least, the deer flies can't bite through them.)

Perhaps the sound could have been made by a horse or a moose, although we haven't had moose in the region for nearly a century. Anyhow, I could not imagine what either beast would be doing, swimmming to Ten Eyck Island.

The sound was not especially menacing in itself; but in that black night, on that lonely spot, it made my short hair rise. The eyes of Alfred and Mike looked twice their normal size in the lantern light. Alfred handed me the flashlight.

"You fling open the door with your free hand, Willy," he said, "and try to catch whatever-it-is in the beam. Then Mike and I will go after it."

We waited and waited, but the sound did not come again. At last we went out and toured the island with our lights. There was no moon, but the stars shone with that rare brilliance that you get only in clear weather in high country. We found nothing except a racoon, scuttling up a tree and turning to peer at us through his black bandit's mask, with eyes blazing in the flashlight beam.

"That's Robin Hood," said Alfred. "He's our personal garbage-disposal service. It sure wasn't him that made that racket. Well, we've been over every foot of the island without seeing anything, so I guess. . . ."

There were no more phenomena that night. The next day, we cleaned the lamp some more. It turned out quite a handsome little article, hardly corroded at all. The metal was pale, with a faint ruddy or yellowish tinge, like some grades of white gold.

I also took a swim, more to show that I was not yet middle-aged than for pleasure. I never cared much for swimming in ice water. That is what you get in the Adirondack lakes, even in the hottest weather, when you go down more than a foot or so.

That night, I had another dream. The thing on the throne was in it. This time, however, instead of standing in front of it, I seemed to be off to one side, while Alfred stood in front of it. The two were conversing, but their speech was too muffled for me to make out the words.

At breakfast, while demolishing the huge stack of pancakes that Mike set before me, I asked Alfred about it.

"You're right," he said. "I did dream that I stood before His Tentacular Majesty."

"What happened?"

"Oh, its Yuskejek, all right—unless we're both crazy. Maybe we are, but I'm assuming the contrary. Yuskejek says he'll make me a winner instead of a loser, only I have to offer him a sacrifice."

"Don't look at me that way!" I said. "I've got to get back to my job Monday—"

"Don't be silly, Willy! I'm not about to cut your throat, or Mike's either. I have few enough friends as it is. I explained to this spook that we have very serious laws against human sacrifice in this country."

"How did he take that?"

"He grumbled but allowed as how we had a right to our own laws and customs. So he'll be satisfied with an animal. It's got to be an animal of real size, though—no mouse or squirrel."

"What have you got? I haven't seen anything bigger than chipmunks, except that coon."

"Jeepers, I wouldn't kill Robin Hood! He's a friend. No, I'll take the outboard down to Gahato and buy a pig or something. You'd better come along to help me wrassle the critter."

"Now I know we're nuts," I said. "Did you find out where the real Atlantis was?"

"Nope, didn't think to ask. Maybe we'll come to that later. Let's shove off right after lunch."

"Why not now?"

"I promised to help Mike on some work this morning."

The work was cutting up a dead poplar trunk into firewood lengths. With a powered chain saw, they could have done the job in minutes; but Mike distrusted all newfangled machinery. So they heaved and grunted on an old two-man crosscut saw, one on each end. I spelled Alfred until my blisters from rowing began to hurt.

The weather had other ideas about our afternoon's trip to Gahato. It is a safe rule that, if it rains anywhere in New York State in summer, it also rains in the Adirondacks. I have known it to rain some every day for eight weeks running.

We had had two fine days, and this one started out clear and balmy. By ten, it had clouded over. By eleven, thunder was rumbling. By twelve, it was raining pitchforks with the handles up, interrupting our woodcutting job on the poplar.

Looking out the windows, we could hardly see to the water's edge, save when a particularly lurid flash lit up the scene. The wind roared through the old pines and bent them until you thought that any minute they would be carried away. The thunder drowned half of what we said to one another. The rain sprayed against the windows, almost horizontally, like the blast from a fire hose.

"Yuskejek will have to wait, I guess," I said.

Alfred looked troubled. "He was kind of insistent. I told him there might be a hitch, and he mumbled something about 'Remember what happened last time!' "

The rain continued through the afternoon. The thunder and lightning and wind let up, so that it became just a steady Adirondack downpour. Alfred said:

"You know, Willy, I think we really ought to take the boat to Gahato—"

"You *are* nuts," I said. "With this typhoon, your boat would fill before you got there."

"No, it's an unsinkable, with buoyancy tanks, and you can bail while I steer."

"Oh, for God's sake! If you're so determined on this silly business, why don't you take Mike?"

"He can't swim. Not that we're likely to have to, but I don't want to take the chance."

We argued a little more, in desultory fashion. Needless to say, neither of us really wanted to go out in that cataract. Alfred, though, had become obsessed with his Atlantean lamp and its attendant spirit. Perhaps the god had been evoked by our rubbing the lamp, like the jinn in the *Arabian Nights*.

Then Alfred grabbed my arm and pointed. "Look at that!"

I jumped as if stuck; the spooky atmosphere had begun to get to me. It was a relief to see that Alfred was pointing, not at the materialized form of Yuskejek, but at an enormous snapping turtle, plodding across the clearing in front of the house.

"There's our sacrifice!" cried Alfred. "Let's get him! *Mike!*"

We tore out the front door and went, slipping and sliding in the wet, down the bank to Lower Lake in pursuit of this turtle. We ringed the beast before it reached the lake. Looking almost like a small dinosaur, it dodged this way and that, showing quite a turn of speed. When we got close, it shot out its head and snapped its jaws. The *glop* of the snap sounded over the noise of the rain.

The turtle was snapping at Mike when Alfred caught it by the tail and hoisted it into the air. This took considerable strength, as it must have weighted at least twenty pounds. Alfred had to hold it almost at arm's length to keep from being bitten. The turtle kept darting that hooked beak in all directions, *glop, glop!* and flailing the air with its legs.

"Watch out!" I yelled. "That thing can castratc you if you're not careful!"

"Mike!" shouted Alfred. "Get the ax and the frog spear!"

We were all soaked. Alfred cried, "Hurry up! I can't hold this brute much longer!"

When the tools had been brought, Alfred said, "Now, Mike, you get him to snap at the end of the spear and catch the barbs in his beak. Willy, stand by with the ax.

When Mike hauls the head as far out of the shell as it'll go, chop it off!"

I had no desire to behead this turtle, which had never done anything to me. But I was a guest, and it was just possible that the lamp and its nightmares were kosher after all.

"Don't you have to do some ritual?" I asked.

"No, that comes later. Yuskejek explained it to me, Ah, got him!"

The turtle had snapped on the frog spear. By twisting the little trident, Mike hauled the head out out of the shell. Then—

"Mother of God!" shouted Mike. "He's after biting off the spear!"

It was true. The turtle had bitten through one of the tines of the trident—which may have been weakened by rust—and freed itself.

Instantly came a wild yell from Alfred. The turtle had fastened its beak on the flesh of his leg, just above the knee. In the excitement, Alfred had forgotten to hold the reptile out away from his body.

As the turtle bit into his leg through his trousers, Alfred danced about, tugging at the spiny tail. Then he and the turtle let go together. Alfred folded up on the ground, clutching his wounded leg, while the turtle scuttled down the slope and disappeared into the rain-beaten waters of Lower Lake.

Mike and I got Alfred back to Camp Ten Eyck, with a big red stain spreading down the front of his soaking pants leg. When we got the pants off, however, it did not look as if a trip to the doctor in Gahato would be needed. The turtle's jaws had broken the skin in four places, but the cuts were of the sort that a little disinfectant and some Band-Aids would take care of.

With all the excitement, we more or less forgot about Yuskejek and his sacrifice. Since Alfred was limping, he let Mike get dinner. Afterwards we listened to the radio a bit, read a bit, talked a bit, and went to bed.

The rain was still drumming on the roof when, some hours later, Alfred woke me. "It's that stamping noise again," he said.

As we listened, the bump—bump—bump came again, louder than before. Again we jerked open the door and sprayed the light of the flash and the lantern about. All we saw was the curtain of rain.

When we closed the door, the sound came again, louder. Again we looked out in vain. When we closed the door again, the noise came louder yet: boom—boom—boom. The whole island seemed to shake.

"Hey!" said Alfred. "What the hell's happening? It feels like an earthquake."

"Never heard of an earthquake in this country," I said. "But—"

There came a terrific *boom*, like a near-miss of a lightning bolt. The house shook, and I could hear things falling off shelves.

Mike risked a quick look out and wailed, "Mr. Ten Eyck! The lake's coming up!"

The shaking had become so violent that we could hardly stand. We clutched at the house and at each other to keep our balance. It was like standing in a train going fast on a bad old roadbed. Alfred looked out.

"It *is*!" he shrieked. "Let's get the hell out of here!"

Out we rushed into the merciless rain, just as the water of Lower Lake came foaming up to the porch of Camp Ten Eyck. Actually, it was not the lake that was rising but the island that was sinking. I stumbled off the porch to find myself knee-deep in water. A wave knocked me over, but I somehow shed my bathrobe.

I am, luckily, a fairly good swimmer. Once I was

afloat, I had no trouble in keeping on the surface. There were no small waves of the kind that slap you in the face, but big, long, slow surges, which bobbed me up and down.

There was, however, a vast amount of debris, which had floated off the island when it submerged. I kept bumping into crates, shingles, sticks of firewood, tree branches, and other truck. I heard Mike Devlin calling.

"Where are you, Mike?" I yelled.

By shouting back and forth, we found each other, and I swam to him. Remembering that Mike could not swim, I wished that I had more lifesaving practice. Fortunately, I found Mike clutching a log—part of that poplar they had been sawing up—for a life preserver. With some pushing on my part, we got to shore half an hour later. Mike was sobbing.

"Poor Mr. Ten Eyck!" he said. "Such a nice, kind gentleman, too. There must have been a curse on him."

Whether or not there was a curse on Alfred Ten Eyck, his corpse was recovered the next day. He was, as he had admitted, a loser.

The surges had done many thousands of dollars' damage to other people's docks, boats, and boathouses on Upper and Lower Lakes and the Channel. Because of the downpour, however, all the other camp owners had stayed in and so had not been hurt.

The stage geologist said the earthquake was a geological impossibility. "I should have said, an anomaly," he corrected himself. "It was obviously possible, since it happened. We shall have to modify our theories to account for it."

I did not think it would do any good to tell him about Yuskejek. Besides, if the story got around, some camp owner might be screwy enough to sue me for damages to his boathouse. He would have a hell of a time proving anything, but who wants even the silliest lawsuit?

The Atlantean lamp is, I suppose, at the bottom of the lake and I hope that nobody dredges it up. When Yuskejek threatens to sink an island if disappointed of his sacrifice, he is not fooling. Perhaps he can no longer sink a place so large as the supposed Atlantis. A little islet like Ten Eyck is more his present-day speed.

I do not, however, care to needle that testy and sinister old deity to find out just what he can do. One such demonstration is enough. After all, Atlantis is supposed to have been a *continent*. If he got mad enough . . .

THE SHADOW KINGDOM

by Robert E. Howard

1. King Comes Riding

The blare of the trumpets grew louder, like a deep golden tide surge, like the soft booming of the evening tides against the silver beaches of Valusia. The throng shouted, women flung roses from the roofs as the rhythmic chiming of silver hoofs came clearer and the first of the mighty array swung into view in the broad white street that curved round the golden-spired Tower of Splendor.

First came the trumpeters, slim youths, clad in scarlet, riding with a flourish of long, slender golden trumpets; next the bowmen, tall men from the mountains; and behind these the heavily armed footmen, their broad shields clashing in unison, their long spears swaying in perfect rhythm to their stride. Behind them came the mightiest soldiery in all the world, the Red Slayers, horsemen, splendidly mounted, armed in red from helmet to spur. Proudly they sat their steeds, looking neither to right nor to left, but aware of the shouting for all that. Like bronze statues they were, and there was never a waver in the forest of spears that reared above them.

Behind those proud and terrible ranks came the motley files of the mercenaries, fierce, wild-looking warriors, men of Mu and of Kaa-u and of the hills of the east and the isles of the west. They bore spears and heavy swords, and a compact group that marched somewhat apart were the bowmen of Lemuria. Then came the light foot of the nation, and more trumpeters brought up the rear.

A brave sight, and a sight which aroused a fierce thrill in the soul of Kull, king of Valusia. Not on the Topaz Throne at the front of the regal Tower of Splendor sat Kull, but in the saddle, mounted on a great stallion, a true warrior king. His mighty arm swung up in reply to the salutes as the hosts passed. His fierce eyes passed the gorgeous trumpeters with a casual glance, rested longer on the following soldiery; they blazed with a ferocious light as the Red Slayers halted in front of him with a clang of arms and a rearing of steeds, and tendered him the crown salute. They narrowed slightly as the mercenaries strode by. They saluted no one, the mercenaries. They walked with shoulders flung back, eyeing Kull boldly and straightly, albeit with a certain appreciation; fierce eyes, unblinking; savage eyes, staring from beneath shaggy manes and heavy brows.

And Kull gave back a like stare. He granted much to brave men, and there were no braver in all the world, not even among the wild tribesmen who now disowned him. But Kull was too much the savage to have any great love for these. There were too many feuds. Many were age-old enemies of Kull's nation, and though the name of Kull was now a word accursed among the mountains and valleys of his people, and though Kull had put them from his mind, yet the old hates, the ancient passions still lingered. For Kull was no Valusian but an Atlantean.

The armies swung out of sight around the gem-blazing shoulders of the Tower of Spendor and Kull reined his stallion about and started toward the palace at an easy gait, discussing the review with the commanders that rode with him, using not many words, but saying much.

"The army is like a sword," said Kull, "and must not be allowed to rust." So down the street they rode, and Kull gave no heed to any of the whispers that reached his hearing from the throngs that still swarmed the streets.

"That is Kull, see! Valka! But what a king! And what a man! Look at his arms! His shoulders!"

And an undertone of more sinister whisperings: "Kull! Ha, accursed usurper from the pagan isles"—"Aye, shame to Valusia that a barbarian sits on the Throne of Kings." . . .

Little did Kull heed. Heavyhanded had he seized the decaying throne of ancient Valusia and with a heavier hand did he hold it, a man against a nation.

After the council chamber, the social palace where Kull replied to the formal and laudatory phrases of lords and ladies, with carefully hidden, grim amusement at such frivolities; then the lords and ladies took their formal departure and Kull leaned back upon the ermine throne and contemplated matters of state until an attendant requested permission from the great king to speak, and announced an emissary from the Pictish embassy.

Kull brought his mind back from the dim mazes of Valusian statecraft where it had been wandering, and gazed upon the Pict with little favor. The man gave back the gaze of the king without flinching. He was a lean-hipped, massive-chested warrior of middle height, dark, like all his race, and strongly built. From strong, immobile features gazed dauntless and inscrutable eyes.

"The chief of the Councilors, Ka-nu of the tribe,

right hand of the king of Pictdom, sends greetings and says: "There is a throne at the feast of the rising moon for Kull, king of kings, lord of lords, emperor of Valusia.' "

"Good," answered Kull. "Say to Ka-nu the Ancient, ambassador of the western isles, that the king of Valusia will quaff wine with him when the moon floats over the hills of Zalgara."

Still the Pict lingered. "I have a word for the king, not"— with a contemptuous flirt of his hand—"for these slaves."

Kull dismissed the attendants with a word, watching the Pict warily.

The man stepped nearer, and lowered his voice: "Come alone to feast tonight, lord king. Such was the word of my chief."

The king's eyes narrowed, gleaming like gray sword steel, coldly.

"Alone?"

"Aye."

They eyed each other silently, their mutual tribal enmity seething beneath their cloak of formality. Their mouths spoke the cultured speech, the conventional court phrases of a highly polished race, a race not their own, but from their eyes gleamed the primal traditions of the elemental savage. Kull might be the king of Valusia and the Pict might be an emissary to her courts, but there in the throne hall of kings, two tribesmen glowered at each other, fierce and wary, while ghosts of wild wars and world-ancient feuds whispered to each.

To the king was the advantage and he enjoyed it to its fullest extent. Jaw resting on hand, he eyed the Pict, who stood like an image of bronze, head flung back, eyes unflinching.

"Across Kull's lips stole a smile that was more a sneer.

"And so I am to come—alone?" Civilization had taught him to speak by innuendo and the Pict's dark eyes glittered, though he made no reply. "How am I to know that you come from Ka-nu?"

"I have spoken," was the sullen response.

"And when did a Pict speak truth?" sneered Kull, fully aware that the Picts never lied, but using his means to enrage the man.

"I see your plan, king," the Pict answered imperturbably. "You wish to anger me. By Valka, you need go no further! I am angry enough. And I challenge you to meet me in single battle, spear, sword or dagger, mounted or afoot. Are you king or man?"

Kull's eyes glinted with the grudging admiration a warrior must needs give a bold foeman, but he did not fail to use the chance of further annoying his antagonist.

"A king does not accept the challenge of a nameless savage," he sneered, "nor does the emperor of Valusia break the Truce of Ambassadors. You have leave to go. Say to Ka-nu I will come alone."

The Pict's eyes flashed murderously. He fairly shook in the grasp of the primitive blood-lust; then, turning his back squarely upon the king of Valusia, he strode across the Hall of Society and vanished through the great door.

Again Kull leaned back upon the ermine throne and meditated.

So the chief of the Council of Picts wished him to come alone? But for what reason? Treachery? Grimly Kull touched the hilt of his great sword. But scarcely. The Picts valued too greatly the alliance with Valusia to break it for any feudal reason. Kull might be a warrior of Atlantis and hereditary enemy of all Picts, but too, he was king of Valusia, the most potent ally of the Men of the West.

Kull reflected long upon the strange state of affairs that made him ally of ancient foes and foe of ancient friends. He rose and paced restlessly across the hall, with the quick, noiseless tread of a lion. Chains of friendship, tribe and tradition had he broken to satisfy his ambition. And, by Valka, god of the sea and the land, he had realized that ambition! He was king of Valusia—a fading, degenerate Valusia, a Valusia living mostly in dreams of bygone glory, but still a mighty land and the greatest of the Seven Empires. Valusia —Land of Dreams, the tribesmen named it, and sometimes it seemed to Kull that he moved in a dream. Strange to him were the intrigues of court and palace, army and people. All was like a masquerade, where men and women hid their real thoughts with a smooth mask. Yet the seizing of the throne had been easy—a bold snatching of opportunity, the swift whirl of swords, the slaying of a tyrant of whom men had wearied unto death, short, crafty plotting with ambitious statesmen out of favor at court—and Kull, wandering adventurer, Atlantean exile, had swept up to the dizzy heights of his dreams: he was lord of Valusia, king of kings. Yet now it seemed that the seizing was far easier than the keeping. The sight of the Pict had brought back youthful associations to his mind, the free, wild savagery of his boyhood. And now a strange feeling of dim unrest, of unreality, stole over him as of late it had been doing. Who was he, a straightforward man of the seas and the mountain, to rule a race strangely and terribly wise with the mysticisms of antiquity? An ancient race—

"I am Kull!" said he, flinging back his head as a lion flings back his mane. "I am Kull!"

His falcon gaze swept the ancient hall. His self-

confidence flowed back. . . . And in a dim nook of the
hall a tapestry moved—slightly.

2. Thus Spake the Silent Halls of Valusia

The moon had not risen, and the garden was lighted
with torches aglow in silver cressets when Kull sat
down in the throne before the table of Ka-nu, ambassador of the western isles. At his right hand sat the
ancient Pict, as much unlike an emissary of that fierce
race as a man could be. Ancient was Ka-nu and wise
in statecraft, grown old in the game. There was no
elemental hatred in the eyes that looked at Kull ap-
praisingly; no Tribal traditions hindered his judgments.
Long associations with the statesmen of the civilized
nations had swept away such cobwebs. Not: who and
what is this man? was the question ever foremost in
Ka-nu's mind, but: can I use this man, and how?
Tribal prejudices he used only to further his own
schemes.

   And Kull watched Ka-nu, answering his conversation briefly, wondering if civilization would make of
him a thing like the Pict. For Ka-nu was soft and
paunchy. Many years had stridden across the sky-rim
since Ka-nu had wielded a sword. True, he was old,
but Kull had seen men older than he in the forefront
of battle. The Picts were a long-lived race. A beautiful
girl stood at Ka-nu's elbow, refilling his goblet, and she
was kept busy. Meanwhile Ka-nu kept up a running
fire of jests and comments, and Kull, secretly contemptuous of his garrulity, nevertheless missed none
of his shrewd humor.

   At the banquet were Pictish chiefs and statesmen,
the latter jovial and easy in their manner, the warriors
formally courteous, but plainly hampered by their tribal

affinities. Yet Kull, with a tinge of envy, was cogni-
zant of the freedom and ease of the affair as con-
trasted with like affairs of the Valusian court. Such
freedom prevailed in the rude camps of Atlantis—Kull
shrugged his shoulders. After all, doubtless Ka-nu,
who had seemed to have forgotten he was a Pict as far
as time-hoary custom and prejudice went, was right
and he, Kull, would better become a Valusian in mind
as in name.

At last when the moon had reached her zenith,
Ka-nu, having eaten and drunk as much as any three
men there, leaned back upon his divan with a comfortable sigh and said, "Now, get you gone, friends, for
the king and I would converse on such matters as
concern not children. Yes, you too, my pretty; yet first
let me kiss those ruby lips—so; now dance away, my
rose-bloom."

Ka-nu's eyes twinkled above his white beard as he
surveyed Kull, who sat erect, grim and uncompromising.

"You are thinking, Kull," said the old statesman,
suddenly, "that Ka-nu is a useless old reprobate, fit
for nothing except to guzzle wine and kiss wenches!"

In fact, this remark was so much in line with his
actual thoughts, and so plainly put, that Kull was
rather startled, though he gave no sign.

Ka-nu gurgled and his paunch shook with his mirth.
"Wine is red and women are soft," he remarked toler-
antly. "But—ha! ha!—think not old Ka-nu allows
either to interfer with business."

Again he laughed, and Kull moved restlessly. This
seemed much like being made sport of, and the king's
scintillant eyes began to glow with a feline light.

Ka-nu reached for the wine-pitcher, filled his beaker
and glanced questioningly at Kull, who shook his head
irritably.

"Aye," said Ka-nu equably, "it takes an old head to stand strong drink. I am growing old, Kull, so why should you young men begrudge me such pleasures as we oldsters must find? Ah me, I grow ancient and withered, friendless and cheerless."

But his looks and expressions failed far of bearing out his words. His rubicund countenance fairly glowed, and his eyes sparkled, so that his white beard seemed incongruous. Indeed, he looked remarkably elfin, reflected Kull, who felt vaguely resentful. The old scoundrel had lost all of the primitive virtues of his race and of Kull's race, yet he seemed more pleased in his aged days than otherwise.

"Hark ye, Kull," said Ka-nu, raising an admonitory finger, " 'tis a chancy thing to laud a young man, yet I must speak my true thoughts to gain your confidence."

"If you think to gain it by flattery—"

"Tush. Who spake of flattery? I flatter only to disguard."

There was a keen sparkle in Ka-nu's eyes, a cold glimmer that did not match his lazy smile. He knew men, and he knew that to gain his end he must smite straight with this tigerish barbarian, who, like a wolf scenting a snare, would scent out unerringly any falseness in the skein of his word-web.

"You have power, Kull," said he, choosing his words with more care than he did in the council rooms of the nation, "to make yourself mightiest of all kings, and restore some of the lost glories of Valusia. So. I care little for Valusia—though the women and wine be excellent—save for the fact that the stronger Valusia is, the stronger is the Pict nation. More, with an Atlantean on the throne, eventually Atlantis will become united—"

Kull laughed in harsh mockery. Ka-nu had touched an old wound.

"Atlantis made my name accursed when I went to seek fame and fortune among the cities of the world. We—they—are age-old foes of the Seven Empires, greater foes of the allies of the Empires, as you should know."

Ka-nu tugged his beard and smiled enigmatically.

"Nay, nay. Let it pass. But I know whereof I speak. And then warfare will cease, wherein there is no gain; I see a world of peace and prosperity—man loving his fellow man—the good supreme. All this can you accomplish—*if you live!*"

"Ha!" Kull's lean hand closed on his hilt and he half rose, with a sudden movement of such dynamic speed that Ka-nu, who fancied men as some men fancy blooded horses, felt his old blood leap with a sudden thrill. Valka, what a warrior! Nerves and sinews of steel and fire, bound together with the perfect co-ordination, the fighting instinct, that makes the terrible warrior.

But none of Ka-nu's enthusiasm showed in his mildly sarcastic tone.

"Tush. Be seated. Look about you. The gardens are deserted, the seats empty, save for ourselves. You fear not *me?*"

Kull sank back, gazing about him warily.

"There speaks the savage," mused Ka-nu. "Think you if I planned treachery I would enact it here where suspicion would be sure to fall upon me? Tut. You young tribesmen have much to learn. There were my chiefs who were not at ease because you were born among the hills of Atlantis, and you despise me in your secret mind because I am a Pict. Tush. I see you as Kull, king of Valusia, not as Kull, the reckless Atlantean, leader of the raiders who harried the western isles. So you should see in me, not a Pict but an international man, a figure of the world. Now to that figure, hark! If you were slain tomorrow who would be king?"

"Kaanuub, baron of Blaal."

"Even so. I object to Kaanuub for many reasons, yet most of all for the fact that he is but a figurehead."

"How so? He was my greatest opponent, but I did not know that he championed any cause but his own."

"The night can hear," answered Ka-nu obliquely. "There are worlds within worlds. But you may trust me and you may trust Brule, the Spear-slayer. Look!" He drew from his robes a bracelet of gold representing a winged dragon coiled thrice, with three horns of ruby on the head.

"Examine it closely. Brule will wear it on his arm when he comes to you tomorrow night so that you may know him. Trust Brule as you trust yourself, and do what he tells you to. And in proof of trust, look ye!"

And with the speed of a striking hawk, the ancient snatched something from his robes, something that flung a weird green light over them, and which he replaced in an instant.

"The stolen gem!" exclaimed Kull recoiling. "The green jewel from the Temple of the Serpent! Valka! You! And why do you show it to me?"

"To save your life. To prove my trust. If I betray your trust, deal with me likewise. You hold my life in your hand. Now I could not be false to you if I would, for a word from you would be my doom."

Yet for all his words the old scoundrel beamed merrily and seemed vastly pleased with himself.

"But why do you give me this hold over you?" asked Kull, becoming more bewildered each second.

"As I told you. Now, you see that I do not intend to deal you false, and tomorrow night when Brule comes to you, you will follow his advice without fear of treachery. Enough. An escort waits outside to ride to the palace with you, lord."

Kull rose. "But you have told me nothing."

"Tush. How impatient are youths!" Ka-nu looked more like a mishievous elf than ever. "Go you and dream of thrones and power and kingdoms, while I dream of wine and soft women and roses. And fortune ride with you, King Kull."

As he left the garden, Kull glanced back to see Ka-nu still reclining lazily in his seat, a merry ancient, beaming on all the world with jovial fellowship.

A mounted warrior waited for the king just without the garden and Kull was slightly surprised to see that it was the same that had brought Ka-nu's invitation. No word was spoken as Kull swung into the saddle nor as they clattered along the empty streets.

The color and the gayety of the day had given away to the eery stillness of night. The city's antiquity was more than ever apparent beneath the bent, silver moon. The huge pillars of the mansions and palaces towered up into the stars. The broad stairways, silent and deserted, seemed to climb endlessly until they vanished in the shadowy darkness of the upper realms. Stairs to the stars, thought Kull, his imaginative mind inspired by the weird grandeur of the scene.

Clang! clang! clang! sounded the silver hoofs on the broad, moon-flooded streets, but otherwise there was no sound. The age of the city, its incredible antiquity, was almost oppressive to the king; it was as if the great silent buildings laughed at him, noiselessly, with unguessable mockery. And what secrets did they hold?

"You are young," said the palaces and the temples and the shrines, "but we are old. The world was wild with youth when we were reared. You and your tribe shall pass, but we are invincible, indestructible. We towered above a strange world, ere Atlantis and Lemuria rose from the sea; we still shall reign when the green waters sigh for many a restless fathom above the spires of Lemuria and the hills of Atlantis and when the isles of the Western Men are the mountains of a strange land.

"How many kings have we watched ride down these streets before Kull of Atlantis was even a dream in the mind of Ka, bird of Creation? Ride on, Kull of Atlantis; greater shall follow you; greater came before you. They are dust; they are forgotten; we stand; we know; we are. Ride, ride on, Kull of Atlantis; Kull the king, Kull the fool!"

And it seemed to Kull that the clashing hoofs took up the silent refrain to beat it into the night with hollow re-echoing mockery:

"Kull—the—king! Kull—the—fool!"

Glow, moon; you light a king's way! Gleam, stars; you are torches in the train of an emperor! And clang, silver-shod hoofs; you herald that Kull rides through Valusia.

Ho! Awake, Valusia! It is Kull that rides, Kull the king!

"We have known many kings," said the silent halls of Valusia.

And so in a brooding mood Kull came to the palace, where his bodyguard, men of the Red Slayers, came to take the rein of the great stallion and escort Kull to his rest. There the Pict, still sullenly speechless, wheeled his steed with a savage wrench of the rein and fled away in the dark like a phantom; Kull's heightened imagination pictured him speeding through the silent streets like a goblin out of the Elder World.

There was no sleep for Kull that night, for it was

nearly dawn and he spent the rest of the night hours pacing the throneroom, and pondering over what had passed. Ka-nu had told him nothing, yet he had put himself in Kull's complete power. At what had he hinted when he had said the baron of Blaal was naught but a figurehead? And who was this Brule, who was to come to him by night, wearing the mystic armlet of the dragon? And why? Above all, why had Ka-nu shown him the green gem of terror, stolen long ago from the temple of the Serpent, for which the world would rock in wars were it known to the weird and terrible keepers of that temple, and from whose vengeance not even Ka-nu's ferocious tribesmen might be able to save him? But Ka-nu knew he was safe, reflected Kull, for the statesman was too shrewd to expose himself to risk without profit. But was it to throw the king off his guard and pave the way to treachery? Would Ka-nu dare let him live now? Kull shrugged his shoulders.

3. They That Walk the Night

The moon had not risen when Kull, hand to hilt, stepped to a window. The windows opened upon the great inner gardens of the royal palace, and the breezes of the night, bearing the scents of spice trees, blew the filmy curtains about. The king looked out. The walks and groves were deserted; carefully trimmed trees were bulky shadows; fountains near by flung their slender sheen of silver in the starlight and distant fountains rippled steadily. No guards walked those gardens, for so closely were the outer walls guarded that it seemed impossible for any invader to gain access to them.

Vines curled up the walls of the palace, and even as Kull mused upon the ease with which they might be climbed, a segment of shadow detached itself from the darkness below the window and a bare, brown arm curved up over the sill. Kull's great sword hissed halfway from the sheath; then the king halted. Upon the muscular forearm gleamed the dragon armlet shown him by Ka-nu the night before.

The possessor of the arm pulled himself up over the sill and into the room with the swift, easy motion of a climbing leopard.

"You are Brule?" asked Kull, and then stopped in a surprise not unmingled with annoyance and suspicion; for the man was he whom Kull had taunted in the hall of Society; the same who had escorted him from the Pictish embassy.

"I am Brule, the Spear-slayer," answered the Pict in a guarded voice; then swiftly, gazing closely in Kull's face, he said, barely above a whisper:

"Ka nama kaa lajerama!"

Kull started. "Ha! What mean you?"

"Know you not?"

"Nay, the words are unfamiliar; they are no language I ever heard—and yet, by Valka!—somewhere—I have heard—"

"Aye," was the Pict's only comment. His eyes swept the room, the study room of the palace. Except for a few tables, a divan or two and great shelves of books of parchment, the room was barren compared to the grandeur of the rest of the palace.

"Tell me, king, who guards the door?"

"Eighteen of the Red Slayers. But how come you, stealing through the gardens by night and scaling the walls of the palace?"

Brule sneered. "The guards of Valusia are blind buffaloes. I could steal their girls from under their noses. I stole amid them and they saw me not nor heard me. And the walls—I could scale them without the aid of vines. I have hunted tigers on the foggy

beaches when the sharp east breezes blew the mist in
from seaward and I have climbed the steeps of the
western sea mountain. But come—nay, touch this
armlet."

He held out his arm and, as Kull complied wonderingly, gave an apparent sigh of relief.

"So. Now throw off those kingly robes; for there are
ahead of you this night such deeds as no Atlantean
ever dreamed of."

Brule himself was clad only in a scanty loin-cloth
through which was thrust a short, curved sword.

"And who are you to give me orders?" asked Kull,
slightly resentful.

"Did not Ka-nu bid you follow me in all things?"
asked the Pict irritably, his eyes flashing momentarily.
"I have no love for you, lord, but for the moment I
have put the thought of feuds from my mind. Do you
likewise. But come."

Walking noiselessly, he led the way across the room
to the door. A slide in the door allowed a view of the
outer corridor, unseen from without, and the Pict bade
Kull look.

"What see you?"

"Naught but the eighteen guardsmen."

The Pict nodded, motioned Kull to follow him across
the room. At a panel in the opposite wall Brule stopped
and fumbled there a moment. Then with a light movement he stepped back, drawing his sword as he did so.
Kull gave an exclamation as the panel swung silently
open, revealing a dimly lighted passageway.

"A secret passage!" swore Kull softly. "And I knew
nothing of it! By Valka, someone shall dance for this!"

"Silence!" hissed the Pict.

Brule was standing like a bronze statue as if straining every nerve for the slightest sound; something

about his attitude made Kull's hair prickle slightly, not from fear but from some eery anticipation. Then beckoning, Brule stepped through the secret doorway which stood open behind them. The passage was bare, but not dust-covered as should have been the case with an unused secret corridor. A vague, gray light filtered through somewhere, but the source of it was not apparent. Every few feet Kull saw doors, invisible, as he knew, from the outside, but easily apparent from within.

"The palace is a very honeycomb," he muttered.

"Aye. Night and day you are watched, king, by many eyes."

The king was impressed by Brule's manner. The Pict went forward slowly, warily, half crouching, blade held low and thrust forward. When he spoke it was in a whisper and he continually flung glances from side to side.

The corridor turned sharply and Brule warily gazed past the turn.

"Look!" he whispered. "But remember! No word! No sound—on your life!"

Kull cautiously gazed past him. The corridor changed just at the bend to a flight of steps. And then Kull recoiled. At the foot of those stairs lay the eighteen Red Slayers who were that night stationed to watch the king's study room. Brule's grip upon his mighty arm and Brule's fierce whisper at his shoulder alone kept Kull from leaping down those stairs.

"Silent, Kull! Silent, in Valka's name!" hissed the Pict. "These corridors are empty now, but I risked much in showing you, that you might then believe what I had to say. Back now to the room of a study." And he retraced his steps, Kull following; his mind in a turmoil of bewilderment.

"This is treachery," muttered the king, his steel-gray eyes a-smolder, "foul and swift! Mere minutes have passed since those men stood at guard."

Again in the room of study Brule carefully closed the secret panel and motioned Kull to look again through the slit of the outer door. Kull gasped audibly. *For without stood the eighteen guardsmen!*

"This is sorcery!" he whispered, half-drawing his sword. "Do dead men guard the king?"

"Aye!" came Brule's scarcely audible reply; there was a strange expression in the Pict's scintillant eyes. They looked squarely into each other's eyes for an instant, Kull's brow wrinkled in a puzzled scowl as he strove to read the Pict's inscrutable face. Then Brule's lips, barely moving, formed the words:

"The—snake—that—speaks!"

"Silent!" whispered Kull, laying his hand over Brule's mouth. "That is death to speak! That is a name accursed!"

The Pict's fearless eyes regarded him steadily.

"Look again, King Kull. Perchance the guard was changed."

"Nay, those are the same men. In Valka's name, this is sorcery—this is insanity! I saw with my own eyes the bodies of those men, not eight minutes gone. Yet there they stand."

Brule stepped back, away from the door, Kull mechanically following.

"Kull, what know ye of the traditions of this race ye rule?"

"Much—and yet, little. Valusia is so old—"

"Aye," Brule's eyes lighted strangely, "we are but barbarians—infants compared to the Seven Empires. Not even they themselves know how old they are. Neither the memory of man nor the annals of the historians reach back far enough to tell us when the first men came up from the sea and built cities on the shore. But Kull, *men were not always ruled by men!"*

The king started. Their eyes met.

"Aye, there is a legend of my people—"

"And mine!" broke in Brule. "That was before we of the isles were allied with Valusia. Aye, in the reign of Lion-fang, seventh war chief of the Picts, so many years ago no man remembers how many. Across the sea we came, from the isles of the sunset, skirting the shores of Atlantis, and falling upon the beaches of Valusia with fire and sword. Aye, the long white beaches resounded with the clash of spears, and the night was like day from the flame of the burning castles. And the king, the king of Valusia, who died on the red sea sands that dim day—" His voice trailed off; the two stared at each other, neither speaking; then each nodded.

"Ancient is Valusia!" whispered Kull. "The hills of Atlantis and Mu were isles of the sea when Valusia was young."

The night breeze whispered through the open window. Not the free, crisp sea air such as Brule and Kull knew and reveled in, in their land, but a breath like a whisper from the past, laden with musk, scents of forgotten things, breathing secrets that were hoary when the world was young.

The tapestries rustled, and suddenly Kull felt like a naked child before the inscrutable wisdom of the mystic past. Again the sense of unreality swept upon him. At the back of his soul stole dim, gigantic phantoms, whispering monstrous things. He sensed that Brule experienced similar thoughts. The Pict's eyes were fixed upon his face with a fierce intensity. Their glances met. Kull felt warmly a sense of comradeship with this member of an enemy tribe. Like rival leopards turning at bay against hunters, these two savages made common cause against the inhuman powers of antiquity.

Brule again led the way back to the secret door. Silently they entered and silently they proceeded down the dim corridor, taking the opposite direction from that in which they had previously traversed it. After a while the Pict stopped and pressed close to one of the secret doors, bidding Kull look with him through the hidden slot.

"This opens upon a little-used stair which leads to a corridor running past the study-room door."

They gazed, and presently, mounting the stair silently, came a silent shape.

"Tu! Chief councilor!" exclaimed Kull. "By night and with bared dagger! How, what means this, Brule?"

"Murder! And foulest treachery!" hissed Brule. "Nay"—as Kull would have flung the door aside and leaped forth—"we are lost if you meet him here, for more lurk at the foot of those stairs. Come!"

Half running, they darted back along the passage. Back through the secret door Brule led, shutting it carefully behind them, then across the chamber to an opening into a room seldom used. There he swept aside some tapestries in a dim corner nook and, drawing Kull with him, stepped behind them. Minutes dragged. Kull could hear the breeze in the other room blowing the window curtains about, and it seemed to him like the murmur of ghosts. Then through the door, stealthily, came Tu, chief councilor of the king. Evidently he had come through the study room and, finding it empty, sought his victim where he was most likely to be.

He came with upraised dagger, walking silently. A moment he halted, gazing about the apparently empty room, which was lighted dimly by a single candle. Then he advanced cautiously, apparently at a loss to understand the absence of the king. He stood before the hiding place—and—

"Slay!" hissed the Pict.

Kull with a single mighty leap hurled himself into the room. Tu spun, but the blinding, tigerish speed of the attack gave him no chance for defense or counter-attack. Sword steel flashed in the dim light and grated on bone as Tu toppled backward, Kull's sword standing out between his shoulders.

Kull leaned above him, teeth bared in the killer's snarl, heavy brows ascowl above eyes that were like the gray ice of the cold sea. Then he released the hilt and recoiled, shaken, dizzy, the hand of death at his spine.

For as he watched, Tu's face became strangely dim and unreal; the features mingled and merged in a seemingly impossible manner. Then, like a fading mask of fog, the face suddenly vanished and in its stead gaped and leered *a monstrous serpent's head!*

"Valka!" gasped Kull, sweat beading his forehead, and again: "Valka!"

Brule leaned forward, face immobile. Yet his glittering eyes mirrored something of Kull's horror.

"Regain your sword, lord king," said he. "There are yet deeds to be done."

Hesitantly Kull set his hand to the hilt. His flesh crawled as he set his foot upon the terror which lay at their feet, and as some jerk of muscular reaction caused the frightful mouth to gape suddenly, he recoiled, weak with nausea. Then, wrathful at himself, he plucked forth his sword and gazed more closely at the nameless thing that had been known as Tu, chief councilor. Save for the reptilian head, the thing was the exact counterpart of a man.

"A man with the head of a snake!" Kull murmured. "This, then, is a priest of the serpent god?"

"Aye. Tu sleeps unknowing. These fiends can take any form they will. That is, they can, by a magic charm or the like, fling a web of sorcery about their faces, as an actor dons a mask, so that they resemble anyone they wish to."

"Then the old legends were true," mused the king; "the grim old tales few dare even whisper, lest they die as blasphemers, are no fantasies. By Valka, I had thought—I had guessed—but it seems beyond the bounds of reality. Ha! The guardsmen outside the door—"

"They too are snake-men. Hold! What would you do?"

"Slay them!" said Kull between his teeth.

"Strike at the skull if at all," said Brule. "Eighteen wait without the door and perhaps a score more in the corridors. Hark ye, king, Ka-nu learned of this plot. His spies have pierced the inmost fastnesses of the snake priests and they brought hints of a plot. Long ago he discovered the secret passageways of the palace, and at his command I studied the map thereof and came here by night to aid you, lest you die as other kings of Valusia have died. I came alone for the reason that to send more would have roused suspicion. Many could not steal into the palace as I did. Some of the foul conspiracy you have seen. Snake-men guard your door, and that one, as Tu, could pass anywhere else in the palace; in the morning, if the priests failed, the real guards would be holding their places again, nothing knowing, nothing remembering; there to take the blame if the priests succeeded. But stay you here while I dispose of this carrion."

So saying, the Pict shouldered the frightful thing stolidly and vanished with it through another secret panel. Kull stood alone, his mind a-whirl. Neophytes of the mighty serpent, how many lurked among his cities? How might he tell the false from the true? Aye, how many of his trusted councilors, his generals, were men? He could be certain—of whom?

The secret panel swung inward and Brule entered.

"You were swift."

"Aye!" The warrior stepped forward, eyeing the floor. "There is gore upon the rug. See?"

Kull bent forward; from the corner of his eye he saw a blur of movement, a glint of steel. Like a loosened bow he whipped erect, thrusting upward. The warrior sagged upon the sword, his own clattering to the floor. Even at that instant Kull reflected grimly that it was appropriate that the traitor should meet his death upon the sliding, upward thrust used so much by his race. Then, as Brule slid from the sword to sprawl motionless on the floor, the face began to merge and fade, and as Kull caught his breath, his hair a-prickle, the human features vanished and there the jaws of a great snake gaped hideously, the terrible beady eyes venomous even in death.

"He was a snake priest all the time!" gasped the king. "Valka! what an elaborate plan to throw me off my guard! Ka-nu there, is he a man? Was it Ka-nu to whom I talked in the gardens? Almighty Valka!" as his flesh crawled with a horrid thought; "are the people of Valusia men or are they *all* serpents?"

Undecided he stood, idly seeing that the thing named Brule no longer wore the dragon armlet. A sound made him wheel.

Brule was coming through the secret door.

"Hold!" Upon the arm upthrown to half the king's hovering sword gleamed the dragon armlet. "Valka!"

The Pict stopped short. Then a grim smile curled his lips.

"By the gods of the seas! These demons are crafty past reckoning. For it must be that that one lurked in the corridors, and seeing me go carrying the carcass of that other, took my appearance. So. I have another to do away with."

"Hold!" there was the menace of death in Kull's voice; "I have seen two men turn to serpents before my eyes. How may I know if you are a true man?"

Brule laughed. "For two reasons, King Kull. No snakeman wears this"—he indicated the dragon armlet—"nor can any say these words," and again Kull heard the strange phrase: *"Ka nama kaa lajerama."*

"Ka nama kaa lajerama," Kull repeated mechanically. "Now where, in Valka's name, have I heard that? I have not! And yet—and yet—"

"Aye, you remember, Kull," said Brule. "Through the dim corridors of memory those words lurk; though you never heard them in this life, yet in the bygone ages they were so terribly impressed upon the soul mind that never dies, that they will always strike dim chords in your memory, though you be reincarnated for a million years to come. For that phrase has come secretly down the grim and bloody eons, since when, uncounted centuries ago, those words were watchwords for the race of men who battled with the grisly beings of the Elder Universe. For none but a real man of men may speak them, whose jaws and mouth are shaped different from any other creature. Their meaning has been forgotten but not the words themselves."

"True," said Kull. "I remember the legends—Valka!" He stopped short, staring, for suddenly, like the silent swinging wide of a mystic door, misty, unfathomed reaches opened in the recesses of his consciousness and for an instant he seemed to gaze back through the

vastnesses that spanned life and life; seeing through
the vague and ghostly fogs dim shapes reliving dead
centuries—men in combat with hideous monsters, van-
quishing a planet of frightful terrors. Against a gray,
ever-shifting background moved strange nightmare
forms, fantasies of lunacy and fear; and man, the jest
of the gods, the blind, wisdomless striver from dust,
following the long bloody trail of his destiny, knowing
not why, bestial, blundering, like a great murderous
child, yet feeling somewhere a spark of divine fire. . . .
Kull drew a hand across his brow, shaken; these sudden glimpses into the abysses of memory always startled him.

"They are gone," said Brule, as if scanning his
secret mind; "the bird-women, the harpies, the bat-
men, the flying fiends, the wolf-people, the demons,
the goblins—all save such as this being that lies at our
feet, and a few of the wolf-men. Long and terrible was
the war, lasting through the bloody centuries, since
first the first men, risen from the mire of apedom,
turned upon those who then ruled the world. And at
last mankind conquered, so long ago that naught but
dim legends come to us through the ages. The snake-
people were the last to go, yet at last men conquered
even them and drove them forth into the waste lands
of the world, there to mate with true snakes until
some day, say the sages, the horrid breed shall vanish
utterly. Yet the Things returned in crafty guise as men
grew soft and degenerate, forgetting ancient wars. Ah,
that was a grim and secret war! Among the men of the
Younger Earth stole the frightful monsters of the Elder Planet, safeguarded by their horrid wisdom and
mysticisms, taking all forms and shapes, doing deeds
of horror secretly. No man knew who was true man
and who false. No man could trust any man. Yet by
means of their own craft they formed ways by which

the false might be known from the true. Men took for a sign and a standard the figure of the flying dragon, the winged dinosaur, a monster of past ages, which was the greatest foe of the serpent. And men used those words which I spoke to you as a sign and symbol, for as I said, none but a true man can repeat them. So mankind triumphed. Yet again the fiends came after the years of forgetfulness had gone by—for man is still an ape in that he forgets what is not ever before his eyes. As priests they came; and for that men in their luxury and might had by then lost faith in the old religions and worships, the snake-men, in the guise of teachers of a new and truer cult, built a monstrous religion about the worship of the serpent god. Such is their power that it is now death to repeat the old legends of the snake-people, and people bow again to the serpent god in new form; and blind fools that they are, the great hosts of men see no connection between this power and the power men overthrew eons ago. As priests the snake-men are content to rule—and yet—" He stopped.

"Go on." Kull felt an unaccountable stirring of the short hair at the base of his scalp.

"Kings have reigned as true men in Valusia," the Pict whispered, "and yet slain in battle, have died serpents—as died he who fell beneath the spear of Lion-fang on the red beaches when we of the isles harried the Seven Empires. And how can this be, Lord Kull? These kings were born of women and lived as men! This—the true kings died in secret—as you would have died tonight—and priests of the Serpent reigned in their stead, no man knowing."

Kull cursed between his teeth. "Aye, it must be. No one has ever seen a priest of the Serpent and lived, that is known. They live in utmost secrecy."

"The statecraft of the Seven Empires is a mazy,

monstrous thing," said Brule. "There the true men know that among them glide the spies of the serpent, and the men who are the Serpent's allies—such as Kaanuub, baron of Blaal—yet no man dares seek to unmask a suspect lest vengeance befall him. No man trusts his fellow and the true statesmen dare not speak to each other what is in the minds of all. Could they be sure, could a snake-man or plot be unmasked before them all, then would the power of the Serpent be more than half broken; for all would then ally and make common cause, sifting out the traitors. Ka-nu alone is of sufficient shrewdness and courage to cope with them, and even Ka-nu learned only enough of their plot to tell me what would happen—what has happened up to this time. Thus far I was prepared; from now on we must trust to our luck and our craft. Here and now I think we are safe; those snake-men without the door dare not leave their post lest true men come here unexpectedly. But tomorrow they will try something else, you may be sure. Just what they will do, none can say, not even Ka-nu; but we must stay at each other's sides, King Kull, until we conquer or both be dead. Now come with me while I take this carcass to the hiding-place where I took the other being."

Kull followed the Pict with his grisly burden through the secret panel and down the dim corridor. Their feet, trained to the silence of the wilderness, made no noise. Like phantoms they glided through the ghostly light, Kull wondering that the corridors should be deserted; at every turn he expected to run full upon some frightful apparition. Suspicion surged back upon him; was this Pict leading him into ambush? He fell back a pace or two behind Brule, his ready sword hovering at the Pict's unheeding back. Brule should

die first if he meant treachery. But if the Pict was
aware of the king's suspicion, he showed no sign.
Stolidly he tramped along, until they came to a room,
dusty and long unused, where moldy tapestries hung
heavy. Brule drew aside some of these and concealed
the corpse behind them.

Then they turned to retrace their steps, when suddenly Brule halted with such abruptness that he was
closer to death than he knew; for Kull's nerves were
on edge.

"Something moving in the corridor," hissed the Pict.
"Ka-nu said these ways would be empty, yet—"

He drew his sword and stole into the corridor, Kull
following warily.

A short way down the corridor a strange, vague
glow appeared that came toward them. Nerves a-leap,
they waited, backs to the corridor wall; for what they
knew not, but Kull heard Brule's breath hiss through
his teeth and was reassured as to Brule's loyalty.

The glow merged into a shadowy form. A shape
vaguely like a man it was, but misty and illusive, like a
wisp of fog, that grew more tangible as it approached,
but never fully material. A face looked at them, a pair
of luminous great eyes, that seemed to hold all the
tortures of a million centuries. There was no menace
in that face, with its dim, worn features, but only a
great pity—and that face—that face—

"Almighty gods!" breathed Kull, an icy hand at his
soul; "Eallal, king of Valusia, who died a thousand
years ago!"

Brule shrank back as far as he could, his narrow
eyes widened in a blaze of pure horror, the sword
shaking in his grip, unnerved for the first time that
weird night. Erect and defiant stood Kull, instinctively
holding his useless sword at the ready; flesh a-crawl,

hair a-prickle, yet still a king of kings, as ready to challenge the powers of the unknown dead as the powers of the living.

The phantom came straight on, giving them no heed; Kull shrank back as it passed them, feeling an icy breath like a breeze from the arctic snow. Straight on went the shape with slow, silent footsteps, as if the chains of all the ages were upon those vague feet; vanishing about a bend of the corridor.

"Valka!" muttered the Pict, wiping the cold beads from his brow; "that was no man! That was a ghost!"

"Aye!" Kull shook his head wonderingly. "Did you not recognize the face? That was Eallal, who reigned in Valusia a thousand years ago and who was found hideously murdered in his throneroom—the room now known as the Accursed Room. Have you not seen his statue in the Fame Room of Kings?"

"Yes, I remember the tale now. Gods, Kull! that is another sign of the frightful and foul power of the snake priests—that king was slain by snake-people and thus his soul became their slave, to do their bidding throughout eternity! For the sages have ever maintained that if a man is slain by a snake-man his ghost becomes their slave."

A shudder shook Kull's gigantic frame. "Valka! But what a fate! Hark ye"—his fingers closed upon Brule's sinewy arm like steel—"hark ye! If I am wounded unto death by these foul monsters, swear that ye will smite your sword through my breast lest my soul should be enslaved."

"I swear," answered Brule, his fierce eyes lighting. "And do ye the same by me, Kull."

Their strong right hands met in a silent sealing of their bloody bargain.

4. Masks

Kull sat upon his throne and gazed broodingly out upon the sea of faces turned toward him. A courtier was speaking in evenly modulated tones, but the king scarcely heard him. Close by, Tu, chief councilor, stood ready at Kull's command, and each time the king looked at him, Kull shuddered inwardly. The surface of court life was as the unrippled surface of the sea between tide and tide. To the musing king the affairs of the night before seemed as a dream, until his eyes dropped to the arm of his throne. A brown, sinewy hand rested there, upon the wrist of which gleamed a dragon armlet; Brule stood beside his throne and ever the Pict's fierce secret whisper brought him back from the realm of unreality in which he moved.

No, that was no dream, that monstrous interlude. As he sat upon his throne in the Hall of Society and gazed upon the courtiers, the ladies, the lords, the statesmen, he seemed to see their faces as things of illusion, things unreal, existent only as shadows and mockeries of substance. Always he had seen their faces as masks, but before he had looked on them with contemptuous tolerance, thinking to see beneath the masks shallow, puny souls, avaricious, lustful, deceitful; now there was a grim undertone, a sinister meaning, a vague horror that lurked beneath the smooth masks. While he exchanged courtesies with some nobleman or councilor he seemed to see the smiling face fade like smoke and the frightful jaws of a serpent gaping there. How many of those he looked upon were horrid, inhuman monsters, plotting his death, beneath the smooth mesmeric illusion of a human face?

Valusia—land of dreams and nightmares—a kingdom of the shadows, ruled by phantoms who glided back and forth behind the painted curtains, mocking the futile king who sat upon the throne—himself a shadow.

And like a comrade shadow Brule stood by his side, dark eyes glittering from immobile face. A real man, Brule! And Kull felt his friendship for the savage become a thing of reality and sensed that Brule felt a friendship for him beyond the mere necessity of statecraft.

And what, mused Kull, were the realities of life? Ambition, power, pride? The friendship of man, the love of women—which Kull had never known—battle, plunder, what? Was it the real Kull who sat upon the throne or was it the real Kull who had scaled the hills of Atlantis, harried the far isles of the sunset, and laughed upon the green roaring tides of the Atlantean sea? How could a man be so many different men in a lifetime? For Kull knew that there were many Kulls and he wondered which was the real Kull. After all, the priests of the Serpent merely went a step further in their magic, for all men wore masks, and many a different mask with each different man or woman; and Kull wondered if a serpent did not lurk under every mask.

So he sat and brooded in strange, mazy thought ways, and the courtiers came and went and the minor affairs of the day were completed, until at last the king and Brule sat alone in the Hall of Society save for the drowsy attendants.

Kull felt a weariness. Neither he nor Brule had slept the night before, nor had Kull slept the night before that, when in the gardens of Ka-nu he had had his first hint of the weird things to be. Last night nothing further had occurred after they had returned to the study room from the secret corridors, but they had neither dared nor cared to sleep. Kull, with the incredible vitality of a wolf, had aforetime gone for days upon days without sleep, in his wild savage days but now his mind was edged from constant thinking and from the nervebreaking eeriness of the past night. He needed sleep, but sleep was furthest from his mind.

And he would not have dared sleep if he had thought of it. Another thing that had shaken him was the fact that though he and Brule had kept a close watch to see if, or when, the study-room guard was changed, yet it was changed without their knowledge; for the next morning those who stood on guard were able to repeat the magic words of Brule, but they remembered nothing out of the ordinary. They thought that they had stood at guard all night, as usual, and Kull said nothing to the contrary. He believed them true men, but Brule had advised absolute secrecy, and Kull also thought it best.

Now Brule leaned over the throne, lowering his voice so not even a lazy attendant could hear: "They will strike soon, I think, Kull. A while ago Ka-nu gave me a secret sign. The priests know what we know of their plot, of course, but they know not, how much we know. We must be ready for any sort of action. Ka-nu and the Pictish chiefs will remain within hailing distance now until this is settled one way or another. Ha, Kull, if it comes to a pitched battle, the streets and the castles of Valusia will run red!"

Kull smiled grimly. He would greet any sort of action with a ferocious joy. This wandering in a labyrinth of illusion and magic was extremely irksome to his nature. He longed for the leap and clang of swords, for the joyous freedom of battle.

Then into the Hall of Society came Tu again, and the rest of the councilors.

"Lord king, the hour of the council is at hand and we stand ready to escort you to the council room."

Kull rose, and the councilors bent the knee as he passed through the way opened by them for his passage, rising behind him, and following. Eyebrows were raised as the Pict strode defiantly behind the king, but no one dissented. Brule's challenging gaze swept the smooth faces of the councilors with the defiance of an intruding savage.

The group passed through the halls and came at last to the council chamber. The door was closed, as usual, and the councilors arranged themselves in the order of their rank before the dais upon which stood the king. Like a bronze statue Brule took up his stand behind Kull.

Kull swept the room with a swift stare. Surely no chance of treachery here. Seventeen councilors there were, all known to him; all of them had espoused his cause when he ascended the throne.

"Men of Valusia—" he began in the conventional manner, then halted, perplexed. The councilors had risen as a man and were moving toward him. There was no hostility in their looks, but their actions were strange for a council room. The foremost was close to him when Brule sprang forward, crouched like a leopard.

"*Ka nama kaa lajerama!*" his voice crackled through the sinister silence of the room and the foremost councilor recoiled, hand flashing to his robes; and like a spring released Brule moved and the man pitched headlong to the glint of his sword—headlong he pitched and lay still while his face faded and became the head of a mighty snake.

"Slay, Kull!" rasped the Pict's voice. "They be all serpent men!"

The rest was a scarlet maze. Kull saw the familiar

faces dim like fading fog and in their places gaped
horrid reptilian visages as the whole band rushed forward. His mind was dazed but his giant body faltered
not.

The singing of his sword filled the room, and the
onrushing flood broke in a red wave. But they surged
forward again, seemingly willing to fling their lives
away in order to drag down the king. Hideous jaws
gaped at him; terrible eyes blazed into his unblink-
ingly; a frightful fetid scent pervaded the atmosphere—
the serpent scent that Kull had known in southern
jungles. Swords and daggers leaped at him and he was
dimly aware that they wounded him. But Kull was in
his element; never before had he faced such grim foes
but it mattered little; they lived, their veins held blood
that could be spilt and they died when his great sword
cleft their skulls or drove through their bodies. Slash,
thrust, thrust and swing. Yet had Kull died there but
for the man who crouched at his side, parrying and
thrusting. For the king was clear berserk, fighting in
the terrible Atlantean way, that seeks death to deal
death; he made no effort to avoid thrusts and slashes,
standing straight up and ever plunging forward, no
thought in his frenzied mind but to slay. Not often did
Kull forget his fighting craft in his primitive fury, but
now some chain had broken in his soul, flooding his
mind with a red wave of slaughter-lust. He slew a foe
at each blow, but they surged about him, and time and
again Brule turned a thrust that would have slain, as
he crouched beside Kull, parrying and warding with
cold skill, slaying not as Kull slew with long slashes
and plunges, but with short overhand blows and upward thrusts.

Kull laughed, a laugh of insanity. The frightful faces
swirled about him in a scarlet blaze. He felt steel sink
into his arm and dropped his sword in a flashing arc

that cleft his foe to the breast-bone. Then the mists faded and the king saw that he and Brule stood alone above a sprawl of hideous crimson figures who lay still upon the floor.

"Valka! what a killing!" said Brule, shaking the blood from his eyes. "Kull, had these been warriors who knew how to use the steel, we had died here. These serpent priests know naught of swordcraft and die easier than any men I ever slew. Yet had there been a few more, I think the matter had ended otherwise."

Kull nodded. The wild beserker blaze had passed, leaving a mazed feeling of great weariness. Blood seeped from wounds on breast, shoulder, arm and leg. Brule, himself bleeding from a score of flesh wounds, glanced at him in some concern.

"Lord Kull, let us hasten to have your wounds dressed by the women."

Kull thrust him aside with a drunken sweep of his mighty arm.

"Nay, we'll see this through ere we cease. Go you, though, and have your wounds seen to—I command it."

The Pict laughed grimly. "Your wounds are more than mine, lord king—" he began, then stopped as a sudden thought struck him. "By Valka, Kull, this is not the council room!"

Kull looked about and suddenly other fogs seemed to fade. "Nay, this is the room where Eallal died a thousand years ago—since unused and named 'Accursed'."

"Then by the gods, they tricked us after all!" exclaimed Brule in a fury, kicking the corpses at their feet. "They caused us to walk like fools into their ambush! By their magic they changed the appearance of all—"

"Then there is further deviltry afoot," said Kull,

"for if there be true men in the councils of Valusia they should be in the real council room now. Come swiftly."

And leaving the room with its ghastly keepers they hastened through halls that seemed deserted until they came to the real council room. Then Kull halted with a ghastly shudder. *From the council room sounded a voice speaking, and the voice was his!*

With a hand that shook he parted the tapestries and gazed into the room. There sat the councilors, counterparts of the men he and Brule had just slain, and upon the dais stood Kull, king of Valusia.

He stepped back, his mind reeling.

"This is insanity!" he whispered. "Am I Kull? Do I stand here or is that Kull yonder in very truth and am I but a shadow, a figment of thought?"

Brule's hand clutching his shoulder, shaking him fiercely, brought him to his senses.

"Valka's name, be not a fool! Can you yet be astounded after all we have seen? See you not that those are true men bewitched by a snake-man who has taken your form, as those others took their forms? By now you should have been slain and yon monster reigning in your stead, unknown by those who bowed to you. Leap and slay swiftly or else we are undone. The Red Slayers, true men, stand close on each hand and none but you can reach and slay him. Be swift!"

Kull shook off the onrushing dizziness, flung back his head in the old, defiant gesture. He took a long, deep breath as does a strong swimmer before diving into the sea; then, sweeping back the tapestries, made the dais in a single lionlike bound. Brule had spoken truly. There stood men of the Red Slayers, guardsmen trained to move quick as the striking leopard; any but Kull had died ere he could reach the usurper. But the sight of Kull, identical with the man upon the dais, held them in their tracks, their minds stunned for an instant, and that was long enough. He upon the dais snatched for his sword, but even as his fingers closed upon the hilt, Kull's sword stood out behind his shoulders and the thing that men had thought the king pitched forward from the dais to lie silent upon the floor.

"Hold!" Kull's lifted hand and kingly voice stopped the rush that had started, and while they stood astounded he pointed to the thing which lay before them—whose face was fading into that of a snake. They recoiled, and from one door came Brule and from another came Ka-nu.

These grasped the king's bloody hand and Ka-nu spoke: "Men of Valusia, you have seen with your own eyes. This is the true Kull, the mightiest king to whom Valusia has ever bowed. The power of the Serpent is broken and ye be all true men. King Kull, have you commands?"

"Lift that carrion," said Kull, and men of the guard took up the thing.

"Now follow me," said the king, and he made his way to the Accursed Room. Brule, with a look of concern, offered the support of his arm but Kull shook him off.

The distance seemed endless to the bleeding king, but at last he stood at the door and laughed fiercely and grimly when he heard the horrified ejaculations of the councilors.

At his orders the guardsmen flung the corpse they carried beside the others, and motioning all from the room Kull stepped out last and closed the door.

A wave of dizziness left him shaken. The faces turned to him, pallid and wonderingly, swirled and mingled in a ghostly fog. He felt the blood from his wound trickling down his limbs and he knew that what he was to do, he must do quickly or not at all.

His sword rasped from its sheath.

"Brule, are you there?"

"Aye!" Brule's face looked at him through the mist, close to his shoulder, but Brule's voice sounded leagues and eons away.

"Remember our vow, Brule. And now, bid them stand back."

His left arm cleared a space as he flung up his sword. Then with all his waning power he drove it though the door into the jamb, driving the great sword to the hilt and sealing the room forever.

Legs braced wide, he swayed drunkenly, facing the horrified councilors. "Let this room be doubly accursed. And let those rotting skeletons lie there forever as a sign of the dying might of the serpent. Here I swear that I shall hunt the serpent-men from land to land, from sea to sea, giving no rest until all be slain, that good triumph and the power of Hell be broken. This thing I swear—I—Kull—king—of—Valusia."

His knees buckled as the faces swayed and swirled. The councilors leaped forward, but ere they could reach him, Kull slumped to the floor, and lay still, face upward.

The councilors surged about the fallen king, chattering and shrieking. Ka-nu beat them back with his clenched fists, cursing savagely.

"Back, you fools! Would you stifle the little life that is yet in him? How, Brule, is he dead or will he live?"—to the warrior who bent above the prostrate Kull.

"Dead?" sneered Brule irritably. "Such a man as this is not so easily killed. Lack of sleep and loss of blood have weakened him—by Valka, he has a score of deep wounds, but none of them mortal. Yet have those gibbering fools bring the court women here at once."

Brule's eyes lighted with a fierce, proud light.

"Valka, Ka-nu, but here is such a man as I knew not existed in these degenerate days. He will be in the saddle in a few scant days and then may the serpent-men of the world beware of Kull of Valusia. Valka! but that will be a rare hunt! Ah, I see long years of prosperity for the world with such a king upon the throne of Valusia."

THE NEW ATLANTIS

by Ursula K. Le Guin

Coming back from my Wilderness Week I sat by an odd sort of man in the bus. For a long time we didn't talk; I was mending stockings and he was reading. Then the bus broke down a few miles outside Gresham. Boiler trouble, the way it generally is when the driver insists on trying to go over thirty. It was a Supersonic Superscenic Deluxe Longdistance coal-burner, with Home Comfort, that means a toilet, and the seats were pretty comfortable, at least those that hadn't yet worked loose from their bolts, so everybody waited inside the bus; besides, it was raining. We began talking, the way people do when there's a breakdown and a wait. He held up his pamphlet and tapped it—he was a dry-looking man with a schoolteacherish way of using his hands—and said, "This is interesting. I've been reading that a new continent is rising from the depths of the sea."

The blue stockings were hopeless. You have to have something besides holes to darn onto. "Which sea?"

"They're not sure yet. Most specialists think the Atlantic. But there's evidence it may be happening in the Pacific, too."

"Won't the oceans get a little crowded?" I said, not

taking it seriously. I was a bit snappish, because of the breakdown and because those blue stockings had been good warm ones.

He tapped the pamphlet again and shook his head, quite serious. "No," he said. "The old continents are sinking, to make room for the new. You can see that that is happening."

You certainly can. Manhattan Island is now under eleven feet of water at low tide, and there are oyster beds in Ghirardelli Square.

"I thought that was because the oceans are rising from polar melt."

He shook his head again. "That is a factor. Due to the greenhouse effect of pollution, indeed Antarctica may become inhabitable. But climatic factors will not explain the emergence of the new—or, possibly, very old—continents in the Atlantic and Pacific." He went on explaining about continental drift, but I liked the idea of inhabiting Anarctica and daydreamed about it for a while. I thought of it as very empty, very quiet, all white and blue, with a faint golden glow northward from the unrising sun behind the long peak of Mount Erebus. There were a few people there; they were very quiet, too, and wore white tie and tails. Some of them carried oboes and violas. Southward the white land went up in a long silence toward the Pole.

Just the opposite, in fact, of the Mount Hood Wilderness Area. It had been a tiresome vacation. The other women in the dormitory were all right, but it was macaroni for breakfast, and there were so many organized sports. I had looked forward to the hike up to the National Forest Preserve, the largest forest left in the United States, but the trees didn't look at all the way they do in the postcards and brochures and Federal Beautification Bureau advertisements. They were spindly, and they all had little signs on saying which union they had been planted by. There were actually a lot more green picnic tables and cement Men's and Women's than there were trees. There was an electrified fence all around the forest to keep out unauthorized persons. The forest ranger talked about mountain jays, "bold little robbers," he said, "who will come and snatch the sandwich from your very hand," but I didn't see any. Perhaps because that was the weekly Watch Those Surplus Calories! Day for all the women, and so we didn't have any sandwiches. If I'd seen a mountain jay I might have snatched the sandwich from his very hand, who knows. Anyhow it was an exhausting week, and I wished I'd stayed home and practiced, even though I'd have lost a week's pay because staying home and practicing the viola doesn't count as planned implementation of recreational leisure as defined by the Federal Union of Unions.

When I came back from my Anarctican expedition, the man was reading again, and I got a look at his pamphlet; and that was the odd part of it. The pamphlet was called "Increasing Efficiency in Public Accountant Training Schools," and I could see from the one paragraph I got a glance at that there was nothing about new continents emerging from the ocean depths in it—nothing at all.

Then we had to get out and walk on into Gresham, because they had decided that the best thing for us all to do was get onto the Greater Portland Area Rapid Public Transit Lines, since there had been so many breakdowns that the charter bus company didn't have any more buses to send out to pick us up. The walk was wet, and rather dull, except when we passed the Cold Mountain Commune. They have a wall around it to keep out unauthorized persons, and a big neon sign out front saying COLD MOUNTAIN COMMUNE and there were some people in authentic jeans and ponchos by the highway selling macrame belts and sandcast candles and soybean bread to the tourists. In Gresham, I took the 4:40 GPARPTL Superjet Flyer train to Burnside and East 230th, and then walked to 217th and got the bus to the Goldschmidt Overpass, and transferred to the shuttlebus, but it had boiler trouble, so I didn't reach the downtown transfer point until ten after eight, and the buses go on a once-an-hour schedule at 8:00, so I got a meatless hamburger at the Longhorn Inch-Thick Steak House Dinerette and caught the nine o'clock bus and got home about ten. When I let myself into the apartment I flipped the switch to turn on the lights, but there still weren't any. There had been a power outage in West Portland for three weeks. So I went feeling about for the candles in the dark, and it was a minute or so before I noticed that somebody was lying on my bed.

I panicked, and tried again to turn the lights on.

It was a man, lying there in a long thin heap. I thought a burglar had got in somehow while I was away and died. I opened the door so I could get out quick or at least my yells could be heard, and then I managed not to shake long enough to strike a match, and lighted the candle, and came a little closer to the bed.

The light disturbed him. He made a sort of snorting in his throat and turned his head. I saw it was a stranger, but I knew his eyebrows, then the breadth of his closed eyelids, then I saw my husband.

He woke up while I was standing there over him with the candle in my hand. He laughed and said still half-asleep, "Ah, Psyche! From the regions which are holy land."

Neither of us made much fuss. It was unexpected, but it did seem so natural for him to be there, after all, much more natural than for him not to be there, and he was too tired to be very emotional. We lay there together in the dark, and he explained that they had released him from the Rehabilitation Camp early because he had injured his back in an accident in the gravel quarry, and they were afraid it might get worse. If he died there it wouldn't be good publicity abroad, since there have been some nasty rumors about deaths from illness in the Rehabilitation Camps and the Federal Medical Association Hospitals; and there are scientists abroad who have heard of Simon, since somebody published his proof of Goldbach's Hypothesis in Peking. So they let him out early, with eight dollars in his pocket, which is what he had in his pocket when they arrested him, which made it, of course, fair. He had walked and hitched home from Coeur D'Alene, Idaho, with a couple of days in jail in Walla Walla for being caught hitchhiking. He almost fell asleep telling me this, and when he had told me, he did fall asleep. He needed a change of clothes and a bath but I didn't want to wake him. Besides, I was tired, too. We lay side by side and his head was on my arm. I don't suppose that I have ever been so happy. No; was it happiness? Something wider and darker, more like knowledge, more like the night: joy.

It was dark for so long, so very long. We were all blind. And there was the cold, a vast, unmoving, heavy cold. We could not move at all. We did not move. We did not speak. Our mouths were closed, pressed shut by the cold and by the weight. Our eyes were pressed shut. Our limbs were held still. Our minds were held still. For how long? There was no length of time; how long is death? And is one dead only after living, or before life as well? Certainly we thought, if we thought anything, that we were dead; but if we had ever been alive, we had forgotten it.

There was a change. It must have been the pressure that changed first, although we did not know it. The eyelids are sensitive to touch. They must have been weary of being shut. When the pressure upon them weakened a little, they opened. But there was no way for us to know that. It was too cold for us to feel anything. There was nothing to be seen. There was black.

But then—"then," for the event created time, created before and after, near and far, now and then—"then" there was the light. One light. One small, strange light that passed slowly, at what distance we could not tell. A small, greenish white, slightly blurred point of radiance, passing.

Our eyes were certainly open, "then," for we saw it. We saw the moment. The moment is a point of light. Whether in darkness or in the field of all light, the moment is small, and moves, but not quickly. And "then" it is gone.

It did not occur to us that there might be another moment. There was no reason to assume that there might be more than one. One was marvel enough: that in all the field of the dark, in the cold, heavy, dense, moveless, timeless, placeless, boundless black, there should have occurred, once, a small slightly blurred, moving light! Time need be created only once, we thought.

But we were mistaken. The difference between one and more than one is all the difference in the world. Indeed, that difference is the world.

The light returned.

The same light, or another one? There was no telling.

But, "this time," we wondered about the light: Was it small and near to us, or large and far away? Again there was no telling; but there was something *about the way it moved, a trace of hesitation, a tentative quality, that did not seem proper to anything large and remote. The stars, for instance. We began to remember the stars.*

The stars had never hesitated.

Perhaps the noble certainty of their gait had been a mere effect of distance. Perhaps in fact they had hurtled wildly, enormous furnace-fragments of a primal bomb thrown through the cosmic dark; but time and distance soften all agony. If the universe, as seems likely, began with an act of destruction, the stars we had used to see told no tales of it. They had been implacably serene.

The planets, however . . . We began to remember the planets. They had suffered certain changes both of appearance and of course. At certain times of the year Mars would reverse its direction and go backward through the stars. Venus had been brighter and less bright as she went through her phases of crescent, full, and wane. Mercury had shuddered like a skidding drop of rain on the sky flushed with daybreak. The light we now watched had that erratic, trembling quality. We saw it, unmistakably, change direction and go backward. It then grew smaller and fainter; blinked—an eclipse?—and slowly disappeared.

Slowly, but not slowly enough for a planet.

Then—the third "then"!—arrived the indubitable and positive Wonder of the World, the Magic Trick, watch now, watch, you will not believe your eyes, mama, mama, look what I can do—

Seven lights in a row, proceeding fairly rapidly, with a darting movement, from left to right. Proceeding less rapidly from right to left, two dimmer, greenish lights. Two-lights halt, blink, reverse course, proceed hastily and in a wavering manner from left

*to right. Seven-lights increase speed, and catch up.
Two-lights flash desperately, flicker, and are gone.*

*Seven-lights hang still for some while, then merge
gradually into one streak, veering away, and little by
little vanish into the immensity of the dark.*

*But in the dark now are growing other lights,
many of them: lamps, dots, rows, scintillations—some
near at hand, some far. Like the stars, yes, but not
stars. It is not the great Existences we are seeing, but
only the little lives.*

In the morning Simon told me something about the
Camp, but not until after he had had me check the
apartment for bugs. I thought at first he had been
given behavior mod and gone paranoid. We never had
been infested. And I'd been living alone for a year and
a half; surely they didn't want to hear me talking to
myself? But he said, "They may have been expecting
me to come here."

"But they let you go free!"

He just lay there and laughed at me. So I checked
everywhere we could think of. I didn't find any bugs,
but it did look as if somebody had gone through the
bureau drawers while I was away in the Wilderness.
Simon's papers were all at Max's, so that didn't matter. I made tea on the Primus, and washed and shaved
Simon with the extra hot water in the kettle—he had a
thick beard and wanted to get rid of it because of the
lice he had brought from Camp—and while we were
doing that he told me about the Camp. In fact he told
me very little, but not much was necessary.

He had lost about 20 pounds. As he only weighed
140 to start with, this left little to go on with. His
knees and wrist bones stuck out like rocks under the
skin. His feet were all swollen and chewed-looking
from the Camp boots; he hadn't dared take the boots

off, the last three days of walking, because he was afraid he wouldn't be able to get them back on. When he had to move or sit up so I could wash him, he shut his eyes.

"Am I really here?" he asked. "Am I here?"

"Yes," I said. "You are here. What I don't understand is how you got here."

"Oh, it wasn't bad so long as I kept moving. All you need is to know where you're going—to have someplace to go. You know, some of the people in Camp, if they'd let them go, they wouldn't have had that. They couldn't have gone anywhere. Keeping moving was the main thing. See, my back's all seized up, now."

When he had to get up to go to the bathroom he moved like a ninety-year-old. He couldn't stand straight, but was all bent out of shape, and shuffled. I helped him put on clean clothes. When he lay down on the bed again, a sound of pain came out of him, like tearing thick paper. I went around the room putting things away. He asked me to come sit by him and said I was going to drown him if I went on crying, "You'll submerge the entire North American continent," he said. I can't remember what he said, but he made me laugh finally. It is hard to remember things Simon says, and hard not to laugh when he says them. This is not merely the partiality of affection: He makes everybody laugh. I doubt that he intends to. It is just that a mathematician's mind works differently from other people's. Then when they laugh, that pleases him.

It was strange, and it is strange, to be thinking about "him," the man I have known for ten years, the same man, while "he" lay there changed out of recognition, a different man. It is enough to make you understand why most languages have a word like "soul." There are various degrees of death, and time spares us none of them. Yet something endures, for which a word is needed.

I said what I had not been able to say for a year and a half: "I was afraid they'd brainwash you."

He said, "Behavior mod is expensive. Even just the drugs. They save it mostly for the VIPs. But I'm afraid they got a notion I might be important after all. I got questioned a lot the last couple of months. About my 'foreign contacts.' " He snorted. "The stuff that got published abroad, I suppose. So I want to be careful and make sure it's just a Camp again next time, and not a Federal Hospital."

"Simon, were they . . . are they cruel, or just righteous?"

He did not answer for a while. He did not want to answer. He knew what I was asking. He knew by what thread hangs hope, the sword, above our heads.

"Some of them . . ." he said at last, mumbling.

Some of them had been cruel. Some of them had enjoyed their work. You cannot blame everything on society.

"Prisoners, as well as guards," he said.

You cannot blame everything on the enemy.

"Some of them, Bell," he said with energy, touching my hand—"some of them, there were men like gold there—"

The thread is tough; you cannot cut it with one stroke.

"What have you been playing?" he asked.

"Forrest, Schubert."

"With the quartet?"

"Trio, now. Janet went to Oakland with a new lover."

"Ah, poor Max."

"It's just as well, really. She isn't a good pianist."

I make Simon laugh, too, though I don't intend to. We talked until it was past time for me to go to work.

My shift since the Full Employment Act last year is ten to two. I am an inspector in a recycled paper bag factory. I have never rejected a bag yet; the electronic inspector catches all the defective ones first. It is a rather depressing job. But it's only four hours a day, and it takes more time than that to go through all the lines and physical and mental examinations, and fill out all the forms, and talk to all the welfare counselors and inspectors every week in order to qualify as Unemployed, and then line up every day for the ration stamps and the dole. Simon thought I ought to go to work as usual. I tried to, but I couldn't. He had felt very hot to the touch when I kissed him good-bye. I went instead and got a black-market doctor. A girl at the factory had recommened her, for an abortion, if I ever wanted one without going through the regulation two years of sex-depressant drugs the fed-meds make you take when they give you an abortion. She was a jeweler's assistant in a shop on Alder Street, and the girl said she was convenient because if you didn't have enough cash you could leave something in pawn at the jeweler's as payment. Nobody ever does have enough cash, and of course credit cards aren't worth much on the black market.

The doctor was willing to come at once, so we rode home on the bus together. She gathered very soon that Simon and I were married, and it was funny to see her look at us and smile like a cat. Some people love illegality for its own sake. Men, more often than women. It's men who make laws, and enforce them, and break them, and think the whole performance is wonderful. Most women would rather just ignore them. You could see that this woman, like a man, actually enjoyed breaking them. That may have been what put her into an illegal business in the first place, a preference for the shady side. But there was more to it than that. No doubt she'd wanted to be a doctor, too; and the Federal Medical Association doesn't admit women into the medical schools. She probably got her training as some other doctor's private pupil, under the counter. Very much as Simon learned mathematics, since the universities don't teach much but Business Administration and Advertising and Media Skills any more. However she learned it, she seemed to know her stuff. She fixed up a kind of homemade traction device for Simon very handily and informed him that if he did much more walking for two months he'd be crippled the rest of his life, but if he behaved himself he'd just be more or less lame. It isn't the kind of thing you'd expect to be grateful for being told, but we both were. Leaving, she gave me a bottle of about two hundred plain white pills, unlabeled. "Aspirin," she said. "He'll be in a good deal of pain off and on for weeks."

I looked at the bottle. I had never seen aspirin before, only the Super-Buffered Pane-Gon and the Triple-Power N-L-G-Zic and the Extra-Strength Apansprin with the miracle ingredient more doctors recommend, which the fed-meds always give you prescriptions for, to be filled at your FMA-approved private enterprise friendly drugstore at the low, low prices established by the Pure Food and Drug Administration in order to inspire competitive research.

"Aspirin," the doctor repeated. "The miracle ingredient more doctors recommend." She cat-grinned again. I think she liked us because we were living in sin. That bottle of black-market aspirin was probably worth more than the old Navajo bracelet I pawned for her fee.

I went out again to register Simon as temporarily domiciled at my address and to apply for Temporary Unemployment Compensation ration stamps for him. They only give them to you for two weeks and you have to come every day; but to register him as Temporarily Disabled meant getting the signatures of two fed-meds, and I thought I'd rather put that off for a while. It took three hours to go through the lines and get the forms he would have to fill out, and to answer the 'crats' questions about why he wasn't there in person. They smelled something fishy. Of course it's hard for them to prove that two people are married and aren't just adultering if you move now and then and your friends help out by sometimes registering one of you as living at their address; but they had all the back files on both of us and it was obvious that we had been around each other for a suspiciously long time. The State really does make things awfully hard for itself. It must have been simpler to enforce the laws back when marriage was legal and adultery was what got you into trouble. They only had to catch you once. But I'll bet people broke the law just as often then as they do now.

The lantern-creatures came close enough at last that we could see not only their light, but their bodies in the illumination of their light. They were not pretty. They were dark colored, most often a dark red, and they were all mouth. They ate one another whole. Light swallowed light all swallowed together in the vaster mouth of the darkness. They moved slowly, for nothing, however small and hungry, could move fast under that weight, in that cold. Their eyes, round with fear, were never closed. Their bodies were tiny and bony behind the gaping jaws. They wore queer, ugly decorations on their lips and skulls: fringes, serrated wattles, featherlike fronds, guads, bangles, lures. Poor little sheep of the deep pastures! Poor ragged, hunch-jawed dwarfs squeezed to the bone by the weight of the darkness, chilled to the bone by the cold of the darkness, tiny monsters burning with bright hunger, who brought us back to life!

Occasionally, in the wan, sparse illumination of one of the lantern-creatures, we caught a momentary glimpse of other, large, unmoving shapes: the barest suggestion, off in the distance, not of a wall, nothing so solid and certain as a wall, but of a surface, an angle . . . Was it there?

Or something would glitter, faint, far off, far down. There was no use trying to make out what it might be. Probably it was only a fleck of sediment, mud or mica, disturbed by a struggle between the lantern-creatures, flickering like a bit of diamond dust as it rose and settled slowly. In any case, we could not move to go see what it was. We had not even the cold, narrow freedom of the lantern-creatures. We were immobilized, borne down, still shadows among the half-guessed shadow walls. Were we there?

The lantern-creatures showed no awareness of us. They passed before us, among us, perhaps even through us—it was impossible to be sure. They were not afraid, or curious.

Once something a little larger than a hand came crawling near, and for a moment we saw quite distinctly the clean angle where the foot of a wall rose from the pavement, in the glow cast by the crawling creature, which was covered with a foliage of plumes, each plume dotted with many tiny, bluish points of light. We saw the pavement beneath the creature and the wall beside it, heart-breaking in its exact, clear linearity, its opposition to all that was fluid, random, vast, and void. We saw the creature's claws, slowly reaching out and retracting like small stiff fingers, touch the wall. Its plumage of light quivering, it

*dragged itself along and vanished behind the corner
of the wall.*

*So we knew that the wall was there; and that it was
an outer wall, a housefront, perhaps, or the side of
one of the towers of the city.*

*We remembered the towers. We remembered the
city. We had forgotten it. We had forgotten who we
were; but we remembered the city, now.*

When I got home, the FBI had already been there.
The computer at the police precinct where I registered
Simon's address must have flashed it right over to the
computer at the FBI building. They had questioned
Simon for about an hour, mostly about what he had
been doing during the twelve days it took him to get
from the Camp to Portland. I suppose they thought he
had flown to Peking or something. Having a police
record in Walla Walla for hitchhiking helped him es-
tablish his story. He told me that one of them had
gone to the bathroom. Sure enough I found a bug
stuck on the top of the bathroom door frame. I left it,
as we figured it's really better to leave it when you
know you have one, than to take it off and then never
be sure they haven't planted another one you don't
know about. As Simon said, if we felt we had to say
something unpatriotic we could always flush the toilet
at the same time.

I have a battery radio—there are so many work
stoppages because of power failures, and days the
water has to be boiled, and so on, that you really have
to have a radio to save wasting time and dying of
typhoid—and he turned it on while I was making
supper on the Primus. The six o'clock All-American
Broadcasting Company news announcer announced that
peace was at hand in Uruguay, the president's confi-
dential aide having been seen to smile at a passing

blonde as he left the 613th day of the secret negotiations in a villa outside Katmandu. The war in Liberia was going well; the enemy said they had shot down seventeen American planes but the Pentagon said we had shot down twenty-two enemy planes, and the capital city—I forget its name, but it hasn't been inhabitable for seven years anyway—was on the verge of being recaptured by the forces of freedom. The police action in Arizona was also successful. The Neo-Birch insurgents in Phoenix could not hold out much longer against the massed might of the American army and air force, since their underground supply of small tactical nukes from the Weathermen in Los Angeles had been cut off. Then there was an advertisement for Fed-Cred cards, and a commercial for the Supreme Court: "Take your legal troubles to the Nine Wise Men!" Then there was something about why tariffs had gone up, and a report from the stock market, which had just closed at over two thousand, and a commercial for U.S. Government canned water, with a catchy little tune: "Don't be sorry when you drink/It's not as healthy as you think/Don't you think you really ought to/Drink coo-ool, puu-uure U.S.G. water?"—with three sopranos in close harmony on the last line. Then, just as the battery began to give out and his voice was dying away into a faraway tiny whisper, the announcer seemed to be saying something about a new continent emerging.

"What was that?"

"I didn't hear," Simon said, lying with his eyes shut and his face pale and sweaty. I gave him two aspirins before we ate. He ate little, and fell asleep while I was washing the dishes in the bathroom. I had been going to practice, but a viola is fairly wakeful in a one-room apartment. I read for a while instead. It was a best seller Janet had given me when she left. She thought it was very good, but then she likes Franz Liszt too. I don't read much since the libraries were closed down, it's too hard to get books; all you can buy is best sellers. I don't remember the title of this one, the cover just said "Ninety Million Copies in Print!!!" It was about small-town sex life in the last century, the dear old 1970s when they weren't any problems and life was so simple and nostalgic. The author squeezed all the naughty thrills he could out of the fact that all the main characters were married. I looked at the end and saw that all the married couples shot each other after all their children became schizophrenic hookers, except for one brave pair that divorced and then leapt into bed together with a clear-eyed pair of government-employed lovers for eight pages of healthy group sex as a brighter future dawned. I went to bed then, too. Simon was hot, but sleeping quietly. His breathing was like the sound of soft waves far away, and I went out to the dark sea on the sound of them.

I used to go out to the dark sea, often, as a child, falling asleep. I had almost forgotten it with my waking mind. As a child all I had to do was stretch out and think, "the dark sea . . . the dark sea . . ." and soon enough I'd be there, in the great depths, rocking. But after I grew up it only happened rarely, as a great gift. To know the abyss of the darkness and not to fear it, to entrust oneself to it and whatever may arise from it—what greater gift?

We watched the tiny lights come and go around us, and doing so, we gained a sense of space and of direction—near and far, at least, and higher and lower. It was that sense of space that allowed us to become aware of the currents. Space was no longer entirely still around us, suppressed by the enormous pressure of its own weight. Very dimly we were aware that the cold darkness moved, slowly, softly, pressing against us a little for a long time, then ceasing, in a vast oscillation. The empty darkness flowed slowly along our unmoving unseen bodies; along them, past them; perhaps through them; we could not tell.

Where did they come from, those dim, slow, vast tides? What pressure or attraction stirred the deeps to these slow drifting movements? We could not understand that; we could only feel their touch against us, but in straining our sense to guess their origin or end, we became aware of something else: something out there in the darkness of the great currents: sounds. We listened. We heard.

So our sense of space sharpened and localized to a sense of place. For sound is local, as sight is not. Sound is delimited by silence; and it does not rise out of the silence unless it is fairly close, both in space and in time. Though we stand where once the singer stood we cannot hear the voice singing; the years have carried it off on their tides, submerged it. Sound is a fragile thing, a tremor, as delicate as life itself. We may see the stars, but we cannot hear them. Even were the hollowness of outer space an atmosphere, an ether that transmitted the waves of sound, we could not hear the stars; they are too far away. At most if we listened we might hear our own sun, all the mighty, roiling, exploding storm of its burning, as a whisper at the edge of hearing.

A sea wave laps one's feet: It is the shock wave of a volcanic eruption on the far side of the world. But one hears nothing.

A red light flickers on the horizon: It is the reflection in smoke of a city on the distant mainland, burning. But one hears nothing.

Only on the slopes of the volcano, in the suburbs

of the city, does one begin to hear the deep thunder, and the high voices crying.

Thus, when we became aware that we were hearing, we were sure that the sounds we heard were fairly close to us. And yet we may have been quite wrong. For we were in a strange place, a deep place. Sound travels fast and far in the deep places, and the silence there is perfect, letting the least noise be heard for hundreds of miles.

And these were not small noises. The lights were tiny, but the sounds were vast: not loud, but very large. Often they were below the range of hearing, long slow vibrations rather than sounds. The first we heard seemed to us to rise up through the currents from beneath us: immense groans, sighs felt along the bone, a rumbling, a deep uneasy whispering.

Later, certain sounds came down to us from above, or borne along the endless levels of the darkness, and these were stranger yet, for they were music. A huge, calling, yearning music from far away in the darkness, calling not to us. Where are you? I am here.

Not to us.

They were the voices of the great souls, the great lives, the lonely ones, the voyagers. Calling. Not often answered. Where are you? Where have you gone?

But the bones, the keels and girders of white bones on icy isles of the South, the shores of bones did not reply.

Nor could we reply. But we listened, and the tears rose in our eyes, salt, not so salt as the oceans, the world-girdling deep bereaved currents, the abandoned roadways of the great lives; not so salt, but warmer.

I am here. Where have you gone?

No answer.

Only the whispering thunder from below.

*But we knew now, though we could not answer,
we knew because we heard, because we felt, because
we wept, we knew that we were; and we remembered
other voices.*

Max came the next night. I sat on the toilet lid to
practice, with the bathroom door shut. The FBI men
on the other end of the bug got a solid half hour of
scales and doublestops, and then a quite good performance of the Hindemith unaccompanied viola sonata.
The bathroom being very small and all hard surfaces,
the noise I made was really tremendous. Not a good
sound, far too much echo, but the sheer volume was
contagious, and I played louder as I went on. The man
up above knocked on his floor once; but if I have to
listen to the weekly All-American Olympic Games at
full blast every Sunday morning from his TV set, then
he has to accept Paul Hindemith coming up out of his
toilet now and then.

When I got tired I put a wad of cotton over the bug,
and came out of the bathroom half-deaf. Simon and
Max were on fire. Burning, unconsumed. Simon was
scribbling formulae in traction, and Max was pumping
his elbows up and down the way he does, like a boxer,
and saying "The e - lec - tron emis - sion . . ."
through his nose, with his eyes narrowed, and his
mind evidently going light-years per second faster than
his tongue, because he kept beginning over and saying
"The e - lec - tron emis - sion . . ." and pumping his
elbows.

Intellectuals at work are very strange to look at. As
strange as artists. I never could understand how an
audience can sit there and *look* at a fiddler rolling his
eyes and biting his tongue, or a horn player collecting
spit, or a pianist like a black cat strapped to an electri-

fied bench, as if what they *saw* had anything to do with the music.

I damped the fires with a quart of black-market beer—the legal kind is better, but I never have enough ration stamps for beer; I'm not thirsty enough to go without eating—and gradually Max and Simon cooled down. Max would have stayed talking all night, but I drove him out because Simon was looking tired.

I put a new battery in the radio and left it playing in the bathroom, and blew out the candle and lay and talked with Simon; he was too excited to sleep. He said that Max had solved the problems that were bothering them before Simon was sent to Camp, and had fitted Simon's equations to (as Simon put it) the bare facts, which means they have achieved "direct energy conversion." Ten or twelve people have worked on it at different times since Simon published the theoretical part of it when he was twenty-two. The physicist Ann Jones had pointed out right away that the simplest practical application of the theory would be to build a "sun tap," a device for collecting and storing solar energy, only much cheaper and better than the U.S.G. Sola-Heetas that some rich people have on their houses. And it would have been simple only they kept hitting the same snag. Now Max has got around the snag.

I said that Simon published the theory, but that is inaccurate. Of course he's never been able to publish any of his papers, in print; he's not a federal employee and doesn't have a government clearance. But it did get circulated in what the scientists and poets call Sammy's-dot, that is, just handwritten or hectographed. It's an old joke that the FBI arrests everybody with purple fingers, because they have either been hectographing Sammy's-dots, or they have impetigo.

Anyhow, Simon was on top of the mountain that

night. His true joy is in the pure math; but he had been working with Clara and Max and the others in this effort to materialize the theory for ten years, and a taste of material victory is a good thing, once in a lifetime.

I asked him to explain what the sun tap would mean to the masses, with me as a representative mass. He explained that it means we can tap solar energy for power, using a device that's easier to build than a jar battery. The efficiency and storage capacity are such that about ten minutes of sunlight will power an apartment complex like ours, heat and lights and elevators and all, for twenty-four hours; and no pollution, particulate, thermal, or radioactive. "There isn't any danger of using up the sun?" I asked. He took it soberly—it was a stupid question, but after all not so long ago people thought there wasn't any danger of using up the earth—and said no, because we wouldn't be pulling out energy, as we did when we mined and lumbered and split atoms, but just using the energy that comes to us anyhow: as the plants, the trees and grass and rosebushes, always have done. "You could call it Flower Power," he said. He was high, high up on the mountain, ski-jumping in the sunlight.

"The State owns us," he said, "because the corporative State has a monopoly on power sources and there's not enough power to go around. But now, anybody could build a generator on their roof that would furnish enough power to light a city."

I looked out the window at the dark city.

"We could completely decentralize industry and agriculture. Technology could serve life instead of serving capital. We could each run our own life. Power is power! . . . The State is a machine. We could unplug the machine, now. Power corrupts; absolute power corrupts absolutely. But that's true only when there's a price on power. When groups can keep the power to themselves; when they can use physical power-to in order to exert spiritual power-over; when might makes right. But if power is free? If everybody is equally mighty? Then everybody's got to find a better way of showing that he's right . . ."

"That's what Mr. Nobel thought when he invented dynamite," I said. "Peace on earth."

He slid down the sunlit slope a couple of thousand feet and stopped beside me in a spray of snow, smiling. "Skull at the banquet," he said, "finger writing on the wall. Be still! Look, don't you see the sun shining on the Pentagon, all the roofs are off, the sun shines at last into the corridors of power . . . And they shrivel up, they wither away. The green grass grows through the carpets of the Oval Room, the Hot Line is disconnected for nonpayment of the bill. The first thing we'll do is build an electrified fence outside the electrified fence around the White House. The inner one prevents unauthorized persons from getting in. The outer one will prevent authorized persons from getting out . . ."

Of course he was bitter. Not many people come out of prison sweet.

But it was cruel, to be shown this great hope, and to know that there was no hope for it. He did know that. He knew it right along. He knew that there was no mountain, that he was skiing on the wind.

The tiny lights of the lantern-creatures died out one by one, sank away. The distant lonely voices were silent. The cold, slow currents flowed, vacant, only shaken from time to time by a shifting in the abyss.

It was dark again, and no voice spoke. All dark, dumb, cold.

Then the sun rose.

It was not like the dawns we had begun to remember: the change, manifold and subtle, in the smell and touch of the air; the hush that, instead of sleeping, wakes, holds still, and waits; the appearance of objects, looking gray, vague, and new, as if just created—distant mountains against the eastern sky, one's own hands, the hoary grass full of dew and shadow, the fold in the edge of a curtain hanging by the window—and then, before one is quite sure that one is indeed seeing again, that the light has returned, that day is breaking, the first, abrupt, sweet stammer of a waking bird. And after that the chorus, voice by voice: This is my nest, this is my tree, this is my egg, this is my day, this is my life, here I am, here I am, hurray for me! I'm here!—No, it wasn't like that at all, this dawn. It was completely silent, and it was blue.

In the dawns that we had begun to remember, one did not become aware of the light itself, but of the separate objects touched by the light, the things, the world. They were there, visible again, as if visibility were their own property, not a gift from the rising sun.

In this dawn, there was nothing but the light itself. Indeed there was not even light, we would have said, but only color: blue.

There was no compass bearing to it. It was not brighter in the east. There was no east or west. There was only up and down, below and above. Below was dark. The blue light came from above. Brightness fell. Beneath, where the shaking thunder had stilled, the brightness died away through violet into blindness.

We, arising, watched light fall.

In a way it was more like an ethereal snowfall than like a sunrise. The light seemed to be in discrete *particles, infinitesimal flecks, slowly descending, faint, fainter than flecks of fine snow on a dark night, and tinier; but blue. A soft, penetrating blue tending to the violet, the color of the shadows in an iceberg, the color of a streak of sky between gray clouds on a winter afternoon before snow: faint in intensity but vivid in hue: the color of the remote, the color of the cold, the color farthest from the sun.*

On Saturday night they held a scientific congress in our room. Clara and Max came, of course, and the engineer Phil Drum and three others who had worked on the sun tap. Phil Drum was very pleased with himself because he had actually built one of the things, a solar cell, and brought it along. I don't think it had occurred to either Max or Simon to build one. Once they knew it could be done they were satisfied and wanted to get on with something else. But Phil unwrapped his baby with a lot of flourish, and people made remarks like, "Mr. Watson, will you come here a minute," and "Hey, Wilbur, you're off the ground!" and "I say, nasty mould you've got there, Alec, why don't you throw it out?" and "Ugh, ugh, burns, burns, wow, ow," the latter from Max, who does look a little pre-Mousterian. Phil explained that he had exposed the cell for one minute at four in the afternoon up in Washington Park during a light rain. The lights were back on on the West Side since Thursday, so we could test it without being conspicious.

We turned off the lights, after Phil had wired the table-lamp cord to the cell. He turned on the lamp switch. The bulb came on, about twice as bright as before, at its full forty watts—city power of course was never full strength. We all looked at it. It was a dime-store table lamp with a metallized gold base and a white plasticloth shade.

"Brighter than a thousand suns," Simon murmured from the bed.

"Could it be," said Clara Edmonds, "that we physicists have known sin—and have come out the other side?"

"It really wouldn't be any good at all for making bombs with," Max said dreamily.

"Bombs," Phil Drum said with scorn. "Bombs are obsolete. Don't you realize that we could move a mountain with this kind of power? I mean pick up Mount Hood, move it, and set it down. We could thaw Antarctica, we could freeze the Congo. We could sink a continent. Give me a fulcrum and I'll move the world. Well, Archimedes, you've got your fulcrum. The sun."

"Christ," Simon said, "the radio, Belle!"

The bathroom door was shut and I had put cotton over the bug, but he was right; if they were going to go ahead at this rate there had better be some added static. Although I liked watching their faces in the clear light of the lamp—they all had good, interesting faces, well worn, like the handles of wooden tools or the rocks in a running stream—I did not much want to listen to them talk tonight. Not because I wasn't a scientist, that made no difference. And not because I disagreed or disapproved or disbelieved anything they said. Only because it grieved me terribly, their talking. Because they couldn't rejoice aloud over a job done and a discovery made, but had to hide there and whisper about it. Because they couldn't go out into the sun.

I went into the bathroom with my viola and sat on the toilet lid and did a long set of sautillé exercises. Then I tried to work at the Forrest trio, but it was too assertive. I played the solo part from *Harold in Italy*, which is beautiful, but it wasn't quite the right mood either. They were still going strong in the other room. I began to improvise.

After a few minutes in E-minor the light over the shaving mirror began to flicker and dim; then it died. Another outage. The table lamp in the other room did not go out, being connected with the sun, not with the twenty-three atomic fission plants that power the Greater Portland Area. Within two seconds somebody had switched it off, too, so that we shouldn't be the only window in the West Hills left alight; and I could hear them rooting for candles and rattling matches. I went on improvising in the dark. Without light, when you couldn't see all the hard shiny surfaces of things, the sound seemed softer and less muddled. I went on, and it began to shape up. All the laws of harmonics sang together when the bow came down. The strings of the viola were the cords of my own voice, tightened by sorrow, tuned to the pitch of joy. The melody created itself out of air and energy, it raised up the valleys, and the mountains and hills were made low, and the crooked straight, and the rough places plain. And the music went out to the dark sea and sang in the darkness, over the abyss.

When I came out they were all sitting there and none of them was talking. Max had been crying. I could see little candle flames in the tears around his eyes. Simon lay flat on the bed in the shadows, his eyes closed. Phil Drum sat hunched over, holding the solar cell in his hands.

I loosened the pegs, put the bow and the viola in the case, and cleared my throat. It was embarrassing. I finally said, "I'm sorry."

One of the women spoke: Rose Abramski, a private student of Simon's, a big shy woman who could hardly speak at all unless it was in mathematical symbols. "I saw it," she said. "I saw it. I saw the white towers,

and the water streaming down their sides, and running
back down to the sea. And the sunlight in the streets,
after ten thousand years of darkness."

"I heard them," Simon said, very low, from the
shadow. "I heard their voices."

"Oh, Christ! Stop it!" Max cried out, and got up
and went blundering out into the the unlit hall, without his coat. We heard him running down the stairs.

"Phil," said Simon, lying there, "could we raise up
the white towers, with our lever and our fulcrum?"

After a long silence Phil Drum answered, "We have
the power to do it."

"What else do we need?" Simon said. "What else
do we need, besides power?"

Nobody answered him.

*The blue changed. It became brighter, lighter, and
at the same time thicker: impure. The etheral lumi-
nosity of blue-violet turned to turquoise, intense and
opaque. Still we could not have said that everything
was now Turquoise-colored, for there were still no
things. There was nothing, except the color of
turquoise.*

*The change continued. The opacity became veined
and thinned. The dense, solid color began to appear
translucent, transparent. Then it seemed as if we
were in the heart of a sacred jade, or the brilliant
crystal of a sapphire or an emerald.*

*As at the inner structure of a crystal, there was no
motion. But there was something, now, to see. It was
as if we saw the motionless, elegant inward structure
of the molecules of a precious stone. Planes and
angles appeared about us, shadowless and clear in
that even, glowing, blue-green light.*

*These were the walls and towers of the city, the
streets, the windows, the gates.*

We knew them, but we did not recognize them. We did not dare to recognize them. It had been so long. And it was so strange. We had used to dream, when we lived in this city. We had lain down, nights, in the rooms behind the windows, and slept, and dreamed. We had all dreamed of the ocean, of the deep sea. Were we not dreaming now?

Sometimes the thunder and tremor deep below us rolled again, but it was faint now, far away; as far away as our memory of the thunder and the tremor and the fire and the towers falling, long ago. Neither the sound nor the memory frightened us. We knew them.

The sapphire light brightened overhead to green, almost green-gold. We looked up. The tops of the highest towers were hard to see, glowing in the radiance of light. The streets and doorways were darker, more clearly defined.

In one of those long, jewel-dark streets something was moving—something not composed of planes and angles, but of curves and arcs. We all turned to look at it, slowly, wondering as we did so at the slow ease of our own motion, our freedom. Sinuous, with a beautiful flowing, gathering, rolling movement, now rapid and now tentative, the thing drifted across the street from a blank garden wall to the recess of a door. There, in the dark blue shadow, it was hard to see for a while. We watched. A pale blue curve appeared at the top of the doorway. A second followed, and a third. The moving thing clung or hovered there, above the door, like a swaying knot of silvery cords or a boneless hand, one arched finger pointing carelessly to something above the lintel of the door, something like itself, but motionless—a carving. A carving in jade light. A carving in stone.

Delicately and easily the long curving tentacle fol-

lowed the curves of the carved figure, the eight petal-
limbs, the round eyes. Did it recognize its image?

The living one swung suddenly, gathered its curves
in a loose knot, and darted away down the street,
swift and sinuous. Behind it a faint cloud of darker
blue hung for a minute and dispersed, revealing
again the carved figure above the door: the sea-
flower, the cuttlefish, quick, great-eyed, graceful, eva-
sive, the cherished sign, carved on a thousand walls,
worked into the design of cornices, pavements, handles, lids of jewel boxes, canopies, tapestries, table-
tops, gateways.

Down another street, about the level of the first-
floor windows, came a flickering drift of hundreds
of motes of silver. With a single motion all turned
toward the cross street, and glittered off into the dark
blue shadows.

There were shadows, now.

We looked up, up from the flight of silverfish, up
from the streets where the jade-green currents flowed
and the blue shadows fell. We moved and looked
up, yearning, to the high towers of our city. They
stood, the fallen towers. They glowed in the ever-
brightening radiance, not blue or blue-green, up there,
but gold. Far above them lay a vast, circular, trembling
brightness: the sun's light on the surface of the sea.

We are here. When we break through the bright
circle into life, the water will break and stream white
down the white sides of the towers, and run down
the steep streets back into the sea. The water will
glitter in dark hair, on the eyelids of dark eyes, and
dry to a thin white film of salt.

We are here.

Whose voice? Who called to us?

He was with me for twelve days. On January 28th

the 'crats came from the Bureau of Health, Education and Welfare and said that since he was receiving Unemployment Compensation while suffering from an untreated illness, the government must look after him and restore him to health, because health is the inalienable right of the citizens of a democracy. He refused to sign the consent forms, so the chief health officer signed them. He refused to get up, so two of the policemen pulled him up off the bed. He started to try to fight them. The chief health officer pulled his gun and said that if he continued to struggle he would shoot him for resisting welfare, and arrest me for conspiracy to defraud the government. The man who was holding my arms behind my back said they could always arrest me for unreported pregnancy with intent to form a nuclear family. At that Simon stopped trying to get free. It was really all he was trying to do, not to fight them, just to get his arms free. He looked at me, and they took him out.

He is in the federal hospital in Salem. I have not been able to find out whether he is in the regular hospital or the mental wards.

It was on the radio again yesterday, about the rising land masses in the South Atlantic and the Western Pacific. At Max's the other night I saw a TV special explaining about geophysical stresses and subsidence and faults. The U.S. Geodetic Service is doing a lot of advertising around town, the most common one is a big billboard that says IT'S NOT OUR FAULT! with a picture of a beaver pointing to a schematic map that shows how even if Oregon has a major earthquake and subsidence as California did last month, it will not affect Portland, or only the western suburbs perhaps. The news also said that they plan to halt the tidal waves in Florida by dropping nuclear bombs where Miami was. Then they will reattach Florida to the mainland with landfill. They are already advertising real estate for housing developments on the landfill. The president is staying at the Mile High White House in Aspen, Colorado. I don't think it will do him much good. Houseboats down on the Willamette are selling for $500,000. There are no trains or buses running south from Portland, because all the highways were badly damaged by the tremors and landslides last week, so I will have to see if I can get to Salem on foot. I still have the rucksack I bought for the Mount Hood Wilderness Week. I got some dry lima beans and raisins with my Federal Fair Share Super Value Green Stamp minimal ration book for February—it took the whole book—and Phil Drum made me a tiny camp stove powered with the solar cell. I didn't want to take the Primus, it's too bulky, and I did want to be able to carry the viola. Max gave me a half pint of brandy. When the brandy is gone I expect I will stuff this notebook into the bottle and put the cap on tight and leave it on a hillside somewhere between here and Salem. I like to think of it being lifted up little by little by the water, and rocking, and going out to the dark sea.

Where are you?
We are here. Where have you gone?

DRAGON MOON

by Henry Kuttner

1. Elak of Atlantis

Of great limbs gone to chaos,
  A great face turned to night—
Why bend above a shapeless shroud
Seeking in such archaic cloud
  Sight of strong lords and light?

—Chesterton

The wharf-side tavern was a bedlam. The great harbor of Poseidonia stretched darkly to the southeast, but the waterfront was a blaze of bright lanterns and torches. Ships had made port today, and this tavern, like the others, roared with mirth and rough nautical oaths. Cooking-smoke and odor of sesame filled the broad low room, mingled with the sharp tang of wine. The swarthy seamen of the south held high carnival tonight.

In a niche in the wall was an image of the patron god, Poseidon of the sunlit seas. It was noticeable that before swilling liquor, nearly every man spilled a drop or two on the floor in the direction of the carved god.

A fat little man sat in a corner and muttered under his breath. Lycon's small eyes examined the tavern with some distaste. His purse was, for a change, heavy with gold; so was that of Elak, his fellow adventurer. Yet Elak preferred to drink and wench in this brawl-

ing, smelly tavern, a predilection that filled Lycon
with annoyance and bitterness. He spat, muttered under his breath, and turned to watch Elak.

The lean, wolf-faced adventurer was quarreling with
a sea captain whose huge, great-muscled body dwarfed
Elak's. Between the two a tavern wench was seated,
her slanted eyes watching the men slyly, flattered by
the attention given her.

The seaman, Drezzar, had made the mistake of
underestimating Elak's potentialities. He had cast cov-
etous eyes upon the wench and determined to have
her, regardless of Elak's prior claim. Under other
circumstances Elak might have left the slant-eyed girl
to Drezzar, but the captain's words had been insulting.
So Elak remained at the table, his gaze wary, and his
rapier loosened in its scabbard.

He watched Drezzar, noting the sunburnt, massive
face, the bushy dark beard, the crinkled scar that
swept down from temple to jawbone, blinding the man
in one gray eye. And Lycon called for more wine.
Steel would flash soon, he knew.

Yet the battle came without warning. A stool was
overturned, there was a flare of harsh oaths, and
Drezzar's sword came out, flaming in the lamplight.
The wench screamed shrilly and fled, having little
taste for bloodshed save from a distance.

Drezzar feinted; his sword swept out in a treacher-
ously low cut that would have disemboweled Elak had
it reached its mark. But the smaller man's body writhed
aside in swift, flowing motion; the rapier shimmered.
Its point gashed Drezzar's scalp.

They fought in silence. And this, more than anything else, gave Elak the measure of his opponent.
Drezzar's face was quite emotionless. Only the scar
stood out white and distinct. His blinded eye seemed
not to handicap him in the slightest degree.

Lycon waited for a chance to sheathe his steel in Drezzar's back. Elak would disapprove, he knew, but Lycon was a realist.

Elak's sandal slipped in a puddle of spilled liquor, and he threw himself aside desperately, striving to regain his balance. He failed. Drezzar's lashing sword drove the rapier from his hand, and Elak went down, his head cracking sharply on an overturned stool.

The seaman poised himself, sighted down his blade, and lunged. Lycon was darting forward, but he knew he could not reach the killer in time.

And then—from the open door came the inexplicable. Something like a streak of flaming light lashed through the air, and at first Lycon thought it was a thrown dagger. But it was not. It was—flame!

White flame, darting and unearthly! It gripped Drezzar's blade, coiled about it, ripped it from the seaman's hand. It blazed up in blinding fiery light, limning the room in starkly distinct detail. The sword fell uselessly to the floor, a blackened, twisted stump of melted metal.

Drezzar shouted an oath. He stared at the ruined weapon, and his bronzed face paled. Swiftly he whirled and fled through a side door.

The flame had vanished. In the door a man stood—a gross, ugly figure clad in the traditional brown robe of the Druids.

Lycon, skidding to a halt, lowered his sword and whispered, "Dalan!"

Elak got to his feet, rubbing his head ruefully. At sight of the Druid his face changed. Without a word he nodded to Lycon and moved toward the door.

The three went out into the night.

2. Dragon Throne

Now we are come to our Kingdom,
And the Crown is ours to take—
With a naked sword at the Council board,
And under the throne the snake,
Now we are come to our Kingdom!

—Kipling

"I bring you a throne," Dalan said, "but you must hold it with your blade."

They stood at the end of a jetty, looking out at the moonlit harbor waters. The clamor of Poseidonia seemed far away now.

Elak stared at the hills. Beyond them, leagues upon leagues to the north, lay a life he had put behind him. A life he had given up when he left Cyrena to gird on an adventurer's blade. In Elak's veins ran the blood of the kings of Cyrena, northernmost kingdom of Atlantis. And, but for a fatal quarrel with his stepfather, Norian, Elak would have been on the dragon throne even then. But Norian had died, and Elak's brother, Orander, took the crown.

Elak said, "Orander rules Cyrena. Do you ask me to join a rebellion against my brother?" An angry light showed in the adventurer's cold eyes.

"Orander is dead," the Druid said quietly. "Elak, I have a tale to tell you, a tale of sorcery and black evil that has cast its shadow over Cyrena. But first—" He fumbled in his shapeless brown robe and drew forth a tiny crystal sphere. He cupped it in his palm, breathed upon it. The clear surface clouded, misted—and the fog seemed to permeate the entire globe. The Druid held a ball of whirling gray cloud in his hand.

Within the sphere a picture grew, microscopic but

vividly distinct. Elak peered closely. He saw a throne, and a man who sat upon it.

"South of Cyrena, beyond the mountains, lies Kiriath," Dalan said. "Sepher ruled it. And now Sepher still sits upon his throne, but he is no longer human."

In the globe the face of Sepher sprang out in startling clarity. Involuntarily Elak drew back, his lips thinning. At a casual glance Sepher seemed unchanged, a black-bearded, bronzed giant with the keen eyes of a hawk, but Elak knew that he looked upon a creature loathsome beyond anything on earth. It was not evil, as he knew it, but a thing beyond good and evil as it was beyond humanity or deity. A Presence from Outside had touched Sepher and taken Kiriath's king for its own. And Elak knew this was the most horrible being he had ever seen.

Dalan hid the crystal. He said coldly, "Out of the unknown has come a being named Karkora. What he is I know not. I have cast the runes, and they say little to me. The altar fires have whispered of a shadow that will come upon Cyrena, a shadow that may spread over all Atlantis. Karkora, the Pallid One, is not human, nor is he a demon. He is—alien, Elak."

"What of my brother?" the adventurer asked.

"You have seen Sepher," Dalan said. "He is possessed, a vessel of this entity called Karkora. Ere I left Orander, he, too, had—changed."

A muscle twitched in Elak's brown cheek. The Druid went on.

"Orander saw his doom. Day by day the power of Karkora over him increased, and the soul of your brother was driven further into the outer dark. He died—by his own hand."

Elak's face did not change expression. But for minutes he was silent, a deep sorrow in his gray eyes.

Lycon turned to look out across the sea.

The Druid went on, "Orander sent a message to you, Elak. You, in all Atlantis, are of the royal line of Cyrena. Yours, therefore, is the crown. It will not be easy to hold. Karkora is not defeated. But my magic will aid you."

Elak said, "You offer me the dragon throne?"

Dalan nodded.

"The years have changed me, Dalan. I have gone through Atlantis a vagabond and worse. I put my birthright behind me and forgot it. And I'm not the same man who went from Cyrena years ago," Elak said softly, laughing a little bitterly, and looking over the jetty's edge at his face reflected in the dark swell of the water. "Only a king may sit on the dragon throne. For me—it would be a jest. And a sorry one."

"You fool!" the Druid whispered—and there was rage in the sibilant sound. "Blind, mad fool! Do you think the Druids would offer Cyrena to the wrong man? Blood of kings is in your veins, Elak. It is not yours to deny. You must obey."

"Must?" The word was spoken lightly, yet Lycon felt a tenseness go through him, tightening his muscles. "Must?" Elak asked.

"The decision is mine, Druid. By Mider! The throne of Cyrena means much to me. Therefore I shall not sit in it!"

Dalan's toad face was gargoylish in the moonlight. He thrust his bald, glistening head forward, and his thick, stubby fingers twisted.

"Now am I tempted to work magic on you, Elak," he said harshly. "I am no—"

"I have given you my answer."

The Druid hesitated. His somber eyes dwelt on Elak. Then, without a word, he turned and went lumbering off into the night. His footsteps died.

Elak remained staring out at the harbor. His cheeks
were gray, his mouth a tortured white line. And he
whirled, abruptly, and looked at the hills of Poseidonia.

But he did not see them. His gaze went beyond
them, far and far, probing through all Atlantis to the
kingdom of the north—Cyrena, and the dragon throne.

3. *The Gates of Dream*

> Churel and ghoul and Djinn and sprite
> Shall bear us company tonight,
> For we have reached the Oldest Land
> Wherein the powers of Darkness range.

—Kipling

Elak's sleep that night was broken by dreams—flashing,
disordered visions of many things. He stared up at the
white moonlit ceiling of the apartment. And—it was
changed. The familiar room was gone. Light still existed, but it was oddly changed—grayish and unreal.
Unearthly planes and angles slipped past Elak, and in
his ears a low humming grew. This changed to a
high-pitched, droming whine, and died away at last.

The mad planes reassembled themselves. In his dream
Elak saw a mighty crag upthrust against cold stars—
colossal against a background of jagged mountain
peaks. Snow dappled them, but the darkness of the
crag was unbroken. On its top was a tower, dwarfed
by distance.

A flood seemed to lift Elak and bear him swiftly
forward. In the base of the crag, he saw, were great
iron gates. And these parted and swung aside, yawn-
ing for him as he moved through.

They shut silently behind him.

And now Elak became conscious of a Presence. It
was stygian black; yet in the tenebrous darkness there

was a vague inchoate stirring, a sense of motion that was unmistakable.

Without warning Elak saw—the Pallid One!

A white and shining figure flashed into view. How tall it was, how close or distant, the man could not tell. Nor could he see more than the bare outlines. A crawling, leprous shimmer of cold light rippled over the being; it seemed little more than a white shadow. But a shadow—three-dimensional, alive!

The unearthly terror of Karkora, the Pallid One!

The being seemed to grow larger. Elak knew he was watched, coldly and dispassionately. His senses were no longer dependable. It did not seem as though he beheld Karkora with his eyes alone—he was no longer conscious of his body.

He remembered Dalan, and Dalan's god. And he cried silently upon Mider for aid.

The shuddering loathing that filled him did not pass, but the horror that tore at his mind was no longer as strong. Again he cried to Mider, forcing himself to concentrate on the Druid god.

Once more Elak called out to Mider. And, silently, eerily, a wall of flame rose about him, shutting off the vision of Karkora. The warm, flickering fires of Mider were a protective barrier—earthly, friendly.

They closed in—drew him back. They warmed the chill horror that froze his mind. They changed to sunlight—and the sunlight was slanting in through the window, beside which Elak lay on his low bed, awake and shuddering with reaction.

"By the Nine Hells!" he cursed, leaping up swiftly. "By all the gods of Atlantis! Where's my rapier?" He found it, and whirled it hissing through the air. "How can a man battle dreams?"

He turned to Lycon, slumbering noisily nearby, and kicked the small man into wakefulness.

"Hog-swill," said Lycon, rubbing his eyes. "Bring another cup, and swiftly, or I'll—eh? What's wrong?"

Elak was dressing hastily. "What's wrong? Something I didn't expect. How could I know from Dalan's words the sort of thing that's come to life in Atlantis?" He spat in disgust. "That leprous foulness shall never take the dragon throne!"

He slammed his rapier into its scabbard. "I'll find Dalan. I'll go back with him. To Cyrena."

Elak was silent, but deep in his eyes was a black horror and loathing. He had seen the Pallid One. And he knew that never in words could he hope to express the burning foulness of alien Karkora.

But Dalan had vanished. It was impossible to find the Druid in teeming Poseidonia. And at last Elak gave up hope and determined to take matters into his own hands. A galley called *Kraken* was leaving that day, he learned, and would beat up the western coast. In fact, by the time Elak had hired a boatman to take him and Lycon to the vessel, the galley's oars were already dipping into the swells.

Elak's cockleshell gained its side, and he clambered over the gunwale, hoisting Lycon after him. He tossed a coin to the boatman and saw the man depart.

The sweating backs of slaves were moving rhythmically under the lash of the overseers. One of these came forward at a run, his bronzed face angry.

"Who are you?" he hailed. "What do you seek on the *Kraken*?"

"Take us to your captain," Elak said shortly. His hand touched the heavy purse at his belt, and coins jingled. The overseer was impressed.

"We're putting to sea," he said. "What do you want?"

"Passage to Cyrena," Lycon snapped. "Be—"

"Bring them here, Rasul," a gruff voice broke in.

"They are friends. We'll give them passage to Cyrena—aye!"

And Drezzar, Elak's opponent in the tavern brawl, hastened along the poop toward them, teeth gleaming in his bushy beard.

"Ho!" he yelled at a nearby group of armed seamen. "Seize those two! Take them—alive! You dog," Drezzar said with cold rage. He stood before Elak and lifted his hand as though to strike the captive.

Elak said stoically, "I want passage to Cyrena. I'll pay well for it."

"So you will," Drezzar grinned, and ripped off Elak's purse. He opened it and ran golden coins through his thick fingers. "You'll work for it, too. But you'll not reach Cyrena.

"Two more oarsmen for you, Rasul. Two more slaves.

"See that they work!"

He turned and strode away. Unresisting, Elak was dragged to a vacant oar and chained there, Lycon shackled beside him. His hands fell in well-worn grooves on the polished wood.

Rasul's whip cracked. The overseer called, "Pull! Pull!"

The *Kraken* sped seaward. And, chained to his oar, straining at the unaccustomed toil, Elak's dark wolf-face bore a smile that was not pleasant to see.

4. The Ship Sails North

Orpheus has harped her,
Her prow has sheared the spray,
Fifty haughty heroes at her golden
　　　oarlocks sway,
White the wave before her flings,
Bright from shore she lifts and swings,

Wild he twangs the ringing strings—
Give way! Give way!

—Benet

They drove down along the coast and skirted the
southern tip of Atlantis. Then the galley crept northwest, up the long curve of the continent, and all the
while the days were cloudless and fair, and the skies
blue as the waters of the Ocean Sea.

Elak bided his time until the *Kraken* dropped anchor one afternoon at an uninhabited island, to re-
plenish the water supply. Drezzar went ashore with a
dozen others, leaving only a few men in charge of the
ship. This was apparently safe enough, with the slaves
chained. Moreover, Drezzar had the only keys. But,
at sunset, Elak nudged Lycon awake and told him to
keep watch.

"What for?" Lycon's voice was surly. "Do you—"
He broke off, staring, as Elak took a tiny twisted bit
of metal from his sandal and inserted it delicately in
the lock of his ankle-cuff. "Gods!" Lycon cursed.
"You had that all the time—and you waited till now!"

"These locks are easy to pick," Elak said. "What?
Of course I waited! We've only a few enemies aboard
now, instead of more than a dozen. Keep watch, I tell
you."

Lycon obeyed. Footsteps creaked upon the deck
occasionally, and there were lanterns here and there
on the ship, but their illumination was faint enough.
The lapping of water against the hull drowned the soft
scrape and click as Elak worked. Presently he sighed
in satisfaction and opened the cuff.

Metal clicked and scraped. Elak was free. He turned
to Lycon—and then hurrying footsteps sounded on
the raised deck. Rasul, the overseer, ran up, dragging
his long whip. He peered down—and dragged out his
sword, cursing. With the other hand he swept the

whip in a great singing blow, smashing down on Elak's unprotected shoulders.

Lycon acted. In one swift motion he flung himself forward, guarding Elak; the lash ripped skin and flesh from Lycon's side. And then Elak's sinewy hand closed on the tough hide; he pulled mightily—pulled it from Rasul's grasp.

"Ho!" the overseer shouted. "Ho! To me!" His voice roared out over the dark sea. His long sword was a pale flickering light in the glow of the lanterns.

Two more men, armed, came running up behind Rasul. They spread out and closed in on Elak. He grinned unpleasantly, as a wolf smiles. The whip was coiled in his hand.

It spring out suddenly, like a striking snake. The fanged, vicious tip hissed shrilly. In the dimness the lash was difficult to see, impossible to dodge. Rasul roared in pain.

"Slay him!" the overseer shouted.

The three ran in, and Elak gave way, his wrist turning as he swung the whip. A thrown dagger brought blood from the Atlantean's shoulder. And a man staggered back, screaming shrilly, clawing at his eyes that were blinded by the tearing rip of the lash.

"Slay me, then," Elak whispered, cold laughter in his eyes. "But the dog's fangs are sharp, Rasul."

He caught a glimpse of Lycon, bent above his bonds, busily manipulating the bit of metal that would unlock them. Voices called from the shore. Rasul shouted a response, and then ducked and gasped as the whip shrieked through the dark air.

" 'Ware my fangs, Rasul!" Elak smiled mirthlessly.

And now the two—Rasul and his companion—were in turn giving way. Step by step Elak forced them back, under the threat of the terrible lash. They could not guard against it, could not see it. Out of the gloom it would come striking, swift as a snake's thrust, leaping viciously at their eyes. The slaves were awake and straining in their chains, calling encouragement to Elak. The man who had been blinded made a misstep and fell among the rowers. They surged up over him; lean hands reached and clawed in the lantern-light. He screamed for a time, and then made no further sound.

Lycon's voice rose, shrill and peremptory, above the tumult.

"Row!" he yelped. "Row, slaves! Ere Drezzar returns—row for your freedom!" Alternately he cursed and threatened and cajoled them, and worked at his bonds with flying fingers.

Elak heard a whisper at his side, saw a slave thrusting a sword at him, hilt-first—the blade the blinded one had dropped. Gratefully he seized it, hurling the whip away. The feel of the cool, leather-bound hilt was grateful. Tide of strength surved up Elak's arm from the sharp steel.

It was not his rapier—but it would do.

"My fangs, Rasul," he said, laughing—and ran in. His two opponents spread out, but he had forseen that move. He turned his back on Rasul, cut at the other, and almost in the same motion whirled and leaped past, dodging a thrust by a hair's-breadth. And now Rasul only faced him. The other man was down, tearing at a throat sliced through to the spine.

Lycon shouted, "Row, slaves! For your lives!"

The long oars clacked and moved in confusion; then habit stepped in, and rhythmically, slowly, the blades dug into the sea. Lycon yelled a chant, and the slaves kept time to it. Gradually the galley gained way.

On the deck swords flamed and clashed. But Elak was not fated to slay Rasul. The overseer stumbled, dropped to one knee—and hands reached for him out of the dark. Shouting, he was dragged down among the slaves. Voices rose to a yelping crescendo of hate. Rasul screamed—and was silent.

Lycon leaped up, free from his chains. He cursed the rowers; their momentary inattention to their duty had caused confusion. An oar, caught among others, splintered and broke. The butt bent like a bow, snapped back, and smashed a slave's face to bloody ruin. From overside came cries and commands.

The face of Drezzar rose above the rail, hideous, contorted, the scar flaming red. He gripped his sword between his teeth. After him armed men came pouring.

Lycon, a captured blade bare in his hand, ran toward them, yelling objurgations at the slaves. The oars moved again, tore at the sea, sent the galley through the waves once more. A slave had long since cut the anchor-rope.

A dozen armed men, swords gleaming, were ringed about Lycon, who, his back against the mast, was valiantly battling and cursing in lurid oaths. A few steps away Drezzar came catlike, and murder was in his eyes. He saw Elak stir, and ran in, blade ready.

Elak did not stoop to recover his sword. He sprang forward, under the sweep of the steel, which Drezzar had not expected. The two men went down together, rolling on the blood-slippery deck.

Drezzar tried to reverse the sword in his hand and stab Elak in the back. But Elak's supple body writhed aside, and simultaneously his lean, sinewy fingers closed on Drezzar's, above the hilt of the blade.

Drezzar tried to turn the blow, but could not. Elak continued his enemy's thrust. And the sword went smoothly into Drezzar's belly, without pausing till it grated against the backbone.

"My fangs, Drezzar," Elak said very softly, and with no expression on his wolf-face—and then drove the sword further in till it pinned the captain, like a beetle, to the deck. Drezzar's mouth opened; a roaring exhalation of breath, fraught with ghastly agony, seemed torn out of the man. His hands beat the deck; his body doubled up and arched like a bow.

He coughed blood, gnashed his teeth till they splintered and cracked—and so died.

Elak sprang up. He saw a heavy iron key hanging at Drezzar's belt. This he tore away and cast down among the slaves. A grateful clamor came in response.

Lycon called frantically for aid. Elak responded. But now the outcome of the battle was a foregone conclusion. One by one the freed slaves passed the iron key to their neighbors and came springing up to add their numbers to Elak's cause. And, presently, the last of the ship's masters lay dead on deck, and the oarsmen—no longer in chains, no longer slaves—sent the galley plunging through the dark sea to the north.

5. Aynger of Amenalk

For the man dwelt in a lost land
  Of boulders and broken men . . .
                                        —Chesterton

They came to a forbidding, bleak coast that loomed high above the galley. The cold winds of Autumn filled the sails and let the weary oarsmen rest. The sea turned smoothly gray, surging in long, foamless swells under a blue-gray sky. The sun gave little heat. The crew turned gratefully to the ship's stock—oil and wine and woven stuff, finding warmth and comfort in it.

But Elak was chafed by inaction. He longed to reach Cyrena; endlessly he paced the decks, fingering his rapier and pondering on the mystery of the thing

called Karkora. What was this Pallid One? Whence
had it come? These problems were insoluble, and
remained so till, one night, Elak dreamed.

He dreamed of Dalan. The Druid priest seemed to
be standing in a forest glade; before him a fire flickered redly. And Dalan said:

"Leave your ship at the red delta. Seek Aynger of
Amenalk. Tell him you seek the throne of Cyrena!"

There was no more. Elak awoke, listening to the
creaking of the galley's timbers and the whisper of
waves against the side. It was nearly dawn. He rose,
went on deck, and searched the horizon under a shield-
ing palm.

To the right, breaking the gray cliffs, was a gap.
Beyond it—an island. And on the island a castle
loomed, part of the rock, it seemed, growing from it.

The galley swept on. And now Elak saw that a river
ran between the broken cliffs. At its mouth was a
delta, made of reddish sand.

So, in the cold, lowering dawn, Elak and Lycon left
the galley. Willing oarsmen rowed them to shore. The
two climbed the northern cliff and stood staring around.
Inland the plateau stretched unbroken by tree or bush,
windswept and desolate. To the west lay the Ocean
Sea, chill and forbidding.

"Perhaps this Aynger of your dream dwells in that
castle," Lycon said, pointing and shivering. "One of
the men told me this is Kiriath. To the north, beyond
the mountains, lies Cyrena."

Elak said somberly, "I know. And Sepher rules
over Kiriath—Sepher, whom Karkora has taken for
his own. Well—come on."

They set out along the edge of the cliff. The wind
blew coldly, and brought to them a thin, high piping
that seemed to come out of nowhere. Sad, mournful,

weird, it murmured half-heard in the air about the two.

And across the plateau a man came—a great gray man, roughly clad, with unkempt hair and iron-gray beard. He played upon a set of pipes, but put these away as he saw Elak and Lycon. He came closer and halted, with folded arms, waiting.

The man's face might have been chipped from the rough rocks of this land. It was harsh and strong and forbidding, and the cool gray eyes were like the sea.

"What do you seek here?" he asked. His voice was deep and not at all unpleasant.

Elak hesitated. "Aynger. Aynger of Amenalk. Do you know of him?"

"I am Aynger."

For a heartbeat there was silence. Then Elak said, "I seek the throne of Cyrena."

Laughter sprang into the gray eyes. Aynger of Amenalk reached out a huge hand and gripped Elak's arm, squeezing it painfully. He said, "Dalan sent you! Dalan!"

Elak nodded.

"But it is not me you seek. It is Mayana—the daughter of Poseidon. You must seek her there." He pointed to the distant castle on the island. "Her power alone can aid you. But first—come."

He led the way to the cliff's edge. A perilous, narrow path led down the jagged face; Aynger started along it with sure-footed ease, and Elak and Lycon followed more gingerly. Far below, the breakers tore upon the rocks; seabirds called shrilly.

The path ended at a cave-mouth. Aynger entered, beckoning to the others. The cavern widened into a high-arched chamber, obviously Aynger's home. He gestured to a heap of furs and gave each of his guests a great horn of mead.

"So. Dalan sent you. I had wondered. Orander is dead. Once the Pallid One has set his seal on a man, there is escape in death alone."

"Karkora," Elak said musingly. "What is he? Do you know, Aynger?"

"You must seek your answer from Mayana, on the isle. Only she knows. Mayana—of the seas. Let me tell you." The gray eyes grew bright with dream. A softness crept into the deep voice. "This land, on the western shore, is Amenalk. Not Kiriath. Once, long ago, Amenalk stretched far to the east. We were a great people then. But invaders come conquering, and now only this bit of land is left to us. Yet it is Amenalk. And I dwell here because in my veins runs the blood of kings."

Aynger flung back his gray, tousled head. "And for ages the castle on the isle had existed. None dwelt there. There were legends that even before the Amenalks held this land, an ancient sea-people made it their home. Sorcerers they were, warlocks and magicians. But they died and were forgotten. So, in time, my own people were scattered through Kiriath, and I dwelt here alone.

"Sepher ruled, well and wisely. One night he walked alone on the cliffs of Amenalk, and when he returned to his palace, he brought a bride with him. The bride was Mayana. Some say he found her in the island castle. Some say she rose from the waves. I think she is not human. She is one of the old sea-race—

"A shadow fell on the land. Out of the dark, out of the unknown, came Karkora. He took Sepher for his own. Mayana fled here, and dwells now in the castle, protected by her sorcery. And Karkora rules."

Aynger's gray beard jutted; his eyes were lambent pools. He said, "My people were a Druid race. We worshipped great Mider, as I do now. And I tell you that Karkora is a foulness and a horror—an evil that will spread through all the world if the Druids fail to destroy him. Mayana holds his secret. Mayana knows. You must go to her on her isle. For myself—" A mighty hand clenched. "I have king's blood, and my people live, though in bondage. I shall go through Kiriath and gather men. I think you will need armies, ere you sit on Cyrena's dragon throne. Well, I have an army for you, and for Mider."

Aynger reached behind him, brought out a huge war-hammer, bound with thongs. Laughter touched his grim face.

"We shall fight in the old way, woad-painted, without armor. And I think Helm-Breaker will taste blood again. If you get aid from Mayana—well. But with you or without you, man of Cyrena, Amenalk will go forth to battle!"

The great gray man towered against the cave-mouth, a grim, archaic figure, somehow strong with primeval menace. He stood aside, pointing.

"Your way lies there, to the isle. Mine lies inland. When we meet again, if we do, I shall have an army to give you."

Silently Elak moved past Aynger and went up the cliff path. Lycon trailed him. On the windy, treeless plateau he stood unmoving, while the gray giant passed him without a word and strode away, his war-hammer over one muscular shoulder, beard and hair flying in the wind.

Aynger grew small in the distance. Elak nodded to Lycon.

"I think we have a strong ally there. We'll need him. But now—this Mayana. If she can solve the riddle of Karkora, I'll find her though I have to swim."

"You won't have to," Lycon said, wiping his mouth. "Gods, that mead was good! There's a bridge to the isle—see? A narrow one, but it will serve. Unless she's set a dragon to guard it."

6. Mayana

By the tall obelisks, all seaweed-girt,
    Drift the pale dead of long and long ago,
Lovers and kings who may not more be hurt,
    Wounded by lips or by the dagger's blow.
                                —*The Sunken Towers*

From the cliff's edge a narrow bridge of rock jutted, a natural formation worn by wind and rain. It ended on a jagged ledge, at the back of which a black hole gaped. Elak said, "Lycon, wait here. I must take this road alone."

The little man disagreed profanely. But Elak was firm.

"It will be safer. So we won't both fall into the same trap. If I'm not back by sundown, come after me— you may be of aid then." Lycon could not help but realize the truth of this. He shrugged his fat shoulders.

"Very well. I'll wait in Aynger's cave. His mead was potent; I'm anxious to sample more. Luck, Elak."

Nodding, the Atlantean started along the bridge. He found it safer not to look down, but the surging roar of the breakers sounded disquietingly from beneath. Sea-birds mewed and called. The wind tore at his swaying body.

But at last he was across, and felt the firm stability of the rocky ground under his sandals. Without a backward glance he entered the cave-mouth. Almost immediately outside sounds dimmed and quieted.

The road led down—a natural passage, seemingly, that turned and twisted in the rock. Sand was gritty underfoot, with bits of shell here and there. For a time it was dark, and then a greenish, vague luminous glow appeared, apparently emanated by the sand on which he trod.

It was utterly silent.

Still the tunnel led down, till Elak's feet felt moisture beneath him. He hesitated, staring around. The rocky walls were dewed and sweating. A dank, salty odor was strong in his nostrils. Loosening his rapier in its scabbard, he went on.

The green glow brightened. The passage turned; Elak rounded the corner, and stood motionless, staring. Before him a vast cavern opened.

It was huge and terrifyingly strange. Low-roofed, stalactites hung in myriad shapes and colors over the broad expanse of an underground lake. The green shining was everywhere. The weight of the island above seemed to press down suffocatingly, but the air, despite a salt sea-smell, was fresh enough.

At his feet a sandy half-moon of a beach reached down to the motionless surface of the water. Further out, he could see, far down, vague shadows that resembled sunken buildings—fallen peristyles and columns; and far away, in the center of the lake, was an island.

Ruined marble crowned it. Only in the center a small temple seemed unharmed; it rose from shattered ruins in cool, white perfection. All around it the dead and broken city lay, to the water's edge and beyond. A submerged, forgotten metropolis lay before Elak.

Silence, and the pale green expanse of the waveless lake.

Softly Elak called, "Mayana." There was no response.

Frowning, he considered the task before him. He felt an odd conviction that what he sought lay in the temple on the islet, but there was no way of reaching it save by swimming. And there was something ominous about the motionless green of the waters.

Shrugging, Elak waded out. Icy chill touched his legs, crept higher about his loins and waist. He struck out strongly. And at first there was no difficulty; he made good progress.

But the water was very cold. It was salt, and this buoyed him up somewhat; yet when he glanced at the islet it seemed no nearer. Grunting, Elak buried his face in the waters and kicked vigorously.

His eyes opened. He looked down. He saw, beneath him, the sunken city.

Strange it was, and weird beyond imagination, to be floating above the wavering outline of these marble ruins. Streets and buildings and fallen towers were below, scarcely veiled by the luminous waters, but possessing a vague, shadowy indistinctness that made them half-unreal. A green haze clothed the city. A city of shadows—

And the shadows moved and drifted in the tideless sea. Slowly, endlessly, they crept like a stain over the marble. They took shape before Elak's eyes.

Not sea-shapes—no. The shadows of men walked in the sunken metropolis. With queer, drifting motion the shadows went to and fro. They met and touched and parted again in strange similitude of life.

Stinging, choking cold filled Elak's mouth and nostrils. He spluttered and struck out, realizing that he was far beneath the surface, that, unconsciously holding his breath, he had drifted into the depths. He fought his way up.

It was oddly difficult. Soft, clinging arms seemed to touch him; the water darkened. But his head broke the surface, and he drank deeply of the chill air. Only by swimming with all his strength could he keep from sinking. That inexplicable drag pulled him down.

He went under. His eyes were open, and he saw, far below, movement in the sunken city. The shadow-shapes were swirling up, rising, spinning like autumn leaves—rising to the surface. And shadows clustered about Elak, binding him with gossamer fetters. They clung feathery and tenacious as spider-webs.

The shadows drew him down into the shining depths. He struck out frantically. His head broke water once more; he saw the islet, closer now.

"Mayana!" he called. *"Mayana!"*

Rustling movement shook the shadows. A ripple of mocking laughter seemed to go through them. They closed in again, dim, impalpable, unreal. Elak went under once more, too exhausted to fight, letting the shadows have their will with him. Only his mind cried out desperately to Mayana, striving to summon her to his aid.

The waters brightened. The green glow flamed emerald-bright. The shadows seemed to pause with odd hesitation, as though listening.

Then suddenly they closed in on Elak. They bore him through the waters; he was conscious of swift movement amid whirling green fire.

The shadows carried him to the islet, bore him up as on a wave, and left him upon the sands.

The green light faded to its former dimness. Choking, coughing, Elak clambered to his feet. He stared around.

The shadows had vanished. Only the motionless lake stretched in the distance. He stood amid the ruins of the islet.

Hastily he staggered away from the water's marge, clambering across broken plinths and fallen pillars, making his way to the central temple. It stood in a tiny plaza, unmarred by time, but stained and discolored in every stone.

The brazen door gaped open. Unsteadily Elak climbed the steps and paused at the threshold. He looked upon a bare room, lit with the familiar emerald glow, featureless save for a curtain, on the further wall, made of some metallic cloth and figured with the trident of the sea-god.

There was no sound but Elak's hastened breathing. Then, abruptly, a low splashing came from beyond the curtain. It parted.

Beyond it was green light, so brilliant it was impossible to look upon. Silhouetted against the brightness for a moment loomed a figure—a figure of unearthly slimness and height. Only for a second did Elak see it; then the curtain swung back into place and the visitant was gone.

Whispering through the temple came a voice, like the soft murmur of tiny, rippling waves. And it said:

"I am Mayana. Why do you seek me?"

7. Karkora

And I saw a beast coming up out of the sea, having ten horns and seven heads, and on his horns ten diadems, and upon his heads names of blasphemy . . . and the dragon gave him his power, and his throne, and great authority.

—Revelations 13:1

Elak's wet hand crept to his rapier. There had been no menace in the whisper, but it was strangely—inhuman. And the silhouette he had seen was not that of any earthly woman.

Yet he answered quietly enough, no tremor in his voice:

"I seek the dragon throne of Cyrena. And I come to you for aid against Karkora."

There was silence. When the whisper came again, it had in it all the sadness of waves and wind.

"Must I aid you? Against Karkora?"

"You know what manner of being he is?" Elak questioned.

"Aye—I know that well." The metallic curtain shook. "Seat yourself. You are tired—how are you named?"

"Elak."

"Elak, then—listen. I will tell you of the coming of Karkora, and of Erykion the sorcerer. And of Sepher, whom I loved." There was a pause; then the low whisper resumed.

"Who I am, what I am, you need not know, but you should understand that I am not entirely human. My ancestors dwelt in this sunken city. And I—well, for ten years I took human shape and dwelt with Sepher as his wife. I loved him. And always I hoped to give him a son who would some day mount the throne. I hoped in vain, or so I thought.

"Now in the court dwelt Erykion, a wizard. His magic was not that of the sea, soft and kindly as the waves, but of a darker sort. Erykion delved in ruined temples and pored over forgotten manuscripts of strange lore. His vision went back even before the sea-folk sprang from the loins of Poseidon, and he opened the forbidden gates of Space and Time. He offered to give me a child, and I listened to him, to my sorrow.

"I shall not tell you of the months I spent in strange temples, before dreadful altars. I shall not tell you of Erykion's magic. I bore a son—dead."

The silver curtain shook; it was long before the unseen speaker resumed. "And this son was frightful. He was deformed in ways I cannot let myself remember. Sorcery had made him inhuman. Yet he was my son, my husband's son, and I loved him. When Erykion offered to give him life, I agreed to the price he demanded—even though the price was the child himself."

" 'I shall not harm him,' Erykion told me. 'Nay, I shall give him powers beyond those of any god or man. Some day he shall rule this world and others. Only give him to me, Mayana.' And I hearkened.

"Now of Erykion's sorcery I know little. Something had entered into the body of my son while I bore him, and what this thing was I do not know. It was dead, and it awoke. Erykion awoke it. He took this blind, dumb, maimed man-child and bore it to his home in the depths of the mountains. With his magic he deprived it of any vestige of the five senses. Only life remained, and the unknown dweller within.

"I remember something Erykion had once told me. 'We have in us a sixth sense, primeval and submerged, which can be very powerful once it is brought to light. I know how to do that. A blind man's hearing may become acute; his power goes to the senses remaining. If a child, at birth, be deprived of all five senses, his power will go to this sixth sense. My magic can insure that.' So Erykion made of my man-child a being blind and dumb and without consciousness, almost; for years he worked his spells and opened the gates of Time and Space, letting alien powers flood through. This sixth sense within the child grew stronger. And the dweller in his mind waxed great, unbound by the earthly fetters that bind humans. This is my son—my man-child—Karkora, the Pallid One!"

And silence. And again the whisper resumed.

"Yet it is not strange that I do not entirely hate and loathe Karkora. I know he is a burning horror and a thing that should not exist; yet I gave him birth. And so, when he entered the mind of Sepher, his father, I fled to this my castle. Here I dwell alone with my shadows. I strove to forget that once I knew the fields and skies and hearths of earth. Here, in my own place, I forgot.

"And you seek me to ask my aid." There was anger in the soft murmur. "Aid to destroy that which came from my flesh!"

Elak said quietly, "Is Karkora's flesh—yours?"

"By Father Poseidon, no! I loved the human part of Karkora, and little of that is left now. The Pallid One is—is—he has a thousand frightful powers, through his one strange sense. It has opened for him gateways that should remain always locked. He walks in other worlds, beyond unlit seas, across the nighted voids beyond earth. And I know he seeks to spread his dominion over all. Kiriath fell to him, and I think Cyrena. In time he will take all Atlantis, and more than that."

Elak asked, "This Erykion, the wizard—what of him?"

"I do not know," Mayana said. "Perhaps he dwells in his citadel yet, with Karkora. Not for years have I seen the sorcerer."

"Cannot Karkora be slain?"

There was a long pause. Then the whisper said, "I know not. His body, resting in the citadel, is mortal, but that which dwells within it is not. If you could reach the body of Karkora—even so you could not slay him."

"Nothing can kill the Pallid One?" Elak asked.

"Do not ask me this!" Mayana's voice said with angry urgency. "One thing, one talisman exists—and this I shall not and cannot give you."

"I am minded to force your talisman from you," Elak said slowly, "if I can. Yet I do not wish to do this thing."

From beyond the curtain came a sound that startled

the man—a low, hopeless sobbing that had in it all the bleak sadness of the mournful sea. Mayana said brokenly:

"It is cold in my kingdom, Elak—cold and lonely. And I have no soul, only my life, while it lasts. My span is long, but when it ends there will be only darkness, for I am of the sea-folk. Elak, I have dwelt for a time on earth, and I would dwell there again, in green fields with the bright cornflowers and daisies gay amid the grass—with the fresh winds of earth caressing me. The hearth-fires, the sound of human voices, and a man's love—my Father Poseidon knows how I long for these again."

"The talisman," Elak said.

"Aye, the talisman. You may not have it."

Elak said very quietly, "What manner of world will this be if Karkora should rule?"

There was a shuddering, indrawn breath. Mayana said, "You are right. You shall have the talisman, if you should need it. It may be that you can defeat Karkora without it. I only pray that it may be so. Here is my word, then: in your hour of need, and not until then, I shall send you the talisman. And now go. Karkora has an earthly vessel in Sepher. Slay Sepher. Give me your blade, Elak."

Silently Elak unsheathed his rapier and extended it hilt-first. The curtain parted. Through it slipped a hand.

A hand—inhuman, strange! Very slender and pale it was, milk-white, with the barest suggestion of scales on the smooth, delicate texture of the skin. The fingers were slim and elongated, seemingly without joints, and filmy webs grew between them.

The hand took Elak's weapon and withdrew behind the curtain. Then it reappeared, again holding the rapier. Its blade glowed with a pale greenish radiance.

"Your steel will slay Sepher now. And it will give him peace." Elak gripped the hilt; the unearthly hand made a quick archaic gesture above the weapon.

"So I send a message to Sepher, my husband. And—Elak—kill him swiftly. A thrust through the eye into the brain will not hurt too much."

Then, suddenly, the hand thrust out and touched Elak upon the brow. He was conscious of a swift dizziness, a wild exhaltation that surged through him in hot waves. Mayana whispered:

"You shall drink of my strength, Elak. Without it, you cannot hope to face Karkora. Stay with me for a moon—drinking the sea-power and Poseidon's magic."

"A moon—"

"Time will not exist. You will sleep, and while you sleep strength will pour into you. And when you awake, you may go forth to battle—strong!"

The giddiness mounted; Elak felt his senses leaving him. He whispered, "Lycon—I must give him a message—"

"Speak to him, then, and he will hear. My sorcery will open his ears."

Dimly, as though from far away, Elak heard Lycon's startled voice.

"Who calls me? Is it you, Elak? Where—I see no one on this lonely cliff."

"Speak to him!" Mayana commanded. And Elak obeyed.

"I am safe, Lycon. Here I must stay for one moon, alone. You must not wait. I have a task for you."

There was the sound of a stifled oath. "What task?"

"Go north to Cyrena. Find Dalan, or, failing that, gather an army. Cyrena must be ready when Kiriath marches. Tell Dalan, if you find him, what I have done, and that I will be with him in one moon. Then let the Druid guide your steps. And—Ishatar guide you, Lycon."

Softly came the far voice: "And Mother Ishtar be your shield. I'll obey. Farewell."

Green darkness drifted across Elak's vision.

Dimly, through closing eyes, he vaguely saw the curtain before him swept aside, and a dark silhouette moving forward—a shape slim and tall beyond human stature, yet delicately feminine withal. Mayana made a summoning gesture—and the shadows flowed into the temple.

They swept down upon Elak, bringing him darkness and cool, soothing quiet. He rested and slept, and the enchanted strength of the sea-woman poured into the citadel of his soul.

8. The Dragon's Throne

Dust of the stars was under our feet,
    glitter of stars above—
Wrecks of our wrath dropped reeling
    down as we fought and we
    spurned and we strove.
Worlds upon worlds we tossed aside,
    and scattered them to and fro,
The night that we stormed Valhalla, a
    million years ago!

                    —Kipling

The moon waxed and waned, and at last Elak awoke, on the further shore, by the cavern mouth that led to the upper world. The underground mere lay silent at his feet, still bathed in the soft green glow. In the distance the islet was, and he could make out the white outline of the temple upon it. The temple where he had slept for a month. But there was no sign of life. No shadows stirred in the depths beneath him.

Yet within himself he sensed a secret well of power that had not been there before.

Pondering, he retraced his steps through the winding passage, across the rock bridge to the high ramp of the plateau. The plain was deserted. The sun was westering, and a cold wind blew bleakly from the sea.

Elak shrugged. His gaze turned north, and his hand touched the rapier-hilt.

"First, a horse," he grunted. "And then—Sepher! A blade for the king's throat!"

So within two hours a mercenary soldier lay dead, his blood staining a leathern tunic, and Elak galloped north on a stolen steed. Hard and fast he rode, through Kiriath, and whispers were borne to his ears on the gusting winds. Sepher was no longer in his city, they said. At the head of a vast army he was sweeping north to the Gateway, the mountain pass that led to Cyrena. From the very borders of Kiriath warriors were coming in answer to the king's summons; mercenaries and adventurers flooded in to serve under Sepher. He paid well and promised rich plunder—the sack of Cyrena.

A trail of blood marked Elak's path. Two horses he rode to death. But at last the Gateway lay behind him; he had thundered through Sharn Forest and forded Monra River. Against the horizon towered a battlemented castle, and this was Elak's goal. Here Orander had ruled. Here was the dragon throne, the heart of Cyrena.

Elak rode across the drawbridge and into the courtyard. He cast his mount's reins to a gaping servitor, leaped from the horse, and raced across the yard. He knew each step of the way. In this castle he had been born.

And now the throne room, vast, high-ceilinged, warm with afternoon sunlight. Men were gathered there. Princes and lords of Cyrena. Barons, dukes, minor chieftains. By the throne—Dalan. And beside him, Lycon, round face set in unaccustomed harsh lines, for once sober and steady on his feet.

"By Mider!" Lycon roared. "Elak! *Elak!*"

The Atlantean pushed his way through the murmuring, undecided crowd. He came to stand beside the throne. His hand gripped Lycon's shoulder and squeezed painfully. The little man grinned.

"Ishtar be praised," Lycon murmured. "Now I can get drunk again."

Dalan said, "I watched you in the crystal, Elak. But I could not aid. The magic of the Pallid One battled my own. Yet I think you have other magic now—sea-sorcery." He turned to the mob. His lifted arms quieted them.

"This is your king," Dalan said.

Voices were raised, some in approbation, some in angry protest and objection. A tall, lean oldster shouted, "Aye—this is Zeulas, returned once more. This is Orander's brother."

"Be silent, Hira," another snapped. "This scarecrow Cyrena's king?"

Elak flushed and took a half-step forward. Dalan's voice halted him.

"You disbelieve, Gorlias?" he asked. "Well—d'you know of a worthier man? Will you sit on the dragon throne?"

Gorlias looked at the Druid with an oddly frightened air; he fell silent and turned away. The others broke into a renewed chorus of quarreling.

Hira silenced them. His lean face was triumphant. "There's one sure test. Let him take it."

He turned to Elak. "The lords of Cyrena have fought like a pack of snarling dogs since Orander's death. Each wanted the throne. Baron Kond yelled louder than the rest. Dalan offered him the dragon throne, in the name of Mider, if he could hold it."

From the others a low whisper went up—uneasy, fearful. Hira continued: "Kond mounted the dais a month ago and sat on the throne. And he died! The fires of Mider slew him."

"Aye," Gorlias whispered. "Let this Elak sit upon the throne!"

A chorus of assent rose. Lycon looked worried.

He murmured, "It's true, Elak. I saw it. Red fire came out of nowhere and burned Kond to a cinder."

Dalan was silent, his ugly face impassive. Elak, watching the Druid, could not read a message in the shallow black eyes.

Gorlias said, "If you can sit on the throne, I'll follow you. If not—you'll be dead. Well?"

Elak did not speak. He turned and mounted the dais. For a moment he paused before the great throne of Cyrena, his gaze dwelling on the golden dragon that writhed across its back, the golden dragons on the arms. For ages the kings of Cyrena had ruled from this seat, ruled with honor and chivalry under the dragon. And now Elak remembered how, in Poseidonia, he had felt unworthy to mount the throne.

Would the fires of Mider slay him if he took his dead brother's place?

Silently Elak prayed to his god. "If I'm unworthy," he told Mider, with no thought or irreverence, but as one warrior to another, "then slay me, rather than let the throne be dishonored. Yours is the judgment."

He took his place on the dragon throne.

Silence fell like a pall on the great room. The faces of the crowd were intent and strained. Lycon's breath came fast. The Druid's hands, hidden under the brown robe, made a quick, furtive gesture; his lips moved without sound.

Red light flashed out above the throne. Through the room a cry rose and mounted, wordless, fearful. The fires of Mider flamed up in glaring brilliance and cloaked Elak!

They hid him in a twisting crimson pall. They swirled about him, blazing with hot radiance.

They swept into a strange, fantastic shape—a coiling silhouette that grew steadily more distinct.

A dragon of flame coiled itself about Elak!

And suddenly it was gone. Lycon was gasping oaths. The others were milling about in a confused mob. Dalan stood motionless, smiling slightly.

And on the dragon throne Elak sat unharmed! No breath of fire had scorched or blistered him; no heat had reddened his skin. His eyes were blazing; he sprang up and unsheathed his rapier. Silently he lifted it.

There was a clash of ringing blades. A forest of bright steel lifted. A great shout bellowed out.

The lords of Cyrena swore allegiance to their king!

Now, however, Elak found that his task had scarcely begun. The armies of Sepher were not yet in Cyrena; the king of Kiriath was waiting beyond the mountain barrier till he had gathered his full strength. But he would march soon, and Cyrena must by then be organized to resist him.

"Karkora didn't invade Kiriath," Elak said to Dalan one day as they rode through Sharn Forest. "He invaded the mind of the king instead. Why does he depend on armies to conquer Cyrena?"

Dalan's shapeless brown robe flapped against his horse's flanks. "Have you forgotten Orander? He tried there, and failed. Then there was no single ruler here. If he'd stolen the mind of Kond or Gorlias he'd still

have had the other nobles against him. And conquer
Cyrena he must, for it's the stronghold of Mider and
the Druids. Karkora knows he must destroy us before
he can rule this world and others, as he intends. So he
uses Sepher and Kiriath's army. Already he's given
orders to slaughter each Druid."

"What of Aynger?" Elak demanded.

"A message came from him today. He has gathered
his Amenalks in the mountains beyond the Gateway.
They wait for our word. Barbarians, Elak—but good
allies. They fight like mad wolves."

Cyrena rose to arms. From steading and farm, castle
and citadel, city and fortress, the iron men came streaming. The roads glittered with bright steel and rang to
the clash of horses' hoofs. The dragon banners fluttered in the chill winds of winter.

Rise and arm! In the name of Mider and the Dragon,
draw your blade! So the messengers called; so the
word went forth. Rise against Kiriath and Sepher!

The defending swords of Cyrena flashed bright. They
thirsted for blood.

And Sepher of Kiriath rode north against the Dragon.

9. The Hammer of Aynger

And a strange music went with him,
    Loud and yet strangely far;
The wild pipes of the western land,
Too keen for the ear to understand,
Sang high and deathly on each hand
    When the dead man went to war.

—Chesterton

The first snows of winter lay white on the Gateway.
All around towered the tall, frosted peaks of the mountain barrier, and a bitter wind gusted strongly through

the pass. Within a month deep snow and avalanches would make the Gateway almost impassable.

The sky was cloudless, of chill pale blue. In the thin air everything stood out in startling clarity; voices carried far, as did the crunching of snow underfoot and the crackle of rocks deep-bitten by the iron cold.

The pass was seven miles long, and narrow in only a few spots. For the most part it was a broad valley bounded by the craggy cliffs. Canyons opened into it.

Dawn had flamed and spread in the east. The sun hung above a snow-capped peak. South of a narrow portion of the Gateway, part of Cyrena's army waited. Behind them were reinforcements. Upon the crags were archers and arbalesters, waiting to rain death upon the invaders. Steel-silver moved against a background of white snow and black grim rocks.

Elak was astride a war-horse upon a small hillock. Hira rode up, gaunt old face keenly alert, joy of battle in the faded eyes. He saluted swiftly.

"The bowmen are placed and ready," he said. "We've got rocks and boulders into position to crush Sepher's army, should it get too far."

Elak nodded. He wore chain-armor, gold encrusted, with a close-fitting helm of gleaming steel. His wolf face was taut with excitement, and he curbed the steed as it curvetted.

"Good, Hira. You are in command there. I trust your judgment."

As Hira departed, Dalan and Lycon arrived, the latter flushed and unsteady in his saddle. He gripped a drinking-horn and swilled mead from it occasionally. His long sword slapped the horse's flank.

"The minstrels will make a song of this battle," he observed. "Even the gods will eye it with some interest."

"Don't blaspheme," Dalan said, and turned to Elak. "I've a message from Aynger. His savage Amenalks wait in that side canyon—" The Druid flung out a pointing hand—"and will come when we need them."

"Aye," Lycon broke in, "I saw them. Madmen and demons! They've painted themselves blue as the sky and are armed with scythes and flails and hammers, among other things. And they're playing tunes on their pipes and bragging, each louder than the other. Only Aynger sits silent, fondling his Helm-Breaker. He looks like an image chipped out of gray stone."

At the memory Lycon shivered and then gulped the rest of the mead. "Faith," he said sadly, "the horn's empty. Well, I must get more." And off he went, reeling in the saddle.

"Drunken little dog," Elak remarked. "But his hand will be steady enough on the sword."

Far away, a trumpet shouted shrilly, resounding among the peaks. Now the foreguard of Sepher's army was visible as a glitter of steel on casques and lifted spearheads. Along the pass they came, steadily, inexorably, in close battle formation. The trumpet sang and skirled.

In response, drums of Cyrena snarled answer. They rose to a throbbing, menacing roar. Cymbals clashed resoundingly. The banners of the dragon flung out stiffly in the cold blast.

Kiriath rode without a standard. In silence, save for the clashing of metallic hoofs and the angry screaming of the trumpet, they came, a vast array that flooded into the valley. Pikemen, archers, knights, mercenaries—on they came, intent on conquest and plunder. Elak could not see Sepher, though his gaze searched for the king.

And slowly the invaders increased their speed, almost imperceptibly at first, and then more swiftly till through the Gateway Kiriath charged and thundered, lances lowered, swords flashing. The trumpet shouted urgent menace.

Dalan's gross body moved uneasily in his saddle. He unsheathed his long blade.

Elak looked around. Behind him the army waited. Everything was ready.

The king of Cyrena rose in his stirrups. He lifted his rapier and gestured with it. He shouted:

"Charge! Ho—the Dragon!"

With a roar, Cyrena swept forward down the pass. Closer and closer the two vast forces came. The drums roared death. From the icy peaks the clamor resounded thunderously.

A cloud of arrows flew. Men fell, screaming. Then, with a crash that seemed to shake the mountainous walls of the Gateway, the armies met.

It was like a thunderclap. All sanity and coherence vanished in a maelstrom of red and silver-steel, a whirlpool, an avalanche of thrusting spears, speeding arrows, slashing blades. Elak was instantly surrounded by foes. His rapier flew swift as a striking snake; blood stained its length. His horse shrieked and fell hamstrung to the ground. Elak leaped free and saw Lycon charging to the rescue. The little man was wielding a sword almost as long as himself, but his pudgy fingers handled it with surprising ease. He lopped off one man's head, ruined another's face with a well-placed kick of his steel-shod foot, and then Elak had leaped astride a riderless steed.

Again he plunged into the fray. The brown bald head of Dalan was rising and falling some distance away; the Druid roared like a beast as his sword whirled and flew and bit deep. Blood soaked the brown robe. Dalan's horse seemed like a creature possessed; it screamed shrilly blowing through red, inflamed nostrils, snapped viciously and reared and struck with knife-edged hoofs. Druid and charger raged like a burning pestilence amid the battle; sweat and blood mingled on Dalan's toad face.

Elak caught sight of Sepher. The ruler of Kiriath, a bronzed bearded giant, towered above his men, fighting in deadly silence. Smiling wolfishly, Elak drove toward the king.

From the distance came the thin high wailing of pipes. Out of the side canyon men came pouring—barbarous men, half naked, their lean bodies smeared blue with woad. The men of Aynger! At their head ran Aynger himself, his gray beard flying, brandishing the hammer Helm-Breaker. The gray giant leaped upon a rock, gesturing toward the forces of Kiriath.

"Slay the oppressors!" he bellowed. "Slay! Slay!"

The weird pipes of the Amenalks shrilled their answer. The blue-painted men swept forward—

From the ranks of Sepher an arrow flew. It sped toward Aynger. It pierced his bare throat and drove deep—deep!

The Amenalk leader bellowed; his huge body arched like a bow. Blood spouted from his mouth.

A battalion charged out from the ranks of Kiriath. They sped toward the Amenalks, lances lowered, pennons flying.

Aynger fell! Dead, he toppled from the rock into the lifted arms of his men. The pipes skirled. The Amenalks, bearing their leader, turned and fled back into the valley!

Cursing, Elak dodged a shrewd thrust, killed his assailant, and spurred toward Sepher. The hilt of his rapier was slippery with blood. His body, under the chain-armor, was a mass of agonizing bruises; blood gushed from more than one wound. His breath rasped in his throat. The stench of sweat and gore choked him; he drove over ground carpeted with the writhing bodies of men and horses.

Down the valley Dalan fought and bellowed his rage. The battle-thunder crashed on the towering crags and sent deafening echoes through the Gateway.

Still the trumpets of Kiriath called; still the drums and cymbals of Cyrena shouted their defiance.

And still Sepher slew, coldly, remorselessly, his bronzed face expressionless.

Kiriath gathered itself and charged. The forces of Cyrena were forced back, fighting desperately each step of the way. Back to the narrowing of the pass they were driven.

High above the archers loosed death on Kiriath.

With ever-increasing speed Sepher's army thrust forward. A gust of panic touched the ranks of Cyrena. A dragon banner was captured and slashed into flying shreds by keen blades.

Vainly Elak strove to rally his men. Vainly the Druid bellowed threats.

The retreat became a rout. Into the narrow defile the army fled, jammed into a struggling, fighting mob. An orderly retreat might have saved the day, for Kiriath could have been trapped in the narrow pass and crippled by boulders thrust down by the men stationed above. As it was, Cyrena was helpless, waiting to be slaughtered.

Kiriath charged.

Quite suddenly Elak heard a voice. In through the mountains. Above the call of trumpets came the thin wailing of pipes. Louder it grew, and louder.

From the side canyon the blue barbarians of Amenalk

rushed in disorderly array. In their van a group ran together with lifted shields. Upon the shields was the body of Aynger!

Weirdly, eerily, the ear-piercing skirling of the pipes of Amenalk shrilled out. The woad-painted savages, mad with blood-frenzy, raced after the corpse of their ruler.

Dead Aynger led his men to war!

The Amenalks fell on the rear of the invaders. Flails and scythes and blades swung and glittered, and were lifted dripping red. A giant sprang upon the shield-platform, astride the body of Aynger. In his hand he brandished a war-hammer.

"Helm-Breaker!" he shouted. "Ho—Helm-Breaker!"

He leaped down; the great hammer rose and fell and slaughtered. Casques and helms shattered under the smashing blows; the Amenalk wielded Helm-Breaker in a circle of scarlet death about him.

"Helm-Breaker! Ho—slay! Slay!"

Kiriath swayed in confusion under the onslaught. In that breathing-space Elak and Dalan rallied their army. Cursing, yelling, brandishing steel, they whipped order out of chaos. Elak snatched a dragon banner from the dust, lifted it high.

He turned his horse's head down the valley. One hand lifting the standard, one gripping his bared rapier, he drove his spurs deep.

"Ho, the Dragon!" he shouted. *"Cyrena! Cyrena!"*

Down upon Kiriath he thundered. Behind him rode Lycon and the Druid. And after them the remnants of an army poured. Hira led his archers from the cliffs. The arbalasters came bounding like mountain goats, snatching up swords and spears, pouring afoot after their king.

"Cyrena!"

The drums and cymbals roared out again. Through the tumult pierced the thin, weird calling of the pipes.

"Helm-Breaker! Slay! Slay!"

And then madness—a hell of shouting, scarlet battle through which Elak charged, Dalan and Lycon beside him, riding straight for the bushy beard that marked Sepher. On and on, over screaming horses and dying men, through a whirlpool of flashing, thirsty steel, thrusting, stabbing, hacking—

The face of Sepher rose up before Elak.

The bronzed face of Kiriath's king was impassive; in his cold eyes dwelt something inhuman. Involuntarily an icy shudder racked Elak. As he paused momentarily, the brand of Sepher whirled up and fell shattering in a great blow.

Elak did not try to escape. He poised his rapier, flung himself forward in his stirrups, sent the sharp blade thrusting out.

The enchanted steel plunged into Sepher's throat. Simultaneously Elak felt his back go numb under the sword-cut; his armor tore raggedly. The blade dug deep into the body of the war-horse.

The light went out of Sepher's eyes. He remained for a heart-beat upright in his saddle. Then his face changed.

It darkened with swift corruption. It blackened and rotted before Elak's eyes. Death, so long held at bay, sprang like a crouching beast.

A foul and loathsome thing fell forward and tumbled from the saddle. It dropped to the bloody ground and lay motionless. Black ichor oozed out from the chinks of the armor; the face that stared up blindly at the sky was a frightful thing.

And without warning darkness and utter silence dropped down and shrouded Elak.

10. The Black Vision

And the devil that deceived them was cast into the lake
of fire and brimstone, where are also the beast and the
false prophet; and they shall be tormented day and night
for ever and ever.

—Revelations 20:10

He felt again the dizzy vertigo that presaged the coming of Karkora. A high-pitched, droning whine rang
shrilly in his ears; he felt a sense of swift movement.
A picture came.

Once more he saw the giant crag that towered amid
the mountains. The dark tower lifted from its summit.
Elak was drawn forward; iron gates opened in the
base of the pinnacle. They closed as he passed through.

The high whining had ceased. It was cimmerian
dark. But in the gloom a Presence moved and stirred
and was conscious of Elak.

The Pallid One sprang into view.

He felt a sense of whirling disorientation; his thoughts
grew inchoate and confused. They were slipping away,
spinning into the empty dark. In their place something
crept and grew; a weird mental invasion took place.
Power of Karkora surged through Elak's brain, forcing back the man's consciousness and soul, thrusting
them out and back into the void. A dreamlike sense of
unreality oppressed Elak.

Silently he called upon Dalan.

Dimly a golden flame flickered up, far away. Elak
heard the Druid's voice whispering faintly, out of the
abyss.

"Mider—aid him, Mider—"

Fires of Mider vanished. Elak felt again the sense of
swift movement. He was lifted—

The darkness was gone. Gray light bathed him. He

was, seemingly, in the tower on the summit of the crag—the citadel of Karkora. But the place was unearthly!

The planes and angles of the room in which Elak stood were warped and twisted insanely. Laws of matter and geometry seemed to have gone mad. Crawling curves swept obscenely in strange motion; there was no sense of perspective. The gray light was alive. It crept and shimmered. And the white shadow of Karkora blazed forth with chill and dreadful radiance.

Elak remembered the words of Mayana, the sea-witch, as she spoke of her monstrous son Karkora.

"He walks in other worlds, beyond unlit seas, across the nighted voids beyond earth."

Through the whirling chaos a face swam, inhuman, mad, and terrible. A man's face, indefinably bestial-ized and degraded, with a sparse white beard and glaring eyes. Again Elak recalled Mayana's mention of Erykion, the wizard who had created the Pallid One.

"Perhaps he dwells in his citadel yet, with Karkora. Not for years have I seen the sorcerer."

If this were Erykion, then he had fallen victim to his own creation. The warlock was insane. Froth dribbled on the straggling beard; the mind and soul had been drained from him.

He was swept back and vanished in the grinding maelstrom of the frightful lawless geometrical chaos. Elak's eyes ached as he stared, unable to stir a muscle. The shadow of the Pallid One gleamed whitely before him.

The planes and angles changed; pits and abysses opened before Elak. He looked through strange gateways. He saw other worlds, and with his flesh shrinking in cold horror he stared into the depths of the

Nine Hells. Frightful life swayed into motion before his eyes. Things of inhuman shape rose out of nighted depths. A charnel wind choked him.

The sense of mental assault grew stronger; Elak felt his mind slipping away under the dread impact of alien power. Unmoving, deadly, Karkora watched—

"Mider," Elak prayed. "Mider—aid me!"

The mad planes swept about faster, in a frantic saraband of evil. The dark vision swept out, opening wider vistas before Elak. He saw unimaginable and blasphemous things, Dwellers in the outer dark, horrors beyond earth-life—

The white shadow of Karkora grew larger. The crawling radiance shimmered leprously. Elak's senses grew dulled; his body turned to ice. Nothing existed but the now gigantic silhouette of Karkora; the Pallid One reached icy fingers into Elak's brain.

The assault mounted like a rushing tide. There was no aid anywhere. There was only evil, and madness, and black, loathsome horror.

Quite suddenly Elak heard a voice. In it was the murmur of rippling waters. He knew Mayana spoke to him by strange magic.

"In your hour of need I bring you the talisman against my son Karkora."

The voice died; the thunder of the seas roared in Elak's ears. A green veil blotted out the mad, shifting planes and angles. In the emerald mists shadows floated—the shadows of Mayana.

They swept down upon him. Something was thrust into his hand—something warm and wet and slippery.

He lifted it, staring. He gripped a heart, bloody, throbbing—alive!

The heart of Mayana! The heart beneath which

Karkora had slumbered in the womb! The talisman against Karkora!

A shrill droning rose suddenly to a skirling shriek of madness, tearing at Elak's ears, knifing through his brain. The bleeding heart in Elak's hand drew him forward. He took a slow step, another.

About him the gray light pulsed and waned; the white shadow of Karkora grew gigantic. The mad planes danced swiftly.

And then Elak was looking down at a pit on the edge of which he stood. Only in the depths of the deep hollow was the instability of the surrounding matter lacking. And below was a shapeless and flesh-colored hulk that lay inert ten feet down.

It was man-sized and naked. But it was not human. The pulpy arms had grown to the sides; the legs had grown together. Not since birth had the thing moved by itself. It was blind, and had no mouth. Its head was a malformed grotesquerie of sheer horror.

Fat, deformed, utterly frightful, the body of Karkora rested in the pit.

The heart of Mayana seemed to tear itself from Elak's hand. Like a plummet it dropped, and fell upon the breast of the horror below.

A shuddering, wormlike motion shook Karkora. The monstrous body writhed and jerked.

From the bleeding heart blood crept out like a stain. It spread over the deformed horror. In a moment Karkora was no longer flesh-colored, but red as the molten sunset.

And, abruptly, there was nothing in the pit but a slowly widening pool of scarlet. The Pallid One had vanished.

Simultaneously the ground shook beneath Elak; he felt himself swept back. For a second he seemed to view the crag and tower from a distance, against the background of snow-tipped peaks.

The pinnacle swayed; the crag rocked. They crashed down in thunderous ruin.

Only a glimpse did Elak get; then the dark curtain blotted out his consciousness. He saw, dimly, a pale oval. It grew more distinct. And it was the face of Lycon bending above Elak, holding a brimming cup to the latter's lips.

"Drink!" he urged. "Drink deep!"

Elak obeyed, and then thrust the liquor away. He stood up weakly.

He was in the pass of the Gateway. Around him the men of Cyrena rested, with here and there a blue-painted warrior of Amenalk. Corpses littered the ground. Vultures were already circling against the blue.

Dalan was a few paces away, his shallow black eyes regarding Elak intently. He said, "Only one thing could have saved you in Karkora's stronghold. One thing—"

Elak said grimly, "It was given me. Karkora is slain."

A cruel smile touched the Druid's lipless mouth. He whispered, "So may all enemies of Mider die."

Lycon broke in, "We've conquered, Elak. The army of Kiriath fled when you killed Sepher. And, gods, I'm thirsty!" He rescued the cup and drained it.

Elak did not answer. His wolf face was dark; in his eyes deep sorrow dwelt. He did not see the triumphant banners of the dragon tossing in the wind, nor did he envision the throne of Cyrena that waited. he was remembering a low, rippling voice that spoke with longing of the fields and hearth-fires of earth, a slim, inhuman hand that had reached through a curtain—a sea-witch who had died to save a world to which she had never belonged.

The shadow was lifted from Atlantis; over Cyrena the golden dragon ruled under great Mider. But in a sunken city of marble beauty the shadows of Mayana would mourn for Poseidon's daughter.

THE BRIGADIER IN CHECK— AND MATE

by Sterling E. Lanier

First Move

It was a windy and wild March evening in lower Manhattan. As I went along the canyons of what was once a familiar Greenwich village area, or its western fringe, I looked despairingly for any sign of a vacant taxi. The few that passed were always full and their lights were smudged by the wind-blown dirt and water. I had come from a meeting of major shareholders near 12th St. and had tried then to walk to Fifth Ave. It grew very dark quickly and began both to rain and blow together as it did. It was not a part of New York I'd been in for years, and though I had a hat and light raincoat, I soon became half-lost and thoroughly miserable. It was not really cold, being in the mid-forties Fahrenheit, but it was the classic English term for a Winter's day, or "short, dark and dirty."

As I groped futilely along the sloshy streets, I cursed my own stupidity for not having arranged some kind of a car pick-up. There were few people about and that made me feel a little safer, since this was a known haunt of drug addicts and the nastier lunatic fringe of the once-famous Art World of the old Greenwich Vil-

lage. I kept well out toward the curb and the running
gutters anyway, and avoided the dark alley mouths
which gaped like black funnel vents between the dirty
and narrow house fronts. I glanced at my wrist watch
and saw that it was after 6:30 already. While the dirty
rain blew in my face, I wondered if I ought to try one
of the local bars, if I could find one, and risk being
mugged or poisoned, just to get out of this blowing
murk and trying to find out exactly where I was, as
well as how to leave it as quickly as possible.

I skirted a pile of soaked paper bags, crammed with
filth and garbage, then almost tripped over what might
still be *live* garbage, a ragged body coiled around the
far side of the trash mountain on the wet pavement.
Its bearded mouth was open and moved faintly so I
guess it was still alive.

Half a block further on, the blurred light of a passing car suddenly showed me a possible shelter, at least
of a sort, quite close to me.

It was a larger opening, between two narrow houses,
each of at least six-story height. This opening was not
an alley, though quite dark, but had a smooth pavement with a worn, brick walk running down its center.
I had heard that a few, old, set-back houses of the
1840 period, or what the English still call "mews," still
existed in lower Manhattan, though I'd never seen
one. I turned left into this one, hopefully as well as
carefully, keeping my left arm up before my eyes and
my body bent as well, in case a blow should come out
at me suddenly. The rain still fell steadily but at least I
was out of that lousy, gale wind.

Ahead of me, down the path, I could see a faint
light, though it came from one side rather than straight
ahead. As I walked slowly and carefully forward, I
saw that the little walkway curved to the right around
one of the two flanking houses, and that the dim light

came from around this corner. Keeping to the exact center of the brick strip, I moved cautiously around the curve, wondering what I would find.

There before me was a little house! It was about fifty feet away and the light came from a couple of curtained windows on the ground floor, for it had two floors under a low, peaked roof. There was even a minute garden or at least two tiny plots with some plants in them, one on each side of the front step and guarded by wooden fencelets a foot high. I gaped at this refugee from Grimm's fairy tales in astonishment. A thing like this buried in the canyons of lower New York City was indeed a thing to gape at.

My surprise and amusement got a quick ending and a scary one, too. One corner of my right eye suddenly picked up movement and my head swivelled to focus while my knees bent as well. Not ten feet away, in a darker angle of tall building was a metal fence, which I guessed was iron. Against this stood two tall, shrouded figures, silent and yet poised. They made no move, though one must have done so earlier to catch my attention, and simply watched me steadily. They were at least as tall as I am and I'm just under six feet. They made no forward movement, just watched, but in a way that somehow conveyed menace.

While the water ran down my hat brim and the moaning of the wind yowled far overhead and the faint noises of intermittent traffic barely pierced the noises of the natural world, I stared at the two silent shapes through the rainy gloom and they stared back at me. The only light, that of the shaded windows, made it possible to see only that two dim figures were watching one. At last, my nerve broke, which, in my own defense, is something it had never done under night attacks in Korea.

"I beg your pardon," I called out. "I'm afraid I got

lost and came in here looking for a phone and directions." I kept my voice from cracking, but it was an effort. The response was startling. One of the two stepped forward instantly, revealing itself as a man my size and also wearing a slouch hat and belted raincoat, a man who held out his right hand in welcome. When he spoke, my tight control of my nerves almost dissolved at the shock.

"My dear Parker," said a very familiar voice, "I fear we appeared a bit dangerous. There are folk in your city, and not far off either, whom one would rather not meet at night, eh? Well, Old man, you've found my private digs which is more than anyone else has done, at least so far."

By this time, my rather limp hand was being firmly clasped by that of Donald Ffellowes, lately a Brigadier General of the British Army and, at this range, I could see the glitter of his blue eyes and the grin on his smooth face.

"My God, Sir," I stammered, "I thought you stayed in hotels and we all know you like privacy and I assure you that I never, I mean I really am lost and I . . ."

The Brigadier laughed out loud or rather, gave a deep chuckle. He pointed at the tiny house and said, "I own the place and have for some years. I want your word that you'll tell no one else of it and (here, he paused a second) about anything else, right?" I could do nothing but nod my spinning head in response.

"Good man. My wife and I were getting a breath of fresh air and then I was going up town to the club. Come and meet her."

Another jolt to my already dazed brain! "My wife!" None of us at the club had ever known Ffellowes was married! He had never so much as mentioned a wife, past or present, any more than he'd mentioned owning a very old house in the labyrinths of lower Manhattan!

I'm not a money-minded person as a rule but I was a bit staggered by another idea. Every surface foot of the Brigadier's property could have been layered in platinum and even then the land itself would have been worth more!

As we walked forward together, the second figure never moved to meet us but remained tall and silent in the shadows. Tall indeed. In the bad and angled light and through the screen of falling water, I could see her head was bare and the glint of a copper color. She wore a long cloak, of something dark and almost ankle-length. A ray of light caught the shine of ordinary rubbers and a hint of wooly socks, heavy ones.

Ffellowes' hand stopped us both when we were about six feet away from the lady but I am not sure that had I been alone, I would have come even that close. I saw great eyes, lambent and fiery, which seemed to have a luminescence of their own and broad cheekbones. The mouth too was broad but closed and there was another strange feature. The facial skin was not pale but a strange neutral hue and it was not shining from the rain but somehow, well, dull and sombre. But these thoughts came late. Just then, all I could think of were those great, burning eyes, wide apart and fixed on a level with my own or even above my own, in a steady, unwinking stare that was almost hypnotic. They were not the so-called "cat eyes" and had normal pupils but there was a glowing lambency about them, so that even in the murk and shadow, they seemed to glow with a sort of brown heat. Imagine a mildly luminous, chocolate milk shake and you'll get some idea how it affected me.

Ffellowes' voice shook me out of my paralysis, or, to use a better phrase, in its older and better meaning, Glamour. "This is Jim Parker, Love. You've heard me speak of him often. A good friend, remember?"

His wife bowed her head in a way that was both casual and somehow condescending, and even almost disdainful. I was damn glad to be free of those strange, flowing eyes but found myself just a little bit irritated, both at the regal head movement and the failure to even try to shake hands. *Grand Duchess meets loathsome peasant to whom she must be polite,* was the thought that flickered through my brain at that point.

The Brigadier either saw something he didn't like or used some ESP. One never knew what he was capable of or what he saw. "My dear Parker, my wife's a foreigner. Doesn't grip hands, you know. Just as bad as the British in that respect."

Then for the first time, I heard her voice. Never had I heard anything like it before and what with my surprise, the wild evening and this very odd meeting, well, it was really one more shock!

"I know very well, My Dear, who Mr. Parker is. He writes those tales for magazines. Those stories about you, he writes and then calls you by a name that is not yours in them, so that no one will ever know your real name or what your real family is." If it were possible to contemplate a very large cat's purr, mingled with a deep contralto, that would give one a vague idea. My own thought as she spoke conveyed my instant feeling: *Lioness Diva;* just those two words.

Ffellowes (which he will remain, now and in the future) was not a bit embarrassed. He grinned at me and stepped back just a little, anticipating his wife's next move.

She stepped forward, her right hand out now, and I instinctively shook it. It was as large as mine, with a smooth-palmed, tight-glove, as warm as flesh, though I could feel the edge of the furry backing. Those feelings came later for then I could only stare into the broad-cheeked face and the great, glowing eyes.

"You two go on away now, Donald. Take Mr. Parker up to your club and tell him some other histories of your past that he can write about." With that, she nodded to me, her wide, full-lipped mouth pleasant but with no trace of a smile, turned on her heel and headed up the path. In seconds the cottage door of the fabulous little house had opened and shut behind her stately back. I was left with the Brigadier in the shadowed court, frankly struck dumb and trying as hard as I could to keep my mouth tight shut so that it wouldn't fall open and leave me gaping.

The Brigadier's chuckle helped somewhat. "We'll take her at her word, Parker, Old fellow. Don't look so staggered. Few folk meet my Phaona but those who have were all a bit numbed by it. Frankly, I am at times myself. She takes one that way and it makes no mind whether it's Manhattan or a remote hamlet in the woods." He turned and led me along the far side of the alley to where a recessed door stood open just enough to show it was a hidden garage. In three minutes we were out on the murky street in his beautiful old Lagonda and humming our way uptown.

Before we had parked two blocks away from the club's front door, he said only one more thing.

"I've known those printed stories of yours since the first one came out, Parker. Very good, too. As long as you kept my title and real name and rank out of 'em and scramble the dates and areas as you do so neatly, I haven't the slightest objection." His head turned and the blue eyes fixed on mine for just one second only. They were utterly cold and frozen. "You're a gentleman and a man of honor. Please remain so."

It took a real effort to get out of the car but I managed it and in five minutes we were alone in a corner of the Club Library.

The Brigadier called for hot coffee and when we'd

been served he leaned back in his leather chair and looked at me with his old smile.

"Parker, I'm going to tell you and you alone, the story of my wife. It should interest you, I think. And I, My dear fellow, will be most intrigued indeed to see how you deal with this tale in one of your charming romances." Again the deep chuckle.

Counter Move

It was a windy March afternoon in the Club. I had got out of my office a trifle earlier than I should, simply out of restlessness. Maybe it was a sign of Spring but the gloomy, windy, cold city sure didn't look it.

I wandered into the library with a drink, thinking I might find an entertaining foreign journal or something, just to kill an hour with. I found something better. *Much* better.

The big room was empty except for one reading alcove where a small light illumined a bent-over shape I knew well and had missed for months.

"Brigadier!" I let out a joyful yelp. "Where you been, Sir? We were afraid you'd gone abroad for good or something. How are you, anyway?"

Brigadier Donald Ffellowes' cold, blue eyes took me in and I thought or maybe hoped, warmed a bit. His smooth reddish face had no lines but it never did and his short-cut, white hair was neatly combed as always. He had a pile of battered-looking books next to him and had one open on his lap which he'd just been leafing through.

"Hullo, Parker. Nice to see you too. Just been havin' a dekko at some oldish stuff, mostly fiction here. I picked up a batch of things I wanted down in one of those caves on, where is it? Oh yes, 4th Ave.

Take a look, My lad. Sort of thing I expect would interest you perhaps."

By the desk lamp on the small table in the alcove, I could indeed see familiar names on the covers, though most of the titles were unknown to me. There was, for God's sake, *Tarzan and the Jewels of Opar!* Next to Burroughs lay a Rider Haggard I'd never seen, titled *Heu-Heu or the Monster.* Finally, there was something by one McNeile, whom I didn't know, called *Island of Terror.* Just a collection of old time thrillers, that was all.

The Brigadier smiled at the perplexity in my face, and shut the rather massive tome in his lap. He then held that one up for me to see the somewhat lurid jacket plainly. I read *Abominable Snowmen; legend come to life.*

Ffellowes laughed gently. "It's all right, Parker. I'm not zany yet. Let's say I am doing a spot of research and using some rather odd sources for my digging at, eh?"

Behind me, I heard movement and then before I could even turn, a cry or several cries of delight. "He's back, you guys! The Brigadier's come back. Come on over, come on up and let's see what he's been doing. Parker's got to him but so can the rest. Come on!"

I was happy to see that Mason Williams was not in the crowd. It was just the gang of four or five of the "regulars," the fans who would have walked fifty miles and back for a chance at one of Ffellowes' stories. Some were very important men, in finance, law and medicine but around the Brigadier they were a gang of eager kids, tongues hanging out, waiting, hoping, ready to beg, just anything, if only to hear one of his quietly-told tales of strange and lurid adventure. In his years in the service of the British Crown, the Brigadier had been damned near everywhere and it seemed, had been attached to every branch of the British Services or if not attached, then loaned to them, or maybe "it."

"Hullo, hullo, Chaps. Nice to see you all again" was the greeting they got as they pulled up chairs and formed a circle around his bay. "Parker here was wonderin' what I was doin' with these books, which are the rankest kind of escape literature, eh? Well," he went on, "I was doing a bit of pseudo-research. Frankly, I was wondering if any of these authors had any real idea of what they were writing about, you know, any actual facts on which to base these bits of wild and wooly fiction."

The others had all been looking as hard as they could at the books he had started to show me and now Westcott spoke up. He was a very top lawyer in one of the big firms, I think maybe Silliman & Cramwell, but I knew he had once been a very sharp D.A. as well and his question proved the point.

"There must be some connecting link, I should think, Sir, between those old novels and your own life. Maybe that big book in your lap is another?"

"Very quick, Mr. Westcott," smiled Ffellowes. "Good, shrewd thinking you attorneys have." Ffellowes never forgot a thing about anyone he'd ever met, no matter how minor it was. Now he looked at the last book again for a second, before continuing.

"Have any of you chaps read much of this sort of thing? This one," and he tapped the fat book about Abominable Snowmen, "is not fiction at all. The man who wrote it, who's now dead, was a scientist himself, though he had imagination. He was trying to gather all the legends from every place on the planet, plus any facts he could find, and make an amalgam. These creatures, these hairy, ape-like, primitive things, are reported from damn near every place on Earth. Did you fellows know that? They are not just glimpsed or rumored in the Himalayas. No indeed! This man Sanderson in this book I have has Russian reports, Chinese reports, African reports and South American sightings. Oh yes, and the most reportage of all comes from of all places, this country we are sitting in." There was a brief silence in the big room and the Fifth Ave. traffic outside provided the only sound. For several moments no one spoke.

Then a man on the other side of the group, a new member of the club, said something. "Isn't there that thing out in California or maybe it was Oregon. They call it 'Bigfoot' and I think it has other names. All they find is footprints and they fake pictures and claim they took them of a real animal."

"Quite possibly correct," said Ffellowes. "Another name out there is 'Sasquatch.' American Indian dialect, one supposes."

"But Brigadier Ffellowes," said Westcott, "what has this idea of some actual ape thing in the woods, this, well this monkey version of Loch Ness or supposed dinosaurs alive, what has any of it got to do with those old novels you were reading? Didn't Burroughs write *Tarzan* and that man Haggard, *King Solomon's Mines*?"

"Yes indeed to both," said Ffellowes. "But consider this. In *Tarzan*, there are tribes of intelligent giant apes, creatures which don't exist in reality. This novel of Rider Haggard's is called *Heu-Heu or the Monster*. Same thing again, intelligent, man-sized ape things. This last one is by the chap who wrote those old detective thrillers about Bulldog Drummond. Stuff I grew up on, myself. But this one's about an island off South America, and guess what? On that remote, little islet lives a mob of nasty, giant apemen. D'you begin to see why I'm interested?"

I seldom talk when the Brigadier's around but I had

a great idea and I had to speak. "What about Conan Doyle's adventure novel, Brigadier? What about the tropical tribe of apemen in the Matto Grosso in *The Lost World*?" I felt I had made a score, had finally caught the Brigadier out in a bit of arcane and useless knowledge.

He smiled gently. "My dear fellow, I know the book by heart. I used it long ago on this pursuit of the nonsensical." Seeing my face fall, he went on. "Not to feel badly though. That book may have started all the other ideas and I've had it on my own mind for years."

He put all the books away on the side table and shoved that aside as well. "Sun's over the Yardarm, Gentlemen. Let's have a small dose of the usual medicine. Then, if you're interested at all, I'll tell you why I have such a personal interest in this problem."

If we'd all been dogs, you could have heard the sound of panting and slavering, felt the eagerness and the electricity that his words had released. We were going to get a story, a Ffellowes story and the Brigadier never told the same one twice!

After the club waiter had brought the tray of cocktails and then gone away, we all started sipping, smoking and waiting. Ffellowes, who was having a glass of ale, gave us all a thoughtful stare and then began.

"Haven't been down that way in years. Any of you fellows know the little colony that used to be British Honduras? It's called Belize now but that was only the name of the capital and the one town of any size in the whole place then. Just a flyspeck colony of ours, which never paid for itself and which the neighboring country of Guatemala wanted. Still does I think, but it was never theirs or even really Spanish before them. It was settled by a bunch of ex- and not so ex-pirates and judicially run from Jamaica for a couple of centuries. Sole export was mahogany. No oil, no minerals, no nothing. Now that it's allegedly independent, I wonder how it supports itself? Just north of it is that Quintana Roo place of Mexico's. Currently a big resort area now with Can Cun and all that." He took a sip of his ale and went on.

"It was in '47 I was sent there. It was an odd sort of job but the big war was over and I did often get the odd ones. I was technically or officially under the Foreign Office, if anyone really cared.

"It seems that during the war, there was a lot of murmur about the locals selling food and drummed petrol to German subs. Nothing ever came of it and I think that fellow Stevenson, the one now called Intrepid, had some of his folk there, checking up and keeping an eye on matters for the Crown and its allies. In fact, this author, that chap Sanderson once was one of 'em.

"Well, it seems a new message had come out of the place and it was this message that got me sent there. The message itself was very odd. It was in an obsolete code form, addressed to a man in MI-6 who'd been dead for three years and it didn't come through any channels at all. What happened was this:

"A local skipper of a coasting schooner had got the message. He, the skipper, was a Bayman, as they're called down there. A big black, and I mean big, because I saw the man later. These folk, the Baymen, are very loyal to the idea of being 'British.' They once helped fight a whole Spanish fleet off, back in the 18th Century. I think myself they're the descendants of runaway slaves from the islands or maybe Spanish territory, but they don't like *mestizos* or Latins of any sort much. They speak good, if jumbled, English, though most can get along in some Spanish too. They usually live by or near the sea and are fine swimmers, boatmen and water people. The remaining inhabitants of the country are simply a straggle of southern Mayans, Maya Indians that is, just like the same folk over the border in Mexico but poorer and more spread out. There are a couple of modest Mayan temples in the back country but nothing very grand, like the ones in Mexico. Don't think anyone from a university ever bothered to do much digging, though a few gave the area a looksee on occasion.

"Well, this skipper, whose name was Ambrose Hooper, had come up the coast in his old piece of floating junk and did a lot of small-time trading as he came. He could have started in Panama for all I know. Many of them did and paid small attention to customs, port duties or any other regulation. The whole coast of Central America was like that once. His story was this:

"One night, while at anchor off the Monkey River, down off the mangroves in the south of the colony, he heard someone swimming out to him from the local mangrove belt. He quietly roused the crew, which meant one son and two nephews and they got their cane knives ready. That's what they call machetes and they all wear them, or used to.

"It was a dark, overcast night and they could see little or nothing. The sound of someone swimming— and they had good ears—was that of a man, not an animal, and they finally called out, asking who and what it was.

"For answer, they got something thrown neatly at them, right into the old schooner, barely missing Captain Hooper's head. They ducked and waited but that was all. Except that in the following quiet they heard the same sound of someone swimming, only this time it was away, back to the hot, black shoreline, the steaming mangrove coast from which it had come in the first place. Slowly, it seemed to them, the sound faded into the fetid night, until once more only the hum of countless mosquitoes and sandflies was audible.

"When they could hear nothing more, Captain Hooper used a flashlight and they looked for whatever had been thrown into their vessel. They found it finally in the bilges and it was a small package, tied with twine, and wrapped in a filthy scrap of oilskin, which had kept the interior almost completely dry. In it was a scruffy pack of crude papers of some kind, very coarse stuff with frayed edges. On the paper was writing, blurred and in some brownish, dark ink of some sort.

"Now what got the men excited was this. On the outside of the bundle, in the same ink, but printed, not written, was the following: 'On His Majesty's Service. Take to English Consul at once!' Oh yes, and below that was printed equally bold, 'MOST SECRET.'

"Well, I've told you how loyal to England these Baymen were and for all I know, still are. The Captain rewrapped the package and tied it up again and then swore his crew of relatives to silence. Nothing more was said and at daybreak they sailed north again but with not a stop until they made the port town and/or capital of Belize. Remember, that was only a town name then and the whole dinky colony was called British Honduras or 'BH' locally. Captain Hooper took the package himself to the Consul and insisted on giving it to him in person and not to his one secretary. Then he left, his duty to the Crown accomplished.

"The Consul thought it was some sort of joke induced by tropical fever, but he looked carefully at it and he found a London address clearly printed. The rest of the scrawled pages were in English but in some sort of code, and no sort he had ever seen."

The Brigadier took a pull of his ale and stared past or through us at the library wall. Outside the street noises penetrated faintly but in the big room, empty save for our small group, there was only silence. We all knew that he was seeing something none of us ever would or could see and that he was far away mentally, lost in some vision of the past, in some "lost world" of his own. Then he straightened again and his cold blue eyes flickered over us in casual appraisal, before he started to talk and to resume his tale.

"I'll cut a few corners here, Gentlemen. The bundle of papers got to first, the Foreign Office and then trickled through several others in turn. They finally ended up in the place they were meant to go and there they caused both laughter and incredulity. Let's call that last despository one or another HQ of a foreign-related intelligence division, eh? That tells you all you need to know." He didn't add "or ever will," but it didn't need adding.

"The papers were in a code, but a long-expired one. It was one of the codes given to agents in the field at a time of confusion, early in World War II. It had a use then, for it was easy to memorize, and even at that was only given to chaps who were considered of small importance and whose work was largely routine. A typical type would be some "small-timer" whose job was reporting shipping movements from obscure Portugese coastal areas of Africa, say. Once in a great while, these men and/or women in a few cases, would come up with something arresting, such as news of a Kraut surface raider or submarine, but this was not normal."

The Brigadier lifted his eyes and stared at the ceiling. A faint but audible sigh came from his lips. Then he went on.

"The agent who had signed this package was interesting to the bureau involved for a couple of reasons. First, he was low on the scale, having been nothing but a very modest coastal trader along the Caribbean littoral for five years before WW II. But, long before a misspent life had commenced, he'd been a, well, to be a bit obsolete, a "gentleman." He was, in fact, a latterday survival of an old Victorian custom, being a 'Remittance Man' of sorts, who had left his family, his country and all that when he got a bit embarrassing. His family, which we'll call 'Jones,' heard little from him but sent him small sums of money through a lawyer at intervals, with the unspoken agreement that he would stay away, far away, and not bother them. One found these oddities here and there, mostly in the Tropics, to a much later date than is generally realized. Their offenses ranged from drink and women to actual criminality, though that was the rarest."

Ffellowes paused here, and reaching down beside his leather armchair, pulled up another book, a very long and very thick book, which looked both used and used hard, being scuffed and with tiny holes in it. He held it up, facing outward, so that with a little leaning from those on the edge, we could all read the words printed under the stained crown on the cover. They were simple, being *Atlas of British Honduras* and the date, *1939*.

"Here's the old official map book," he said. "It was all we had until quite a while after. If I refer to something, it might make it easier on you fellows for me to indicate it on this thing than something more up-to-date, which I don't have anyway, at least here."

He eyed the book with amusement and affection for a moment. "Full of rot and a few wormholes, this one. Any book carried into real tropical bush doesn't last long." He flicked it open and held it up and rotated it for us to see a map of the entire tiny country, which looked a bit like a shortened, bent version of the state of Vermont. Then, with his forefinger, he indicated a certain area, a largely blank area, two thirds of the way down or South and also in the center.

"This patch is all hills, covered with limestone crags, domes and heavy bush. There are bits of real tropical rain forest in places but a lot of it's scrub jungle. Full of ravines and also streams, being quite well watered. There are swamps also in places in depressions in the hills or where the ravines broaden. The area's known, or was known then, as 'The Maya Mountain.' Well, the whole country inland was full of Amerindians of Mayan stock and probably still is. They have strong kinship systems, and now and again will leave their *milpas*, their corn patches, and go off visiting relatives on foot, some of whom are a long way off, such as due North up in Mexican Quintana Roo where famous ancient Mayans lived. You men have heard about Chichen Itza and all that. Or, they might drift due South or Southwest and end up in Guatemala with still other relatives. Made little of borders they did, and as the news tell us, they have not changed since the place became independent around 1971." He sipped his ale and went on, a reflective tone now in his voice.

"An odd folk and keep very much to themselves, unless they've changed a lot. In B.H. very few spoke any English and their Spanish was archaic and full of loan words of Mayan. They preferred that and didn't care much for anyone who was not Mayan. A dour, silent people, hard-working and living on tiny corn patches and a little hunting and fishing. They did not live on or even near the coast, leaving that to the negro Baymen and mestizo mixed-blood and the few Caucasians who were there, either for official reasons or for private ones.

"Now this brings us back to the mysterious message thrown on the boat by that unknown swimmer. Look at this map and see a lot of creeks hitting the sea almost due East of the Maya Mountains? See that area marked *Seine Bight?* All heavy swamp on that stretch and that's where the Baymen's coaster was moored when that message arrived.

"So then, we can get back to the message itself and to Jones, the supposedly dead and certainly vanished agent of the British Government, who had sent it, or at least had signed it with his long-defunct, assigned number. His first name was really Percy, I mean *really*. Sticks in my mind, it does, being rather effete for a man of this sort.

"The message was scrawled with some very crude sort of implement, perhaps a split piece of reed. It was, to put it mildly, confused as well as confusing, that is, to those who had to decipher and make what sense they could out of it." The Brigadier stared away again, obviously trying to coax his memory.

"Well it went something like this, and I'm giving you a digest of what I can recall: 'Send Troops to B.H. in secret! Send at least one half Batt., well-trained in Bush Fighting, artillery not needed. Send at once! Send to compass bearing XYZ, in the heart of Maya Mountains.' "

Ffellowes chuckled grimly at this point. "Good thing he thought to put in the country involved and the Maya Mountains. The compass bearing was wildly askew and the latitude-longitude readings were someplace off Cape Horn in the sea. The whole thing seemed to indicate a very sick man, probably writing in the grip of some fever or other, or perhaps wounded or maybe both.

"There was a bit more to come and the next and last bit was the wildest and most weird of the lot. It went on in this way, all broken up, you know and not consecutive, like shorthand taken by a drunk stenographer. Here are enough pieces to give you some indication of what it was like: 'Devils! They hate us and all like us! If the scientists are correct, though, they *are* us! Us as we were and they know it, by God!' " A strange smile flickered briefly over the Brigadier's smooth face. "I'm not gassing you people when I use points of emphasis, this is verbal exclamation points and such. There are ways in a code of doing just that, to mean something's most important and/or vital. Well, poor Percy Jones used that mark on every line, every scratched sentence, in fact on every place he could fit it in at all." He sighed again, sadly, and we all felt his sympathy in our own minds as well for that poor lost man and his strange plight.

"Not too much more," went on Ffellowes. "A few bits like this though: 'They can see in the dark, better than cats; they have keen noses and can hear an ant crawling; they eat meat whenever they can get it and they don't care what sort; they eat green stuff mostly, all kinds of plants; I think they raid a few lonely farms for corn and for other purposes; they *must* do that! How else could they get those other blank-blank?' Now *here*," The Brigadier went on, "one word was very hard to get straight. The best opinions seemed to be a mix. Some of the backroom boys thought it was 'female,' either singular or plural. Other opinions give it as 'rulers' or even 'female rulers.' Then there was another word that cropped up all the time and that was often blurred or run. This was something or appeared to be, olfactory. It was translated as 'stench,' 'smelling' and even 'perfume.' There were continued references to 'night,' to 'dark' and to the apparent proclivities of 'them,' whoever 'they' might be for darkness or the dark hours."

He looked down at the open map book for a second and then up again quickly. "Oh yes, there was or

were, still other repeated phrases of some sort. One
was to 'breeding' and also 'trying to breed.' That came
in a lot, rather at random. With it were words like
'peril' and 'danger.' 'War' and 'revolution' were not
absent. And finally, there were constant references to
some sort of hirsuteness. 'Hair' and 'fur' appeared a
lot and also 'pelt.'

"It didn't really come to an end at all. There was
some scribble about 'Danger!' and mixed in was 'Hurry!'
and 'Act at once!' and more like that, all with the
emphasis on *Now, Urgent, Instantly,* and in general,
'Hurry Up' plus 'Move!' "

He stopped talking for a moment and there was
silence in the big room. The noise of traffic was audible through the curtained windows, the roar of New
York that never stops. But no one felt like talking and
we simply waited. The Brig. didn't like being inter-
rupted at any time but it was more than that. We were
all far away, trying to hear a strange message in our
minds from a lost soul.

"At any rate," he finally went on, "Certain powers
that be, or were then, got mildly intrigued. The bloody
place *was* still a sort of dubious possession of the
Crown. Somewhere in it, a long-lost man had tried to
communicate. It ought to get a quick look, if no more."
He chuckled quietly. "I had always been noted as an
oddity, if no more and I happened to have no current
job. So, to make a long story one inch longer, I was
off to Belize, the then capital and only sizeable town
in all B.H.

"I found it dismal enough when I got there. Built at
sea level, it had little paving and open sewers that
emptied into a sluggish little river also called 'Belize.'
The sewers and the river were both full of rubbish,
including dead cats, pigs, dogs and possibly people. It
all went out to sea but slowly and not much to sea,

with each tiny tide. There were few if any decent buildings and fewer Caucasians, though that meant little to me. I had chats with the Governor, the Consul and the local police chief, saying little myself but learning a lot about the country. I had impressive but vague papers, which said I was from the Foreign Office on inspection duty. What I really wanted I kept to myself. I had to tell one chap only, and I chose the policeman. Like a lot of Colonial Cops, he was a splendid chap and had started long before as a London Bobby. I told him the whole thing, except for the meaningless bits of message, the stuff about 'hair' and such. And I had him arrange a meeting with Captain Hooper, the skipper who'd got the actual message so strangely. The police chief was the only one in the country who knew even vaguely what my job *really* was and he'd been cleared by my own H.Q.

"We ended up by having a very quiet meeting one evening, Captain Hooper, his oldest son, George, and I. Over vast glasses of appalling beer, which did not help much with the tropic stench in the still air, but some, we talked. Police Chief Plover, by agreement, kept watch outside the little hut on the town's edge where we met.

"I got the whole story from Hooper and his son, the latter a big, really big, young Black. His rippling muscles were impressive but the steady eyes over the high cheek-bones and the soft, deep voice were more so. The father had both and only a little grey in his cropped curls. They were far better material than I'd hoped for. I noticed their cheap clothes were clean and that they were also.

"I told them what I wanted and they promptly agreed with enthusiasm. They and the rest of the crew had been back from a trip down the Coast for over a week and were loading goods on their schooner, named

Windsor incidentally (they pronounced it 'Weensore' in their deep tones) for another. Whatever I wanted was mine and they even argued about my offer to pay a price for charter! This was 'Guvmint Wuhk' and they wanted no pay. A refreshing note of loyalty for the battered Empire in those Post-War days but I'd found it elsewhere in the world before this and later as well. They were clever men and they could reason. When I'd sketched what my plans were, they had thought of some helpful ideas of their own and I *do* mean helpful.

"Captain Hooper summed it up and I'll give it to you in his words. 'You wanna go inshore to where that man swim out wit that lettah. Then, Cap'n, (I was that rank) you wanna go afta that mon all the way in to them Mayan Mountain, where you feel he come from? Okeh, gettin you theyah, thass easy. You come on wit us in the dahk and none know this. But when you go ashoah, thass vurry difficull. Bad country, fulla bugs, snake and sickness. If you goes through to them hills, mebbe it get worse. No one go up there, cep' a few hunter now and then. Clean air, plenty watah, good ground and animals too, mebbe even a few 'Panther cats' or even 'Tygrees.' (He meant Puma and Jaguar, the latter being *Tigre* to Spanish speakers.) But, Sah, they ain't why I'm worried, nor Jawge neither. Nobody like the inside of them hills and nobody, not the lousiest 'Injun' corn digger, go there for mor'n a day or two. No one *live* theah! That *Baaad* Place and it always been so. A littul huntin, thass OK, but some folks won't even go in there foh just that even.' Captain Hooper stopped here and looked at his son. I could see them both clearly in the light of the paraffin or kerosene lamp.

"George was ready for the pause. 'You'se watched, is what I heah,' came from his own deep tones. "Somfin's in theah that watches folks. If they stays on the edges like and don' stay long, then's all right. If should be they goes in deep or mebbe tries to live there permanent, thass a diffrunt thing, Cap'n. They just vanish, like a Duppy got 'm. Whoosh!'

"His father took a giant gulp of beer, emptied the bottle in fact, and nodded to me. 'He say right, Cap'n. Thass no place to go, not nobody. And nevah *alone*, Suh. Too easy foh the Duppies, one puhson all by hisself!' "

Ffellowes leaned back and his blue eyes twinkled at us. "A 'Duppy,' my friends, is an evil spirit. It's simply Anglic dialect for what the Haitians call a 'Zombie' or one of their own spirit terrors. Cheery news, eh, in that smoky hut?" Then the humor left his eyes and he continued. "I was making mental notes over what I heard when George spoke again.

" 'I go wit the Cap'n, Dadee. I ain't no Bushman, jus' a sayluh boy but I got good legs. An' we take Lucas Payrfit. He part Spaniol, mebbe part Injun, but he my fren' also. An' he *do* know the Bush. He hunt evr'thin they is an' he know to live theyah an' go quiet-like. Wit us two, mebbe they's a chanct. Lemme ask Lucas to come ovah and talk wit usn's.'

"I strongly suspect," Ffellowes continued, "that all this had been pre-talked over before we met. I feel that George had already got his father's permission to escort me and that the mysterious Lucas had already been sounded and had agreed."

He fell silent, gazing at the rug and we stayed immobile in our circle. Once again Ffellowes had captured our spirits and we all were far away and long ago with him in that steamy, tropical hut, planning a venture into the unknown. The street noises and the faint sounds from the other parts of the Club were mentally shut out and meaningless, not registering on our tensed-up sense patterns. We also saw and heard the two black giants as they calmly offered to risk their lives for Ffellowes and that sacred (to them) intangible, the British Government.

The Brigadier gave a sigh and then resumed. "Well, at Dawn, two days later, we cast off from a battered, mooring post and were off to the South. All had been taken care of that could be. I'd left a complete report of my findings, which were largely speculative and also my intentions, possibly even more so. All that was with Plover the Top Cop. A good chap and he'd served a term not long before in the police of one of the Malay States, in Borneo I believe. He knew something thus of both traveling and looking for trouble in uncharted rain forests.

"As the *Windsor* chugged out, sails down, on her battered auxiliary, there were two of us below decks, sweating in the still heat and stench. We'd come on board in the thick dark at 3:00 A.M. and with us a lot of equipment we needed. The other man was the mysterious 'Lucas Pairfit.' His name was really of French derivation and spelled correctly, was 'Peyrefitte.' The Hoopers had summoned him quietly at dusk on the previous day and he'd just appeared, equally silent.

"I had given him the once over, since we were to be companions and I was rather impressed. He too was tall, perhaps 6'2" but lean and not burly. He had a hawk face and bronzy-red skin. There was some negroid strain, as evinced by the close-cut, tight curls, but the rest? At a guess, French and Amerindian. He moved like a great cat and he had piercing black eyes. His voice was a purring growl, very sinister at first, but his grip was firm and hard. We chatted while trying to breathe as the schooner cleared the river with me putting the questions and him the answers. George Hooper was on deck with his father and two husky cousins, but that was the normal thing and thus not worth disguising.

"Lucas had guided more than one hunting party into the edge of the Maya Mountain country but as he put it, 'I don' stay long. I keep the white folks who hire me movin' fast and when they want rest, I always tell 'em this Bad Place. Sometime I say fevah, some-time bad watah, sometime no animal to hunt, some-time too many buggses. But, mos' imphtant, we keep on the move.'

"When I asked him about the feelings the others had told me of, those of being *watched*, I could see the whites of his eyes flicker, even in the fetid dark of the little cargo space.

" 'Oh yes,' he said, this time with a real snarl. 'They is somethin' that see you. You don' notice much in the day time, jus' now an then. But aftah dark, then it get bad. You look to me Sah like a man what's done a bit of huntin', right?' At my grunt of assent, he went on. 'Then maybe you have feel this thing too. All huntah have. But, lookee, Cap'n, did you evah have *this* feelin', that a smaht *tigre* watch you, one that don' like you and can think about it, like a man think?'

"When he'd finished that particular comment, there was silence between us, broken only by creaking tim-bers and our breathing. His next comment anticipated my next question but was quite logical in so doing. 'I nevah find any tracks, not a one. But I do fin' where a place where something heavy, maybe man size, squat down. An in sof' groun' close by, I find where a branch been use to rub out track. Jus' like you or me would if we don' wanna be seen or notice we been theyah at all.'

"Again there was a brief pause and again he went on, but doing no thought reading this time. 'Theah was also a stink. Vurry light and not one I evah smell.

If it were people, then they got a very nasty smell to 'em. They got that smell, like somethin' that live in the woods, some wil' animal, d'you see an' they got a lot of weight, more than us and they like the dahk, jus' like a cat do.'

"Once more there was silence and I noticed the engine was off and that we were heeling a little, obviously under sail. He pulled his thought-reading trick again. 'I speak pretty fayuh Maya, Cap'n. They tell me I mus' be part Maya and mebbe so. I don' look like the Hooper men and that help, not lookin' so much like a Bayman, wit' this thin nose and mouth and all. Anyhow, they talk to me, some of 'em do. I ask a lot about these Maya Mountains and the things I notice. Man, do they *freeze* up! That's bad country in the inside, fulla devils! They are bad devils and they steal Maya girls mebbe to eat. They ain't nevah seen again, not evah! They's a vurry few ol' men, who can remembah times they was told of befoh the whites come here. Any whites at all, Spanish, English or any and that mean any black men too, cause they had black men as slaves. An' these ol' mens, onect in a while, but rare, they would tell me a few things they been tol' by *their* ol' men when *they* little kids. This place we headed now was always the bad place! Them ol' injuns they always stay out too even back when they was the bossmen of this whole country and the other countries round about like Guatemala an' Mexico too. So what do that tell us, Cap'n?' He was silent and waiting and my answer was obvious, as obvious as it must be now to you fellows. 'Old,' I said, 'very old. Whatever makes them afraid of that country has been there a long time indeed, Lucas.' His grunt of assent was loud and clear.

"At this point, a bolted hatch on the foredeck was slid open and we both took deep breaths of the gust of fresh air. Whatever the Hooper clan had carried in that little ship, including partly-cured hides, it didn't make for easy breathing with the hatches shut.

"Young George Hooper's head appeared and he hailed us with a smile and told us to come up and relax. We were well out of the river now and sailing South under a gentle breeze, with not another craft of any sort in sight, not even a canoe. So we climbed out and went aft in the sun to the after cockpit. There we settled down with Captain Hooper and the two other cousins ran the boat. We began to plan our own moves and coordinate them.

"It was obvious that we could not plan too much, since there were so many unknowns in the whole thing. But we did the best we could and as carefully as possible. Then, we simply ran South, aiming for the area where the strange message had been thrown aboard ship in the steaming night.

"For two days and nights we dawdled on, following the coastline and well inside the fringing reefs that lie up to ten miles off that same coast. It was work for experts only, since there were plenty of local obstacles, from bars of mud and sand to clumps of local coral heads, floating logs out of the forest and occasional fishing boats without lights, the latter probably smuggling something. The Hoopers had done this trip many many times before though and laughed uproariously when I joshed them about their varied cargoes and His Majesty's Revenue Inspectors.

"As a cruise for honeymooners, I would fault it. The breeze was erratic and never strong and we were close enough to shore for sand flies and mosquitoes to pick us up with ease. We slapped, swore and smoked steadily. There was nothing else to do.

"Eventually at dawn, we arrived, having passed Stann Creek in the night where there's a small port whose lights we could see at a distance. When the *Windsor* was anchored, close to where the older man said the message had come, young George Hooper, Lucas Peyrefitte and I collected our gear, prepared a spare dinghy which we'd towed for this purpose, and went ashore if you call a healthy mangrove swamp 'shore,' which I don't. The skipper and the other two were to call back at this point in two days and then in two more days, a job to be repeated until they saw us or a signal from us. Very simple arrangement compared to jobs I had during the war, off the Norwegian coast, say, but it was the best we could do.

"We got the dinghy as far up a muddy creek as we could and then had to slog through a lot more mud, plus clouds of stinging bugs, until we finally hit solid ground and collapsed. We had blazed mangrove trees with our machetes as a backtrail guide. Now we spit out bugs, wiped the worst mud off with leaves and looked at each other ruefully.

"We all had Winchester carbines slung on our shoulders and ammo, in pouches, plus oil and cleaning stuff. All three also had Webley .455 revolvers in flap holsters and full belts as well plus heavy hunting knives and the local machetes. We had full canteens as well and light packs, also shoulder-slung. In the packs were mosquito nets and food, *charqui* which is dried beef and crude tortillas baked to iron hardness. Most folk who know nothing of the tropics think being lost is the problem. It's one, but the least thought-of is more dangerous yet. Quite simply, thirst. Just because you have tons of greenery, that doesn't always mean water, reachable water. In this country, a mixture of sand, dirt, limestone and granite, it was even more chancy. Little streams and brooks are there and lots of them. But they take finding. Rain is common and heavy as well but it can hold off for weeks at the wrong season, always when you most want it.

"I looked at my team and felt pretty good. George, to my delight, had once done a short term in the local 'Territorials,' a mob we raised during the war for local defense. Lucas was a hunter and a 'bushman.' We were all in tough khaki trousers and shirts, commandeered from the Belize cops by Inspector Plover, my 'link' to the Crown. He had got Army laced boots for us too, just now soaking wet but we had grease to reproof 'em and keep them from cracking. I had a slouch hat, my own *shikari* hat from India, but the other two didn't want any or ever wear them. We all had compasses and they could read theirs as well as I. I had what local maps the Crown had had done, but these were vague and not much use.

"Looking at mine, I found that we were, or thought we were, south of a maze of creeks, the largest of which was labelled 'Jenkins,' named after God knows who. I discussed our position with the others and we set off, bearing West by Northwest.

"There were no trails in this country and Lucas went first, me next and George last. It was up-and-down trekking, with lots of low ridges, some with bare rock spines protruding. The trees, Waha palms, tropical pines and a few mahoganys, weren't too tall, except for a rare one but there was lots of low stuff under many of them and a lot was spiny and nasty. Lucas, who knew this stuff best, was simply to hold course and pick the clearest path possible.

"We soon ran into another blight, one they had warned me of many times. It was tick country and several sizes and types were plentiful, from big black ones to minute red pests. We ignored them mostly, and when we stopped for breaks, scraped them off or held lit smokes to the most bloated until they popped bloodily. Mosquitoes were rare, save near water in the low bits, that is, rare by our standards here only. To reinforce them came a nasty group of large, biting flies. I was the chief sufferer, since the two young men seemed to ignore the damn things. Still, I've been in a lot of tropical bush and/or jungle and some was worse. There were at least no leeches.

"Actually, had we not been pressing on fast, the country was lovely. On top of sandy ridges, where the pines predominated, one could see a lot, especially as we were climbing steadily as we went inland in our torturous, up-and-down path. We saw few animals, save for a rare glimpse of an armadillo and once a tapir clumping away up a wet ravine. Birds were everywhere though, vultures or *zopilotes* sailing over us and lots of little things warbling and chirping below, some with very bright colors, other as drab as sparrows.

"On one of these ridges, Lucas called a halt and pointed. Far down a series of tangled ridges we could see patches of small corn fields spread over flat country and out of the heavy bush. This was to the North.

"Then, he whirled and we looked West. Here the summits of much higher, though rounded hills capped the view. 'Maya Mountains,' he growled. 'None of these Injun live any closer than those field we jus' look over. We in the bad country right now, the land where no one go except to hunt and for not long even then. We mus' be careful from now on, Cap'n. Already we might be seen.' He paused then and added, 'by sump'n, sump'n bad.'

"When night came, which meant less heat but only a different variety of biting bugs, we camped in a little gully, having found a niche on one side where three smooth rock walls twenty feet high gave us some feeling of protection. There was a tiny stream trickling down the ravine bed so we had water. We grilled our *charaqui*, very good but tough, over one of the cans of American Sterno, a thought of mine to bring. It weighed little and though there was a smell of meat perceptible, there was no fire and no woodsmoke. The latter can be detected miles away by sensitive noses.

"We picked off all the ticks we could find and George and I spread our one-man mosquito nets. We were keeping what the navy calls 'watch on watch' and Lucas had the first round. Then, after four hours, he'd wake me and after my four, I'd get George up. None of us wanted there to be no sentry at *any* time.

"Next day, after a quick meal, varied by an antiscorbutic, what you men pay for as 'Heart of Palm salad,' or the little growing heads of some small palm trees, we set off West again. It was much the same going, into ravines and up tangled slopes, with breaks only where the pines, now getting fewer, dominated on the sandy ridge tops. Lucas used his machete with great skill and also his experience, and we seldom had to cut any tangles away from in front. He was a real bushman, with a keen eye for selecting the best track both for footing and also for the fewest tangles of vegetation.

"All day we went on in our usual way, which might be described as being alternate verticals or half verticals, mixed with spirals and right angle shifts. The only constant in the whole mess was the gradual but neverceasing upward slant. In one way and another, we climbed steadily to higher ground. As we paused in the later afternoon for some deticking and arrest on a lofty ridge, I was amazed by a Westward glance. Through the taller and heavier trees, I could see rounded summits, little higher than our own position, though far larger and looking quite close. I mentioned it to the others and they seemed surprised I had just noticed.

"Lucas did not look elated and he continually darted his sharp eyes in every direction, up, down and sideways. 'We is deep in the bad country now, Suh, and well in it. We keep a good look out or we never come out. Now we be real quiet and we look for a good place to camp, some kin' of place we can't be jump on by dem thing what live here.' His voice had lost all of the growl and was now a low, hissing purr. George Hooper, usually a cheery lad, quick to laugh and talk, was also suddenly silent and his seaman's eyes were as wary as the hunter's.

"Lucas shortly found the place he wanted, but he told me he had been on the watch for such a site for two hours past. I checked my compass and got rough bearings, using the map, the setting sun and my own skill. We were about 16-1/2 degrees North and maybe 88-2/3 West. This certainly put us in the Maya Mountains, all totally unmarked territory.

"Lucas' find for a campsite was another notch in a cliff, with bare or mossy rock behind and no big trees close. It was only a gap and about ten feet square. The rock walls for it arced out on each side, went up into darkness and there were no vines running down them. In front we had a clear view in daylight of 30 feet of open space, being rock slabs and shale with nothing higher than low bunches of grass. It made us all feel better when we got in and faced out.

"If any of you know the Tropics, you know there is no real 'evening.' The dark fell like a cloud and we could hardly see one another save with our flashes, which we were careful not to use at more than three feet.

"The usual night noises rang out as we quietly used our Sterno and did not talk as we ate. Lots of bird calls, an insect vibrato and now and then the cry of some mammal. I heard a distant scream once and nudged Lucas. He nudged back and muttered *Tigre* under his breath. It had been a jaguar after all. There must have been a stream in the gully below us and to our left for the chorus of frog voices grew steadily louder during our meal, until it had almost blanketed the birds and the bugs through sheer volume.

"Suddenly, as we sat silent and listening, the batrachian calls stopped. It was an instant cut-off. So did the birds and even the insects seemed muted. In this silence came a new sound. It was not near or seemed not near but, oh how it carried! It was a strange cross between a moan and a roar. It gave the impression of immense volume somehow and more, for intermingled was a savagery, a terrible wild and forsaken anger, which rather chilled the blood. Quite unconsciously, I found myself huddling close to young Hooper, who sat to my left. His great body was trembling like a leaf and I could smell his sweat as no doubt he could smell mine.

"Finally that appalling sound died away in a series of rumbling grunts whose volume was not lessened much from that of the roaring wail which had begun the whole thing. There was silence and then the frogs took up their chorus again, with new members joining in until the night was once more echoing with croaks and trills in which insect stridulation was mixed again.

"The voice of Lucas Peyrefitte struck George and myself, though it was soft, so that we started and almost jumped away from one another. 'Not to clost,' it came. 'Jus' set still now an' don't talk nor move.' He said no more for a second, and then continued. 'Someone far off, he think that that noise come from them Howly Monkey. But it don', not *that*. This come from somethin' much bigger and meaner.'

"I had forgot, d'you fellows know, that Howler Monkeys were found in these parts. Never heard a Howler and I understand they can make a good, loud racket but I never thought they'd give one a chill to the marrow.

"Mind you, as some of you know, I'm not exactly inexperienced in living in the Tropics. I've heard leopards cough and grunt many times and the same with tigers and lions roaring. I'd picked up that jaguar scream back earlier and identified it by an educated guess. This was something I'd never heard before or wanted to hear again.

"Then Lucas spoke once more before falling silent. 'Set still and use your ear an' your nose till I say it OK. And keep you pistol handy too.' I got my Webley cautiously in my grip and could feel George Hooper doing the same. Then we simply obeyed orders and sat listening. I'd forgot part of the order until I heard George sniffing deeply at intervals. I did the same without even thinking about it. And, deep in my subconscious memory, an alarm was triggered. Had there not been something about 'smells' or 'stinks' in that weird report signed by the man I call 'Jones'? In fact, in the very report that had got me here in this wilderness in the first place?

"Well, gentlemen, God knows how long we three sat there, as relaxed as possible but more than alert. I checked my luminous watch hand at intervals and at least one hour had passed when something else began to happen.

"I'd given up sniffing the jungle air which was lovely but so full of bugs that I'd inhaled several gnats without meaning to. But the other two were tougher and they had not. I heard and almost felt my neighbor George increase his sniffs and I started to do so too. One deep breath was enough.

"It was a most unpleasant odor that now wafted our way. It was wild, ferel if you like, but mainly a sort of concentrated garbage sort of reek. There was none of the ammonia smell of the big cats; what you can get in any zoo, though I've had it close to in the bush myself. Oh no, this was another new one for me. Mix a filthy athletic locker room with the stench of uncleaned dog kennels and add rotten garbage. That's the best I can do to describe it.

"And with this foul effluvium there was something else. This was more of a feeling than anything else. We were under intent and malign observation, that was it. Someone or something was looking at us and it was the look of a predator. You'll recall that Lucas and I'd had a conversation on this point before we started. Well, as any real hunter knows, one can feel this sort of thing, if one's lucky that is. Not very pleasant in that hot, damp dark, to feel that some 'presence,' something deadly and predatory had one under observation!

"It was Lucas's voice that broke the dead hush. And it was no whisper but a shout. 'Look *up*,' he yelled, almost in my ear. 'That stink come from up, down the rock behin' us!'

"Well, the three of us whirled as one man and young Hooper, God bless him, flicked on his torch as he did. And so we weren't taken too much by surprise." The Brigadier paused for thought but there wasn't a breath expelled in the Club library. We were all rivetted by the imagined horror of his tale and all mentally in that black, steaming forest, long ago in an unknown land, holding our breath and with racing pulses, all desperate to find out what followed.

The silence grew unbearable and Ffellowes' smooth pink cheeks finally loosened and he resumed his tale.

"Something huge and covered with matted hair was

dropping down that cliff face behind us, on what we'd all thought was the one safe side. How it found grip, I'll never know, and it was half-falling and half-climbing, I think, now.

"I saw its turned head in the torchlight, the great fangs and the red, glaring eyes between the mighty shoulders and the vast arms and crook-clawed hands, the huge straight legs and the claws on the toes as well. It was an instant, glaring picture of primal terror, caught as one catches a flash bulb photo, all in a split second.

"The oddest thoughts tend always to surface in a time of crisis. No doubt those of you who've seen combat in a war have noticed the phenomena. I had the weirdest flash then and it went like this: 'There are no reddish-blond gorillas in Central America. And its legs are much too long anyway!

"For the matted pelt that covered the hide of this monster was the color I've just used, a sort of reddish yellow and it was short, not like the longer hair of a gorilla or chimp you know.

"I had my gun drawn but frankly not levelled. It was Lucas, that trained hunter, who was ready, not I. His Webley .455 went off with a roar and young Hooper's was not much behind. It was I, the supposedly trained soldier and the leader of the group, who finally fired third. I will say that I fired at the demon head, just in my own defense, you know and to demonstrate to you fellows that I wasn't totally panicked. Damned lucky I finally came to, I might add.

"That huge, ghastly vision never let out one cough or even a grunt. It simply collapsed and fell, from perhaps eight feet up on that rock wall. One moment it was alive and about to leap on us, the next it was a huddled pile of reeking, bloody fur, clearly seen in the torch light for all three of us now had our flash buttons out and down. It was odd that the frog orchestra never stopped even for those three shots. The night was returned in an instant to the sounds of its normal voices while the three of us just stood frozen, staring at what we'd killed. I holstered my gun and started swatting mosquitoes without even thinking about it. I felt like a moron later when I thought of what might have happened had there been more than one of those things!

"Now we come to more of my stupidity. It was not the trained Intelligence *wallah* who spotted the next piece of evidence but young Hooper who at this moment had both sharper eyes and quicker wits. He bent and held his light close to the outflung right hand, for claws, size and all, it *was* a hand, of the dead thing. I almost choked when I saw what he'd noticed. To prove it was a 'hand' and not a paw, it was clenched tight in a death spasm and clenched around the shaft of a weapon too. That dead grip was around the wood of a short and incredibly massive spear! A further glance along the shaft showed the glittering, broad point, which gleamed black in the torch light. As heavy and broad as the wood was massive, so too was the obsidian blade, sharpened by clearly-seen chipping and flaking to razor edges!

"Well, that chap Lucas read my mind at this point. 'I listen good,' he said, almost casually. 'Dis the onliest one around. Maybe more come but I think this one find us alone by himself and try kill us quick.'

While Lucas spoke, though I heard him clearly, I was looking hard at other things, details that fit nothing I'd ever dreamt of, let alone heard about. The hairy hand that retained its weapon had a thumb as long and human in shape as mine. I'm sure you men know that no ape, gorilla or other, has anything but a short peg, a stump that can't grip or even bend. That dispelled any thought of the lower primates on the spot. You could, I suppose, teach a trained ape to carry a weapon but you can't train him into growing a thumb!

"Next, I carefully examined the head, which happened to lie face up so that I didn't have to move anything or touch the foul-smelling bulk. Oh, did it stink, a feral reek of everything wild, mixed with rank garbage! But I breathed through my mouth and carefully looked at that head. Oddly, the more I looked, the less horrid it got. Here's why.

"Under that curious pelt, which was longer on the top just like a man's hair, was a large, but not abnormally-shaped skull. There was a big hole in it where my bullet had gone home and I hate to think what would have happened if I'd missed. One of the other shots had hit an arm and only by a narrow margin, while the third had gone high and to the right in the chest. If that thing had been given a few seconds in that little rock bay with that great spear, well, I think the whole party would have lost a few guests.

"The head of this creature grew more interesting every second I was staring at it. It had a small but adequate nose. The canines were very large and pointed, easy to see since the mouth gaped open in death. But, and this interested me even more, there was a highish forehead, a well-rounded chin, such as no ape or monkey possesses, and glimpsed through the dirty head hair, ears not unlike those of, say Parker here," and he nodded at *me*.

I must have turned purple or something because they all laughed but the Brigadier held up one hand and the laughter died. "I only meant," he said, "that they were quite normal ears, that's all, but you don't see yet, any of you, what I'm getting at, nor should you, I suppose." He paused to collect his thoughts and then continued.

"There was a frontal brow ridge on this thing's forehead, which I think now nothing more than the Neanderthal Man had. But it was a high forehead, not ape-like. And there was a goodish bump at the skull's back, which I believe is the occiput."

He paused again and then came out with his full thought, once he'd apparently been skirting for some reason. "What I'm driving at is this: Aside from the enormous size, for the creature was seven foot tall at least, and the massive bulk and the pelt of course, what I was looking at was no ape at all but a crudish sort of very large *man*, a giant man with fur all over him."

I must have been brooding subconsciously about my own ears and Ffellowes' remark, because I saw a point or two I thought he'd missed and that made me bold, bold enough to interrupt, something I had seldom dared as did few others when one of the Bridgadier's stories was in progress.

"Excuse me, Sir," I said quickly, "but what about those great claws you said you'd seen. Claws on both toes and fingers, wasn't it?"

I was afraid I'd made the greatest tale-teller I ever knew angry when those blue eyes hit mine as he was about to speak. He only smiled a little though and just kept talking.

"Parker has a point there," he said to all of us. "Glad he made me think and remember. They weren't claws, they were immense, crooked fingernails, uncut, sharp and filthy." He ruminated a moment and then went on. "I may be wrong but they looked as if they'd been *filed* sharp, you know and I looked carefully. Yet, that wasn't the main reason I looked so long at those great hairy hands. On the right middle finger, clenched in that death grip around the spear handle, I saw a glint of something bright. I parted the fur with my pistol barrel and there it was, a huge gold ring!

"It was quite smooth, though very large and had a big green stone in the center, a dull circle of what looked to me like jade. It made me catch my breath to see it on the hand of this awful brute and I turned to point it out to Lucas and George.

"Neither one seemed much surprised. I guess they had lived too long with the thought of marvels to be as impressed as I was. Lucas gave a purring chuckle and then said, 'These bad place thing, these killer men of the mountain dark, they rich. They got gol' and jewel to hide, mebbe an' that why then don' come out and kill whoever try come in here.' What it was that stuck in my throat about his comment was not the idea of a hidden treasure. No, it was the way both he and the younger chap quietly and directly took the thing I had killed to be . . . a *man!*

"I mentioned this, commenting on the fur and the lack of any clothes as well. They were not impressed, either of them, by these arguments. 'They wild things, bad things, these men,' said Hooper. 'Try to kill us or anyone that come here, Cap'n. Look hard at that shape, the head, that shahp speeah he got. An' the fingah ring too. That ain't no animal, Sah. No way. In ol' time, the Bible say these men live an' whatever live in his mountain, it very ol'. Remember, Cap'n, it tell in the Book "an' Esau were a hairy man"?'

"That remark finished the argument for me. I'd come to much the same conclusion anyway, and if the Bible were going to be quoted against me, I'd better keep my trap shut. Frankly, you chaps, I thought I'd found a member of some lost race of what used to be called Missing Links, some creatures that had survived in a lost wilderness long after *Homo sapiens* had risen and cleared the Earth of his more brutish relatives, save for the few lingering colonies of great apes like the gorillas. The thought of what a great discovery we'd made danced through my brain but Lucas' next words drove the idea far away.

"He wasted little time. 'We got to get rid of this 'un,' he said bluntly. 'Mebbe other ones come aftah him and follow he tracks. Bury him quick, that what did ought to be did!'

"I had no argument with this remark either. Guns or no guns, we'd stand no chance against a mob of these creatures even in daylight, not in this thick bush, while at night they'd smother us.

"Working by the light of our torches, always kept pointed down, we scratched up the soft earth and moved the rocks in it until we had a pit three feet deep cleared. Before we shoved the reeking body into it, I used my big knife, of which more later, and hacked off that ring, throwing the severed finger into the pit. I pocketed the ring. I was going to have some evidence of something, anyway. The other two said nothing and for all I know, assumed I had just used the rank I had as leader to grab a piece of loot first.

"When we'd finally got that enormous body dumped in and wiped our hands on leaves and grass, we simply stamped the earth hard and flat for we'd shoved the loose dirt and rocks back in and covered our work as thoroughly as we could.

"It wouldn't have deceived a policeman or even a skilled woodsman, not for long, but in a jungle where rot works fast and growth faster, both Lucas and I knew it would soon be quite unfindable.

"Then, I raised another point I had overlooked in the excitement and which I'm sure all of you have been puzzling over. I asked Lucas, the skilled woodsman, what he thought about the sound of our three shots.

"He didn't seem concerned or even much worried. 'Remembah, Captain, what I tell you about hunting along the edge of this bad place? Lots of them Injun down in the low country got guns. Here in this little hole, wit all those frog an' bug sounds, if anyone, even us like, heah a shot or two, it soun' far off and not clost.' He thought for a minute and then added a word. 'Somehow, I feel shuah this killer man come alone an' he won' be missed by them other things till day come or mebbe longer.'

"We were all silent then and deep in thought. My own ideas were simple for the hunter's last words had brought out another thing I'd managed not to consider.

"Whatever we had killed, it could not be alone. To keep a whole area inviolate and under a blanket of fear and avoidance for countless years, perhaps count-less centuries, there had indeed to be more than once specimen of whatever *he* had been. I was now thinking of *he* and not *it* myself, you see.

"Well, dawn finally came, as it does in the Tropics, as fast as the dark falls. A red glow in the East changed to bright morning sunlight in a few seconds. We packed our stuff and set off again, but I had them both do as I did and unfasten and tuck back the flaps on their pistol holsters, for a quick draw if needed.

"We climbed slowly and watchfully for three hours and I then called Lucas back and George up from the rear. I explained that we needed two things, a rest and a 'clean-off.' The ticks and crawling bugs had got all over me during the night and were driving me wild. Also, we'd had no morning grub, having decamped in a hurry from our haunted lair under the cliff.

"We were following up a fair-sized stream at the time and Lucas looked at the water thoughtfully. Suddenly his face lit up and he slapped his leg. He said only one word, unintelligible to me and that was 'Billums!' I had no idea what he meant, but dutifully followed as he set off at a tremendous pace, still following the noisy brook up and over the rocks and screens and ducking under tree branches and vines as we did so.

"About 10:00 A.M. we suddenly hit the top of the biggest rise we had yet seen. Lucas waved us down flat on our stomachs and we all peered over the rim of sharp rock. The stream, now icy-cold and ten feet across, was pouring over the cliff or hill edge very close on our right.

"There before us lay a broad stretch of savannah, mostly tall grasses and a few scrub trees. On the far side, almost half a mile away, a belt of tall forest began again. But what Lucas was looking for lay much closer, no more than a hundred yards off. It was a long, crystalline pool, fringed by ferns and aquatic shrubs, all low except at the upper end where the stream entered and the lower where it left to flow over the hill. But we were at an angle and could see it clearly, all sixty feet or so of its length. At a signal from Lucas we sneaked over to the taller shrubs near us and then to the lower edge of this lovely water.

"Lucas said he would take first watch and told both George, who was equally at a loss, and I to take off everything and lie in the pool with only our heads out. We were not to move, even though things tickled us! We would come to no harm and we would have no bugs left in a minute, or even less. While on watch, he, Lucas would debug our clothes and then we would watch while he immersed himself in turn.

"Ye Gods that water was cold! Not icy but we were hot and sweaty and plain filthy as well. After a second shock, it felt heavenly and I lay back to watch a pair of hummingbirds, flickering close by over some arum plants growing from the water. Then, suddenly, I felt a series of tugs all over, as if someone were pulling my body hairs in six different places.

"Both George and I jumped with a start, for he'd felt the same thing! I looked at Lucas on the bank above me and he was grinning widely, a thing I seldom saw that impassive chap do. Then I looked down at my body, all visible in the utterly clear water. I was surrounded by little fishes, some very brightly colored. They were darting in and out all over me and pulling off every tick, ant or bug on my body. Sometimes, they would grab a hair by mistake and that was the 'tickling.' Lucas murmured his word again and I had my first experience with the 'Billums,' the tiny, tropical fish he had been looking for to get us all clean. I relaxed again for I knew the piranhas of the Amazon did not come this far to the North.

"Well, he was right again. In five minutes we were quite clean and we climbed out and traded places while he went in himself. Once in our now debugged clothes again, we felt wonderful, being clean as well. Lucas had not been in the water a minute and I was searching out food with George when we heard an acid hiss like that of a huge snake. It was Lucas and his immobile head was facing the other end of the pool We had slacked on our sentry job but he had not.

"We flattened ourselves behind a bank of foot-long, giant arum leaves and slid our Enfields forward. I saw nothing at first but soon noticed a waving of leaves coming our way down from where the upper stream entered the pool. The motion stopped near the water and we waited, ready, we thought, for anything.

"We were wrong. No one was ready for the most wonderful sight I ever saw. The bushes parted suddenly and out stepped a woman, the most glorious sight of my not too hum-drum life.

"She was nearly nude and very tall. She wore golden breastplates and a broad golden belt, all set with pieces of jade and what looked like dark shining stones, not the dull glint of jade. When I say she was nude, I felt for a moment I had made a mistake. Mind you, she was no more than seventy-five feet from my hiding place and I could see every detail plainly. Was she wearing a fur suit of golden red colour? Her face, both broad and high-cheekboned, was an ochre of red tinted with bronze and as smooth as any baby's. Only then did I see the fur 'suit' was nothing but her own lovely pelt, of a dense but close-clipped hair, body hair, you know. I could see her glorious eyes plainly as she faced the Sun; narrow and long though they were, they were a blazing brownish tint."

The Brigadier paused here and looked off across the big room. He was plainly lost in memories and we all sat—waiting. Then he took a deep breath and went on.

"Her hair, combed back straight, was straight itself and went to just above her waist. It was a reddish gold and shimmered in the sun. With her size and blazing good looks and coloring, she looked like the living figurehead of some ancient, royal ship, absolutely staggering!

"That, gentlemen, was my first sight of Fayuna, the glorious, lost queen of Conhung-At'lantz, and mind the last half of that place name.

"But though George Hooper and I had been simply gawping in total amazement, the real hunter among us had been thinking and moving. Lucas' head popped up right under my nose, silently as an eel's. 'Watch all behind her,' he purred. 'I think she take bath. In the watah, I get her quiet like and bring her here.'

"I could only nod and he vanished again under overhanging leaves while George and I took up our watch, though I don't think we'd have noticed anything short of a mad, pink elephant. Our male eyes were set hard on one thing only.

"Surely enough, the glorious young avatar of womanhood, and I could see by many indications, including her movements, that she *was* young, had come for a bathe. She only took one thing off. That gold belt and the jewel-studded gold bra were hardly clothing, but she unhooked the breast plates, laid them on the bank and stepped into the shallows, waded deeper and began to swim in our direction as it got deeper. She wasn't much of a swimmer and it was nothing but what we'd call a 'dog paddle,' but it was slow and graceful even so.

"As she swam, her deep husky voice sounded for the first time in a sort of gentle song. I couldn't get a word but they were words nevertheless. It was kind of a chant and I could even catch sounds that seemed to rhyme, though not in any tongue that sounded even vaguely familiar and I've heard quite a few.

"Closer and closer she came and now she was on the edge of a tall patch of some reed which threw a shadow over the water below them. I was holding my breath for I'd seen one of those reeds move just a second earlier.

"Then, Lucas struck! He'd got in front of the reeds and slid under water until he was behind that great, red-gold shape and then he rose like a dark copper eel, suddenly and smoothly at her back. His long, strong arms locked about her upper torso, sliding under her arms and up behind her neck, a lovely neck but large, suiting the rest of her more-than-normal female proportions. They were so close now that as we waited breathless, her young, pointed breasts thrust at us and I saw the pink of the nipples rising out of that sleek, golden pelt which garbed her body. In a split second Lucas had the woman in the hold Americans call 'Full Nelson,' his hands locked at the back of her neck, holding her pinned fast to his own body, unable to even move.

As her wide and full-lipped mouth opened, I saw the white teeth, and they looked sharp, the canines almost those of a carnivore. Her great eyes, as strange as a cat's but smokier looking, were wide in shock and surprise. I knew a yell was coming and I determined to try and prevent it. I rose from the cover of leaves and leapt forward into the water. It was not deep and the two in front of me were waist deep only. At the sight of me, her huge, lovely eyes widened even further and almost rolled upward in shock. I had one hand raised, palm out and up, and I hissed 'Quiet' at the frozen face before me.

"Lucas's voice came from behind her shoulders. 'Don' worry, Sah, I got her good! She don't move unless I let go.' The woman's, or rather girl's—for that was what she was, despite her size, a great girl—mouth closed in despair. I had my finger at my own closed lips now and it took no knowledge of English to know that I wanted silence from her. In another instant I had one of her upper arms in one of mine and Lucas and I began to push and pull her into the shallows and up on our bank. George came down to help and we soon had her in the ferns where we had been hidden, concealed from sight by greenery from all but a careful search.

"She stared wildly at first from George to myself and back. Lucas had never slackened his firm grip but had allowed her head to come erect so that it was not bent over, and since he was still crouched behind her, she could see nothing of him.

"I decided to try my crude Spanish on her. I spoke no Indian tongues and the local Mayas all spoke a crude Spanish, when they felt like it, that is. 'Amigos,' I said, trying to keep my eyes fixed on hers. It wasn't easy. That great, female body, lean-hipped and long-legged and all covered with that extraordinary pelt, like a close-furred golden cat's but even shorter, the amazing hair, the oval face and the full lips, now slightly parted as she panted softly. But the fear and horror were gone from the eyes now and they were sharp eyes, studying us, though still surprised. And, when I'd said 'Friends' in Spanish, they flickered and she stopped twisting her neck and focussed on me alone. At this point, so odd is the human mind, I registered in my mind that below the massive golden belt, the lady wore a smooth leather loin cloth, which was tucked under and up again over her rounded rump. For some reason, this made me feel better, as if things were more proper this way!

"That thought only took a split second. Then, my brain wiped all else away. For she was talking to me and I could at least partially make sense out of what she was saying. There, if you like, men, was a *real* thrill and one I had never expected.

"She kept those extraordinary eyes glued on mine, not looking at all at either Lucas or George, though both were helping keep her pinned. Her voice, which I'd already heard when she was carolling to herself, was deep and throaty. She spoke slowly, as if trying to deal with both unfamiliar speech and concepts. It was an odd tangle, being largely crude Spanish but with many pauses. Mixed in were clicks and gutturals which I guessed were Mayan and Lucas told me I was right later on. Rarely, she'd be at a complete loss and then would come some word utterly alien even to Lucas. This, we soon learnt, was in her own tongue.

"What I got was roughly this: 'Who are you? Are you from the Land of my people? Are you another of those who writes scrolls? Your eyes, they are of *our* ancient, lost color! Only once have I ever seen a man like you and those who advise, they killed him. I tried to stop them (it) but it was not good. The poor Pursee!'"

"Even with all the garbled language, that last word got to me. Pursee! That was the first name, even mispronounced, of our long-lost agent, the chap I've called Jones, the man who wrote the report that was so strangely delivered to the Hoopers' boat at night off the mangrove coast. Percy, eh?

"I spoke finally, when she fell silent at last and simply stared up at me. 'What do you know of Percy?' I said in my very crude Spanish. I had no Mayan and her own language was a total blank. 'Who killed Percy? He was my friend. I came to find him. Was it your people?'

"Those great, smoky-brown eyes widened even more, and that gorgeous mouth opened again. 'He spoke like you do. He did not speak like those young girls the Plan has us take from down below. He spoke like that too, the other man who came and went away when I was little, the one who made our High Women so sick and angry, the one who wrote all the scrolls.'

"Here she looked thoughtful as one does who tries to remember some forgotten name. She no longer seemed upset or even afraid of us. Then the eyes cleared. 'Labrador, that was his name, my aunt told me. Three names this strange man who escaped us had, Felipe Jose Labrador!'"

"So, someone else had come and seen this weird bunch at close range and even got away with it, which seemed more than our lost agent had done. No doubt some peon or mestizo, some wandering laborer, maybe even a bandit. 'Philip Joseph Farmer indeed! As common as Smith in New York and probably an alias, as Pancho Villa had been. But what *was* that about this unknown's writing scrolls? I asked the lady as best I could, and made sure that Lucas was also listening to it, so that any Mayan that crept in might have a chance of being understood.

"What came out was a real melange of everything: Spanish, Mayan and her own gabble—a real linguistic stew. I finally put my hand gently over her open mouth to shut her up and nodded to Lucas to tell me what, if anything, he'd got out of this. It was more certainly than I had, but puzzled us both.

" 'She talk very fast, Sir, and there is much words I don' know at all. But she say this man she call Labrador, he get everyone all excited so they wan' kill him, but he was clever and get out anyway. He tell them the country they come from it sink in the ocean, it don' exist any longer. Then he tell them a man name of Ee Are Bee, he know all about it. And he say, this Labrador fellah, he say maybe there is other city and this other city over in Africa! Yes, a city from this country that sink in the ocean long ago, he say, and his other city it called "Opar." I don' understand what this woman talkin' about, except it mus' be very old.'

"Now that word 'Opar' stirred some lost memory in my own mind. I took my hand away and our captive raced off into more of her excited speech. I listened to it for a minute and then put my palm back and again looked at Lucas. He seemed more confused than before, but he tried.

" 'Now she say the people here worship the sun, jus' like them ol' Indios did, them Mayans befoh the priest come. And this place in Africa they do that too.' He paused a second, then scratched his head. 'This man Labrador, he mus' be *big* liar but they think he smart. He tell them the name of their country that sink in the ocean and they say that is *right* name, the old name, almost the same as the way they say thot name. An' the name of this country they say sink in the ocean is some funny one. They call the place "Aztlante" or "Atlantaz," something like that anyways. I think this Felipe Jose Labrador, whoever he was, was some big liar and a bigger storyteller than anyone. But he fool these funny folks good wit' all his talk about sunk countries and cities in Africa called "Opars" or somethin'. Anyway, Captain, that's what I get out of her talk now and I think I get most of it.' Lucas fell silent and three pair of eyes studied my face. I looked down at the giant, chocolate and milk orbs of our captive and made it four pairs studying.

"Frankly, I was just a bit numb, you know. This weird trip, that peculiar message that started it all, the ape-man monster we'd killed and finally this extraordinary female revelation. Only one continent of civilized humans was ever supposed to have sunk in the sea, as any child knows. Atlantis! The greatest legend of all time, left to future ages by Plato, and no one has ever known whether that Greek genius was writing of actual history or simply inventing mythical utopias for his own personal philosophy.

"So there we stayed, for what seemed an hour but was only a minute really, four people full of varying degrees of puzzlement, while the tropic sun beat down and small insects bit us and buzzed off.

"Finally, I woke myself out of my dreams and returned to reality or what passed for it in this place. I can tell you, it wasn't easy with all of what I'd just heard and what I'd guessed, all churning through my mind."

The Brigadier sipped from his glass and fell silent, looking off over the library mantle, seeing far-off things we could only imagine. But at this point, my own memory stirred and I recalled something read as a boy in the 10th grade.

"Excuse me, Sir, but wasn't one of those lost cities in Africa that Tarzan's author invented, wasn't that called Opar?" I shut up as soon as those glacial blue eyes met mine, but then I could see he was laughing and felt a bit easier. The Brigadier didn't like interruptions when he was telling one of his yarns and I was afraid I'd goofed badly, especially since I was often telling the others never to interrupt him.

"You may have noticed that I was looking at Burroughs' stuff, along with a lot more light fiction when you came in, Parker," he said and now there was an open grin on his smooth face. He looked around, to take in the rest of the listeners.

"I have a rather good memory, Gentlemen. Intell Training, you know, but some of it's natural, especially for what is now called 'trivia.' That name, the one Lucas had caught 'Opar,' supposedly a place in Africa, that rang an old bell in my mind. That was a so-called 'lost city' of the Ancients in a number of the Tarzan tales, by a writer whose initials were E.R.B.

"Did this mean that old Burroughs knew a few secrets of the unexplored? No, not to me. To me, it meant this unknown chap Labrador, whoever he was— the name means nothing but 'farmer' or 'agricultural laborer' in Spanish, you know, so it was probably an alias—but whoever and whatever he was, he must have thought very quickly and stuck in that name from his memory to sway the rulers of this strange area into believing he knew all about 'em and that their alleged culture and ancestry was well known too.

"Pretty clever, the fellow must have been, since according to our fair captive, he'd impressed the locals well enough to escape from them, which seemed not the normal event at all!

"When I got this array of thoughts a tiny bit digested, I looked down at our scrumptious prisoner and thought quickly for a change.

"I told Lucas to try and ask what the woman's name was first and also how she should be addressed, assuming there was some title or other, from 'Your Grace' to 'Madam.' Always best to be polite to women, I've found, and I've been in a few odd places. What we finally got was several long and difficult words in her own tongue, but which ended in "Loosheer' or at least something like that. I tried calling her 'Lucia' and she smiled and seemed to enjoy my pronunciation. She had lovely white teeth but the carnassials or canines were a bit longer than normal and frankly looked as if they might be lethal in biting.

"It was time to do something. I checked my watch and it was close to Noon. We'd spent over an hour getting this muddled story sorted out and while there was still a lot missing, especially concerning our lost agent, I thought we'd sat around in dangerous country long enough, if not too long. A pack of those giant ape-men, like our visitor of the night before, might appear and we needed nothing less. But what to do next and especially what on Earth could we do with our oversized dazzler, our bepelted figurehead?

"We all three must have been on at least similar thought tracks. It was young Hooper who cleared the air. 'Lookee heah, Sah. You an' Lucas tell this lady to stay wit' me an' stay quiet 'til you two come back.' He waved his drawn Webley. 'You tell her what this is an' that I kill her dead if she run away or scream out or make trouble. You two better bush men an' can get around faster in this bush than me. So you go take a looksee maybe while I stay an' keep guard here.'

"Couldn't have been better put, really. The youngest of us was the coolest at this juncture. I thanked him and then Lucas and I, both speaking slowly and carefully, gave the lady orders. She wasn't pleased but she understood them. She said a couple of words, looking at our revolvers, and it was plain even to me that she knew something about firearms, whether her tribe had any or not. And something had to be done soon. The day was drawing on and we had to try and decide something about the future and do it quickly.

"Between us, we finally got the message across and though she seemed a bit hurt, she finally settled down and curled up. We three synchronized watches and agreed to come back to this spot in two hours or less. We ought to be able to learn *something* in that amount of time.

"With Lucas leading, we set off, following the upper steam flowing into the big pool, the path by which our captive had approached it. We kept low, using all the cover there was and along the brook there was a fairish bit. Ducking under big ferns, arums and shrubs that liked damp, we soon found a path, though a little-used one from the look of it. It made me wonder just how important locally our prisoner was. Was this her private trail?

"Lucas led and I brought up the rear. In no time at all we came to the forest across the plain, following the weedy little gorge of the brook bed the whole way.

"The sudden shade of the big tropical trees did not make us relax at all. Now we had to look *up* as well as on all sides. We all recalled our attacker of the previous night. When we finally got to looking about us and down as well, we found we were at what could only be a sort of junction. From a flat place between several towering boles, five or six paths and very well-beaten paths at that, led off like the ribs of a fan, all going somewhat forward. We looked at each other in silence. It was a silent place, with only a few insect hums and distant bird calls. Finally, Lucas crouched and studied the ground at close range.

"I heard him sniff several times too before he spoke. 'I'm pretty suah she come this way,' he said, pointing at a left-of-center trail. 'That's my best guess anyway.' Then he looked at me, waiting for orders.

"I nodded. 'Very well,' I said. 'Let's go as we did by the stream, one following the other. But we'll go slow and keep on the very edge of the path, on the left side as close to the trees as one can get.' I checked my watch. We'd been away for one quarter of an hour so far. We unclipped our holster flaps and tucked them behind the revolver grips as well as shifting both rifles to the left hand. Then we moved out.

"For about a half hour there was nothing. Deep green shadows shading to black in places and that winding path. There was no undergrowth, only the great trees, whose trunks and leaves cut off any direct light save for rare gaps where stray sunbeams wandered down through lianas and bromeliads from far above. Then, suddenly, we both halted in our tracks. I didn't need Lucas for we both saw a blaze of light ahead which could only mean a clearing.

"Lucas fell back to my side and without a word we began to advance in line, slowly and also moving from tree shadows and root boles in an irregular, shifting manner. I noticed in passing that we were now under the reddish, oily boles of a grove of absolutely giant, mahogany trees, the sole decent cash export of this odd little colony. We were moving under the shadows of twenty thousand Hepplewhite or Chippendale chairs and tables.

"As the light grew closer ahead, so did something else, which was an odor. The other man noticed it before I did but soon even I got it hard and strong. It needed no breeze to bring us that smell and there was none in any case. We halted in silence again and looked at one another. No words were needed. Whatever we were approaching bore the reek of that monstrous humanoid we had buried only a few hours before!"

Fellowes stopped his story at this point and shifted a little in his chair. I saw an odd look come over his face, one almost of chagrin or even embarrassment, both rare to the Brigadier in my experience. Then the expression vanished and in his even tones he began to talk again.

"I thought of something just now, Gentlemen, a small thing but I should have mentioned it earlier. That unholy stink we had learnt to dread so had *not* been even faintly apparent on that great, furry beaut' whom we'd taken prisoner." Pause. "If anything at all could be said about the lady's odor, it was very faintly that of a house cat, a pampered one, with a sort of wild, floral trace intermingled." Pause. "Not in the slightest bit repellent, you know. If anything, quite the reverse. Sorry I forgot to mention it earlier.

"Well, Lucas held up one hand to me in silence. Then he pointed to the forward path and tapped his own chest and shaded his brows with the other hand. Finally he pointed to me and then to the ground behind a giant tree. The whole message took one second. He would scout and I would remain and wait. I simply nodded and got behind the tree. I'm fairish in the woods but was not a patch on Lucas and we both recognized the fact.

"It seemed a long time to me, once he had gone, moving off in the direction we'd been going, not on the path but near it and silently as any native hunter I've ever seen. I've seen a goodish few in many parts of the world, so that's no mean compliment!

"It wasn't really much actual time at all, no more

than a few moments, he suddenly reppeared from
behind the next tree to mine, coming back as noiselessly as he had left. 'Follow now, Captain,' he murmured, his mouth next to my ear. 'Is very old city,
close in front; very old, broken-up place, the kind
place science men come from all over to look at an'
study.'

" 'Do you mean an ancient Mayan ruin?' I whispered back. 'No!' came the quick reply. 'I got Mayan
blood with French an' Spaniol too. I know the Mayan
stuff an' I got plenty Mayan frens' too, and I can
speak Mayan a bit. I *know* their old places, like
Xunantunich, which is not too far Nort' of where we
are an' I been to lots more up in Quintana Roo. This
place, she's, well, *different*.'' He paused a second,
obviously trying to find some descriptive phrase in his
slurred English. He soon gave up and shrugged. 'I tell
you this, Sar. This place no more like any Mayan
place than that stink of that hairy man we kill, the
stink we smell now, like a *puta's* perfume!'

"I couldn't help smiling and he gave one of his rare
half-smiles back. The analogy was crude but effective.
If the place he was describing was no more Mayan
than that foul odor we'd learnt to know was like a
whore's perfume, it must be *very* different indeed!

"Well, there was no time for being humorous. I, in
turn, tapped his shoulder and pointed to the trail's
right, then tapped my chest and pointed to its left. 'Go
very slow and stay even with me,' I breathed. He
understood at once that I was telling him I couldn't
match his pace or his stealth in his own jungles and
nodded. And so we set off, one on either side of the
path where there was little scrub due to the dense
foliage overhead and the shade it gave. The chief
obstacles were the giant tree roots, some types of

which spread out in huge flanges, tall as a man where they joined the tree."

The Brigadier took a long drag on one of his thin cigars. Around us the big room was quiet, the few lamps illuminating only their own corners. I think the thick, old carpets added to the hush by absorbing sound. The roar of New York traffic was a monotonous and unheard or unnoticed hum, and only an occasional siren or police car whoop-whoop even drew one's attention to it. We, his audience, were like children told to be quiet or we'd get no story. We moved only when we had to, breathing as quietly as we could.

"I got to hate those damned trees," he resumed. "The giant roots were a nuisance and so were the bunches of vines, some large and some thread-like, which hung to the ground in many places. But the real reason was simple fear of what might be up above, ready to drop on our backs and even worse, might be watching us and stalking us from up above. I had seen that great monkeyman we'd shot and knew quite well how quietly and agilely *he* had moved down a vertical rock face. Only his appalling odor had alerted me, though the others, the two younger men with their keen senses, had felt that we were under observation long before I did." He looked around at the intent faces and smiled.

"I've been on *shikar* up in Garwhal after a man-eater, a tiger who'd already got two experienced hunters. That was bad but this was worse, I can tell you. My own view is that we're too used to danger from two dimensions only. A bomb or a diving plane or even rocket or missile is different. One knows the danger but it is still a mechanism at its worse. No one thinks of an *animal* striking from above, save for a few folk in the world who live in leopard country. Aside from *Panthera pardus* there ain't no such animal, as you might say in this country. Despite a lot of nonsensical and faked stories by so-called 'explorers,' pythons do *not* drop from trees on human beings, of whom they have a very sensible fear. Very rarely, a big one may use that method on a small antelope, but I've never come across such a case aside from occasional comments by old hunters which are at least *meant* to be the truth and I mean not told to impress the ignorant or to make a news story.

"From time to time I could see Lucas, though damn seldom hear him, as we both climbed over roots and ducked tangles of liana on opposite sides of the narrow trail.

"In case either of us should forget where we were and why, that foul stench, the odour of those man-apes or ape-men, was a persistent and excellent reminder to stay alert. It didn't seem to increase or get worse or such. It didn't need to. It was just there, all about us or rather about that track we were skirting. Once or twice a vast root led me a bit away from our route and it grew fainter rather swiftly. That to me clearly meant one thing. What we were sliding along was *their* path, and the smell was a result of constant usage.

"We hadn't actually gone far when we checked and halted, both of us. I daresay Lucas alone could have done it in half the time and been not a bit less silent about it either. I suddenly saw his hand across the trail, just the hand projecting from a clump of glossy green bromeliads or something. I stopped short and saw one finger point ahead. It stayed that way for a second; then the hand flattened, fingers pointing ahead and all together. That gesture was held for a second too; then the whole palm, fingers and all, made a downward motion. It made the motion three times. I held a hand up so he could see it and made a circle with forefinger and thumb. Everyone seems to know *that* gesture. He'd told me that we were almost there, that we'd move ahead but would do so at a crawl. I'd answered that his signal was received. End of exchange.

"So I went into a Boy Scout or, if you prefer, a Commando crawl at the very left edge of the path. Lucas appeared and did the same on the other side. We moved out.

"It wasn't far or even much of a muscle strain for me. I'm sure that it was nothing to my partner. In about two hundred feet, the path made an almost right-angle curve. I got my head carefully around the corner as did Lucas. And there it was, a sight that any museum in the world would have given its last cent for and perhaps 5/6 of its endowment for even a verified set of photographs!

"In front of us, a couple of hundred yards away, lay a hidden city. And I *do* mean hidden. The ground sloped down in front of us at about a 45° pitch. The trees stopped where we were concealed, leaving only low forms of vegetation, none over knee height, mixed with patches of smooth, damp, black rock and stretches of equally damp, brown sand. A couple of hundred yards away, the slope ceased and the ground became level. Well beyond the point where this started, there rose a high, stone wall, made of vast, reddish-hued blocks. Behind this obstacle and starting almost next to the wall were tall, cylindrical towers.

"And, Gentlemen, why do I emphasize the phrase *hidden?* Simply due to one fact. A cliff lay just behind the city, a cliff perhaps a sixth of a mile high. Now, due to some earlier convulsion of Nature, of God knows how long ago—and Central America is still a great, active, volcanic spine—the cliff had leaned out and *over* the strange metropolis. Much more likely, of course, this very odd formation had been discovered in ancient times by whomever built the perishing place to begin with. They'd simply used the cover of this, well, call it a geologic scoop turned parasol. They found the place and built their lair under it to suit. The result was, among other forms of protection, such as a weather shield and such, they had a place that enemies could only approach from one direction. Plus an added benefit and one they couldn't, and in this case I'm frankly guessing, since there were strange things about this place, have calculated on it at least in their day. From the air, the whole complex was invisible! Nothing but smoke could give anything away, and planes over Central America were and are most unlikely to notice smoke. What with endless patches of vulcanism and thousands of unknown and/or tiny villages in dense rain forest or scrub forest, why should any pilot even bother?

"I looked at my watch. It was midafternoon and we could see very well how this extraordinary place was built, or rather had been built, for it was certainly very old indeed. And gone somewhat to ruin as well. There was a vast wooden gate in the wall's center. It was shut tight, but there were gaps in it where the wood had rotted and they were unfilled gaps, some big enough to take a small car and with ragged edges. Some parts of the upper tier of the giant wall blocks were simply gone, leaving a broken, crenellated effect. I could see a number of the great squares of stone lying outside the wall with grass growing around and over them but not enough to fill all those empty spaces by far. It was puzzling.

"Lucas, who was lying beside me now behind a clump of bushes, was the faster thinker at this point, as he was in others. 'Not enough stone in front, right,

Captain? Not to fill them holes?' I simply nodded, having nothing to say.

" 'I don't think that breakings were done by people, Captain,' he continued. 'Them stones they mus' weigh a half ton mebbe, each one. Well, mebbe I crazy but I think those other stones that don' be out front where we see them, I think they inside, behin' that monstruss wall. I don't think people done it, Nossuh. I think there be an earthquake, mebbe long time gone. Some of those ol' temple things that stick up behind, they look the same, I think.'

"As his very shrewd reasoning proceeded, he grew quite excited and talked faster as well as pointing to what he meant. 'See that tall towah on the lef'? It still got a round top on but it ain't straight up and down. It lean a bit. There's two more like that in the middle an' on the right two that leaned over too much an' break halfway up.' The clever fellow looked at me with a rather pathetic inquiry in his eyes. 'I'm not much educate, not like you, but do that mebbe make a sense, Captain?'

"My answer was enthusiastic and I showed it by punching his near shoulder. 'Dam right it makes good sense, man. You know more about this place than I ever will, Lucas, but by God it's more than that! You can *think* and you make me feel stupid! That's a perfect answer and one I'd never have got on to for months!'

"It was worth a lot to see the broad grin, a thing I'd only seen once before from Lucas. He was a silent man and though always decent, he was both reserved and for this part of the world, very taciturn. Now his pleasure vanished as quickly as it had come, and with one accord we both turned back to study that amazing place before us.

"I was fairly tired, though by no means exhausted,

yet that hidden lair of strange architecture was like a
stimulant, not just to the eye but to all the senses and
of course, especially to the imagination, to what in a
child is called 'a sense of wonder.'

"We could see at least a dozen of the strange,
cylindrical towers, all built of the same reddish stone,
or at least those in front certainly were. Some could
barely be glimpsed at all for they were far back in the
shadow of that bizarre cliff which roofed the whole
thing. The wall ran about three hundred yards on a
flat plane across the front and then curved sharply in
at each end. I imagine it ran right back to the cliff
face, deep in the blackness of the great cavity's back.
In the center, but well back, was a tower which looked
much bulkier than the others. It got just enough of the
brilliant sun so that I could see its domed roof was
colored, and that the color was a golden hue. All the
other intact, dome roofs were of the same red hue as
the towers and the mighty wall. Why not, I thought.
Gold-plated temples ranged from central Mexico all
the way to southern Peru in the Andes. The old Meso-
Americans used the precious metal the way we Euro-
peans used bronze or even tin. No doubt this was the
main temple, the religious and political HQ. of the
entire culture which had built the place. And who
could they be? Just as I was slowly returning to the
present, two things brought me back with a rush!

"One was Lucas. 'Howcome there is no plant on
them walls?' he whispered, 'an' I don' see any peoples
at all. We can smell 'em good back on that track.
Where they is, d'you think? All inside now?'

"The other stimulant to end daydreams followed
like an answer to his questions. I had just realized that
the walls must have been cleaned to stay so free of any
growth, when out of the depths of that incredible,

cave city there came a sound. And what a sound! It was a long, howling wail.

"How one noise, obviously from a throat not an instrument, could express all that this one did, I can't conceive still. It held menace, it held despair, it held defiance and even triumph, all in one hellish, ululating wail! I've heard badly-played bagpipes playing laments, gentlemen, but their bad mix of sadness and off-key notes was 'Merry Christmas' by comparison. And it had great depth and volume, too. Lucas and I cocked an eye at each other, at the same time we stopped slapping bugs, wiping sweaty faces and froze where we lay, listening and staring. We guessed what kind of throat *that* was!

"The appalling sound died slowly away and once again one became aware of insect hums and bird calls. The pause was brief. Then it came again, exactly the same. Another brief pause and repeated a third time.

"In bright sunlight, tropical too, I felt as chilled and numbed by that ghastly sound as if I'd been plunged into an Arctic night. As the third cry died slowly away, neither of us had any inclination to move. We waited, just lay there, not even hearing the normal forest sounds as they became audible again. My head was buzzing and not with deafness or shock either but with scrambled thoughts and recollections.

"I thought of the long-lost 'Jones,' our sometime area agent, and the strange code message tossed into the Hooper's trading schooner. All stirred up in that was a mess of other points; the apeman thing we'd killed, my giant, lovely 'catgirl' we'd caught and left behind, the vague but quite definite avoidance of the whole region we were in, all of that and more. That lost and hidden site before us and its architecture, unlike anything I'd ever glimpsed, anywhere in the world, jumbled with 'Jones' and the warnings of danger and the demand for troops, fast, plus my own memories of reading the Tarzan stories and their 'lost city in central Africa' that Burroughs had named Opar, in his wonderful, self-taught, imaginative fiction. Fiction? Was it *all* fiction? Had he heard rumors or tales of something *real?* And then there was my recently-acquired 'catgirl' and the jumble of what might be legend and/or fact Lucas and I had got from her through the maze of partial comprehension. Through that last, ran another thought or rather a feeling, you know, an emotion so to speak. Very strong one, too; I felt that adjective 'my' and 'mine' to the depths of my being. *My* girl, that incredible, tall, female thing! And with that came more lunacy, such as her comparing me to another man, her alleged 'tale teller,' whose name in English came out as 'Philip Joseph Farmer,' and who 'knew all about everything and who had escaped her people.' "

Here Ffellowes stopped for breath and a quick drink. The library stayed utterly quiet. Then he began again.

"Must really sound as if I was and am still batty, eh? Felt a bit that way myself, though hopelessly confused, hyper-nerved up and more than a bit scared as well, might sum up what I was feeling then. The twin blows on eyes and ears at this point, staring at this weird, shrouded city with its aura of abnormal age, and then those shocking sounds too. You fellows would have had to be there to understand.

"Then I checked my watch for something to do that was normal. Damn if a full twenty minutes had passed since that third, moaning yell had quit. I looked at Lucas but his eyes were fixed in front, locked on that great stone wall. I looked back at it too, as if pulled by the thing, sort of mesmerized. So I also saw it all, from the start.

"As if laid on for an instant vision, pre-ordered by Fate or God, the great, half-rotted gates in the wall began to open!

"My jaw must have dropped and Lucas' did because I saw it, out of the corner of my eye. Sort of thing one sees unconsciously and only recalls as fact long afterward. In any case, and my apologies for these random divergencies, slowly and creakingly the bloody things opened, shoving back built-up soil and plants as they did. There *must* have been one or more other exits from that cavernous fort and it really was more of a huge fort than a city. In a second, you'll hear and realize why there had to be."

He took a long breath, the only one to be heard in that big room, and continued. "Shocking the way I forget to tell details. Those gates were not pushed open by machines or electricity. On the inside of each half, exerting three times at least the strength that the same numbers of men could have done, were five goldy-red pelted bipeds. I didn't need to look at my neighbor. We knew what they were as if we'd smelt 'em. But these specimens were dressed, unlike what had fallen upon us earlier. They had short kilts of stuff that glittered like woven metal, which in fact it was, as we soon saw. There were things hanging from heavy belts as well, things that had to be weapons and some of them glinted brightly also. One had something strapped to his or her back which looked awfully familiar to me. If it wasn't a rifle it was a close copy, and I could discern the breech and metaltipped butt easily.

"This was all happening rather fast, but I'm trying to keep my tale a bit slow deliberately, so as not to miss anything else as I almost just did. Next, the ten gate openers fell back and lined up, each bunch of five with backs to its own half of the gate. There was a hush and even the distant birds seemed to shut up. All at once, there was movement in the shadowy opening, movement and noise. Barking cries, the clank of metal, the thudding of feet, all came at once. No problem for me to construe. I'd heard variants of that noise all my life. An armed body of considerable size had begun to move. If my eyes had been shut it might have been the Scots Guards, same number of U.S. Marines or probably even a gang of Alexander's hoplites for that matter. Any troops make the same noises at times. I expect Chaka's Zulu regiments would have sounded much the same when moving out. Because one thing allies all such groups, which is discipline and a cadence, a rhythm. And what was now appearing through the gate had it. The strangest little army on our planet was marching, not walking, marching out, and they were in both a formation, a column of fives, and in step to boot. Lousy pun, that, since they were barefoot.

"About a hundred came with officers on the flanks and one in front. Half way to our position, they stopped on a barked command as if a lion had been Regimental Sgt. Major—or a gorilla. Just what the Guards would like, unless they've changed. Behind this advance now came the cavalry, the most amazing body of mounted troops that ever existed, past or present.

"When I saw the first one, the leader or colonel or whatever, appear, I damned near choked. T'wasn't the rider, and I don't say 'man' for all the infantry who'd come first were our giant ape men. And so were the lines of mounted troops, and they *were* troops, now emerging. But that first one!

"*She* was another of these ultra females, gold breastplates and all, who might at a distance have been a twin to my big catgirl!

"Have you noticed I've carefully said 'mounts' and not 'horses' once? No, they weren't mules, donkeys or even zebras. They were massive, with legs like elephants, though smaller, hair like coarse, greyish wire and long noses like pigs, noses that were pink and twitched but with broad, flat muzzles and nostrils set side by side. And tiny, short tails that hung straight. They each weighed about as much as a medium horse but had narrow, ridged backs and the massive legs were so short that the riders' bare feet almost hit the ground, even though their knees were pulled up high.

"In short, Lucas and I were observing a force, the only such there ever was, of jungle cavalry, designed for the rain forest. Their mounts were not equids at all but *tapirs!*"

Ffellowes stopped and looked around at us, a grin on his face as he watched our reaction to this fantastic story. In the silence that followed, someone else cleared his throat and then spoke quickly. It was an older man named deCamp, an economist I believe for the U.S. Government. "I'm a student of zoology as a hobby, Brigadier," he said. "Did you know, by any chance, that tapirs, rhinoceroses and all types of horses, asses, donkeys and so on are all related? They're the only living mammals, I mean those three groups, that *are* related, each to the other two sets. I mean like rats and squirrels both being members of the Rodentia?"

Ffellowes laughed aloud. "Yes, My dear man, I do know it; know it *now*, that is. I certainly didn't at the time, and would have had you clapped into bed or a hospital due to either alcohol or fever if you had ventured to tell me such a thing in those days.

"And now, my friends, I suddenly understood a lot of what I had heard, and more than that. I knew a lot that made perfect sense from the very beginning, from the story of 'Jones' for instance and the secret message thrown aboard the Hooper vessel.

"There *was* an army, a secret army, which had given

our poor ex-agent the fits when he somehow discovered it. There *were* actual and very real reasons for the Amerindians to avoid this territory and there always *had been*, since the dawn of human civilization. Certainly since the Classic Age of Greece. Aristotle and Plato *had* known what they were talking about, gentlemen. There had been a great culture far to the West, whose name at least had come to them. I was standing in its lost and last colony, preserved through the ages. There *was* an Atlantis!

"All of this data flashed through my mind at once, as lightning comes through a cloud. I knew it all. And I knew more. Alone in the world, the world of *Homo sapiens*, the world of what Science calls Reasoning Man or Modern Man, Man the gorilla hunter, the Orangutan shooter, the Chimpanzee trapper, there had been one wiser branch long ago. And this one, isolated by its home's disappearance under the Atlantic waves, had survived!

"Like the British garrison at Lucknow in the Indian Mutiny of 1857, this colony too had survived. In this case, they had been surrounded by the oncoming hordes of alien Amerindians who were pouring down from North America to the end of South America at Cape Horn. Some, perhaps many, had already gone past the lost colony of Atlantis, gone South forever. But more would come and Home could never now send help or even exist as a place to go back to, if evacuation had been possible at all.

"What to do, when all seemed lost, for these isolated men and women and probably some children too? What help was there in this hostile world? Think of it, men, think of it. Picture perhaps a few lonely ships, the last galleys perhaps, but possibly better ships than galleys, for the Atlanteans were wise, far ahead of the Minoans, the Egyptians and the south-migrating

Dorian Greeks. Read Plato, who knew something of them. Can you see those lonely vessels and their crews with straining eyes, as they used the stars to navigate and again and again, crossed and recrossed the stormy Atlantic, looking, always looking, for the Home that now was not, the Home that Never Was, for them?"

As the Brigadier brought that tragic story, one of the greatest human tragedies ever, to life again and I thought of those gallant and forever lost seamen, my own eyes filled with moisture and my breath caught. I could hear some vigorous nose-blowing and throat clearing nearby, and I knew that I was neither a hurt child nor alone in my feelings.

Like the born tale spinner he was, Ffellowes gave it a moment to sink in. Then he started again, his calm uninflected voice as soothing and quieting as some old nurse's. There is some child in every thinking man, I am sure.

"You may ask, did these folk know Europe? Did they know that behind the Gates of Hercules lay the Mediterranean and its peoples, the ones I have mentioned? Why of course they did. No doubt they took them for slaves on occasion and traded with some of them on others. How else could the bare knowledge of that lost and mighty realm have come to Plato and to others from whom he, in turn, got it? Consider two facts, taken in order. First, the far-ranging and skilful seamen of Carthage, Hannibal's city which Rome killed; plowing the levelled ground with salt and obliterating her great foe forever.

"We know from the Greek historians that the Carthaginians rounded the tip of Africa, going South down the East Coast and North up the West Coast. We know they reached the Canary Islands, whose still extant natives, the caucasoid or 'white' if you like, Guanches have never had any boats, not so much as a

raft and still speak a dialect or rather their own language related to the mountaineers of the Moroccan
Rif. Who put them there? Carthage or perhaps an
earlier race of seamen? And remember this, too. The
men of Carthage were most secretive. They did not
and would not say where they had been and especially how one got to any trading place by sea. They
kept the secret of British tin, vital to the ancient
world, for centuries. And why were they always want
to go West? All the other seamen of the ancient Mediterranean and the Black and Red Seas too, knew
about this obsession of the Carthage rovers. They
were thought to be, and were called by others, mad.
What were they seeking? Hell, Gentlemen, those folk
knew the world was round, a knowledge later lost.
There was regular sea trade with India and Ceylon,
now called by its name of those days, Sri Lanka.
Could they have learnt of this lost colony?

"Fact two. Why were *blond* Spaniards, starting with
that greedy bastard Alvarado, Cortez' lieutenant,
revered by the Aztecs and other Amerindians of Central America? Not North, mind you or South. Only by
the MesoAmerican folk, from Aztec to Mayan, and
many more minor tribes. What was so holy about
blonds and redheads? A lot of that scrambled mythos
of *Quetzalcoatl* has to do with fair skins and light hair.

"So—back to my own story. All of the above hit me
at once and in one orderly, intelligible blast, as in the
aforesaid lightning bolt. And more besides, the ulti-
mate key to the whole mystery and it was a complex
key, a mix of Genetics, Myth and Anthropology, all
fused together. As another detective that imaginary,"
(Ffellowes paused a strangely long time at this point in
the sentence which was odd) "chap S. Holmes, was
wont to remark, 'When one has eliminated the impossible, whatever remains, however improbable, must be

the answer.' I had it now. What about the long-rumored Sasquatch, the 'Big Foot,' the Wendigo of the northern Amerindians? There are clever men, scientists, who are still searching and sure that a few are alive and in hiding. And if so, who and what might *they* be?

"Having just shot a cross-bred specimen and captured another, I had no doubts on the matter. The male I had shot had more of the early strain in him, call it *Gigantopithecus, Pithecanthropus* or whatever. My catgirl had far less. Probably a caste system existed, with those who had more of the ancient genes of Atlantis running things on an hereditary basis. Logical isn't it? We Britons have had an absurd passion for logic, always.

"So there's the key, Chaps. Lost Atlanteans, mostly fair-skinned, on one side. On the other, primitive apemen, not lost but frightened and in hiding. Because, like our cousins the anthropoid apes I named above, they got killed mercilessly whenever Modern Man, be his skin red, yellow, black or white, in short, *our* nice ancestors, found them around. And that was true on any part of the planet from the Himalayas and Alaska up north, to Capes Horn and Good Hope in the southern reaches." He sighed and looked weary before going on.

"A lovely example is modern Germany. Hitler and his fellow crooks were warped fanatics in the bargain. And they were reverting to a *very* old and horrible idea. The Past is unsleeping. It never dies.

"What was the greatest crime a German could then commit? Male or female, sleeping with and/or breeding with a Jew of the opposite sex. To our remote forbears it must have been quite similar. Sleeping with, and/or breeding with intelligent hominids, who still lived in the wilder places and, mark you, had enough of the *same* genes to produce fertile offspring!" He sighed again and was silent. His eyes saw nothing as he mused on human cruelty and racism. Then he shook himself out of it and resumed.

"One gets hints in the Old Testament of all places. I was given one earlier that same day. 'For Esau was an hairy man.' How about, 'There were giants on the earth in those days?' To me, that's just another one.

"But those lost Atlanteans had another idea. Their isolated, cut-off group needed men. Here were strange folk, also in hiding, who knew the rain forest and how to live in it better than anyone. Why not use logic and do some cross-breeding? Those leaders of the abandoned survivors were eminently practical and must have been real leaders and damn persuasive as well, to get those two sets of isolated aliens to do it. But they had. And I was at this point, along with another modern man, looking at the result of that ancient decision. Its last and only army, officers and NCOs, rulers and ruled, was parading in front of me, having emerged from their place of refuge and ancient retreat to do so.

"And who knew where this very dangerous force was going next? Or why and what they would do, or had plans to do when they got there? I was back in our time and place and taking a deep series of gulps of air as I recalled who I myself was and the fact that I could hardly die now and here, not because of any scientific discoveries of fabled realms which had become real. I was an officer of the British Army, sent on a scout, and I had found an unknown and wickedly-effective-looking *foreign* army on British territory and totally unknown to any branch of His Majesty's Government!

"I tapped Lucas's shoulder and his head turned. 'Crawl back to the curve,' I murmured in his ear, 'and then run like Hell back to George and the girl. I'll be doing the same, but do *not* wait for me, understand?

You can run quicker. Wait with George and the other for three minutes by your watch. Not a second longer. If I haven't come, get out and head for the coast and that Hooper boat *fast!* The Government *has* to know about this! That's *all* that's important. Understand? Let's go!'

"We crawled back, going backward, always a slow job, but it wasn't far. All the time our eyes never left that incredible army that was still issuing from the gate and forming up in the little valley below us. At last we reached the trail at the last curve, went around it, stood up and began to run.

"As I knew he would, Lucas took an instant lead and within a minute was out of sight, though I was doing my best and the trail, for a jungle trail, was good and firm with no obstacles. God, how I ran! All the time I was listening intently for any sound from behind me, checking my watch as my left arm flailed up and down and burning every ounce of energy I possessed in the process. Despite tobacco and alcohol, I was in pretty good shape, though nothing like that of my vanished woodsman whom I'm sure could have done anything he was trained to do in the Olympics for an equally sure gold medal.

"I was racing through the trail junction and fifty feet into the small trail, the one down which my catgirl had come and up which we two had retraced her steps, when I heard the first noise that was not that of a bird or insect. Ahead of me and not too far away there came the sound of a rifle shot. Just the one shot and no more, but that was enough to make me race even faster, faster than I'd known that I could. I burst out on the little savannah and tore through the grass, ignoring the cover of the stream up which Lucas and I had come. I was at the big pool in seconds and saw just what I'd feared I'd find.

"My two stalwart friends were standing together, looking sadly down at a long, still shape on the water's edge. George kept looking down and away from me but Lucas, who wasn't even breathing hard, by the way, met my eyes directly and stood erect as he did so. 'Jawj had to do it, Captain,' he said quietly. 'She tried to run the minute I come in sight. She move quick too, maybe quicker than me even an' much too quick foh Jawj. But it was me, too, Suh. I yelled to him to shoot an' he done it. It was the orders an' what I knew you wanted, after what you said an' what we seen back there.'

"Well, I'd got some breath back and I stepped over and put my arm around George's big shoulder. He was crying, poor lad. 'Lucas was right, Son,' I said. 'War is sometimes Hell, like this, but we're alone in enemy country. If they've heard that shot, they'll be coming fast on our tracks, I think. We'll leave her right here. Her own folk can bury her. We three have to move and move fast or they'll get us too, so let's go. Lucas, take the lead again!

"That splendid young man straightened up. He wiped his eyes once with the back of his arm and we moved out and over the cliff edge, doing a dog trot whenever possible. I had looked just once at the shape in the grass and never again. If I had, I don't think I could have left at all, except manacled and under restraint. Frankly, in a rather full life, never before had my sworn duty seemed so hard, so ugly and so meaningless.

He stopped talking and the silence in that big room was such that the sound of one cockroach crawling would have seemed like a train coming by five feet away.

At least two minutes of the utter quiet went by while the Brigadier stared at the floor. No one could have spoken, I think, even had they tried.

Then, he lifted his head again, and the even, level tones resumed. "Since I'm here in this room, Gentlemen, you can see we got away. All three got away and back to George's father's boat.

"What came next? That's locked in Her Majesty's most thoroughly guarded files. Certain picked units of paratroops, allegedly training for jungle warfare in one of our quieter possessions, found a hilltop in one of the remoter areas, quite by accident, of course, where there had been a recent minor earthquake. This in turn seemed to have been followed by a subsidence of soil and rock over a wide area, as much as five square miles. Fortunately no one lived anywhere near the place. Simply a lot of ruined jungle and twisted rock was absolutely all there was to be seen. Wouldn't have made a line in the papers if it had been reported, but since the troop training was secret, only the War Office ever heard about it." He smiled a little. "I do hear the Mayan Indians still don't like that area, or ever go there. They must have knowledge of seismic forces and the danger of earthquakes, eh?

"Well, I've got to go now and can't say when I'll be back. I need a vacation and I'm thinking of the Caribbean shores. Probably why I recalled this tale just now."

I went to the club's front door with him and we two were alone. He shook my hand very hard indeed and something hard hurt my unready fingers. It was a massive ring, a huge gold thing with a great green stone set in the top. There was odd carving on the stone, but I could hardly study it then, could I?

ABOUT THE EDITORS

ISAAC ASIMOV has been called "one of America's treasures." Born in the Soviet Union, he was brought to the United States at the age of three (along with his family) by agents of the American government in a successful attempt to prevent him from working for the wrong side. He quickly established himself as one of this country's foremost science fiction writers and writes about everything, and although now approaching middle age, he is going stronger than ever. He long ago passed his age and weight in books, and with some 250 to his credit, threatens to close in on his I.Q. His sequel to *The Foundation Trilogy—Foundation's Edge—* was one of the best-selling books of 1982 and 1983.

MARTIN H. GREENBERG has been called (in *The Science Fiction and Fantasy Book Review*) "The King of the Anthologists"; to which he replied, "It's good to be the King!" He has produced more than 150 of them, usually in collaboration with a multitude of co-conspirators, most frequently the two who have given you MAGICAL WISHES. A Professor of Regional Analysis and Political Science at the University of Wisconsin–Green Bay, he is still trying to publish his weight.

CHARLES G. WAUGH is a Professor of Psychology and Communications at the University of Maine at Augusta who is still trying to figure out how he got himself into all this. He has also worked with many collaborators, since he is basically a very friendly fellow. He has done some fifty anthologies and single-author collections, and especially enjoys locating unjustly ignored stories. He also claims that he met his wife via computer dating—her choice was an entire fraternity or him, and she has only minor regrets.